HALO BREAKER

Feathers and Fire Book 10

SHAYNE SILVERS

ARGENTO
PUBLISHING

CONTENTS

This is a work of fiction. Names, characters, businesses, places, events, and incidents are either the products of the author's imagination or used in a fictitious manner. Any resemblance to actual persons, living or dead, or actual events is purely coincidental.

Shayne Silvers

Halo Breaker

Feathers and Fire Book 10

A TempleVerse Series

ISBN 13: 978-1-947709-56-0

HARK! THE HERALD ANGELS SCREAMED...

War is coming to the City of Fountains.

The Four Legendary Creatures are free, the Seven Sins are running wild, the vampires are getting thirsty, and the Vatican is ready to enter the front lines.

And Callie Penrose is at the heart of it all. The Horsewoman of Despair flicked the first domino, and the consequences are echoing throughout the various halls of power in all corners of the world. As the streets of Kansas City threaten to become raging rivers of blood, one of those closest to Callie is kidnapped, and she is forced to choose between her heart and the people who depend on her to keep them safe.

To value **duty** over **love**.

As the pillars of Heaven begin to crumble, it becomes increasingly obvious that all these events are coordinated rather than coincidental. Callie may have flicked that first domino, but how much can her heart handle when she learns that some of her closest friends set all the dominos up in the first place.

Now is the time when success truly depends on how Lucky Callie can be, and whether she can determine which friends have been paid thirty pieces of silver to stab her in the back. Angels shall weep, and demons shall laugh.

Humanity will burn and gods shall die in the wake of a Horsewoman betrayed.

DON'T FORGET!

VIP's get early access to all sorts of book goodies, including signed copies, private giveaways, and advance notice of future projects. AND A FREE NOVELLA! Click the image or join here:
www.shaynesilvers.com/l/219800

FOLLOW and LIKE:
Shayne's FACEBOOK PAGE:
www.shaynesilvers.com/l/38602

I try my best to respond to all messages, so don't hesitate to drop me a line. Not interacting with readers is the biggest travesty that most authors can make. Let me fix that.

I

M aster Dracula faced the crowd of silent, bloodthirsty monsters surrounding her on all sides. Then she uncapped the permanent marker in her hand and drew a dick on the decapitated Archdemon's forehead.

Thankfully, it had only been a few hours since I had removed it, so it was particularly fresh.

The crowd exploded with laughter and screams, roars and cheers, hurling wreaths of white and red roses into the arena of the Coliseum. It was Fight Night and I had requested the first bout.

I calmly sat down in the center of the Coliseum as Xylo scooped up Envy's severed head from my arms, winked at me with his smoking black eyes, and then he said, "Ryuu's strike teams are in place."

I nodded subtly, feeling a burden lifted from my shoulders. "Let's hope for the best," I told him. If all went well, Ryuu, Samael, and Lilith would secretly raid the nephilim hideouts in Kansas City and take them hostage so I could increase my nephilim army. My job was to keep everyone here distracted while they did it. Who knew how many spies were lurking in the stands? Minions of the other Sins or even Archangels. Only a handful of my trusted allies knew about Ryuu's strike teams so no one could blab. "Is Sanguina still gone?" I asked him, hoping I hid my concern.

Xylo nodded uneasily. "Yes." She had left earlier today and I could not sense where she'd gone or why. Xylo took my silence as the end of our conversation, turned, and jogged away with Envy's head under his arm like it was a football. I pushed back my concerns for Sanguina to deal with later. She would return.

I closed my eyes and formed a black void of nothingness in my mind, muting the sounds around me, squashing the scents pervading my nostrils, and even the gentle breeze kissing my skin. The pains of Envy kidnapping Claire and then murdering Solomon and Last Breath burned freshly in my heart, but I managed to shove all those thoughts, emotions, and desires for vengeance into my black void of focus. I watched them burn. Within seconds, nothing else existed in the void except a gleaming white rose and a pair of lazily flapping angel wings.

I was finally at peace. I calmly began my mantra, committing myself to what would come next while keeping my mind muted and silent. A singularity in a mad, bloodthirsty realm of monsters.

A singularity is the state or condition of being singular. Impossibly unique.

Yet some believe that a singularity is also the point at which a function takes an infinite value, especially in space-time when matter is infinitely dense—like the center of a black hole.

The White Rose grew out from the center of a field of dust, ash, blood, bones, and rock.

It was the only flower to be seen in this desolate land and it should have never survived such an inhospitable environment. Yet it *flourished*.

No.

She flourished. Radiant. Chilling. Riveting.

She was beautiful and she was death.

Her barbed thorns were silver points of dread.

Her once-white petals were now coated with dried blood from killing Envy, yet there was a haunting beauty to her luminescence. A finality to the singularity.

There were no water and nutrients to hydrate and feed this rose, but there were oceans of blood buried deep within the ground. The pulverized bones and long-rotted remains of hundreds upon hundreds of dead warriors from centuries of death and murder and execution provided every nutrient needed to sustain this lone flower.

The circle of death had given birth to a rose of life.

There was no sunlight, but this exotic flower needed only the icy beams of moonlight to grow.

Serenity rippled through my body as I slowly breathed in through my nose, seated in the center of the Coliseum's fighting arena. I knew the Minotaur was watching me, but my eyes were closed. Still, I could sense his anxiety and fear. He had wanted to wait to test out the newest Dueling Grounds—a place where creatures could fight to the death without the risk of actually dying. I had disagreed. Here we were.

The thought was distant and abstract to me in my current state.

I waited.

The stadium seats of the Coliseum were full of all manner of monsters: storybook nightmares who had chosen to be refugees at Castle Dracula, vampires and members of the Sanguine Council, shifters of all flavors— bears, wolves, jaguars, coyotes, rhinos, gorillas, and even a chimera—and my newly acquired nephilim vampires. Alucard had even mentioned some guests from St. Louis, but I hadn't pressed him for details.

Thousands of Freaks filled the stadium, holding their breaths in a pregnant hush as they stared down at the White Rose seeming to grow out of the dusty ground. They knew not why I had summoned them here yet they had obeyed without question.

King Solomon—my legendary ancestor—and Last Breath were dead at Envy's hands mere hours ago.

She was now dead by *my* hands, bringing the number of surviving Seven Deadly Sins to five: Wrath, Greed, Sloth, Gluttony, and Lust. Envy's halo was perched in my lap where everyone could see it and I gripped the Spear of Destiny in one hand, shoving the butt of the staff into the dirt with the point sticking straight up into the air.

I'd single-handedly executed her, startling exactly everyone because it shouldn't have been possible.

Halo Breaker...

The thought drifted across the hills and valleys of my mind like a gentle breeze, doing little more than causing the grassy fields to sway and bend in a rolling wave.

Claire had been abducted by Envy and was either dead or a prisoner.

And now, the newest Master Dracula had some lessons to teach—examples to set for her people.

The fact that I had not taken the time to wash off the blood covering my face, hair, and clothes had generated a pall of anxiety, fear, and anticipation to hang over the Coliseum.

I had just declared war on the Vatican, held a brief war council, and negotiated with Hermes for the Coliseum to be part of the Minotaur's Dueling Grounds franchise so my warriors could fight to the death without actually dying. The ultimate virtual reality experience in some respects.

And my first order of business had been to summon everyone to the Coliseum for them to watch their dread lord, Master Dracula, battle an unknown foe.

I opened my eyes and heard an immediate intake of breath from the thousands of monsters watching me. I ignored them, focusing instead on the entrance to the arena—where the fighters entered. I began counting down in my mind. *Five...four...three...two...one.*

The gate opened to reveal three werebears. A massive Kodiak grizzly bear stood on all fours, staring directly at me. Behind him loomed two larger bears—Armor, the alpha of the Kansas City Cave, and a lieutenant I couldn't name. They looked resigned yet I could see the unspoken questions in their eyes. They had been told to bring the Kodiak here and had not been given an explanation.

Yet they had obeyed Master Dracula without question.

They growled as they ushered their prisoner forward with their snouts. The Kodiak curled his lips reflexively but he obeyed his alpha, Armor, and padded towards me in the center of the ring. His ears twitched and swiveled, taking note of the thousands of spectators, but his eyes stayed fixed on me.

I remained seated, waiting for him to reach me.

Asterion, the Minotaur, gestured at the other two bears, motioning them to join him at the side of the arena, well out of harm's way. They grudgingly obeyed, staring at me with wary expressions on their furry faces.

I stared at the massive Kodiak as he approached.

I could see the rage in his eyes.

The fear.

The resignation.

The shame.

To mask those, he tried to make his rage burn hotter, but he failed. I could see the truth.

And I was not satisfied with it.

2

He came to a stop before me and stared at me in silence. I stared back, my face blank.

The hush of the crowd was physically palpable as they collectively held their breaths, not knowing what this was about or why I had apparently singled out one of my staunchest allies for a display of humility. The first such display for the newly minted terms of the Coliseum.

No one could die here—as long as it worked properly.

I could imagine the thoughts of the crowd. *Why had the White Rose summoned this opponent specifically? If she wanted to execute him, she could have done so at the Castle or anywhere else. She purposely invited this man to make an example that he would not be able to hide from in death. He would not be a martyr.*

He would be an example.

I scooped up the black halo from my lap, ignoring the vibrations of darkness emanating from it. The foul whispers I could almost just make out in my mind. Was I merely imagining those? Projecting them since I knew how evil the previous wearer had been?

Or...were those dark whispers my own? My own rage at the deaths of Solomon and Last Breath.

Or my own fury at Claire's possible death or captivity.

"Kenai," I said, rising to my feet. The Spear of Destiny crackled in my grip but I did not lift it from the dirt. Claire's lover studied me warily and gave the faintest of nods. He towered over me, at least ten feet tall and ten times my weight. "You failed her. Claire Stone is dead or being tortured in a dark prison we cannot locate."

His lip curled back at the mention of his lover's name. "You think I do not know that, Master Dracula?" he rasped hoarsely, his muscles visibly shaking. His fur ruffled in the faint breeze.

"I need to remind you until I am satisfied that your shame is burned into your bones," I snarled, blinking slowly. Part of me hated my words, knowing they applied to me just as equally as they applied to Kenai.

More shame applied to me than him, to be honest.

But I was no longer Callie Penrose, the woman. The wizard. The White Rose assassin.

I was Master Dracula, a symbol, and my people needed to see violence, blood, power, and precedent. They needed to know where I stood when one of my people failed. They needed to fear me so much that they never dared failing me in the future. The upcoming war against the Vatican, Heaven, and Hell would demand everything from them, and I knew the Sins were excellent at offering enticing temptations.

I needed to murder those errant hopes so that my people did not succumb to the tantalizing prospects of betrayal if the Sins came knocking at our doors. When they came knocking.

I shut down sudden thoughts of Ryuu and his disapproving frown. He had not agreed with my decision. He did agree that Kenai needed to be reprimanded, but he had strongly disagreed about the public spectacle with everyone at Castle Dracula watching it happen. That was why I had chosen to send him on the nephilim mission. I didn't need his judgy eyes. He was not a flamboyant man. Ryuu knew how to manage a small, secretive army of killers. But I was Master Dracula, and my monsters needed spectacle, flair, and a firm hand. Quietly punishing Kenai would be seen as a weakness. I hated it but I knew it was true.

I walked a thin line in my new position. A dangerous cliff where one misstep either way could result in the hordes of Dracula possibly deciding to set out on their own rather than rallying behind me. I had all the vampires in the world now here at Castle Dracula, and many of them had never seen me before. I needed to show them fear and humility. Show them that the stories they had heard about me were true.

I needed to be relentless and inspire fear in their hearts. That was the only thing holding my ragtag army together for now. Later, in small steps and actions, I could begin to teach them a better way.

But that was not for today. They would rebel against me if they saw me as soft. Because softness resulted in death in their history. Hate it or love it, that was the way things were for them. Their previous masters had been monsters to fear, so that was the only thing they respected. I would teach them better, but not today.

Kenai would become the symbol for failure and, hopefully, redemption— although that seemed unlikely. We had exactly zero leads on Claire's location.

None.

Nada.

Zip.

I gripped Envy's halo in my fist and closed my eyes. It suddenly let out an ear-splitting shriek like nails on a chalkboard and Kenai recoiled, snarling. I opened my eyes and my palm to see a small, dark obsidian ring in my hand. I slipped it on over my finger, warding myself from its whispers. Then I looked back up at Kenai. I let the Spear of Destiny wink out, leaving me barehanded. My chest rose and fell as rage consumed me, causing my vision to narrow and zero in on Kenai so that he was the only thing I saw.

The crowd disappeared in my mind. Asterion and the two bears on the sidelines faded to vague silhouettes. I needed this to be a show. Epic. I needed to entertain. Anything else simply wouldn't do.

It was showtime.

"I will not fight you, White Rose—"

I zipped forward in a blur and punched him in the ribs. His bulk swallowed my hand but not before sinking deeply enough to hammer his ribs and elicit a sharp cracking sound. He roared in pain and lazily swiped at me to get me to back off. I rolled to the side, dodging his blow.

I needed him to fight back rather than simply sitting there as I wailed on him.

"I wonder what Claire is doing right now?" I mused in a taunting tone. "I wonder who she is thinking about. Maybe she's waiting for you to come save her." Kenai roared, spittle flying as he flexed his paws open and closed, but he still made no move to attack. "I wonder how many bones Envy broke. Maybe she used knives. Small ones, so as not to kill her too quickly." Kenai was panting in agony, digging his claws into the earth. He punched the ground and his eyes burned with rage. "Maybe they used fire," I taunted, hating myself more than I ever had before.

Yet at the same time, my words stoked my own fire. I hated myself for failing Claire.

I hated Kenai for failing Claire.

I do not know who I hated more, but the scales seemed to tip more heavily my way. So, my taunting took on a rawer tone, one that hoped to exonerate me of my shame and shovel it all onto Kenai. To bury him alive with my own guilt.

3

I darted forward and kicked him in the thigh, but he took it like a fucking bear, of course, chuffing in annoyance but still not attacking. I snarled, calling up my nephilim claws, and stabbed them deep into the meat of his thigh—once, twice, three times before he howled in rage and slammed his paws down at me.

I lifted my hands in a cross-block over my head and laughed as my claws pierced his paws. He yowled and stumbled back a step, shaking his head violently.

"COME ON, KENAI!" I screamed. "I know you blame me as much as I blame you!"

"YES!" he shouted. "You abandoned her!"

I nodded eagerly, crouching with my claws out. "Yes! I did abandon her, and I *hate* myself for it! I want to feel that pain. Embrace it. Give it to me, Kenai!" The crowd roared and screamed. Gargoyles swooped through the sky, shaking their weapons excitedly. "Let it out, Kenai! Show me *your* pain! Neither of us can die here! Let. It. OUT!"

"NO!" he roared, snapping his teeth at me. "This will solve nothing!"

I pointed my claws out and spun in a circle, indicating the roaring crowds. "They. *Need*. This," I growled. "They know only violence. This will keep them from scattering to the four winds. Love it or hate it, they need a show."

He hesitated, cocking his head thoughtfully as he assessed the crowd. He obviously hadn't thought of it that way. Neither had Ryuu—which was why I'd ordered him to lead the raids at the nephilim hideout right now while I took care of my children here.

I could see the understanding in Kenai's eyes, but I could also see he detested the audience for these faults. Their bloodlust was a weakness, because shifter bears were honorable, noble beasts. He studied me thoughtfully, realizing that my rage towards him was not fully selfish, but an act of what I believed to be for the greater good. Unfortunately, this made me look *more* honorable in his eyes, which defeated the purpose. Now he definitely didn't want to fight me. He respected me for my decision.

I gritted my teeth. Goddamn it.

His shoulders hunched forward and he met my eyes. "I. Will. Not."

I screamed and called up my magic to boost my muscles as I tore forward and shoulder charged him. I struck him in the gut and sent him flying. He landed hard, tumbling and rolling, but I didn't let up. The crowd shrieked in a deafening roar as I leapt into the air, summoning my angel wings. The crowd gasped collectively and the gargoyles cheered a dusty shriek. I came down to the ground, driving my knees directly into Kenai's back hard enough to shatter the bones of a normal man. He bellowed in pain and flung me off with a roar.

I hit the ground and rolled, laughing. I scuttled to my feet and crouched expectantly. "You want my monsters to respect the bears, then you better put up a good fight or they will eat your cave alive!"

He climbed to his feet, panting furiously as he glanced back at Armor. The alpha of the shifter bears gave him a grim nod, agreeing with me even though he was also torn. I grinned maniacally, doing my best to hide my own emotions.

One thing I dared not say was that Kenai was not the only person the crowd needed to see punished today.

They needed to see Master Dracula take her punishment as well. To see me bear the cross of my own failures. Bullying Kenai would help, but it would likely later spark whispers of why I hadn't accepted responsibility for my own failings in protecting Claire.

Because one day...

The people in the crowds might be the ones I failed to protect. They needed to see that I was fair. That I would bleed for them and accept those wounds with honor.

They needed to see me bleed, so I had to get Kenai to hurt me badly. In a real fight, I would have used every weapon at my disposal, but the crowd saw me choosing to only use my claws and magic, evening the fight with Kenai. I was not a bully.

Kenai squared his shoulders in resignation but I could still see the hesitation in his eyes. I stormed forward with my claws out. His ears tucked backwards and he sprinted towards me on all fours, barreling at me like a train.

I laughed. He needed one more push to truly get him over the edge or I knew he would simply put on a good show to honor his cave. An act. He would put up enough of a fight to make the other monsters wary but not enough to make them angry at him for harming their Master Dracula. But they would see through that.

They needed a real fight.

"First was probably the snap of Claire's bones. Then the crackle of Claire's burning flesh. Then, who knows," I shouted furiously, "maybe the pop of the electric shock they ran through her body." He was roaring as he ran and I saw his eyes darken murderously as he flashed his teeth at me. We were only feet away from impact, so I screamed, "Snap! Crackle! Pop!"

We hit each other hard enough to send a shockwave of dust outward. I felt my arm snap as I slashed my claws across his gut, but the pain from my arm was quickly eclipsed by his claws echoing my movement, slicing through my stomach. We stumbled back from each other and I held one hand over my abdomen, feeling many warm, meaty, squishy parts touching air for the first time. I gritted my teeth and stared at Kenai who was standing on his back legs howling as he held his own guts inside. He stumbled and fell back on his rear. I gritted my teeth through my tears, blinking them away as I spun to face the hushed, stunned crowd.

"When one suffers, we all suffer!" I shouted, trying to remain upright through the pain. "Me as well as you. We are family and we failed to protect one of our own. We got vengeance, but that matters not to the dead."

My voice rang out like a bell as I used magic to amplify it to everyone. They stared at me and I saw the awe and surprise in many faces. I switched hands, using my clean one to keep my insides inside so I could lift my bloody hand and claws for all to see bits of viscera from my mortal wound. My broken arm throbbed and flashed with pain, but I managed to swallow the agony down—it was nothing compared to being gored. I spun in a slow circle, feeling dizzy.

Then I pointed at the distant Castle. "This is my home. Our home. I will never deliver punishment I would not accept for myself!" I shouted. "Claire Stone is family. She is my sister. And Kenai failed to protect her from Envy, that is true." I sucked in a breath, wincing at the fire burning through my guts. Blood was pouring down my waist and thighs. I would 'die' soon. I knew it. "But I failed her too. The fact that I was too busy with other fights does not dampen my shame in leaving my family vulnerable. We will not make this mistake again! The forges of Castle Dracula are coming back to life today, and soon Xylo and the skeleton armies will be armed with Eternal Metal to keep our families safe while we go to war against the Conclave and the Shepherds!"

The crowd erupted.

"Against Hell!" I screamed, lifting my hand and letting Envy's Halo expand, for all to see, into a black disc the size of an Aerobee frisbee.

They began chanting in unison, making the very stands shake in thunderous approval.

"And against those in Heaven who claim piety when their actions scream hypocrisy, if they want war, they shall have the hordes of Dracula to contend with!"

The resulting screams were deafening, shifting the air like a tornado and whipping my clothes back and forth. I slowly turned to Kenai and bowed respectfully.

"You have honored me, Kenai." I glanced down at my stomach and let out a weak, painful laugh. "A little too vehemently, but tonight we will feast as we formulate our plan to get Claire Stone back home."

The crowd cheered, but it was stunted and off beat. I managed to hide my grimace of disappointment as I shambled up to Kenai. He stared at me in wonder, blinking slowly. Since he was a bear, his wounds were not as fatal as mine. I was surprised I hadn't passed out already. The pain was like a gnawing monster eating me alive from the center.

I lifted my claws to his throat and smiled proudly. "I will see you back at the Castle. Remember this moment." He stared at my gored stomach with guilt and awe, no doubt wondering how I was still standing.

Great question. Sheer ovarian fortitude.

He finally nodded respectfully, lifting his snout to give me better access to his throat.

I took a calming breath and committed myself to executing him. Strangely, the monsters in the crowd were screaming and it didn't sound like cheer or praise. Had my pain caused me to fumble my speech and say something wrong? I pursed my lips, panting in agony. I couldn't attempt to speak more motivational words. I was almost ready to pass out and it would do no good for their morale to see me die mid-speech.

The crowd suddenly screamed in real terror and fear, and the hairs on the back of my neck abruptly rose up on end of their own accord. I caught the stench of rotten filth suddenly hammering into my nostrils. I felt an icy cold darkness behind me as I stared into Kenai's face. In the reflection of his suddenly widened eyes, I saw myself—a blood-crusted monster with whipping white hair.

But he wasn't staring at me, he was staring *behind* me.

And in his eyes, I saw the reflection of a giant skeletal monster who was twice Kenai's size with antlers as large as small trees. Gargoyles whipped through the night sky, hurling spears at the hulking brute. The beast swatted them away, raised claws the size of my body, and then swung them down towards my back to kill me.

It looked like Castle Dracula had a new neighbor for me to meet.

4

My legs were too weak to move, but Kenai was made of sterner stuff. He rose up and tackled me backwards, wrapping me up in his bulk to protect me from whatever the fuck this giant tree-moose-scarecrow thing actually was.

An explosion of dust, cracking bones, and snapping branches erupted where I'd been standing. Kenai set me down, turned his back to me in a protective stance, and then roared up at the colossal creature. I groaned, still holding my guts inside as my arms and legs shook with blood loss and pain. My world spun as I stared up at what looked like a twenty-foot-tall scarecrow with the head of a skeletal deer. Fiery yellow eyes sparkled with flashes of crimson and his leaf-eating teeth had either been chiseled or broken into jagged, uneven points. He lashed out with one claw, grabbed a werewolf, and then bit him in half, chomping the shifter's bones with two sickening crunches before swallowing him.

The air around him was distorted and warped and I felt myself gritting my teeth at the pervasive feeling of wrongness emanating from him like a visible gas. His shoulders were a mass of matted, filthy fur, looking like a mantle, but his chest was entirely skeletal, flaunting a bloody ribcage with an inky black heart thumping inside his chest. It sounded like a subwoofer. I saw the eaten werewolf slide down his throat but then evaporate to dust within his ribcage. He let out a furious, honking sound, obviously annoyed that the Dueling Grounds had stolen his Scooby Snack.

He looked like a half-rotten zombie. His arms were too long and sinewy, but his thighs were huge and muscular, covered in more fur. His claws had snapped while trying to swipe me from behind, but I watched in dazed fascination as they grew back before my eyes with loud, crackling snaps. He hunched forward rather than standing up straight, as if his body didn't fit together as it should. If he'd let his hands hang by his side, they would have touched the ground.

"What the fuck is *that?*" I croaked, struggling to get to my feet as my mind ran in a million directions. I sat in a growing pool of my own blood, so the ground was becoming slick and muddy.

The monsters in the stands were scattering in all directions and I realized someone else was attacking them, hurling balls of black fire into the Coliseum. I couldn't see who it was beyond the scarecrow monster, but they were doing serious damage, destroying entire sections of the stands with black fire that seemed to crystallize everything it touched. Werewolves and vampires and nephilim huddled together, trying to rally from the unexpected attack. Ninjas and frogmen fought back a wave of red demons who suddenly poured into the stands, battling for all they were worth to protect a mass of fleeing human residents. Asterion and Armor and the unnamed lieutenant had leapt into the fight, hacking the giant skeletal deer with axes and claws, giving me and Kenai a moment of reprieve.

It was madness. And I couldn't make my legs work.

"Wendigo," Kenai growled, taking in all the chaos with a guttural snarl. "Demons and..." he trailed off, apparently getting his first look at whoever was throwing the black fire. I smelled rot like the nastiest swamp coming from the apparent wendigo, but I also caught the sharp, acrid scent of sulfur, and I was betting it wasn't coming from the army of red demons in the stands. They wouldn't make a smell that pungent from this far away.

"One of the Sins," I rasped, trying to rise to my feet. I slipped in my own blood and crashed back down on my ass as my world tipped sideways. I panted desperately, feeling my limbs growing cold and sluggish.

Kenai glanced down at my wound with a sick look on his face. "You cannot fight," he said in a grim tone, still gripping his own stomach closed from the wound I had given him. "I could kill you and hope you wake up in time to come save us from...this," he said, but he sounded desperate and absolutely glum about those prospects.

How quickly would I wake up from death at the Dueling Grounds? I could almost guarantee it would be too late to do any good. Why had one of the Sins chosen to attack in such a flagrant manner? Did they know about the Dueling Grounds and that one could not actually die here? If so, maybe they were hoping to make an example with very little room for loss. If I beat them, they would wake up later none the worse for wear.

But if they won, the crack to the confidence of my monsters would be profound. They would see one of the Sins utterly destroy me and would then become doubtful of my chances going forward into the real fight.

I had to deal with this *now*. And I had to *win*.

"No," I told Kenai. "I will not run." He opened his mouth to argue but I called up a ball of fire and shoved it into my stomach, cauterizing the slash that threatened to deposit my guts to the dirt. I screamed as my flesh and blood burned, and my vision went black for what felt like an eternity. I felt Kenai scoop me up and lope away as I panted and hissed, sealing up the last of my wound. My vision slowly returned as Kenai carried me to relative safety, and I managed a quick glance down to see a bloody, blackened smear across my stomach. It would have to do.

Something hit Kenai and sent us flying. We struck the ground and tumbled, flipping over each other before slamming into the side of the arena. I saw stars even though Kenai had absorbed most of the blow. I lay sprawled atop him, listening to the panting, whimpering bear. He hugged me with one arm but the other was simply missing. I stared, momentarily confused. His arm had been *severed*.

Then I gritted my teeth. "Don't be a bitch about it, Kenai. It's just an arm," I growled. Then I called up a ball of white fire and slammed it down into his empty socket. He roared in pain, thrashing and shaking beneath me, but I didn't let up. I used another ball of fire to seal up his own gut wound, pretending I couldn't feel his intestines beneath my fingers. He roared loud enough to rip his own vocal cords. His fur burned and smoldered as he twitched and spasmed and writhed beneath me, but I didn't let up until his wounds were closed. I rolled off him, feeling relatively better but still incredibly weak. "Even an arm down, we arm up," I said, handing him a discarded spear from a shattered gargoyle that I found lying in the dirt nearby. He accepted it, hoisting himself to his feet with it like it was a walking staff.

He stared at me, panting in horror and shock. "It's still not enough!" he growled, looking pointedly at me as I wobbled on two feet. The wendigo was on the other side of the arena, as was a hulking Sin in obsidian armor at least the same size as the wendigo. I didn't know who it was, but they wore a cloak of blackened skulls woven together like shells on a net. Two massive black horns curled forward and down from the sides of its head, but I couldn't make out its features clearly—the face seemed to smear and shift like wet watercolor paint.

"You need to *feed*," Kenai said, extending his one good arm in front of my mouth. I felt my fangs pop out at the suggestion and a gnawing hunger abruptly teamed up with the aching pain in my gut. He...was right. Even back in action, I was only at a fraction of my usual power. "Before they take away your chance!" he snapped, physically shoving his arm against my lips this time.

With a grim nod, I grabbed onto his arm and sank my fangs into his flesh. His blood hit my mouth and it was like it lit a fuse, racing from my tongue, down my throat, and slamming into my stomach. I gasped at the savory thick blood, lapping it up with a fervor. Kenai trembled and shook, curling his lips as he kept his gaze on our surroundings to make sure we weren't interrupted.

The smell of fire and blood filled the air, and the screams were deafening.

Power roared through me like hot lava and I felt my back arching and my bones knitting back together. The level of pain from my gored stomach had completely overwhelmed the sensation of my fractured arm. How had I even been using it? Adrenaline? I felt steam rising off my skin and my senses exploded, sharper than ever before. My nostrils flared and I released Kenai, stumbling back a step. I lifted my head and screamed in outrage, calling out to my vampires.

"Get to the arena and fight, my children!" I roared, lifting my claws high as I called up a storm of lightning overhead. "Tonight, we FEAST!" I unleashed the storm and a dozen bolts of lightning slammed down into the stands, seeking out demon hearts only. I stumbled dizzily at the sudden expense of power.

Kenai stood before me, trembling with blood loss and pain from his missing arm and burned flesh. He stared at me, awed and horrified.

He stared at a nightmare he apparently found more frightening than the wendigo and the Sin.

Good. "Let's get to work, Loverbear—"

A ball of black fire slammed into him, sending him cartwheeling away even as he burned and shattered into a million crystals.

I stared in disbelief, blinking rapidly at the smear of sparkling black sand that had just been Kenai.

Then I gritted my teeth and slowly turned to stare at the giant Sin who had shimmered into existence behind him. The Sin who had murdered him. The rest of my army were harrying the wendigo, but I saw that Asterion was missing a horn and one arm hung loose.

Chaos reigned supreme.

Like my father had always taught me, I straightened my spine and set my shoulders back.

I glared up at the Sin. "You were not invited to my party," I said with a stern frown. I lifted Envy's halo, which had somehow latched back onto my finger back when I'd prepared to execute Kenai. The strange whispers from earlier were utterly silent, leading me to believe they really had been my own dark thoughts. The Halo was cold and lifeless in the presence of its sibling. "Do you like my new bling? I think it looks better on me than the spineless tramp who wore it before." I bared my fangs at the Sin.

The face continued to shift and move like wet black paint, but I could undoubtedly confirm that it was a woman. Her massive breasts sagged low, looking like rotten melons. Her obsidian armor looked more like a part of her skin rather than a chest plate, as I had earlier assumed, because as she took a threatening step forward, her breasts swayed back and forth and the obsidian armor crinkled like living metal as it readjusted.

"Give me the Halo," she growled, sounding surprised to see the Halo in my hand, "or I will lay waste to Castle Dracula and all your pretty toys, and my wendigo will finally eat his fill."

I knew very little about wendigos, but what I did know was enough to make my stomach roil. They were insatiably greedy and hungry, never able to fill the aching void of starvation in their guts. I wasn't sure where they had come from or how they were made, but some believed they were malevolent spirits who possessed humans and forced them to crave only human flesh. Cannibalism with a healthy dose of karma.

A greedy and insatiably hungry monster working for one of the Sins.

"Well, Titty Galore," I drawled, grimacing at her grotesque chest, "you must be Greed."

She gave me the briefest of nods. "I. Am."

"I didn't take you for the sentimental type," I said, twirling Envy's Halo around my wrist in a playful manner. "And the surprised look on your shit-smear of a face tells me you crashed my party for a different reason entirely."

She snarled at my apparently correct assumption but her shifting face tracked the Halo like a dog eyeing a raw steak. "A trade then," she suggested in a strangely confident tone. I felt my pulse momentarily quicken, not liking her implication.

The wendigo continued to battle and gobble vampires and werewolves behind her, letting out its agonized honking blast as the meals it consumed evaporated to smoke. Was that thanks to the Dueling Grounds or part of the wendigo's curse? I focused back on Greed. "Let me guess. I give you the Halo in exchange for you leaving Castle Dracula with your hangry deer?" I mused, pretending to consider the trade while my mind searched for alternatives. Asterion was still fighting but he was moving sluggishly. Gargoyles screamed through the air but they looked like those fighter planes in the King Kong movies as the wendigo angrily swatted them away, more annoyed than anything.

We were losing.

Greed laughed and I looked up to see her shaking her head. "No. I came for the Divines. Give them to me and we will leave," she said, chuckling wickedly.

She was easily three or four times my size, and I knew my vampire and wizard's powers wouldn't be enough to shut her down. But I had to defeat her here. Even if it wouldn't be permanent, it would inspire confidence in my people. I saw Alucard zipping through the sky in my peripheral vision, clearing exits for the human residents at Castle Dracula to escape the Coliseum. I managed to bite back a smile, realizing he was wearing his Horseman's Mask. *Of course!* But I needed to keep her talking first. Find out what she knew.

"You won't find me such easy meat, Horseman," the Sin said in a serpent-like hiss, following my eyes to look up at Alucard. "Envy *covets*, whereas Greed *takes!*"

"Well, I'm glad that you fell for my trap here," I said in a pleasant tone. "I mean, I worked so hard to lure you in and here you are," I lied. "Now I don't have to waste time hunting you down. Like your spider minion I cooked in the dumpster. I ripped his skull open with my bare hands." I smiled, glancing down at my claws. "Well, I used these to crack that particular chestnut, first." I swept my gaze over the battle raging through the Coliseum. "As you can see, the Divines are not here to laugh at your deal so how about I give you a counter-offer?" I grinned as I looked up to stare at the space above Greed's head where I could see a flickering silhouette of her halo. "I don't want to trade. I really want a matching set, you see," I said, taunting her with Envy's halo. "I will let you die. Like your sister did when I sliced her head off. That's the deal."

Greed laughed wickedly, but I saw two pinpoints of red fire flare up behind her smeared face. Her eyes. Mentioning her sister had pissed her off and she'd tried to cover it up with a laugh. So simple, these unholy beings. They were emotional, fickle things.

"I can return for the Divines, but if you want Claire Stone, you will give me my sister's Halo."

The sounds of chaos and violence abruptly muted and I heard a sharp ringing in my ears. "You...have Claire?" I rasped in a cold, dead voice, feeling like my soul was about to rip out of my chest.

Greed chuckled. "Don't worry. She is not lonely. She and the wendigo have been sharing meals together," she said meaningfully. The wendigo...was feeding on Claire. "He is an excellent dinner companion—"

I hurled a blast of fire at her. It struck her in the chest and washed over her armored melons. She hissed in outrage as I summoned my angel wings and leapt into the air to kick her squarely in the face. She fell back a step, snarling. She spat a gobbet of black blood onto the earth and it sizzled.

"If Greed takes, then take *that*, bitch," I laughed.

6

S he sneered at me through bloody teeth. "Of course, I could be lying. She might already be dead, her flesh filling my wendigo's stomach and her bones draped over my throne. At least Envy managed to take out Solomon and the pathetic cat before she failed," she laughed, referring to Last Breath. I hovered before her, flapping my wings instinctively. My gauntlets and wings wouldn't be enough. I could already feel them waning as a result of my injuries; even though I'd fed upon Kenai, I was still at only a fraction of my usual power. It definitely hadn't healed me as well as it should have. Was that because he was a bear or because Sanguina was on a walkabout? I blocked out the pain of my seared stomach and fragile arm. I felt deep throbbing pain in my thighs as well. I needed my Horseman's Mask, but I needed it at the right *time*.

"I don't know why Envy saw them as such a threat," I admitted, "but she paid for her crime. Her head is on a spike at the Castle," I said with a grim smile. "Bet you didn't think you guys could be taken down so easily."

"The reason you will fail is because you don't understand Envy's gambit. She wasn't punished. She sacrificed herself for the cause. On purpose and with full intent. Why else would she have given Claire to me before completing her project and confronting you?" she asked, cackling.

I kept my face blank, processing her words. What the hell was she talking about? What was Envy's project? Was she lying to confuse me? I needed to keep her talking as long as possible, but I also came to the sudden realization that killing her here would be pointless. Neither of us could actually die here. It was simply a battle of our egos. A warm up for what would come later. And if Envy had indeed sacrificed herself purposefully, what was Greed's angle now? Was this attack intentional as well? How could I throw a wrench in her plans?

She hated me but she didn't fear me right now. She knew she couldn't die here. That was the only explanation. She knew about the Dueling Grounds. I needed to change the game.

"The Divines will never serve you," I vowed. "They don't even serve me!" The fighting had bled into the arena proper and I saw hundreds of demons fighting werewolves and vampires.

"With the right leverage, anyone will serve," Greed snarled. "The Divines will—"

"Never serve you, Sister," a new voice said. I turned to my right to see Lucky in the arena with us, less than ten paces away and glaring up at Greed. Fuck. The Anghellian had arrived. He wore jeans and a fitted tee, his long hair flowing in the wind. His face was utterly calm and he walked through the chaos and fighting like a specter, completely oblivious and apart from the carnage as if they were repelled from reaching him. I saw the Four Divines tearing into the enemy. Xuanwu's black form zipping about with his frosty sword almost too fast to see and Qinglong's serpentine blue dragon form hurling spears the size of trees out of thin air, laughing as they hassled the wendigo, assisting Samael and Lilith. My godparents were in their greater demon forms, almost as tall as the wendigo, but even they were having a hard time pinning him down—

Wait. Samael and Lilith were supposed to be helping Ryuu with the raids on the nephilim hideouts! I scanned the chaos but didn't see Ryuu anywhere. What the hell?

Zoe and Bai had joined the vampires and wolves; the Red Phoenix and White Tiger ripped through the demons with blasts of fire and explosions of metal spikes like they were paper, but more enemies kept pouring in.

I cursed under my breath. Goddamn the Anghellian. Goddamn the Divines. They were all supposed to be tucked away safely at Xuanwu's estate where Heaven and Hell could not reach them!

Greed was staring at Lucky with a baffled frown. A brave human without any weapons was strolling up to one of the strongest demons in Hell without a flicker of fear.

She has no idea what he is, I thought to myself. *I still have a chance to fix this.*

Lucky held up a hand and the Four Divines immediately stopped fighting, turning to face him in silent obedience. Greed gasped, her face shifting from the Divines to the human who had just apparently commanded them. She turned all of her attention on Lucky and I could practically taste the greed in her posture. Control the human and control the Divines by proxy. Lucky had just shown Greed a vulnerability.

And as powerful as Lucky was, his body was basically as fragile as any human. He had a potentially world-ending right hook but a delicate glass jaw.

Shit. I couldn't let her get him. He didn't control the Divines but they had seemed to adopt him as part of their family after he'd assisted me—barely—in saving Zoe and Bai from Purgatory.

Me? *Still* no love from the Divines for my efforts, but that was neither here nor there. I wasn't bitter.

I wasn't afraid that Lucky could die because we were in the Dueling Grounds. None of us could die here. But she could *take* him, which was infinitely worse. My only solution was to take her out, but that was no longer enough because she had seen Lucky. If I killed Greed here, she wouldn't actually die. She would wake up in her hideout, now having information that would put the Divines and Lucky in grave peril.

She needed to die—for real—before she had the opportunity to share the information she'd just learned. I had to get Greed out of the arena and kill her. Now. Before the Divines or Lucky killed her here inside the safety of the arena—

Greed hurled a blast of black fire at him and he absently swatted it aside, sending it into a horde of her own demons, transforming them to black sand. She grunted in disbelief at the bored expression on his face. He snapped his fingers and the Four Divines resumed their fighting. The wendigo honk-screamed again and I heard disgusting chomping sounds and screams as he ate my people alive while battling Xuanwu and Qinglong.

Shit. Shit. Shit.

The ghostly apparitions of Pride and Michael flickered into view over Lucky's shoulders and I groaned. Greed's eyes twinkled with a longing so deep that it overwhelmed her surprise. "What are you?" she demanded, and

I could practically taste the hunger in her voice. There would be no chance at getting her off his scent now. She would do anything to get her hands on this mysterious creature.

"I'm Lucky," he said, facing her with a distant look on his face.

Greed started hurling more blasts of fire at Lucky in rapid succession and I saw his apparitions grow larger and more menacing as they started gathering power to hit Greed back with a haymaker of their own. No! I couldn't let anyone kill her here in the safety of the Dueling Grounds.

I started hurling blasts of my own fire and ice at Greed in hopes of distracting her from Lucky, but she'd been expecting it and held up a shield with one hand as she continued lashing out at Lucky.

I saw Ryuu sprinting towards us and my heart skipped a beat. Him too? Who was watching the captured nephilim? He was covered in blood and held his black blade at his side, intending to stab Greed in the spine from behind while Lucky and I distracted her. I gritted my teeth, focusing on Greed. I couldn't let Ryuu or Lucky kill her.

I called up a massive ball of air and hurled it directly at Lucky. He'd been so focused on Greed that it struck him like a train and sent him cartwheeling thirty yards away where he slammed into the wall of the fighting arena. I grimaced, knowing I would pay for that later.

Greed cocked her head at me as she drifted down to the ground and summoned a massive black sword to her hand. She frowned suspiciously, glancing at the motionless Lucky with concern.

"You fucked up, Greed," I said, slowly drifting back down to the ground.

"Oh?" she asked, amused. "Do enlighten me. Because I so enjoy passing the time by listening to the desecration of your followers who are not in the safety of the arena. I will return for him."

Fuck. She really did know how safe she was in the Dueling Grounds.

I calmly turned my back on her and let out a sigh as I surveyed the chaos behind me. There had to be a few hundred demons in the stands, but Alucard was doing an admirable job keeping them back. "You brought a friend because you are a coward." I let my shoulders sag. "Which means you have something to lose and that you are afraid. Envy covets. Greed takes. But Despair *breaks*," I said, lifting my hand to the side and summoning a massive ball of white fire to throw at Lucky, who was only just now stumbling to his feet. "I would rather permanently break my toys than share them."

"You cannot do such a thing here in your Coliseum, White Rose," she snarled hungrily.

I shrugged. "Watch." The ball of white fire screamed as it ripped through the air for Lucky.

Greed snarled furiously and I felt her lunge to strike my spine. I slipped on the Mask of Despair and made the ball of fire racing towards Lucky wink out of existence.

I spun to face Greed as the transformation took over my body.

I clapped my hands together before me in a praying pose and I caught the tip of her giant black blade between my two palms as the Mask of Despair latched onto my face with the sensation of a thousand silky, groping fingers. My lower body transformed to mist and I calmly rose up into the air, still trapping her sword despite her quivering, straining muscles trying to jerk it free or force it forward into my chest.

I smiled. "How does Despair taste, angel?" I asked in a chiming, singsong tone. Then I tore the sword from her hands and swung it like a baseball bat, cracking her across the jaw with the massive hilt. She flew across the arena just as Ryuu reached her back and lunged forward with the sword known as the Angel Killer.

His black katana struck only empty air and he snarled furiously, glaring up at me.

I blew him a kiss. "I love you," I said.

Then I tore through the air after Greed as she slammed into the bleachers and through the walls of the Coliseum.

Beyond the protections of the Dueling Grounds.

For both of us.

7

I grabbed her by the throat and lifted her off her feet as I hastily tore open a Gateway behind her. It opened up into a distant night sky high above a sleeping city. I used my other hand to punch her in the forehead as hard as I could. I felt her skull crunch as she flew free from my grip on her throat and through my Gateway to...

Well, St. Peter's Square in Vatican City, naturally. My mind had a sick flair for poetic justice. Maybe the Conclave would finally realize who the real enemy was when I dropped a Sin at their front doorstep.

"We're here for the midnight baptism!" I shouted, my voice booming through the night sky like thunder.

Greed flew through the open night sky and slammed into one of the fountains, obliterating it in a spray of water and rubble as she rebounded, skidding across the cobblestones. I winced. Damn it! I hadn't intended to damage any of the beautiful architecture. I also realized that the famous destination was not as sleepy as I had hoped. A few dozen tourists screamed and ran from the sudden chaos. It was still late in the night so there weren't too many people, but even one was more than I had hoped for.

I saw a few couples with strollers and my heart broke. Fuck. I needed to change locations. Now.

I dove through the Gateway after her and I felt my Horseman's skin protect me as I ripped through the protective wards that the Shepherds had placed over the Vatican grounds. I hit the ground on one knee that was aimed for Greed's chest, but she'd rolled away at the last moment.

The cobblestones around me shattered and Greed stumbled to her feet with a horrified look on her face. The smeared, blurry mask over her face was no longer there, having broken after my punch. Instead, I saw the face of an emaciated, gaunt-cheeked woman who reminded me of a crack addict. Her forehead was a shattered mess, leaking black and yellow blood, and her legs wobbled as she glanced left and right, trying to determine where we were and why there were so many screaming people racing in every direction.

She'd obviously wanted me to keep her confined to the safety of the Dueling Grounds.

I heard a shout from the sky behind me and I saw Greed's eyes flick upward as they widened in terror.

I glanced back to see Ryuu falling from my Gateway, his Shadow Skin acting like a parachute as he pursued me across the world. I gritted my teeth in annoyance that I had forgotten to close my Gateway, but I was secretly grateful. He could look after the tourists and keep them safe. I rose to my feet and abruptly felt a wave of exhaustion ripple through me. A very strange, alien sensation in my Horseman form.

What the hell?

I spun back to Greed and tackled her, ripping open a Gateway behind her. Icy snow from a lonely forest in Alaska whipped through the hole in the air, but Greed batted me aside with a powerful claw. I felt my armor ripple strangely, as if flickering in and out of existence. I hit the ground hard and this time there was no imagining it. I actually saw my armor flicker in and out of existence, and my legs materialized for a moment rather than remaining in their mist form.

Greed cocked her head curiously, and then a wolfish smile split her cheeks as she painfully shambled over to me. "Uh-oh. Looks like someone has been naughty, Horseman," she chuckled, rubbing her scaly palms together.

I scrambled to my feet, suddenly alarmed as I felt the pain of my injuries rippling back like a reverberation, each wave hitting harder and harder as my eyes began to water. Greed swung a massive fist at me and I turned into mist to absorb her blow.

Or...I tried to.

I felt all of my ribs crack as the air was sucked from my lungs. I felt my own shattered ribs stabbing and poking me as I flew through the air. Something struck me mid-flight, wrapping me up like a swaddling babe and altering my trajectory. We hit something hard and my vision went white. I felt stone shatter and crack as someone grunted.

More bones cracked as my vision flickered in and out.

Blood flew through the air, actually misting my face, but I couldn't breathe. I couldn't even think straight.

Then we were falling through the air. We hit hard, but my savior cushioned me from the fall by holding me to his chest. The smell was vaguely familiar, but my head spun and I couldn't get enough of a breath to actually recognize the scent. I was lying on top of someone. He was strong.

I looked down, gasping desperately, feeling like I was choking. Ryuu stared up at me with terrified eyes. His face was torn and covered in blood. He gently rolled me to the cold cobblestones and cupped my cheeks. "Hold on, my love."

I could only stare back at him. I found myself staring up at a massive circle of cold marble faces high above in the sky. They perched on the ledges of the buildings surrounding St. Peter's Square and they looked vengeful. Saints and angels passing judgment.

On me.

The screams and shouts of tourists had grown distant but they definitely hadn't ceased. Hell had just fallen through the sky over the Vatican. And a Horseman had brought it.

I tried clutching at my throat but I couldn't move my hands. I could feel the gentle breeze kissing my wet cheeks, so I knew my Horseman's Mask had completely failed at some point during my flight. Ryuu slipped as he tried rising to his feet and he crashed down to one knee with a groan.

He growled and lifted his black katana in one trembling hand. The other hung loose at his side and looked to be missing a significant chunk of muscle. I could see bone and blood dripping freely to the ground at his feet. He lifted the sword towards Greed and hurled it at her. It stabbed into her thigh and she roared in agony, crashing to the ground.

Ryuu held up a bloody hand and the black katana zipped back through the air, hitting his palm. But he fumbled it, dropping the blade from his slick hand. It hit the ground with a chiming sound. He groaned and crashed to one knee again, scrambling for the hilt with his quivering, bloody fingers.

"You stupid motherfuckers," a familiar voice drawled from behind me, and I felt someone grab me by the back of my collar. "The Four Horsemen are coming!" Then a green hand that seemed to be on fire grabbed Ryuu by the Shadow Skin and I heard a glass shatter. I gasped and choked, unable to get a deep breath as my ribs twisted and stabbed, tearing and ripping my insides.

My gut wound had torn open from Greed's punch.

The green man dragged us backwards as Greed screamed in her own agony, looking just as wounded as us. I saw a ring of sparks above me as I was dragged through a Gateway with Ryuu. His eyes were blinking rapidly and he was gritting his teeth as he turned to stare at me.

He took one look at my face and his flesh paled at what he saw.

"Hold on, you two," Alucard drawled as the Gateway winked shut.

I tried to keep my eyes open. I really did.

But my world was pain. Only pain.

The last thing I saw was the Dueling Grounds behind Ryuu, but the pain and horror in his eyes hurt worse than the agony twisting my guts to ribbons.

Everything faded to black and I let go.

I felt like I was falling and no one was left to catch me...

8

I felt myself floating in a pool of warm, syrupy liquid. A neon purple and pink night sky surrounded me, seeming larger than any other I had seen. The moon was luminescent. I felt I could almost reach up and touch it with my fingers, it was so massive. I stared up at the night sky, smiling as I counted the craters on the moon. This was nice—

The moon exploded in a concussive blast and I sat up with a gasp of fright that immediately transformed to one of alarm as I remembered the gaping wound in my stomach. I quickly clutched at my stomach to keep my insides inside after my abrupt movement, but then I frowned and looked down. I...wasn't wounded.

Hadn't I just had my ass kicked...by...

My thoughts went fuzzy and I felt a sharp pain in the back of my neck that made me groan.

I looked down to find myself sitting in a pool of hot black oil that didn't ripple even when I shifted. I dipped my fingers into the liquid yet they came back out clean rather than stained. Not oil. Water. Maybe it just looked black because of how dark it was. I frowned, seeing the reflection of the giant, brilliant, white moon in the perfectly-still water.

I frowned in confusion, recalling that the moon had just exploded moments ago. I glanced back up at the sky to see that the moon had *not* blown up.

"What the hell is going on?" I mumbled, slowly climbing to my feet. Something about the water terrified me. It seemed alien and dangerous for reasons greater than the fact that it didn't ripple. I wanted to go swimming in it but I also wanted to run away from it.

I wore the white suit Aphrodite had made for me and I even had my silver katana tucked into my belt. I glanced down at my hands to see the Seal of Solomon on my finger and another glittering black ring of obsidian on the same finger on my opposite hand. I took a step forward, frowning at the reflection of my foot in the water. Was it my imagination or had I just seen a flicker of light that momentarily made my foot look like a full-plate armored boot? I frowned as the water reflected a similar flicker of light where my hand was, resembling a gauntlet of glowing ice, but when I looked directly at my hands, I saw only my flesh.

The pain in the back of my neck returned and I groaned, blinking my eyes closed tightly until the pain receded. Then I opened my eyes again and took another step forward.

The water still did not ripple and made no sound as I moved, even when I stomped my armored foot down. No, my boot.

Armor?

"What the hell kind of drugs did you give me this time, Starlight?" I heard myself asking as I forcefully shifted my gaze to my surroundings rather than the strange, reflected anomalies of the moon, my hands, and feet. I caught a new flicker of glowing light behind me in a reflection on the pond. I spun abruptly, drawing my katana and snarling at the sneaky threat.

But I was all alone. Had the reflection looked like glowing wings?

I frowned uneasily, staring down at the water again, harboring the sneaking suspicion that the reflections might be more accurate than what my lying eyes could see. After all, the moon hadn't really blown up.

I glanced up at the night sky just to be sure on that last point.

I shouted out in alarm to see the moon exploding in slow motion, hurling meteors of moonstone out into space. I forced myself to look down at the motionless pond again and saw the moon healthy and whole.

I closed my eyes and forced myself to control my breathing, realizing I had been panting hoarsely.

It felt so incredibly good to breathe, but that shouldn't have been something I specifically noticed. Breathing wasn't strange. I did it all the time as a matter of simply existing. "So, Callie," I mused, opening my eyes and keeping them firmly latched onto the pond so as not to give myself another panic attack, "why does it feel so refreshing to finally breathe again?"

I frowned. Breathe *again*? Why had I framed it like that?

"Over here, Callie!" a familiar voice hooted. I flinched, lifting my katana as I zeroed in on the voice.

A mature woman sat beneath a weeping willow tree on a small, nearby island of lush green grass. The drooping branches of the willow tree were loaded with bright pink flowers in full bloom. The small woman was wearing a crown of the pink flowers in a wreath around her head and she was weaving another one in her lap.

She looked up at me with a brilliant, white-toothed smile and I gasped as her eyes hit me like glittering gems. She was...gorgeous and wild and strangely primitive. But she was *much* younger than I had initially thought. At first, I'd taken her for a middle-aged woman but now she looked like one of those barely legal girls with perfect skin and hair who had turned eighteen about four seconds ago. She wore a bright white toga and her long, wavy auburn hair crashed down over her shoulders like a still-shot of a waterfall hitting boulders. Her tan skin was slick and glistened in the moonlight as if she had just taken a dip in the pool, but her toga was dry and practically transparent, shifting in the breeze like a silk scarf. She motioned me over again with a bubbling laugh and waggling fingers. Then she focused back on her work.

I instinctively knelt down and scooped up a palmful of water, feeling I might need the clarity of the water's reflective qualities to see the truth and to keep my sanity.

I slowly approached the woman and used the tip of my katana to part the branches of the willow tree. The beautiful nymphlike girl sat on a boulder, humming to herself as she worked on her second flower wreath. She did not look up, so I glanced down at the water in my palm, angling it to catch the woman's reflection. Her youthfulness remained, letting me know that my eyes and the reflection matched this time.

Except the wreath in her lap was not made of pink flowers and vines from the willow tree.

It was woven from glossy black vines with wicked thorns and tiny white roses. Even as the beautiful girl worked, the thorns stabbed and poked at her fingertips, drawing fresh blood. Even as I watched, the thorns seemed to drink in her blood, causing the tiny white roses to grow larger, brighter, and more vibrant.

"Clever, clever girl, Callie," the girl sang in a light, playful tone. "I must tell you that you are so incredibly high right now, I can hardly believe you are able to communicate with me through meditation. Aala was highly distraught that she was unable to help you with her hot springs, but she was unbelievably smug and proud that her suggestion to tap into your mind worked, despite your intoxication. But after Sanguina disappeared, we had very few options."

I felt a wave of anxiety rock through me at the mention of Sanguina, but I couldn't place why that name seemed familiar. I sat down on the mossy boulder across from her, feeling the sharp pain in the back of my neck again. "Ow," I grumbled, gritting my teeth tightly. "Who...are you?"

She looked up at me and cocked her head with a whimsical smile. "I'm Pandora, silly rabbit." She laughed at herself, finding something incredibly hilarious in her own words. "Well, you're a stone-cold murderer, too, but who can hold *that* against you?"

The pain in my neck escalated to more of a jarring vibration the moment she mentioned her name. Then it abruptly faded and I sucked in a breath, surprised to find myself now sitting on the ground rather than the mossy boulder. I must have slipped off.

Pandora crouched before me, smiling sadly. She hoisted me up by my shoulders and placed me back on the boulder as if I weighed no more than a twig. She straightened my back and shoulders, nodded satisfactorily, and then sat back down across from me on her own boulder, resuming her work on her wreath.

A basin that was large enough for me to dunk my head in sat between us. It hadn't been there before.

I looked back up at Pandora, squinting my eyes. "We are...friends," I mumbled uncertainly.

Pandora laughed delightedly. "Well, you're my landlord, but I do wish to be your friend, Beautiful Death."

I sucked in a breath, feeling another rush of pain in the back of my neck at her last two words. This one almost knocked me back off the boulder, but I'd managed to grasp onto the rock with one hand while stabbing my katana into the ground like an anchor with the other. I panted hoarsely as the world spun and turned crazily.

"Are you all right?" Pandora asked, not looking up at me as she continued weaving.

Her words seemed to settle my vertigo and I felt myself nod. "Why did you call me...*that?*"

"Callie means beautiful in Greek. But in Hindu, Kali refers to the goddess of time, doomsday, and death." She glanced up at me from the corner of her eye. "So, which is it? Or is it both? There's a certain irony to combining them. Beautiful Death. What more could we ask for?" She glanced up at me with a whimsical smirk. "I refuse to call you doomsday. DC is the Green Lantern of bad film franchises."

I nodded numbly, agreeing with her last comment even though I didn't understand it. It felt like a natural law: water was wet, fire was hot, DC films were trash. "What did you give me?" I asked, recalling her mentioning that I was intoxicated.

Pandora laughed lightly. "I didn't give you anything. Starlight gave you something he called *Monday Blues*. It was the only thing we could do for you."

I frowned. "Do for me?" I scowled at her wreath. "Stop lying to me!"

She looked up to see me glaring at the wreath of purple flowers. "You don't find it beautiful? I'm making it for you," she said, sounding hurt. "You need it, Callie. Desperately. I don't know how else to help."

I frowned. "Just...stop lying to me," I said tiredly. "They are not purple flowers. And you're getting blood all over the white petals," I lied, since I no longer held the palmful of water after my fall and couldn't see through whatever illusions surrounded me.

She smiled mischievously. "Even high and on the brink of death you are entirely too clever for your own good." She let out a tired sigh and the wreath in her lap shimmered, revealing the white roses and the black thorns. I gasped to see they really were covered in blood. So was Pandora's beautiful white toga. Her hands were torn and shredded to ribbons. She resumed her work, humming to herself as she wove the thorns together, connecting the two ends. I saw her clenching her jaws from the pain as numerous thorns stabbed into her fingers. Her hands were shaking and I saw a tear roll down her cheek even as she continued her merry humming.

My eyes widened and I looked up at her face, realizing she looked gaunt and pale compared to earlier. Almost sickly. "Pandora! Stop!" I hissed, leaning forward. "You're killing yourself!"

"You have a big and beautiful and terrible future ahead of you, Callie. Unless you fuck it all up," Pandora said, ignoring my plea. "Sanguina left. You are Master Dracula, but your Beast left. Starlight is scouring the Astral Plains for her, but he didn't sound optimistic about his chances." She looked over at me with haunted eyes. "Which is why you need me right now. Or your castle will be a house of cards against a storm."

I shuddered, feeling confused. "As pep talks go, it needs work," I mumbled, not knowing what to make of her strange advice.

She smiled faintly. The wreath clicked together and she let out an exhausted tremble. She took two deep breaths and then turned to look up at me. She extended the wreath to me in silence. Blood dripped freely from the thorns and I felt myself reaching for it, licking my lips for some reason.

I froze, recoiling from the wreath. I shook my head firmly. "No."

Pandora sighed dejectedly. "Callie, you need to feed or you will die. This is your subconscious," she said, lifting the wreath. "I'm whetting your appetite to keep you alive," she said, sounding exhausted. "I came here to convince you that being a monster can still be beautiful." I looked up sharply, pursing my lips. "Your term, not mine," Pandora said with a sympathetic smile.

"I...think I want to go back in the water," I told her, rising to my feet. "It spoke the truth rather than lying to me," I said, pointing at the wreath in her lap.

She smiled sadly. "It is not water, Callie, but it is the truth," she said cryptically. She waved a hand towards the pool and I gasped as it shimmered to reveal something else entirely.

Crimson, steaming water stretched as far as the eye could see. No. Not water.

"Blood," Pandora murmured from directly beside me as she placed the wreath on my head like a tiara. "I'm sorry, Callie, but this is for your own good. Don't clench."

Before I could open my mouth, she picked me up and hurled me into the pool of boiling blood. I struck the hot surface with my mouth open to shout at her and...

The blood hit my tongue.

Lightning hit my soul.

Wind tore at my muscles.

Fire burned through my veins.

And I crashed below the surface, sucked down into the blood like a whirlpool. My fangs erupted from my gums and I guzzled ravenously as I drowned myself in the eternal bliss of power.

9

I woke up with a start and a defensive snarl. A body was draped over me and my fangs were buried into her wrist as I clutched her tightly to my chest. The lights were too bright, and there were many people shouting. I was on a large, lavish white bed that was liberally spattered with blood. The room stank of incense and antiseptic. I saw a large pile of white towels with crucifixes embroidered on them heaped beside my head. They were blood-stained too.

I focused on my meal, devouring and guzzling the blood even as my wild eyes darted around the room, searching for threats that might attempt to take my food.

No, I thought to myself. *Not food. Blood. A woman.*

I glanced down, recognizing the thick, wavy auburn hair and I gasped. My fangs retracted and I recoiled, shoving the woman away from me. The voices rose in volume, too loud for me to separate since they were all screaming at the same time. The limp woman fell off the bed and I saw an arc of half-a-dozen faces staring at me from around the room. Some looked familiar.

Claws ripped out of my knuckles, tearing through the thick blankets covering me, and I sat up with a hiss. Well, I tried to.

What felt like a dozen knives suddenly tore through my stomach and I felt something wet and hot spill from me as my hiss turned into a choking rattling scream. I collapsed to the bed and my back arched as I felt my bones snapping and cracking, my ligaments ripping and tearing, and my muscles burning away like acid.

Rich, beautiful power oozed down my throat, but it moved sluggishly, making me want to gag. I knew it was healing me, but it moved too slowly to completely wash away my pain, only serving to dull it...slightly.

Enough for me to momentarily stop screaming. The room spun in my vision and I panted in short, sharp bursts, afraid of taking too deep a breath and hurting myself again. A man cautiously approached me, but he did so walking backwards, keeping an eye on the others in the room as he came to a stop near my face. His arms were raised as if expecting an attack. He... smelled familiar and I felt my hand reaching for his lower back.

Someone in the room shouted out a warning and the man beside me swiveled his arm toward the voice. A concussive *bang* cracked through the room, making my ears pop and my hand recoil. The voices grew silent as the smell of gunpowder hung heavy. I scrunched up my nose, fearing it might make me sneeze, causing me to crack more bones.

"Fuck, Terry!" a familiar voice snapped. "He was trying to *warn* you! Did you have to shoot him?"

"I'm fine," a voice growled. "It's just a gunshot."

The room was silent. "Yeah. In the forehead, you psychopath. Sit down, and at least pretend you're normal, Samael."

I heard a squelching sound and then the familiar *clink* of a small piece of metal hitting the floor. "There. Happy? What's a bachelor party without a little friendly fire, Dorian?"

"You just plucked a bullet out of your forehead!" Dorian laughed.

"Freedom seed," the shooter corrected.

Samael chuckled, obviously unfazed. "It was only a pistol."

The room was silent for a minute. "This is a Ruger Redhawk. I use it for bears," the shooter replied, sounding slightly troubled. "There are talking grizzly bears in the goddamned hall." Why did he sound familiar to me?

Everyone laughed, easing the tension.

"It's part of the godfather gig," Samael said. "Papa Penrose didn't mean it. Check on the librarian, Dorian. She'll need an IV...and a blood donor or two. Maybe some orange juice?"

"I'm fine, you morons," a woman argued in a weak, sleepy voice. "If you want to get me a drink, give me some Roland. Yum."

Several men burst out laughing.

"Now that she's fed, should we move her again?" someone else asked. "We don't want the Horsemen finding her."

Samael laughed. "Ryuu has a fucking army keeping them back at the gates. Fuck them."

"I can't believe that crazy ninja is walking around after what he went through. Looks like death walking."

Several voices murmured their agreement.

"We'll move her later."

"No one is moving her unless they want a bullet in the eye," the gunslinger warned.

"Any idea if the Sin survived?" Dorian asked.

The room grew silent.

"I hope Lucky stays away. I get a bad feeling around him."

"He's changed."

Someone snorted. "Callie blasted him into a wall. I'd be grouchy too."

"And he walked it off without a scratch."

The room returned to an awkward silence.

"Has Fabrizio returned from the Vatican?" someone else asked warily.

"Don't worry about the Conclave. Yet. We still don't know who alerted all the nephilim about our raids." A pause. "Maybe someone in this room…"

The voices continued to bicker and argue for a few moments as my world spun, and I found it impossible to connect the names I heard to memories that I could actually grasp. They were just barely out of reach, tickling my mind, but the pain swamped me like a lead blanket, preventing me from clearing my head. The blood I had consumed from the…librarian seemed to be helping, but not as fast as I wished.

I found myself staring at the shooter who was still standing with his back to me. His voice reached deepest into my memories, and I recalled sitting on a porch during a thunderstorm, huddled under a thick blanket while sipping hot chocolate. I stretched out my fingers, but I was unable to reach him as I clawed weakly at empty air.

"D-daddy?" I croaked, as my vision started to tunnel to black.

He tensed and spun, suddenly crouching down so that his head was level with mine. The familiar face made me gasp and tears welled up in my eyes. Terry Penrose looked tired, slightly unhinged, and full of love. "Callie!" he rasped, cupping my cheek with one dry, callused hand. "I brought my baseball bat, but I don't know which one of them to hit. Just say a name," he growled.

I blinked away another tear as a halting laugh bubbled up from my belly, which ignited another flare of daggers to my guts and turned my laugh to a sharp gasp. His face started fading from view and I felt him grasp my hand and squeeze it comfortingly. "I'm not going anywhere, Callie."

I smiled as the pain and exhaustion finally took over. "Raised...royal."

He laughed hoarsely. "Damned right," he growled.

Then sleep took me. Or death.

Whichever it was, I invited them into my home like a late-night bad decision, hoping they'd be gone by morning after we'd shared our fleeting moment.

❧ 10 ❧

I woke up with a gnawing hole in my stomach, but I kept my eyes closed, focusing on my surroundings with my other senses. I could smell the same antiseptics and incense in the air, but I couldn't recall why it smelled familiar to me. My mouth was dry and sticky, but I felt a cool sensation within my throat. That also felt familiar for some reason. Like I was drinking something but not actually drinking something. I heard electrical equipment beating and humming nearby and it all clicked into place.

A hospital. The occasional muted beeps, the gentle humming, the smell of antiseptics. The cooling sensation within my throat was from the IV needle plugged into my arm. Except incense wasn't allowed in a hospital and I didn't hear the hum of conversations from nurses or the bad daytime television playing in the background. And this bed was entirely too comfortable and big for a hospital.

I took a light breath, taking stock of my injuries. It hurt, sending pins and needles through my fingers and toes, but it no longer felt like a gang of virginal auto mechanics were working screwdrivers into my lungs in an attempt to unscrew and fine-tune my organs. I took a slightly deeper breath and winced as the sharp pains I remembered from earlier hit me. I reached under the blanket to check my stomach and felt pads taped to my abdomen. They were damp and sodden and...

Very, very big.

My muscles felt shaky and weak, and I knew sitting up would cause me to vomit and pass out in pain—

"Boop!" a baritone voice chimed in a forced falsetto as he pressed a cold finger against my nose.

My eyes shot open, and I instinctively pressed the back of my head deeper into the pillow in an attempt to escape the horrifying visage of an ancient skull beneath a deep, crimson cowl with eyes that were smoking pits of woe. Xylo grinned at me and then spun his head completely backwards to look behind him.

"It worked!" he rasped excitedly in a muffled voice since he still wore the crimson cowl. "I healed her!"

Cain burst out laughing and I heard him hurrying closer. He grabbed the skeleton by the shoulder and shoved him to the side. "Callie!" the big ugly brute whispered, grinning from ear-to-ear.

I felt a tired smile creeping over my face as my memories slowly emerged from the fog of sleep. I was in the Master's Suite at Castle Dracula. "Stop pranking Xylo," I scolded in a weak whisper.

Cain snorted. "It's not like you could have hurt him like you did the others—"

Xylo swatted him hard, shaking his head. Cain's smile slipped and he averted his eyes. "I mean, they're fine *now*, thanks to Aala's healing pool—" Someone cleared their throat out of sight and Cain cut off abruptly.

"You had your fun, now step back," Pandora warned them in a stern tone. "She's recovering, and I doubt you've brushed your teeth or are even remotely hygienic at present—if ever."

Cain scowled over at her, grumbling his displeasure, but then he flashed me one more roguish grin, pressed his finger against my nose and blurted, "Boop!" I snapped my teeth at him but felt like I pulled my groin in the process, so I let out a gasp of pain. Pandora was suddenly there, driving an elbow into Cain's gut and then sweeping his legs out from under him. He crashed to the ground with a gasping curse out of my sight and then I heard him crawling away. Xylo cautiously stepped away from the bed, keeping his smoking eyes on Pandora as if she might attack him. "Leave my brother alone, you tiny bully!"

I heard the door click closed as I recovered from the sharp pain and I found myself staring up at Pandora. She smiled down at me, gently resting the back of her hand against my forehead. She smiled and then used her thumb to brush a few loose strands of hair away from my face.

"Beautiful Death," I murmured, frowning at her. She visibly started but did an admirable job at covering it up. "You...were in my head."

She held her breath for a moment and then let it out, dipping her chin in acknowledgment. "Yes. It was the last thing we attempted when you refused to drink. Someone needed to get through to you, and you have long since proven that your mind is the strongest part of your body."

I grunted, not knowing how I felt about anyone poking around in my head. What else had she seen before I became aware of her in my strange dream?

"I walked in blindly and said nothing when I came out," Pandora said in a soft voice. "A woman's secrets are her own." She smiled wistfully. "That definitely frustrated the menfolk when I refused to divulge what I'd seen or what we discussed."

I closed my eyes, testing my lungs for deeper and deeper breaths. They were still only a fraction of what they should have been, but they seemed better than before. I opened my eyes as a scent in the room tickled my nostrils. I saw hazy ribbons of clear light drifting through the air, reminding me of heat waves off black concrete in the hottest days of summer. I followed them to the source, and I flinched when I realized they emanated from thick bandages taped to Pandora's forearms. I was visibly seeing the scent of her blood.

I scrunched up my nose at the thought of drinking her blood again and managed to shift my head an inch farther from her without sending my body into a seizure.

"Don't hate your nature, Beautiful Monster," Pandora murmured. "It was an honor to help you." She paused, considering. "And to be completely honest, it's probably the rarest blood you will ever taste in your life. You're welcome."

I grimaced. I knew my body occasionally gained power from drinking blood, but I was grateful for the fact that I had not needed to feed on blood to sustain myself. Had that changed? Was I now dependent on blood like my vampires? "Why was drinking your blood even necessary? I died in the Dueling Grounds, didn't I?" I asked her, licking my dry, cracked lips. "I should have woken up healthy and whole."

Pandora reached to the side and picked up a pitcher of cold water. She poured some in a glass, put in a fresh straw, and then held it up to my lips. I eagerly filled my mouth, held it there for a few seconds to let it seep into my gummy tongue, and then I swallowed it hesitantly, hoping I wouldn't cough it up. It easily slid down my throat and I took another few sips.

Pandora finally pulled it away and set it on the nightstand. I saw a few bottles of water with crucifixes stamped on them and I frowned. Pandora followed my gaze and sighed. "To answer your question, Greed broke a claw off in your abdomen. It prevented Aala's healing pool from saving you. It took us some time to even realize it was there and we were obviously startled to find that her water did not immediately restore you. You did not die at the Dueling Grounds, but you were dying. It was almost like your body and soul were fighting the powers of the Dueling Grounds, rejecting them," she said with a frown. "Something was wrong with you and we don't know what it was. Ryuu knew that if he kept you in the Coliseum one moment longer you might die for real. So, he took you to his sister, where he learned her powers could not save you either." She waved a hand, indicating multiple various attempts to care for me. "She inspected your wounds and found Greed's claw, but she could not get it out. Roland collected some holy water and, after irrigating your wound with it, your body rejected the claw on its own. Until that moment, you were calm. The moment the claw came out, you became violent. Starlight gave you something to sedate you. Many somethings, to be completely honest. Your body rejected his drugs just like it did with Aala's pool." She looked haunted and her eyes were distant.

"I hurt people?" I whispered guiltily.

Pandora nodded. "Yes, but they have recovered. No one died, Callie. Do not beat yourself up about it. You were not aware. We tried giving you blood. All kinds of blood. You spit it all out, so they came to ask me for help." She shot me a weak glare. "I tried bringing you to my hot tub in the Armory since they had succeeded in removing Greed's claw, but it did not work either," she said, shaking her head with a troubled look on her face. "That's when I decided to let you try my vintage wine," she said dryly, tapping her savaged wrist. "You accepted it begrudgingly but would not take more. We couldn't get you to latch on and bite me. That's when I decided to enter your mind and see what you were going through. You were refusing the concept of blood. You were swimming in it, seeing truth in it, but your fear and distaste for the concept was forcing you to refuse it. That's when I made your wreath, tricking your subconscious into drinking my blood with each stab of the thorn."

I glanced down at her fingers and was surprised to see faint scars that looked only recently healed. My eyes widened and I looked up at her. She nodded. "You threw me in the pool of blood."

She smirked. "And you took to it like a shark in the ocean."

I shuddered at the visual of me instinctively adapting to the mentality of an apex predator. "Where is everyone? Was my father really here or was that some kind of fever dream?"

Pandora smiled. "Yes. Dorian Gray found Terry Penrose for you. He knew it would be important for both of you." She didn't say it, but I saw the flicker of hesitation in her eyes. They had feared I actually might die from my injuries. "He may have convinced your father that he's your boyfriend," Pandora added as a throwaway.

I groaned. "God damned Dorian," I growled, but I felt a smile tugging at my lips.

Pandora laughed at my condemnation of Dorian. "Your father is now resting. He fell asleep beside your bed, refusing to leave. Raidia is with him now in one of the guest rooms." She saw the concern on my face and smiled reassuringly. "With their own guard of four shifter bears. The father of the White Rose is very popular here at Castle Dracula. The royal family, as it were."

I let out a sigh of relief to consciously process that my father was back in my life and safe from harm. And he'd brought his witchy girlfriend. The same witch who'd helped my mother keep me safe as a baby. I'd almost forgotten about that bizarre coincidence. I'd lost Solomon and Richard, but I'd recovered my dad.

It seemed like years since I had seen him. I'd sent him away to keep him safe, but the city had never really gotten any safer. I hadn't had anywhere to keep him safe, but now I had Castle Dracula and Solomon's Temple. Except...

As Greed and Envy had shown me, even my new homes were not safe. The Sins had entered Castle Dracula and Solomon's Temple without any struggle. So had Archangel Gabriel. I needed to find a way to lock my places down to keep my people—and now my father and Raidia—safe. I forced away the depressing thought, knowing I had a lot more to catch up on before I started making plans.

I found myself smirking about Dorian. Love him or hate him, he always pulled through. Finding my lost father and managing to make him think we were dating. Couldn't have a win without a loss when it came to Dorian Gray. "Tell me that Ryuu didn't kill Dorian for claiming to be my boyfriend."

Her humor abruptly evaporated and her face grew pale.

She saw my sudden anxiety and plastered on a hollow smile. "No. Ryuu did not kill Dorian." Her silence stretched on, letting me know there was a whole lot of subtext left unsaid.

I glanced around the empty room, trying to recall if I had heard Ryuu's voice when I'd first woken up to find myself feeding on Pandora and my father wielding a revolver at my allies. Had he really shot Samael? And hadn't Samael said something about a bachelor party? The voices had said many strange things, but I couldn't quite recall them all. They felt like a swarm of butterflies circling my head, easy to see but hard to grasp.

But I felt my pulse beginning to quicken as I recalled my fight with Greed. How Ryuu had also been severely injured while trying to protect me. "Where is Ryuu?" I hissed. "He was covered in blood!"

Pandora placed a comforting hand on my chest. "He is fine, Callie. The blood was mostly yours. Ryuu has been...busy. When he's not here glaring everyone to death, he has been dealing with the...fallout."

I let out a breath of relief, but her words caused a ball of dread to settle in the pit of my stomach. "Fallout?" I asked, hoping my voice didn't sound as panicked as I felt.

Pandora nodded tiredly. "I will leave that explanation to him so I don't misstate anything, but I can clarify some things I personally learned about your little shit show." I finally took note of how exhausted she truly looked from being my blood donor. "You took quite the beating at the Vatican." She gestured to the side and I saw a collection of x-rays pinned to an illuminated, mobile display stand tucked against the wall. The screens showed the bones of my skull, torso, arms, and legs. I cringed, feeling like every bone I saw cracked and shattered on the sheets suddenly flared inside me, counting off with salutes of fresh pain.

Pandora recited my injuries like she was reading a spreadsheet. "Seven cracked ribs, two entirely broken free and stabbed into your organs, resulting in internal bleeding. Ruptured spleen, lungs, stomach, and intestine. Three shattered vertebrae and a broken collarbone." She turned to the image of one of my arms and I gasped to see a horrifying spiral fracture that sent a throbbing agony through my forearm.

She noticed my reaction and turned to me. "Yes. That one resulted in bones sticking out of your flesh." She pointed at the one of my skull, and I saw jagged lines over my cheek, two chipped teeth, one entirely missing, and my jaw distended. I also saw a hairline fracture on my forehead, but Pandora read them off for me, confirming my own layman's prognosis.

I checked my teeth with my tongue, searching for gaps or jagged breaks, but they were all healed and repaired. I arched an eyebrow at Pandora, and she tapped her bandaged forearm with a hollow smile. "I told you my wine was vintage. Roland had to leave the room once he smelled it. He didn't trust himself near me." A wicked smile crept over her cheeks and she licked her lips. "I offered to let him try a few licks if he let me have a few licks of him, but you took too much of my blood for me to remain upright, so you saved me from a bad decision," she admitted, chuckling huskily.

I smiled, thinking of Roland boinking Pandora. I lived in a crazy world and it was hard to realize how insane things were without stopping to say it out loud every now and then. "Thank you, Pandora," I said. "But I still don't understand what happened. How did I get my ass kicked so hard and why did my Mask fail me so violently?"

Pandora pursed her lips into a thin line. "That is a very good question. It is not my field, but I would recommend reaching out to Nate Temple to see if he knows anything about it. His Mask broke and I managed to help him fix it, but this was something different."

I sighed tiredly, feeling sluggish from so much conversation. My thoughts ran wild as they tried to process the information.

"You should get some more rest. Two days is nothing after what you went through," Pandora said, gently squeezing my palm. "I will send Ryuu over to visit if you promise not to overexert yourself."

I flinched to hear that it had been two days, but I nodded gratefully and obediently to her request. Then again, after seeing my slideshow of injuries, two days was pretty impressive. "Thank you again, Pandora. Don't tell anyone else I woke up. Let them sleep too. I'm sure they spent entirely too much time doting on me and are now half-dead themselves."

Pandora smirked. "I won't tell anyone, but you do remember that Cain and Xylo were here and are likely already planning a parade for you."

I groaned. "You should have let me die," I said, closing my eyes.

Pandora grew stiff. "Do not joke about that, Callie. As close as you were to the abyss...that joke is entirely distasteful because it dances too closely to the truth."

I opened my eyes and winced guiltily. "You're right. I'm still a little foggy."

She smiled warmly, dipped her chin, and then rose. "Master Dracula." Then she strode away.

"Hey, Pandora?" I asked, unable to lift my head high enough to see her across the room. "I'll waive your next year's rent for this," I said, smiling.

Pandora snorted. "Why? Nate Temple pays those bills, and he wasn't the one to help you."

I scowled. "Damn. Well, I'll think of something else then. Don't want him to get a bigger head than he already has."

The room was silent for a few moments. "You should call him, Callie. If he spends too much time alone in his mansion with nothing to do, he starts getting a little Howard Hughes-ey."

I grunted and then hissed at the resulting flash of pain. "He's alone in his mansion?"

Pandora smirked. "Well, Kára is with him, so he's probably busy doing *her*," she admitted, laughing lightly. Then she pursed her lips. "He's *probably* not peeing in empty milk bottles, but I can't be sure."

"Stop," I wheezed, biting back a laugh. "It hurts." But a part of me was happy to hear he'd latched onto some joy in his life after our battle at Olympus.

Pandora nodded apologetically. "What happened that day..." she trailed off, sounding uneasy, "was concerning. The Dread Four must come to understand it. Warriors must know the limits and strengths of their weapons, lest they rely on the wrong one at the wrong time."

I nodded slowly, already having determined the same thing. "I will. Later."

I cringed at my answer, remembering that it was what had pushed Nate and me apart—later.

"One more thing, Pandora," I said, hoping to come across as humorous. "On a scale of *one to Nate*, where would you put the situation out there?" I asked, smiling faintly.

Pandora did not smile. "Nate would suffer an identity crisis if he heard how severely you outperformed him."

I arched an eyebrow, my breath catching. "Oh?"

"It's bad, Callie. Very, very bad. I don't know how to quantify it because this isn't my pantheon." She turned away, reaching for the door. "Get some rest, Callie. I'll be back with more blood soon."

I felt despair seeping into my bones, knowing how helpless and defenseless I currently was. How broken and battered my body and confidence were. "You never told me where Ryuu is," I said, hoping I didn't come across as desperate and afraid as I truly felt.

Pandora hesitated for a moment as if debating whether or not she could pretend she hadn't heard me and slip out the door. I saw her shoulders sag and then she turned to face me. "He is in a meeting."

I nodded, feeling a sense of foreboding in her too-simple answer. "With?"

"The Four Horsemen demanded a debriefing of the fight at St. Peter's Square," she said, lowering her eyes.

I let out a breath of relief. "Oh. Are they finally going to get off their asses, and help me fight the Sins?" I asked, feeling a flicker of hope.

The look in Pandora's eyes doused it with a bucket of cold despair. "They demanded an explanation...from *you*. Ryuu and a small army are stalling them outside the gates of Castle Dracula." I flinched as if struck, staring numbly at the door as Pandora curtsied and left.

The door clicked shut and I closed my eyes, processing her parting comment. The Four Horsemen had come for me? What the ever-loving fuck? I tried to sit up but let out a gasp of agony as my wounds twisted and stabbed. I sank back into the bed, knowing I could do nothing to help Ryuu. I needed to let him handle it.

So, feeling worthless, pitiful, angry, scared, and as weary as I'd ever felt, I committed to the only thing that might change the situation—getting sleep.

Because I knew things were about to get a whole lot worse in the coming days. Greed had already broken into Castle Dracula once and she'd done it with ease...

She could do it again.

She *would* do it again.

"I'm strong," I whispered, lying to myself as I closed my eyes, ignoring the ever-present pain throbbing in my everywhere. "I'm brave," I stammered, hoping the words might give me strength. "And I never give up..." I added. My words echoed in the silent room, taunting me with their impotence.

Master Dracula may have cried before sleep took her, but no one was there to prove it.

Because she was all alone.

I dreamed I was in darkness...hurt, afraid, confused.

Blink.

I dreamed I was none of those things.

Blink.

I dreamed I was out of bed.

Blink.

I dreamed that I was staring at a reflection of myself in silver. My face was calm yet hard, as if someone had just killed my dog. I didn't have a dog.

Blink.

I dreamed that four men stood with their backs to me no more than three paces away. Elegant white wings jutted out from their shoulders. They leaned on spears. They did not notice my presence.

We were in a familiar wasteland. A desert littered with pillars of salt, heaps of bones and forgotten priceless weapons.

I was excited. I was horrified. I was in awe and full of love and despair and hope...but I didn't know why.

An endless, overgrown, wild forest stretched far, far, far into the distance, surrounded by a battered stone wall. A broken gate that had once been elegant and profound.

Before the gate stood two Archangels. Before the Archangels knelt two battered, bloody nephilim bound in shackles of glowing white metal.

They were also ignorant of my presence. It looked interesting. I watched their exchange.

Blink.

"The beast was here!" one of the Archangels snarled. He had long, straight blonde hair. "I assure you."

The other Archangel glanced at the worn gate and shrugged. He had shaggy, curly, raven-black hair. "Not anymore." He glanced at the two shackled nephilim and pursed his lips.

The blonde Archangel followed his gaze and clenched his jaw as he growled at the scrawnier prisoner. "Where does she keep them, boy?"

The prisoner shrugged, meeting his captor's eyes. "Hell if I know, Lord Uranus."

The Archangel kicked him in the gut and screamed savagely, spittle flying from his mouth. "It's Archangel Uriel, you useless sack of meat!" he screamed, his hair snapping with the gesture.

"It's Quentin," the groaning nephilim wheezed, "you feckless sack of feathers."

Uriel's cheeks darkened as he lifted his boot again, but the other Archangel placed a firm hand on Uriel's shoulder and pulled him back at the last moment. "How can you be certain she has what you seek, Brother?" he asked in a firm but calming tone.

The larger nephilim spoke up. "Yeah. Listen to Donatello. He's obviously the smartest Ninja Turtle—"

The curly haired Archangel abruptly held a long thin sword against the nephilim's jugular, cutting him off. "You are not as humorous as the stupid one," he said in an eerily soft tone. "Call me Lord Raphael or I will carve out your tongue. Last warning." The nephilim narrowed his eyes defiantly but remained silent. Archangel Raphael pursed his lips and sheathed his sword, turning back to Uriel. "Explain."

Uriel clenched his jaw at the command. "I've heard multiple reports. There is no other explanation. Michael and Pride are gone. Gabriel and Wrath are gone. Envy is gone. Greed is licking her wounds. What more proof do you need, Brother?"

Raphael grimaced but he shook his head. "You are a fool, Uriel. That is not *proof* of anything. You are obsessed, Brother. Why did you command my guardian angels to kidnap and beat them without my permission?"

Uriel pointed at the nephilim with a furious hiss. "Perhaps you did not notice the missing cuffs, Raphael!" he snapped. "We cannot let her reveal this or we are all doomed."

Raphael looked down at them with a disgusted look and a resigned sigh. "On that, we can agree..."

I had seen enough. I was bored. I looked at the backs of the four guardian angels and hungrily licked my lips. I froze time and the strangely familiar realm obeyed my will.

Blink.

Bloody feathers floated down all around me like falling snow. I was no longer hungry. I held the bony joints of severed, bloody angel wings in each hand but my arms hung loose at my sides as I stared ahead. I retracted my claws into my knuckles without a sound.

The two Archangels did not notice the deaths of their guards. Pity.

The nephilim noticed but they hid their reactions well. I felt proud of them.

Blink.

I felt a strange fog lift from my head, and sudden conscious awareness hit me like a pitcher of cold water. This...wasn't a dream. I was in control of my thoughts again. I froze like a startled rabbit, glancing left and right with wide eyes as I took in my surroundings. I really was standing before the Garden of Eden's battered gate, ten paces away from two very powerful Archangels and two severely beaten nephilim. My nephilim vampires. My family.

Quentin and Adrian.

Bloody feathers still drifted down to the ground all around me. It was time to punish more bullies.

Archangels were no easy meat. I glanced down to assess the weapons at my disposal. I wore only a long white pajama tee and underwear, my usual sleep attire. The shirt was so bloody that it was actually dripping at my feet. I was still gripping the base of a severed angel wing in each hand as if I might start flapping them in an attempt to fly. My lips and chin were also dripping blood, so I accepted the fact that I really had just sampled Eden's courtesy buffet upon my dazed and confused arrival to Hotel Eden.

Four heaps of gory guardian angel pieces surrounded me and I saw that my bare feet were actually standing in the chest cavity of one of the poor bastards. It looked like a pack of wild animals had set upon them, but it had been *me*. How the hell had no one noticed me kill four angels from ten feet away? I bit down my rising panic and took a careful step back. My legs started to shake violently as my subconscious started screaming at me for what I'd done in my sleep.

I drowned it out, staring at my nephilim. They needed me. My violence had been justified. The guardian angels had kidnapped and beaten my nephilim. Bad mommy time.

Something crunched under my bare foot and I bit my lip as the two Archangels spun, drawing wicked swords that gleamed with white light around the edges. They leveled those epic swords my way and stared at me, and then the dismembered bodies at my feet, in stunned, horrified silence.

Quentin grinned at me and Adrian gave me a trusting nod.

Crystalline armor suddenly sprang to life over Raphael, weaving and snaking over his muscles like a sentient creature. Uriel maintained his white robes and settled for glaring at me with raw, unfiltered hatred. Both their eyes glowed with a white light and their faces were perfectly unmarred. Michael had revealed that secret to me. They wore masks. Beneath they were typically scarred with the marks of battle from the Angel Wars that had taken place right here outside the Garden of Eden so long ago.

I looked back up at the two men and winced. "You guys ever woken up to find your pants missing?" I laughed awkwardly, indicating my bare thighs— which were smeared with bloody handprints from the dead guardian angels. "Super embarrassing," I continued, trying to read their body language. "Nothing?" I finally asked. "You two need to get out more."

"How did you *get* here," Raphael demanded, risking a swift glance up at the sky. "And how long have you been standing there?"

I thought about it and finally shrugged. "Dude. I have absolutely *no* idea. One second I was dreaming, and then *wham!*" I said, lifting the wings in the air, making it rain more bloody feathers. They flinched instinctively but I did not laugh at them. "I wake up here," I finished, lowering the wings and shrugging again.

Uriel was staring at my hands and feet with a confused look on his face. "She smells...wrong."

"Did you *eat* my guardian angels?" Raphael demanded, taking an aggressive step forward.

"Well, they weren't very good," I said defensively, glancing down at the bodies. I let out a sudden laugh at my accidental double entendre. "Good at their *jobs*, I mean. They *tasted* superb," I assured him, licking my lips for emphasis.

Quentin howled with laughter and even Adrian started chuckling between coughing sounds.

Raphael's face grew slack and I saw his armor growing spikier. He glanced at Uriel with a grim look. "I think I'm beginning to see the proof you spoke of, Brother—"

"This has been great and all," I said, interrupting him. I pointed one of the severed angel wings at Quentin and Adrian. "But those are mine."

"*Those?*" Quentin snapped sanctimoniously.

Uriel kicked him in the side of the head without even looking, and then he took an aggressive step forward, pointing his sword directly at me.

I narrowed my eyes at him and then cracked my neck from side-to-side. "Yeah. You really shouldn't have kicked that," I growled, dropping one of the wings and summoning my claws from my hand.

"*Him!*" Quentin shouted. "Not *that*! I'm a real boy!"

I grinned, baring my fangs at Raphael and Uriel as they started to spread apart to attack me from two different sides. "Yes, you are, Quentinocchio. Give mommy just a minute and I'll kiss your boo-boos."

I held the bloody angel wing out to my side, facing Uriel, and then I waved it fiercely. "Olé!"

❧ 13 ❧

Raphael lunged at my back and I spun, laughing as I swatted his blade down into the dirt with my claws and then clotheslined him with the wing. His own wingtips furled and stabbed into the ground, preventing him from falling on his ass. But he'd dropped his sword.

I abandoned the wing and replaced it with the sword, rolling it with my wrist to test the balance like Ryuu had taught me. Halfway through the motion, my angel gauntlets flickered into existence, encasing my hands. I grinned and took a step forward, settling into my sword-fighting stance. My heavenly boots crushed a skull beneath me and sent up a faint cloud of dust.

Raphael stared at my hands and feet with horror. "It's true!" he gasped.

Uriel was staring at my hands with feverish eyes, having lowered the tip of his sword to the ground without realizing it. "You will pay for your theft, White Rose," he whispered, and I heard an ominous rumble of thunder in the skies overhead as his eyes flashed brighter.

I straightened, frowning as I looked from one to the other. "Theft of what?" I asked, confused.

Uriel continued to stare at my hands but my eyes shifted to Raphael and his elegant armor. I frowned. I turned back to Uriel and his lack of armor, cocking my head. Then I slowly glanced down at my angelic gauntlets and boots. My eyes widened and I grunted.

"You have *got* to be shitting me," I breathed. I tossed Raphael's sword to the side and lifted one of my hands, inspecting the gauntlet at head level, twisting it back and forth as I compared it to Raphael's Archangel armor. I shifted my eyes to Uriel and saw the desperate look in his eyes. "These were *yours?*"

Instead of answering, the two Archangels crouched defensively, looking terrified and furious at the same time. I smiled and dramatically snapped my fingers. The sound echoed throughout the land like a gunshot, making everyone flinch. I frowned in disappointment. "Well, it's no Infinity Gauntlet," I grumbled, silently cursing my parents for yet another high crime: Grand Theft Archo.

Uriel and Raphael continued to stare at me, but their fear had abated slightly, replaced with curiosity. "You...don't have it all," Uriel murmured, staring at my legs and chest. "No wonder I could not find them!"

Rather than reveal my ignorance, I just stared back. Then I summoned up my wings of ice and fog and launched myself at them with a furious cry.

The two shared a thoughtful, expectant look, and then promptly disappeared.

I swept over the empty space where they'd been standing and landed beside Adrian and Quentin with a sigh of relief. I had known they would flee and had wanted to prevent them from executing my boys.

Adrian let out a tired cheer and I heard Quentin whistling smugly, but my eyes were firmly latched on the gate to the Garden of Eden. Many of the letters were missing or destroyed so it now said *Den of Ed* across the top. The last time I had been here had been when I had my first honest and open talk with Michael.

He had seemed alien and aloof to mankind, like some kind of artificial intelligence or something.

But Uriel and Raphael had seemed...well, like thugs. Gabriel as well, for that matter. Did that mean something significant? Were they more or less dangerous for it? Was that why they seemed bad where Michael had generally seemed good?

I had so many questions, but right now we were standing in enemy territory and I'd just pissed off two new Archangels. We needed to get home. Now.

I shook my head and glanced down at my two nephilim vampires. Adrian was propped up on one elbow, looking a little wild around the eyes, but

Quentin was flat on his back almost directly beneath me, staring up under my shirt at my—

"Hey!" I snapped, tugging my long bloody tee tight against my legs and hurriedly stepping to the side.

Quentin was grinning toothily, even though his teeth were covered in blood. "I'm a real boy!" He hooted, raising his shackled hands in triumph. He cast Adrian a sidelong grin. "Wow. Way better than I'd imagined, and way better than the Garden of Eden."

I kicked an angel femur at him, conking him in the nose since he didn't lift his hands fast enough to block. He cursed with a yelp and then started chuckling weakly. "Worth it," he groaned, painfully rising up to a sitting position.

I shook my head, realizing I was grinning as well. I bent down and inspected Adrian's glowing white shackles. I touched them with my angelic gauntlets and they let out a sharp clicking sound before dimming and snapping open. Adrian rubbed at his wrists with a groan of relief. "They blocked me from calling my claws," he said with a growl. Then he promptly summoned his claws—a matching set to mine—and grinned.

I looked over my shoulder at Quentin's shackles and sighed. "I'm feeling a little too tired to remove yours."

He snorted. "Oh, come on! You can't blame me for an innocent look!"

I arched a stern eyebrow at him. "Want me to tell Phix about your wandering eyes? You still owe her a few bodies before you regain her trust."

He pouted and averted his eyes. "Sorry, Master Dracula," he said in the exact same cadence and tone as 'we love you, Miss Hannigan!' from the orphans in the movie, *Annie*.

I laughed, shaking my head. "You're impossible, Quentin," I growled, very carefully scooting my way towards him so that he saw no more free shows. I broke his shackles and then rose to my feet with a weary sigh. I reached down to my stomach with a concerned frown. I could feel the thick pad of gauze over my wound but it did not hurt. Similarly, my legs and arms were peppered with wounds and stitches from my fight with Greed.

So...why was I not bedridden, and...

"Do either of you know how I got here?" I asked, trying to hide my anxiety from them.

Adrian arched a confused eyebrow at me. "You...stepped through a Gateway."

I squinted doubtfully at him. "Uriel and Raphael would have sensed me the moment I did that. And how did I kill the guardian angels without anyone sensing me or smelling the blood and feathers?"

Adrian glanced at Quentin, looking even more confused. "Is this a test?" Quentin asked me.

"Just entertain me for a minute," I grumbled, rubbing at my temples and closing my eyes.

"Okay..." Adrian said. "I saw a Gateway open up but it looked like a vertical pool of liquid silver rather than the fiery one. It was just suddenly there behind the guardian angels. It didn't make a sound at all. You stepped through and no one sensed a thing. I thought I was imagining it so I only watched you in my peripheral vision as they questioned us. You just stood there as still as a picture. Your hair didn't even move. They started arguing with each other instead of us and I risked a glance at you. I almost let out a shout when I saw you suddenly covered in blood, holding angel wings in your hands, and realized the guardian angels were shredded. I didn't even see you feed, and I still couldn't smell their blood." He was staring at me in awe.

Quentin nodded his agreement. "I only saw it in my peripheral vision too, but it looked like a completely silent explosion of blood and feathers. I thought I was losing my freaking mind until you looked up at me and met my eyes." He eyed my legs again and smirked. "So fucking hot. In a professional way."

Adrian kicked him in the shin and Quentin hissed. "Sorry," Adrian said, wincing at me.

"No. He's right," I murmured, absently waving a gauntlet at him as something in the air caught my nose's full attention. "I am," I heard myself say.

Quentin burst out laughing but I didn't acknowledge him. I took a step towards the gates, sniffing the air. What was that familiar smell? It wasn't necessarily coming from the Garden, but it had been very close to where I now stood. I took another big whiff and something clicked in my mind.

My breath caught and I gasped. "Sanguina?" I whispered, frantically glancing left and right.

But I saw nothing. We were completely alone.

I took another inhale, closing my eyes. It...was an old smell, but it was definitely her. Sanguina had come here in the last day or so. I don't know how I knew that, but I was certain of it. Was that what Uriel had been talking about when he tried to warn Raphael that someone had been here?

I shuddered at the thought of the Archangels hunting her. If they hadn't been before, they definitely would be after this. I glanced down at my gauntlets with a shiver. Tit for tat.

Heaven was definitely gunning for me now.

"How did they find you two?" I asked, frowning.

"Someone warned the nephilim we were coming in KC," Quentin said, narrowing his eyes, "so the raids were a bust. The buildings were all recently evacuated. Ryuu took off back to the Castle to warn you of a likely trap, but Eae sent us to the Vatican to keep an eye on the Conclave," Quentin said.

Adrian nodded. "Seemed the most likely place for nephilim to magically reappear, but we never made it into the Vatican. We were taken in Rome when we were investigating the...battle scene," he said, wincing.

Quentin eyed me curiously. "It looks like a few bombs went off there, boss. Almost broke the obelisk in the center when something shaped like you and Ryuu hit it."

I nodded, feeling a strange flutter in my stomach. Had that been what we hit when Ryuu caught me? "Yeah. It didn't feel great," I said in a soft voice.

Adrian cleared his throat. "Luckily, it started raining hard so the blood washed away, but..." He trailed off, staring at me from head-to-toe. "How are you standing right now?"

I grimaced, glancing down at the dead bodies. "Guardian angels," I said with a hollow smile.

They nodded but I could tell they didn't buy it. "You guys are on a strict censorship about..." I waved a hand disgustedly at our surroundings. "All of this. My ears only."

Quentin nodded, scratching at his chin. "You're covered in angel blood."

I glanced down at my bloody shirt, which was still dripping faintly. "Unidentified flying angels kidnapped you from Rome and took you to an undisclosed location. They were about to anally probe you when I saved your worthless hides," I said with a smile. "Other than that, you are fit to return to duty. Watching the Vatican is a good idea. If the nephilim would show up anywhere, that would be my guess. But don't get caught again if you can help it."

Adrian grinned. "No more UFAs. Got it."

"*And* no more anal probes," Quentin added, smirking. "Got it."

"And on *that* note..." I ripped open a Gateway back to Castle Dracula. "Come on, boys. It's bedtime."

"All right!" Quentin cheered until Adrian punched him in the stomach.

"Just stop, man. It's embarrassing," he grumbled.

I was smiling as I stepped through the Gateway with my nephilim behind me. For whatever reason, I was no longer bedridden, and—

My legs turned to wet noodles and I fell as pain roared through my body from head-to-toe. Someone caught me with a curse and I heard someone else shouting for help. I decided to go swimming in my sea of pain rather than stick around for all that nonsense.

14

I glared at the greater demon from my throne—the bed where I was recuperating from my severe injuries. I felt blood trickling out the side of my mouth as we stared at each other from across the room.

"You've got a little something right there," Lilith cooed as she pointed at my chin. She licked her thumb and made as if to rise so she could wipe it away for me. "You're a messy eater, sulfur sugar."

I narrowed my eyes. "No, godmother."

She sunk back into her chair, meeting my gaze with a faint smile. "*Yes,* goddaughter."

Pandora continued wrapping up her forearm in fresh bandages, watching the two of us like we were two stray cats in an alley that had suddenly became aware of each other's presence. And one was wounded. "Just to clarify," she said in a neutral tone, "was that you denying her help with your drool or are you two still arguing about the celebration?"

"*Wedding,*" Lilith corrected.

"I'm *not* drooling," I growled. "And both."

"Right," Pandora mused. And then she promptly reached over to wipe her own blood off my lip with damp gauze, making me feel like a child and taking away all my authority in my argument with my godmother. "There you are. Cute as a button."

I shifted my scowl towards her for the briefest of moments and she smirked.

Lilith laughed. "We already sent out *hate the date* cards and hung announcements throughout Castle Dracula. We've already booked the virgin sacrifices, exotic dancers, food, alcohol...oh! And flowers," she added, batting her eyelashes. "There is no stopping me, child. It is happening."

"We're in a war. Like, right *now*," I argued for the fifth time, trying not to shudder at the updates I'd finally received after my third day of recovering. "Ryuu only barely kept the Four Horsemen from arresting me."

Lilith leaned forward, her eyes flaring with fire. "He wasn't able to stop you from Shadow Walking in your sleep and returning an hour later covered in angel blood and feathers with two purple nephilim in tow," she said sweetly.

I flinched as if she'd slapped me. "I don't remember any of that," I lied. "And I really wish you wouldn't have told everyone, Pandora," I added with a stern look, even though I pointed specifically at Lilith to clarify who I meant by *everyone*.

The two women studied me pensively but I could sense their fear. How had I left and who the hell had I killed? I hadn't told anyone the particulars of the bizarre experience, and I'd explicitly banned Quentin and Adrian from talking. They quite literally couldn't answer questions unless I said so.

And that had infuriated quite a few people, but I refused to change my mind. Someone had betrayed me at the Coliseum, telling Greed exactly when to attack. Someone had known exactly when Ryuu's strike teams had planned to take down the nephilim hideouts and had alerted them.

After the strange encounter at the Garden of Eden, I was fairly certain it had been Uriel. He'd been furious about me breaking the cuffs of servitude on Quentin and Adrian and had been practically begging Raphael to help him with the cover-up. He obviously had the motive for taking the nephilim away before Ryuu could get them, and he definitely had the means and opportunity. He was an Archangel.

And that meant he, or one of his minions, was here at Castle Dracula or Solomon's Temple. It wasn't that I did not trust my allies, but the Archangels and Archdemons could perfectly shapeshift or possess their targets to such a fine degree that it was almost impossible to notice.

All that was on my mind.

But none of it was as concerning to me as how the fuck I'd wound up in the Garden of Eden at the exact moment I needed to be there in order to eavesdrop on Uriel and Raphael's argument. Just in time to save my nephilim from likely execution.

Sanguina had been there. I knew it. Had she led me there somehow? Spoken to me in my dreams?

But that didn't explain the fact that my injuries had not hampered me but had also not been healed. If Sanguina had helped me, I'd be cured right now. I thought. I tried reaching out to her again and felt nothing.

Come on, Sanguina! Give me something!

Pandora and Lilith were arguing amongst themselves about my nighttime excursion and I let out a tired sigh. "She could have killed herself!" Lilith hissed. "She obviously fed on angels, which is probably the only reason she's conscious right now." She eyed me with a hint of approval. "Took to it like a duck to water, child."

I groaned at my godmother's macabre compliment. "I'm fine. Really."

They ignored me. "As frightening as it was," Pandora mused, "she is in the exact same health she was before she fell asleep and disappeared, so I consider the matter settled." I smiled at her in silent thanks. "But if she killed an angel, we should expect a swift retaliation." I closed my eyes, taking my smile back from her.

"Oh, do stop pouting, goddaughter," Lilith said to me. "The Horsemen would have never succeeded in taking you," she snarled protectively, taking my silence as annoyance caused by her earlier comment.

I shrugged. "And how many of my people would have died in the fallout if they'd pressed the issue?"

"As many as needed to," she said callously. "Your people know the risks. After what they saw you do for them in the Coliseum...they would have burned the whole world to the ground to defend you from the Four Horsemen," she said in a tone of awe. "They truly love you, goddaughter."

AFTER MY SLEEPWALKING EPISODE, I'D FALLEN INTO A SEA OF ALTOGETHER different nightmares. Visions of the Four Horsemen razing Castle Dracula to the ground while I lay helpless had plagued my slumber, but even that hadn't been enough to wake me. However, I had finally recalled the snippets of chaos I'd overheard when I'd woken to find my dad protecting me with his hand cannon. The revelations hadn't improved my mood at all.

I'd finally awoken to find Pandora perched on the bed beside me, humming a Greek lullaby and twining my hair through her fingers in an affectionate, loving gesture. Upon seeing my eyes open, she had grinned happily and reassured me that the Horsemen had finally left after Ryuu told them I was away hunting down Greed. Without waiting for my response to Ryuu's blatant lie, she had torn off her bandage and shoved her forearm in my mouth, giving me the mutually exclusive choice between feeding or blood-boarding.

I'd chosen to drink, and Pandora had given me a brief rundown of Ryuu's confrontation with Death, War, Famine, and Pestilence—although Pestilence had introduced himself as Conquest.

The Four Horsemen of the Apocalypse had indeed faced a front united behind Ryuu. Alucard and Roland, Lucky and the Four Divines, Dorian Gray, Cain and Xylo, Aphrodite, Samael and Lilith in their full Greater Demon forms, and my father with his big-ass pistol. The Four Horsemen had been adamant about their demand to speak with me but they hadn't shown aggression. They had agreed to meet with me later since Ryuu had told them I was off on a mission that he had no authority—or compunction —to explain to them other than to say it would lead to Greed's demise.

It was humbling to hear so many people standing up for me after my colossal failure. It had brought more than one tear to my eye.

When Pandora had casually mentioned that Ryuu was on his way to see me, I had greedily latched onto her forearm, desperately lapping up the blood in hopes that my acceptance might heal me faster. I had drunk until I saw Pandora begin to sway slightly from exhaustion and then I had swiftly retracted my fangs, panting as I felt the power of her blood oozing through me, healing and restoring. Not enough but better than before.

With Sanguina gone, my blood-healing abilities were severely limited and no one knew why. Was I only Master Dracula with her by my side? She still hadn't returned and Starlight's search had been unsuccessful so far. No one knew where she had gone or why, and I could not sense her.

But I had sensed a hint of her trail at the Garden of Eden. I knew it.

Pandora had told me as much as she knew about Sanguina's departure but there wasn't much to tell. The fox had simply walked away from Castle Dracula before disappearing at the gates. My healers had tried feeding me every kind of blood imaginable but I had vomited all of them up, making my wounds tear further with each of the sudden violent expulsions. Only Pandora's blood had bypassed my gag reflex and only because she had reached through to me in my dreams, or whatever that strange place had been. My subconscious?

Then I had woken up unsupervised and subconsciously decided to take a walkabout where I fed on angels and did not throw up. Pandora had asked me about that but I'd shaken my head, refusing to answer. "I don't have any answers, Pandora, and I definitely don't know how it happened. I woke up in a strange place to find Quentin and Adrian in danger. I got us out and then collapsed. That's all I'm going to say right now."

On that light note, Lilith had walked in to deliver me a heated dressing-down and interrogation for sleep-murdering angels before hitting me with the one-eighty that my godmother was planning her goddamned wedding for tomorrow. We'd argued like family.

Pandora broke the current silence by loudly sipping from the straw of her glass of orange juice. I glanced over at the nightstand, but my eyes jerked away as they briefly settled upon Greed's claw that had been extracted from my guts. It had been cleaned and was warded from detection just in case Greed had the ability to track it—track me—but I imagined tendrils of darkness reaching out to me from the inert black claw.

I imagined Greed and Uriel skipping down a beach together with a parasol, laughing happily. It wasn't any crazier than reality. Wrath and Gabriel were pals. I tried not to think of the angelic gauntlets and boots my parents had apparently stolen from Uriel and gifted to me. Was that even possible? How would I even check?

My mother's laboratory might have answers, but I couldn't go anywhere without chaperones. I couldn't even question Quentin and Adrian on their story without someone listening in on me.

I let out a frustrated sigh and gently bumped the back of my head against the headboard. It was still chipped from where I'd buried my katanas the first time I'd taken Ryuu to my sheets. The fact that even that simple joy had been so fleeting—one night—really helped amplify my current mood. I'd been too injured to even play sheath the katana with my ninja lover. *Embrace the suck*, I chided myself.

I finally met my godmother's eyes. "With all of this shit going on, I still can't believe you decided it was the perfect time to plan your wedding. It is quite literally the worst timing. Ever. Were you trying to find a more efficient way for the most people to get killed when Greed returns?"

71

Lilith narrowed her eyes dangerously. *"With all of this shit going on,"* she repeated my phrase, "we thought it would be an excellent opportunity to celebrate why we put up *with all this shit going on."*

I winced, cringing in my everywhere as I acknowledged the precarious footing I was stomping on. I adored the fact that she wanted to marry Samael and even her haste to do so was touching, but the timing couldn't have been worse. "Sorry, Lilith—I mean, Godmother."

"No harm no foul, sulfur sugar," she replied, sounding as if her ire had also faded away. "And it would be an excellent distraction to conceal whatever you are *really* doing."

I sighed tiredly. "Yes. It would." I glared at the door. "As soon as I find out what that is. First, I have to get out of this bed on my own two feet," I growled, feeling a wave of anxiety and fear ripple through me at the thought, "and then I need to hear what's actually been happening while I've been bedridden. Which means the ninja better get his ass here before I start breaking things."

Pandora offered me her empty glass of orange juice with an inviting smile, pointing for me to hurl it at the wall. I accepted it with a thoughtful frown and then felt a smile tug at my cheeks as I shrugged. I very carefully hurled it at the door where it shattered. I felt flashes of sharp pain stab into my wounds but other than shortness of breath, the satisfying act of destruction hadn't killed me and it had improved my mood.

The door opened and a massive shifter bear peered in, checking to see that the sound hadn't been an attack on my life. I smiled, realizing it was Kenai. Greed's attack hadn't truly killed him. He curled his lip in what I hoped was a smile, dipped his chin, and then softly closed the door. I tried to push down the sudden reminder that Claire was still missing before it destroyed me. Greed and the wendigo had her.

Apparently, Greed and the wendigo had disappeared right after I was dragged away from Rome. No one had heard from them since. Two days of silence had everyone on edge. Especially since she now knew about Lucky. Well, she might not know *what* he was, but she knew he was *something.* Might was not a very reassuring word.

Please be okay, Claire. We're coming for you. I'm coming for you, I promised myself, hoping Greed had been lying about the wendigo gnawing on my best friend. I also hoped Greed had been lying about Envy's so-called gambit— voluntarily making herself a martyr for some greater cause.

15

I turned back to Lilith. "Has anyone heard from Greed or the goddamned surprise wendigo?" I asked. "Do we know whether she's alive or dead? If she was lying about holding Claire prisoner?"

Lilith shook her head. "No idea."

"Okay, I need to go—"

"Nowhere," Pandora said in unison with Lilith. The two shared silent looks, as if they were about to come to blows. Then they nodded ever-so-faintly to each other—apparently joining forces—and turned on me in unison.

I felt like a cornered rabbit. "Someone has to find Greed and take her out before she spills the beans about Lucky!" I growled. And if she really was working with Uriel, he would soon know as well.

They shrugged. "Wrath and Gabriel know about Lucky and they have done nothing," Lilith said.

"Unless this *is* their something!" I growled gesturing at the insanity we were dealing with. "What if Greed was following their orders?"

Lilith shrugged. "Greed did not know about the Anghellian when she arrived, so I find that highly doubtful. She sought the Divines, not Lucky."

"And she wanted to avenge her sister, Envy," Pandora added. "If she survived, she likely would have returned to finish you off. Or she is just as wounded as you. Or she's dead." She shrugged. "Did you really shatter her skull with a punch?" she asked curiously.

"Yes. Fat lot of good it did me," I muttered with a resigned sigh, jerking my chin at my broken body.

Pandora winced apologetically. "Sorry."

I had to force myself not to look down at the black ring on my finger. Why had Greed wanted it so badly? If she'd been telling the truth about Envy purposefully sacrificing herself to me, then why had she been surprised to see Envy's Halo? I was missing something. "We can't just sit here and hope for the best," I growled. "I'm taking her out—"

"No. We already dismissed that ill-advised plan," Lilith said calmly. "If you must do something, issue a command and let your people serve you. What good is being Master Dracula if you are the custodian charged with fixing every little problem?"

I stared at her, clenching my fists. I bit back a curse at the pain it caused my abdomen to breathe so angrily but Pandora noticed. She arched an eyebrow as if to say *I told you so*.

I ignored her wisdom. "My people look to me to protect them from the big bads, and Greed is a big bad. When it comes to the smaller things, I've got the nephilim, vampires, and ninjas helping," I explained, reminding her of the numerous other operations I'd immediately set up after killing Envy: investigating the murders of Solomon and Last Breath, staking out and planning raids on known nephilim hideouts, and searching for my best friend, Claire. All those ploys had either failed or come up as goose eggs so far, but I *had* let my people help me. They had failed just like I had failed. "The werewolves and ninjas are guarding the streets and looking for Claire while mapping demon and angel activity in town. But we can't do anything about Heaven and Hell unless we get the nephilim to serve me by breaking them free of their handcuffs," I growled, envisioning the strange bracelets Quentin and Adrian had worn that bonded them to working for the angels while concealing their latent and uniquely unsettling vampire claws. Claws that fed exclusively on angel blood. "And now we find out the nephilim got a hot tip about my raids and fled to God knows where. Then angels try to kidnap the two nephilim I do have."

I didn't say it out loud, but the conclusion was fairly obvious. We either had a traitor in our midst or a lot more spies at Castle Dracula than even I had anticipated. It was quite possible that more Sins or archangels were walking around in doppelgänger bodies since they could shapeshift and possess people so easily.

Like Envy had done to Claire.

Lilith's lips thinned, not appreciating my tone. "I believe the child has overstressed herself and needs some tea," she told Pandora. "If she is finished feeding on you, would you be a dear and—"

The door opened and Ryuu entered the room, speaking softly with Kenai. I let out a breath of relief and flashed a smile at Claire's massive loverbear. The bear smirked back at me, patted his now regrown arm and chuffed. I shrugged guiltily, having forgotten all about cauterizing his stump. "Any news on our girl?" I asked him, figuratively crossing my fingers.

His ears tucked low against his skull and he shook his head. "No, White Rose, but we have over two hundred of the St. Louis werewolves scouring the city with Master Alucard. I'm on the next rotation," he said eagerly. I nodded empathetically at him and he closed the door behind Ryuu. He wore his ninja blacks and I found myself eyeballing his tight pants.

That is Dracula's ass, I thought to myself, feeling territorial, even though I was crippled and couldn't currently entertain hanky-panky time. My ninja took one look at the room and then hesitated, sensing he was outnumbered three-to-one. All three of us folded our arms at him in unison, knowing we would not like what he had to say no matter what he said.

He processed this information with a faint smile and then turned to Lilith. "Samael wishes to speak with you regarding the wedding tomorrow. Something about the altar."

"Better cancel those sacrificial virgins or I'm going to ruin your special day," I murmured, giving Lilith the stink eye.

She smirked faintly—obviously hearing my comment—but her suspicious gaze was firmly locked on Ryuu. She finally gave him a resigned nod. "See that this foolish child remains in bed and does not sleepwalk again. If that means you must orally occupy her to keep her awake or until she fully recovers, then I expect you to man-up and do it. I hope you have a strong jaw. I will send refreshments to keep you nourished but the job itself is up to you."

Orally occupy me? Had she meant to say *talking*? Why had she phrased it so strangely—I froze, my cheeks flushing beet red as my brain's perverted translator kicked in.

Pandora burst out laughing and I blushed harder. "I think I can manage this onerous task," Ryuu said, biting back a grin. I felt steam coming from my ears but I clenched my jaw, glaring at my godmother with pure rage. She blew me a kiss, curtsied, and then exited the room.

Ryuu turned to Pandora with a tired sigh as if to say *one down, one to go.*

She arched a cool eyebrow at him, readying herself for the challenge like it was a duel. He approached the bed and sat on the end, facing her. He dipped his chin respectfully and waited for her to mirror the gesture before speaking. "Thank you for offering up your blood, Pandora," he said solemnly. "She is very precious to us, but to me most of all. She is stubborn, foolhardy—"

My claws erupted out of my knuckles, slicing through the blanket covering me.

Pandora grinned, eyeing my claws sidelong and then arching an inquisitive eyebrow at Ryuu to gauge his reaction. He was also grinning, but pretended not to notice as he continued. "She is reckless and too big-hearted to see the larger picture when those she protects are in danger. She sees herself as a warrior more often than a leader, and that carries its own burdens and considerations. We need her healthy and strong so that she may swiftly return to the fight, and it seems you are the best option to help her do so."

Pandora nodded pensively, likely wondering what he was aiming at with his strangely specific compliments. "I am quite amazing," she said beneficently.

Ryuu nodded solemnly. "You are also one of the brightest—if not *the* brightest—mind we have on our side at the moment. We need to know what Envy was really doing at Solomon's Temple. Why she saw fit to execute Solomon and Last Breath, and whether that was out of personal animosity or a result of what Callie had asked them to research. Greed told Callie that it was a voluntary sacrifice Envy chose to make, but we don't know if she was lying or not. I've heard Callie call you a librarian, and we are sorely in need of such a skill."

Pandora turned to look at me, silently asking my thoughts. I sighed in annoyance and nodded as I retracted my claws. "In addition to letting me feed off your blood, would it be terribly inconvenient if you let us leach off your mind as well?" I asked dryly.

She smirked. "Of course not. Though I will remind you again that this is not my pantheon so I'm not sure how much help I will be. That being said, I am eager to offer my services." She scrunched up her nose. "Not my *oral* services." She pointed a finger at Ryuu. "Because Lilith expects *you* to—"

I managed to throw a pillow at her without rupturing my spleen, and she cut off as she lashed out with a sharp blast of an alien, strange magic. The pillow exploded into feathers a few inches from her face and her triumphant snort turned into a choking wheeze as she immediately inhaled the remains of one thousand dead gooses.

Yes, gooses. Deal with it, Kerri—I mean, *Karen.*

She rose to her feet, swatting at the feathers as she gasped for air and made her way to the door, pretending not to notice my triumphant laughter. It clicked closed after briefly revealing a very puzzled looking Kenai on the other side. I let out a sigh to finally have some privacy and turned to Ryuu. My humor faded even though he was smiling at me. He had bad news to deliver about the fallout, as Pandora had called it.

I hadn't seen him since the fight in Rome, although I had been told he had remained in my rooms to watch over me while I slept—except when I'd sleepwalked to the Garden of Eden to eat angels and save my nephilim. Seeing him healthy rather than covered in blood and barely able to hold his own sword against Greed was like a dream come true. But judging by the dark circles under his eyes, he hadn't slept much in the last few days. Too busy bullying Horsemen, patrolling the streets, or keeping an eye on me.

I realized that he was about to start justifying why it was perfectly okay for me to rest up in bed while everything else fell to pieces. That he was about to sugarcoat the bad news. I opened my mouth to angrily—

"Get up," he said in a firm, no-nonsense tone as he rose to his feet. "We're going for a walk."

My mouth clicked shut and I felt momentarily befuddled. "Wait. *What?*"

He smirked at the bewildered expression on my face and then unceremoniously flung back the corner of my blankets, exposing my broken body. Pandora had bathed and changed me while I slept off my excursion. I wore a fresh sleep tee that Claire had bought me.

In the famous cursive font Disney used, it said *She wants the D.*

Like my outfit in Eden, the shirt only just covered my hips, and that was it. My brief humor swiftly evaporated as I took stock of the bruises, lacerations, stitches, and crusted blood decorating my flesh. In Eden, I had been covered in so much blood that it had disguised how terrible my injuries really looked. I resembled the Bride of Frankenstein. I couldn't remember getting half of my injuries.

Within milliseconds, I felt incredibly helpless and vulnerable, as if a spotlight had suddenly illuminated my failings for all to see. It was humiliating and I realized I hated looking upon myself. This was the first time I was seeing Ryuu and he saw me as a broken creature rather than the powerful, relentless woman he loved.

I felt my eyes grow misty with shame. *I looked powerful in Eden!* I wanted to shout at him.

I wasn't upset at Ryuu, I was disappointed in—and disgusted with—myself. To physically see myself wearing nothing but a t-shirt and underwear while I'd been acting so brave and tough to Pandora and Lilith a few minutes ago was jarring. I hadn't truly accepted how ridiculous my situation was until the protection of my blanket was removed. Like a turtle without its shell or an eagle without its feathers.

Ryuu's face showed no shock or compassion or empathy for my wounded and frail frame; it was a challenging stare directed at my eyes rather than my battered body. "I don't trust anything that isn't broken, White Rose," he growled, staring into my eyes. "Fractured glass makes rainbows while flawless windowpanes are transparent and invisible, holding no secret magic."

My breath caught in my throat and I felt my stomach flutter as another tear dripped down my cheek.

Then he glanced at the pitcher of ice water on the night stand. "I sense a cold rain coming in," he murmured, slowly bending forward to grasp the handle of the pitcher.

﹩ 16 ﹩

I squawked in alarm and shambled upright as carefully as I could, determined to keep myself as decent as possible for some inexplicable reason. I almost cried out in relief to find that the sudden motion hadn't caused me to cry out in pain. He chuckled, abandoning the pitcher.

"Such a jerk," I muttered. Then I gathered my resolve, held my breath, and slung my legs over the edge of the bed. I winced at the echoes of sharp, twisting pains in my stomach and arm, and the faint occasional throbbing of my cheek and jawbone. Pandora's blood was strong, but I was different from most vampires. Drinking blood seemed to dramatically supercharge my magic but it was nowhere near as fast at healing my body like it did for other vampires. Then again, that could have something to do with Sanguina's mysterious absence. So, was I feeling better because of my late-night angel snacks or because of Pandora's breakfast?

Whatever had completely washed away my injuries in Eden was nonexistent now, but I did feel better.

Ryuu smiled, dipping his chin. "Guilty as charged. Do you need your cane?"

I pursed my lips angrily, knowing that the second part was not a joke as I saw him pointing a finger at the floor beside my nightstand. A glistening ivory cane rested against the wood and I frowned, wondering where he'd gotten it and when. I nodded stiffly, still feeling embarrassed and insecure and ashamed.

"Callie," Ryuu said sternly. "Stop pouting. Weakness is giving into fear and remaining in bed when you feel shame; bravery is choosing to face that fear walking on your own two feet even though you might fall flat on your face." Initially, my temper had flared at his harsh reprimand, but then the deeper meaning of his words hit me, resonating with entirely too much truth to deny. Ryuu had not wanted to sugarcoat anything for me or to make excuses for me. He had purposely sent Pandora and Lilith away because he hadn't wanted me to suffer an audience while I faced my fears.

He wanted me strong and confident again.

And if he had to risk my ire to get me there, he would die on that hill. If it made me better, the cost to himself did not matter at all. In that moment of fear and anxiety and shame, I felt my heart grow warmer as I realized Ryuu loved me too much to let me wither and die on the vine of self-doubt.

He held out the ivory cane with a challenging grin on his handsome face. "Oh, and this cane is a weapon used to teach swordplay to young children."

I had been reaching out for the cane—while he slowly pulled it farther and farther from my reach—when I paused to shoot him a wicked scowl and then settled my ass firmly back on the bed. "Are you calling me a young child?" I asked in a dangerous tone.

He nodded sagely. "Congratulations. You have been promoted from insecure invalid to petulant young child. I forgot to bring a belt to signify your new rank," he said, biting back a grin.

I swiveled my head suddenly, sensing danger near the door. Ryuu spun on a heel, drawing his black katana with a grim scowl. I lashed out with a tendril of magic, scooped up the pitcher of ice water, and immediately dumped it over his head. The ice water splashed down around him, soaking him from head-to-toe.

"Ha! Suck on that, tall, dark, and broody!" I said, grinning. "My *magic* isn't broken!"

He slowly turned to shoot me a hungry look that momentarily took my breath away and made my smile falter. "Well done," he said, nodding his approval. "You capitalized on my subconscious reflex to protect you. That was clever."

I nodded smugly, burying the momentary panic and lust that had flared through me upon seeing the dangerous gleam in his eyes.

"You have been promoted past the use of a cane," he said. "Congratulations again." Then he hurled my ivory cane out the open bedroom window. How the hell was I going to walk *now*?

I stared dumbfounded at the sopping wet ninja. He looked utterly ridiculous. He held out his hand and nodded encouragingly to me. "Let's go. They are waiting."

My stomach suddenly fluttered and my heart dropped down a few stories below me as if it was tied to the cane Ryuu had just thrown. "Who is waiting?" I whispered.

"Everyone, White Rose. They are waiting to catch a brief glimpse of their Master Dracula after her glorious adventures across the globe hunting down the Sins."

I licked my lips nervously and realized that I was subconsciously checking my hair. "I don't know, Ryuu. They'll see how weak I am, and I can't afford that right now or else it might attract the Sins—"

He placed a warm finger over my lips, suddenly leaning into my personal bubble. "You will be on the ramparts overlooking the courtyard. Everyone will be down below. You need simply smile and wave at them. This is part of your job as monarch—to show them confidence. *Especially* when you don't truly feel it."

I nodded stiffly, knowing he was right. "No speech?" I asked nervously.

He shook his head. "You are far too busy hunting down Sins to give speeches," he said in a playful tone.

I grabbed his hand and carefully pulled myself to my feet. I sucked in a breath, tensing my muscles in anticipation of the wave of pain that would hit me—

I blinked in confusion, letting out a nervous breath. I reached down to touch my stomach beneath my thin tee and I let out a sob of relief when I felt no immediate pain. If I pressed harder, I would definitely cramp up, but it was no longer painful to the touch. I still wore bandages over my abdomen, but they weren't saturated with blood and discharge anymore.

My arm trembled faintly, already feeling tired, and my legs wobbled dangerously, but that was expected with my first steps out of bed. They would grow stronger and less awkward after a few steps. Ryuu held his arm out for me to use as support as I familiarized myself with the standing position. He did not judge and he did not mock me. He would only do those things when I was lounging, but the moment I showed any initiative to push myself, all mockery would be replaced with encouragement and glowing pride at even the slightest of achievements.

"Okay," I said, "Dracula should probably put some pants on."

Ryuu let out an unexpected laugh and nodded his agreement. I closed my eyes and summoned up the magical white outfit Aphrodite had made for me. I felt it wrap over my body like a bandage and I let out a soft sigh of relief, realizing that the form-fitting outfit actually served to reduce the general aches and pains from my injuries. It didn't get rid of them entirely but it helped, kind of like an ankle wrap after a mild sprain.

I opened my eyes and glanced down, nodding satisfactorily. My muscles were still twitchy and shaky but I looked like a million bucks. Ryuu studied my body, grumbling hungrily under his breath in a way that did more to boost my confidence than I expected. He saw me as sexy and that helped to further reinforce my self-image.

I don't care how self-empowered a man or woman is or how pretty they think they are—when another person looks at you and purrs or growls like they want to lick you from your toes to your lips, it sends an immediate and primal boost to your morale and self-image.

You could feel beautiful by yourself.

But you could feel smoking-hot booty-full when the right man looked at you the right way.

Ryuu pointed at the door to the bathroom. "Put a bow on it, woman."

I turned to look and then I gasped in surprise. A rich, hooded, red cloak hung from the door. The quality was nicer than anything I had ever worn, and the elegant, thick fabric featured a huge, fancy white rose embroidered on the back. The hood and lapels were lined with white fox fur, reminding me of Sanguina, and I felt my throat tighten with concern for her absence even as joy for the beautiful cloak consumed me. My hand had already started reaching for it without my conscious thought, needing to touch the fabric to lay claim to the wonderful garment—like when you spotted the perfect pair of shoes at the sale of the century and rediscovered your Viking DNA that urged you to kill, pillage, and burn in order to take what was yours before another wretched woman could set her eyes on it.

Your purse was your axe and the glory of Valhalla awaited you should you fall—

"Callie?" Ryuu asked curiously, startling me out of my reverie.

I mentally replayed the last few moments to make sure I hadn't verbally impersonated Gollum. I hadn't, thankfully, but I *had* shambled forward three steps before realizing that Ryuu was not supporting me. I froze, sucking in a breath as my mind suddenly screamed at me that I was going to fall.

"Ignore them!" Ryuu barked. "Pain and fear are false gods. Worship them at your own peril."

I flinched at the unexpected authority in his command, and then I grinned broadly, realizing he was right. I hadn't fallen over! My legs were weak and still unsteady, but they were doing their job, even if I did feel like a new fawn taking her first steps. I laughed excitedly and lurched forward into the doorframe, using it to lean against as I snatched the cloak and lifted it to my face. I inhaled deeply and smiled, closing my eyes.

"It smells like you," I whispered, turning to Ryuu.

He grunted. "If it offends your delicate sensibilities, I can throw it out the window and commission a second one."

I opened my mouth to laugh off his joke, but then I processed his last words and it cut me short. I blinked slowly, staring at him as I held the precious cloak to my chest. "You...had this *made* for me?" I asked in a soft tone. I had assumed it to be one of the many random gifts that appeared in my closet from the tailors at Castle Dracula. They'd worked hard to get me a fresh new wardrobe in addition to the elegant selection I'd acquired from Mina Harker, my true predecessor.

But Ryuu had individually chosen to commission this cloak for me? My heart suddenly throbbed deeper, and that loving warmth transformed into lustful fire as it spread to a few notable, under-appreciated, parts of my body that I had been unable to have serviced in my convalescence. I felt my cheeks growing bright red at the thought, and Ryuu grinned knowingly.

"Yes," he admitted to both my spoken question and my nonverbal thought. I watched as his eyes grew distant, using the moment of silence to clear the dirty thoughts out of my brain. "The bravery and fire you showed when pursuing Greed beyond the safety of the Coliseum was both reckless and sensationally smart. It was inspiring. That act alone served to rally your forces to harass the wendigo into fleeing. For your people to see you, injured and on the brink of death, purposely choosing to take the fight outside of the safety of the Dueling Grounds." He shook his head in wonder, smiling faintly. "For the first time, I saw your people actively working together as a team despite their differences. The new vampires from the Sanguine Council huddled around the weak and fought off demons to keep them safe. They worked together because of the bravery you displayed," he said, turning to meet my eyes. "I've never seen your people love you more than they did in that moment."

I blushed with pride and lowered my eyes, drinking in the healing balm of his words. Even though I had failed, I had failed in the best way possible —uniting my monsters.

"And," he continued, "I thought you would look beautiful in it. My decision was mostly selfish because I fantasized about you wearing it for me in private once you are fully recovered," he said, raking his hungry eyes down my chest and legs.

"Stop taunting me, Ryuu!" I growled playfully, brushing my fingers across the plush velvet interior of the cloak. Ryuu's fantasy was a good one. I could imagine this on my bare shoulders after a few glasses of wine and a dim candlelit night in with my ninja. I carefully flung it over my shoulders, leaning against the doorframe so I didn't fall flat on my ass. I slipped on a pair of loose sneakers over my bare feet, flung up the hood to hide my mess of unbrushed hair, took a careful step away from the support of the doorframe, and then turned to him with an expectant look.

He grinned. "A queen."

I shook my head, smiling wickedly as I glanced down at my hands. Envy's Halo and the Seal of Solomon occupied the same finger but on opposite hands. "I'm not a queen, Ryuu. I'm a *Master*," I said, embracing the title of the mysterious forces lining up against us for the upcoming Omega War. I had unintentionally become one, although that had not amounted to anything yet. Nate was also a Master.

Ryuu nodded his agreement and gave me a mock bow. "Master Dracula," he said solemnly.

I rolled my eyes with a faint smile. "Escort me to the ramparts, Halo Breaker," I said in an imperious tone. "And tell me the truth about what kind of fallout we're facing."

Ryuu nodded and grabbed my katana for me before walking towards the door. The first few steps were the hardest but my legs grew steadier with only a low-grade burn of fatigue by the time I reached the door. Ryuu opened it and a colossal bear stood in our way, almost filling the entire hall. Kenai. Ryuu spoke to him in a low tone and I absently reached into my pocket as I felt something poking at my thigh. I felt a somewhat crumpled business card and pulled it out with a frown.

It was simple and plain, but it sent a chill down my spine. *The Toymaker* followed by a contact number. I'd arranged a meeting with her prior to my fight in the Coliseum, but I'd missed our appointment after my injury. Damn it! With how easily Greed had entered my home it was even more important for me to speak with her about installing a security system here, but the fewer who knew about the breach the better. I palmed the card and managed to mask my features as Ryuu turned to check on me. I gave him a nod and a gesture for him to lead the way. The moment he turned around I slapped the card into Kenai's massive paw and breathed a command.

"Tell Dorian Gray to reschedule it for tonight. Period."

He nodded subtly and then I walked past him. I heard him lumbering behind me as another bear stepped out of an adjacent hall to take his place guarding my door. Kenai's claws scraped the stone behind me and I could practically feel his hot breath on my neck as I caught up with Ryuu.

"So. I'm practically crippled, the Four Horsemen want me on trial, the Vatican wants me burned at the stake, Hell wants me to be their new step-mother, Heaven wants me eradicated, we didn't find any nephilim, my Horseman's Mask is out of commission, Greed knows about Lucky, and we still haven't found Claire," I said in a calm, emotionless tone. "What else did I miss?"

When he told me, I felt my heart turning to cold, merciless stone as we walked through the halls of Castle Dracula. I gritted my teeth and willed my muscles to get stronger, my wounds to heal faster, and my fury to burn hotter.

Because my little stunt in Rome had inadvertently started World War Dracula, and the odds weren't looking good for the home team.

17

I had carefully filed Ryuu's data-dump of threats on the near horizon, hoping to let them simmer on my mental back burner as I focused most of my effort on walking with bold, purposeful steps. It worked for a time but once he stopped speaking, they seemed to come creeping back with a vengeance. Not all news was bad but the scales were definitely imbalanced.

Pandora had used her plight as my blood donor to bully Hephaestus into finally committing to firing up the Eternal Metal forges at Castle Dracula, giving him a sense of urgency about it. The blacksmith god had hoped to avoid his wife, Aphrodite, until what he saw as her semi-betrayal—actually an incredibly selfless act of love, in my opinion—had faded from the forefront of his mind.

But this was Aphrodite we were talking about, and now that she was my House Manager at Solomon's Temple, she had her fingers knuckle-deep in all the honeypots of local gossip and had conveniently started making casual appearances at the forge. Aphrodite had found every reason imaginable to saunter on down to the forges and watch her husband work. She brought water, sandwiches, towels, refreshments, and she even hired a pack of goblins to sing raucous songs to her husband and his workers while they struggled to mint the first weapons for the upcoming Omega War.

Hephaestus had grown very twitchy because his wife never actually confronted him. She was just always there to help before anyone else knew help was needed. Unfortunately, the supply of Eternal Metal was lacking as a result of Sanguina's absence, so Hephaestus' resources were limited.

The bears had earned badges of respect for Kenai's performance against both me and Greed, and Armor had fought viciously against the wendigo before it had fled the Coliseum after I tackled Greed through the Gateway to Rome. Most of my residents believed the carefully promoted lie that I had been globetrotting since the fight, smiting down Sins and leaping small churches in single bounds.

Morale was vital. If they saw how easily Greed had slapped me around, learned the severity of my wounds, or heard that my Horsman's Mask had failed, they might get very concerned when they processed the fact that four other Sins were still out there besides Greed.

But word of my battle at St. Peter's Square had definitely spread like wildfire. Thankfully, the less savory details had been omitted and everyone was simply stunned that I had slammed Greed down into the heart of Rome, destroying a fountain with her face.

I had been grateful to hear that only a dozen vampires and werewolves had truly died during the Coliseum attack. Most of the severely wounded had either been brought to the Dueling Grounds and executed—allowing them to wake up healthy and whole—or brought to the healing pool at Xuanwu's estate for a swift recovery.

But twelve dead still injured my heart. I had utterly failed to protect them. What if all five Sins came next time? What if the archangels came as well? The Coliseum would take some time to repair. I'd broken a good chunk of the wall when I'd thrown Greed into the stands and the wendigo had caused plenty of his own damage at the onset of the attack with Greed and her black fire.

But overall, my people were proud of both my theatrics with Kenai and my supposed handling of Greed and her pet wendigo. Cain, Roland, Fabrizio, and Eae had been secretly poring over the libraries inside Solomon's Temple in an effort to investigate Envy's true purpose in murdering Solomon and Last Breath. They'd mentioned specific books for me to look into regarding answers on the Divines, the Seven Sins, and the Archangels. Also, the Anghellian I'd accidentally made with Lucky.

Who, unfortunately, had been absolutely no help in the research depart- ment. Michael had been a warrior and Pride had been an arrogant opportunist. Neither had been scholars. Lucky had grown more and more reclusive and distant since our battle with Greed. He'd been caught walking around talking to himself or hanging out with the four Divines. Strangely enough, he'd even started meditating.

People seemed scared of him. Even Ryuu pursed his lips warily when telling me that Lucky and the Divines were cooped up at Xuanwu's estate most of the time. Whatever that meant.

Despite the number of people searching for answers, they had come up with absolutely nothing helpful. No answers on Wrath's dark prophecy about me, no mention of the Anghellians; plenty of talk about the nephilim and their angel parents, the Watchers, but they had found no books on the Divines or the supposed Azrael Scrolls Last Breath had told me about.

Something about that thought made me want to scratch my head but I couldn't place why. I would do some digging of my own into the dangerous books Last Breath had warned me about once I was finished with my brief appearance at the ramparts.

I reached the last step in my climb, not even having realized I'd been climbing stairs in the first place. I paused to take a breath, feeling my legs quiver warningly from the heavy workout I had given them. I gripped the railing for support as I stared through the archway leading out onto the ramparts. Ryuu held both of our swords in one hand and waited patiently, giving me a nod of encouragement.

I studied him suspiciously. "Why haven't you asked me about my sleep-walking?"

He stared back at me. "By biting my tongue very hard. It's obvious you don't wish to discuss it yet, so I will wait until you think I need to hear it." His lip curled up faintly. "For the record, I am not happy about it." He gestured towards the archway with the swords. "Stop stalling and get your ass out there."

I grinned. "I am Master Dracula, and I will not trip and break my ass-bone in front of my adoring monsters," I vowed. Ryuu covered his mouth with a fist and coughed, trying not to laugh at me.

I took a deep breath and strode through the archway and out into the open night sky of the ramparts.

Crackling torches lined the balustrade overlooking the streets below and cast a crimson glow on my immediate surroundings. Ryuu walked by my side —a step back so as not to share the limelight but close enough to catch me if

I stumbled. I hadn't tripped during our walk and it had given me a boost of confidence for my short-term future. Like justifying how being able to take a shower by myself would logically result in me being able to defeat all of the Seven Sins.

The black night sky seemed so huge, reminding me of my strange dream with Pandora. My red hood was up and I felt it billowing slightly in the breeze that always blew this high up. I was surprised to see Fabrizio standing within the archway of a second staircase that led back down to the castle proper. He studied me intently, looking impressed at my mobility. His hands were still bandaged and apparently useless, reminding me of how I had also failed him, and that had only been against a trash-gobbling demon in an alley.

I shook off the pessimistic thought, wondering if he had any new updates on the future of his hands—like if he would have them or not. Also, what furious threats—missed confessional opportunities—he'd heard from the Conclave as a result of my offense at St. Peter's Square.

I dipped my chin at him, knowing he wanted to speak with me about that. Ryuu had told me that he'd swiftly placed himself in charge of cleaning up that mess for me. Not with the Conclave directly—because he'd apparently been excommunicated from the Shepherds for his proximity to me—but with making an anonymous donation to the Vatican proper to cover repairs on the bizarre attack that was now all over the world news. Thankfully, everyone had been running away and screaming, so no mobile footage had caught clear shots of the demon, or me in my Horseman's Mask, on video. Just a lot of explosions, destruction, screaming, and running. And a heavy rain had washed away DNA, according to Quentin and Adrian.

I hoped they were right about that.

I'd been glad to hear that no one had died and there had only been a few minor injuries caused by people trampling each other in their haste to escape. I again forced myself to swallow the pang of guilt I felt at how foolish of an idea that had been. I'd been seeing the Vatican and the Conclave Shepherds as one unit, but that wasn't entirely true. The Conclave was very independent, and most of the Vatican had no idea it even existed.

By taking my fight with Greed to St. Peter's Square, I had dealt a solid blow to the faiths of billions of normal, God-fearing men and women. In a way, my spite for the Conclave had benefited Hell. That was definitely how the Conclave had seen it.

And probably how Uriel and Raphael had seen it as well since they'd kidnapped my nephilim in Rome.

I reached the balustrade and leaned forward, taking in the expansive crowd gathered in the courtyard below. It was swarming with bears, frog-men, vampires, werewolves, and plenty of witches—members of the Hellfire Club likely brought here by Dorian Gray when he'd collected my father and his lady friend, Raidia.

They looked to be having some kind of street festival because the air smelled of freshly sizzled meats, spices and wine, and music played from several pop-up tents lining the street. Some of them had been looking up so they were the first to see me and the first to erupt in outrageously excited cheers. The rest of the crowd turned and the cheers doubled upon them-selves until it was a startling roar. I gripped the stone with shaking fingers and forced myself to smile down at them.

Gargoyles shrieked overhead, swooping down and up in a Flying V formation and I smiled at the rush of wind from their beating wings.

I heard a scrap of tile shatter on the rampart, sounding like a broken vase, and my smile abruptly fractured as one of my fingers suddenly surged with intense heat. I glanced down and saw that it was the finger wearing Envy's Halo.

I blinked, confused as I heard whispers on the wind, urging me...

Destroy the threat! a strange voice abruptly screamed from within my own head, laughing like a lunatic. I spun on instinct just as I heard Ryuu shout out a warning.

A black silhouette dropped out of the air above and behind me, almost invisible to the naked eye, camouflaged with the dark sky. I could only make it out due to the contrast of its body against the towering spires looming up from the castle. I heard another crash and realized it had been a second roof tile, dislodged from this creature's perch when it had leapt into the air to assassinate me. Its wings were tucked close to increase speed and it was eerily silent as it came for me.

In a perfect Jack Nicholson impersonation, a voice inside my head sneered, *Here's Envy!*

And then I felt Envy's Halo snatch complete control over my body and shove me into the cockpit of my own head to watch the immediate future play out from behind the windows of my own eyes.

I was now simply along for the ride.

It felt eerily similar to my sleepwalking episode last night, except this time I was conscious for it all.

A torrent of power screamed through me, burning my injuries away to ash like the purifying chaos of a forest fire, and I felt new shoots of vibrant life and strength abruptly scream through the powdery wasteland of my smoldering humanity, making me feel like I was about to explode.

My muscles and bones and ligaments sang with joy and I realized my eyes were crying with rapture as I watched my broken body do the impossible.

᠅ 18 ᠅

Ipirouetted with the ease and agility of a professional ballet dancer, hearing myself laugh out loud as my red cloak twirled around me like a matador's cape. The beast grabbed at me with inky black claws as long as my forearm, and the reflection of the crimson torches lining the ramparts finally hit its slick black skin, revealing a demon-pterodactyl hybrid.

A flying maw, Envy's alien voice informed me, sounding terribly amused. *Do try to keep up, dear.*

I was too startled by the direct message to formulate a response, and too rattled by the unexpected attack to do more than simply stare. But what Envy did with my reborn body...

I wasn't sure I had ever moved quite so fluidly before.

The flying maw's long claws slammed closed on empty air, emitting a shower of yellow sparks, but the creature immediately extended them again in an effort to latch onto the balustrade and halt its momentum, scoring deep gouges in the stone as it flexed its legs and launched itself back up into the sky and out over the roaring crowd below.

Said crowd abruptly stopped cheering, suddenly confused to see the monstrosity occupying the space where I had just been standing. It spread massive wings that looked like kites and raced straight for the gargoyles flapping their wings in the air. They held spears and their eyes burned with crimson fire but they couldn't risk hurling the weapons and missing, because that would have put their Master Dracula in danger.

I laughed jubilantly, shaking my head in amusement. Well, Envy puppeteered me to do so.

Realizing that Ryuu still held my katana, I let out an annoyed growl. Instead, I lashed out with my fingers like I was cracking a whip in either hand.

Black chains screamed into existence from the depths of Hell, crackling with electricity—

Sulfuricity, sweetness, Envy corrected without missing a beat or sounding the least bit exhausted.

Sulfuricity. Of course, I thought back at her. The chains wailed like the souls of the damned as they zipped out into the air and wrapped around the demon-dactyl's legs, drawing it up short. It spread its wings further, beating furiously so that it looked like I was flying a kite.

I grinned wolfishly. "Let's have some wind then!"

And I summoned a storm of wind and ash that ripped at the balustrades and shook up the gargoyles as they fought to remain airborne. The demon on my chains let out a honking scream as I tugged on one foot and then another, making him dance and barrel roll in the air even as the arcs of sulfuricity scorched his flesh and danced over the membranes of his wings, causing it to sizzle and burn.

I saw Fabrizio struggling with a tiny candle flame over his bandaged stumps, cursing furiously as his magic failed to work for him. *Amateur,* Envy muttered scathingly.

"Callie!" Ryuu roared in my peripheral vision, hammering a fist at a darkly opaque barrier between us. Inside my own head, I frowned. Had Envy or the flying maw done that? The demon on my chains took advantage of the distraction and tugged me forward.

I snarled and leaned back. The demon was strong, so I wound up skiing across the ground, laughing as my feet tore furrows in the solid stone of the ramparts. I felt none of it. I reached the balustrade and lifted one foot, slamming it against the wall to stop my momentum. Inside my head, I knew this was no ordinary demon—no simple minion of hell looking to capitalize on an opportunity.

One of my brothers or sisters sent us this little gift, lamb, Envy informed me in an overly sweet voice.

Inside my head, I shuddered at the thought. More Sins attacking me on my home turf?

Sloth? Envy mused, either thinking to herself or directly to me, I wasn't sure. *No. He is too lazy to bother. Wrath? He's been laying low for a while.*

Inside my head, I stared up at the flying maw with disbelief, seeing how it was at least twice as large as my gargoyles circling around it with their spears. They didn't want to interrupt their Master Dracula's fun but they didn't want to let the flying maw out of their crosshairs either.

"I'm bored," I heard myself say out loud. "Goodbye, creature. You did well. Die with honor and horror."

Then I heaved my arms to the sides, ripping the flying maw in half with my Hellchains. The creature screamed as it was dismembered. Inky blood showered down over the grounds of Castle Dracula, but most of the remains immediately burst to flame caused by the arcs of sulfuricity crackling up from my chains.

I leaned out over the balustrade as I recalled the chains back to my wrists. They whipped back into me like retractable leashes and I smiled out at the crowd. "Demon meat is poisonous, so don't eat it," I said, grinning madly. "Raise a glass for me and celebrate this crazy thing we call life, my children!"

The crowd stared up at me in awe and disbelief before exploding with an even louder cheer and applause than before. I waved, flashed them another smile, and then I turned around.

Envy's power abruptly winked out like a popped bubble and I fell back on my ass with a grunt as I felt control of my still broken body returned to me like a cold wet slap to the cheek. My eyes were as wide as saucers and I was panting hoarsely as I thumped my back against the balustrade, fighting back a wave of dizziness and confusion. I blinked woozily as the opaque wall keeping Ryuu back evaporated to smoke and he rushed forward, dropping to his knees and skidding to a halt before me.

I leaned to the side and vomited blood, understanding why my mind had blocked out certain events from last night's Envy Special. Thankfully I managed to aim away from Ryuu and away from my fancy new cloak.

Fabrizio let out a startled shout as Envy's block on his magic abruptly evaporated and a loud whoosh! heralded a geyser of fire from all the pent-up energy he'd been pouring into his tiny candle flame. It burned off his eyebrows and he started choking, swatting at his forehead with muttered curses and smoldering bandages.

Ryuu handed me a kerchief and I grabbed it with a shaking hand. I quickly wiped my mouth, embarrassed and terrified and confused. He handed me a flask and I took a quick swig, washing out my mouth and then spitting it out. Then I took another drink, guzzling the cool water down my burning throat.

I handed it back to him and rested the back of my head against the balustrade, blinking slowly as I stared at Ryuu. I felt strangely energetic, almost euphoric, but I was similarly terrified of the fact that Envy's Halo had just fucking puppeteered me without my approval.

I snatched off the ring, panting anxiously as I threw it to the ground a few feet away. It hit the stone hard but stuck fast like a magnet rather than bouncing away. Faint tendrils of smoke rose up from the stone beneath the cursed Halo.

Ryuu pursed his lips at the ring before turning back to me. His eyes were haunted and troubled and I could tell that he had never experienced, never even heard of, such a thing. But he was definitely connecting the dots to my sleepwalking.

"I...didn't try to do that, Ryuu," I whispered, trembling. "It...just *happened*."

He nodded. "It's okay. We will figure it out," he reassured me, placing a palm on my knee. "But we can't just leave it there," he said, turning to look over his shoulder. He stiffened abruptly and then spun back to me, staring down at my hand.

I glanced down and gasped to find the ring back on my finger, pleasantly warm to the touch.

Hello, stepsister, Envy's voice whispered in my mind. *Hope you didn't mind me taking the wheel for a minute back there. It always takes so long to explain to you humans what you can now do with your body once we bond you.*

My eyes bulged and I stared down at my ring as if it was a venomous spider angling to bite me.

"What is it?" Ryuu asked in a low growl.

"It's...talking to me," I whispered. "Again."

Mmmm, the voice purred in my mind. *Halo Breaker looks downright TASTY! I could just gobble him up!* Sensing my abrupt panic at the comment, the voice laughed wickedly. *Oh, no, stepsister. Not killing him. I'm talking about sucking down that long, hard, Halo Breaker—*

I ripped off the ring and shoved it into my pocket. The voice's laughter faded away but it didn't entirely leave. "Just stop!" I snapped.

Okay, stepsister. Remember, I'm only one psychotic breakdown away if you need me! she called out, her voice seeming to echo up and into my mind.

I was panting wildly and Ryuu was staring into my eyes with concern. "No refunds!" I warned him, waggling a trembling finger at him. "Just consider me an investment with unlimited upside potential," I whispered, trying not to break down into tears or cave in to hysteria.

Ryuu grinned and squeezed my thigh. "No refunds," he agreed, chuckling.

I nodded jerkily and let out a sigh of relief. "I think we just figured out why my Horseman's Mask broke," I whispered. "And this is what happened last night, but I wasn't aware of most of it that time."

Ryuu arched a concerned eyebrow. "Is she trying to possess you?"

Ha! the voice belted out. *I don't want to possess you, stepsister. I am fulfilling a vow so we can help each other!*

I blinked, glancing down at my finger again. The ring was back on my finger. I grumbled a curse. "What vow?" I demanded.

In due time, she promised. *We must establish trust first.*

I shuddered at the idea. "Well, if you want me to help you then stop eavesdropping."

Okay, Envy replied.

"And no more taking control of my body without my permission," I added.

Only if you promise not to ignore me, stepsister. That makes me...angry.

"Okay...Envy," I said, recalling all the horrors the Sin had caused. She had murdered Solomon and Last Breath. Kidnapped Claire. And now...she was living in my head.

She snorted. *It's not as simple as that. I'm not the fallen angel who done you wrong. She wasn't able to handle me. I think I broke her. She tripped up and then she fell,* the voice cackled venomously. *Now Envy has a new sister! Yay!*

I blinked, recalling something about Lucky that I had completely overlooked. "If you are Envy, then what...was her real name? The Archdemon," I clarified, remembering that Pride had actually been Lucifer.

Oh, aren't you clever? Envy cooed approvingly. *Leviathan. May she rot in...is there anywhere worse than Hell?*

I shrugged, focusing on steadying my breathing and silencing my emotions. Reason must come first and foremost. Emotions clouded judgment and led to terrible decisions. As alarming as all of this was, I couldn't let it control me. I needed to remain objective or my mind would break, just like Leviathan's had.

You rid me of Leviathan's weak shell the moment you snatched me from the peak of her precious little head. You're not weak, are you White Rose? Please don't be. I see great and terrible things in our future together and I would hate for you to ruin that. It wouldn't be good for our relationship. Or your health...

I pursed my lips, forcing myself to take calming breaths and seek the clarity of my meditative state rather than wading too deeply into her comments. She was trying to scare me. Establish dominance. I'd dealt with that before with Sanguina. "Right. Well, if you want me to trust you, give me something helpful. Where is Claire Stone? You must know what Leviathan did with her."

Envy grew silent as if I'd slapped her. *That...that is a dark story*, she finally murmured. *We hurt the polar bear. A lot. But I finally convinced Leviathan to stop. It wasn't good for business, so we gave her to Greed with orders not to kill her but not to tell us where she put her. A dead polar bear was not useful as insurance.*

My eyes bulged and I felt them burning. *You...bitch*, I thought back at her in my mind this time.

I stopped her, Envy reminded me. *But more importantly, I believe Greed sent the flying maw, so she's still kicking around. Let's go kill her and skip through her blood! Like a trust exercise!*

I closed my eyes, pretending I hadn't picked up on the sheer joy in her suggestion. I frowned, analyzing her comments. She was very similar to me —other than the insanity—mentioning that killing Claire would be a waste. I had determined the same thing while trying to convince myself it wasn't wishful thinking.

Fabrizio made his way over to us, but he hesitated at a sharp warning look from Ryuu.

What if I want to get rid of you, Envy? I asked her. *What if I destroyed this thing or locked it away in Solomon's Temple?*

I felt a sharp flash of pain in the back of my skull and I groaned, feeling my head spin. *Do not threaten me, stepsister. I've been polite*, Envy warned in a low sinister growl. *If you attempt to banish me, I will fight you and tear you apart from the inside out. But even if you win, your Mask will never work again. I broke it. Leverage.*

I sucked in a breath of relief as the pain vanished from my mind. I blinked dazedly, processing her words. Envy really had broken my Mask! Damn it! *Why?* I snapped.

Envy snorted in my mind, making my finger grow warm as she returned to the ring rather than exploring my soul. *Because it wouldn't let me play with it. Or you. I wanted it and couldn't have it. So, I broke it.*

I shook my head in disbelief at the childish answer. Then again, this was Envy. She coveted others' possessions and qualities. *What do you want from me, Envy?*

The ring was silent for a few moments, and I could tell she was considering how to answer. *To be whole again,* she whispered. *You should hurry, though. After I broke the Mask, the Spear became the only thing slowing me down from consuming your soul. But even that can't hold me back for long,* she said in a regretful tone that seemed remarkably genuine. And then I felt her retreating deeper into the ring and out of my reach.

I finally focused back on Ryuu and pursed my lips. "We have a big problem, Ryuu. I'm on the clock. She wants to be whole again, and if I don't hurry, I might wind up a vegetable...or just as bad as one of the Sins."

19

Ryuu clenched his jaw and nodded. He opened his mouth to speak but noticed Fabrizio still standing nearby and hesitated. "Later," he murmured to me, and then he motioned for Fabrizio to approach as he prepared to help pull me up.

Except I leapt to my feet faster and ended up pulling him to his feet, and tugging him hard enough to actually lift him a few feet into the air. He landed with a light grunt, squinting at me warily. I smiled awkwardly, feeling the rush of energy trickling through my muscles from Envy's assistance. It was a relief to no longer be crippled, but I knew it was a slippery slope to accept help from Hell.

Especially from one of the seven strongest demons...or whatever the hell Envy's Halo actually was.

Fabrizio paused, narrowing his eyes at me as he gave me the old horse buyer's once over. His eyebrows had completely burned away in his fiery fiasco, so he looked perpetually startled. I swatted him in the shoulder and he gasped, stumbling back a step. He opened his mouth wordlessly, frowning at my hand and then wincing as he massaged his shoulder with his charred stump of a hand. "What the fuck is going on here? You could barely walk when you first came up those stairs, and then you pulled some magic out of your ass that I've never even heard of. I thought you were practically dead a few hours ago. Now you're bullying us grown men around. Have you no respect for the patriarchy?" he teased, scoffing with faux indignation.

But I could tell part of him was entirely honest. He was merely trying to put me at ease.

I rolled my eyes, shaking my head. "I'm feeling much better now. I was just taking it easy on my way up."

Fabrizio arched a dubious eyebrow—which was now bald, so it was really him arching a thick strip of paler flesh on his olive-skinned face. "Is that why you busted your ass the second you let go of those black and gold chains?" he asked drily, glancing down at the furrows I'd left in the stone when I'd been parasailing with the demon kite. The flying maw, as Envy had called it.

I realized Fabrizio was staring at my feet and I glanced down to see I was barefoot. My sneakers were wedged into the stone near the beginning of my trajectory with the flying maw, and they were smoldering and torn.

"She has calluses on her feet," Ryuu grumbled. "No matter how much lotion she puts on they feel like chapped rhino hide—"

I elbowed him in the gut, laughing. Except he folded in half and dropped to his knees with a wheeze. Fabrizio's eyes threatened to pop out of his head and he actually took a fearful step back from me.

I knelt down to Ryuu, grabbing him by the shoulders. "Oh, god, Ryuu. I'm so sorry," I whispered, staring into his eyes. I didn't see any blood and I hadn't felt any ribs break from my Envy-powered elbow.

He chuckled deeply, stretching out his stomach with a groan. "I am an excellent teacher. You are learning the pressure points entirely too quickly, White Rose," he lied, covering for me.

I nodded sheepishly, plastering on a crooked smile. "Yeah. But I have silky soft feet, jerk." He arched an eyebrow and then rotated to glance down at my feet without Fabrizio seeing him. I flicked my gaze downward, using Ryuu like a shield from Fabrizio's suspicious gaze. My breath caught upon seeing that my feet were bleeding and covered in particularly nasty abrasions. The nail on my big toe was hanging by a thread, but I felt no pain. My eyes widened and I shifted my feet to conceal the missing toenail from Fabrizio, even though he had already taken note of my obviously bloody feet.

"Enough girl talk, Fabio," I growled in a stern tone. "Did you send the money to the Vatican to pay for the damages?"

"Anonymously," Ryuu added, lifting a finger in warning.

Fabrizio snorted. "Fabio. All right. You want to play dirty, I'll play dirty, little Red Riding Hood," he muttered, eyeing my cloak.

I rolled my eyes and waved my hand in a carry-on gesture.

"Yes. They got the money. The Conclave is furious, knowing exactly who was behind your little stunt, but the Vatican at large seems aloof. For whatever reason, the Conclave is helping keep it quiet. Probably because it makes them look incompetent and ill-prepared."

I nodded. "That was actually one of my reasons for taking her there," I admitted. Envy purred her approval at my comment, making me jump.

"You okay?" Fabrizio asked, noticing the look on my face.

I nodded stiffly. "Yes," I said, casting a guilty look down at the charred bandages covering his hands. "Just realizing how many unexpected consequences my actions have. I'm sorry they booted you from the Shepherds, Meatball," I said.

He scoffed. "Lock it down, Girlie Penflower, or I'm going to start asking you to make me sandwiches." My eyes narrowed dangerously and he nodded. "Every. Time. I. See. You."

"Stubborn bastard," I muttered, chuckling. "Fine. Let's wall off all emotions and embrace our inner caveman."

He nodded solemnly. "That's more like it. Testosterone makes the world go 'round." Ryuu snorted, shaking his head in amusement. "Quentin and Adrian were sent *back* to Rome," he said, studying me curiously, letting me know he'd heard something about their adventure with me. "I called in a favor and got them temp jobs as janitors at the Vatican proper where they should be able to keep a distant eye on the Conclave. Eae will keep in contact with them at regular intervals." I frowned at his tone and he winced. "Eae said the Conclave is definitely gathering an army. Lot of shifters hidden within the barracks of the Shepherds' compound," he said in a soft tone.

My eyes widened. The Shepherds hated shifters. "They really are preparing for war," I murmured. "This new Father Ignatius is beginning to sound like a go-getter. I'm going to have to disabuse him of that. Personally."

Fabrizio grimaced but nodded his agreement. "We still haven't found out where the nephilim went or who tipped them off."

Ryuu leaned forward, speaking in an innocent tone. "You should head to Xuanwu's estate for a brief swim. He may know something and it's safe there. Perhaps Aala has something for your hands."

Fabrizio's cheeks reddened slightly and I grinned, turning to Ryuu. "You sunk his battleship."

Fabrizio scoffed, his cheeks puffing defensively. "I might know how to find Greed," he said in a low voice.

He opened his mouth to continue but Ryuu abruptly silenced him. "Whisper it in my ear."

I felt Envy paying very close attention so I started singing the ABC's in my head and I averted my eyes from the very confused Fabrizio and the very intent Ryuu.

I want her dead just as much as you, Envy growled. *Trust, remember?*

I grunted. *Call me old fashioned.*

Fabrizio finished telling Ryuu his secret and the two separated. Ryuu finally nodded. "Pursue it and let me know if it works. Tell no one."

Fabrizio cast me a pensive look and then nodded. "Okay," he said, drawing out the word.

I smiled reassuringly at him. "Precautions."

He nodded slowly. "Against you, though," he said, obviously suspicious.

I shrugged vaguely. "When you visit Aala, see if Lucky knows anything about where the nephilim went."

The moment the words left my mouth, I felt Envy's ears perk up curiously. I didn't know how, but I immediately clamped down on my thoughts, splitting myself off from Envy's ability to seemingly read them. I wasn't sure if she could actually read my thoughts or if she'd simply been listening to me talk, but she was entirely too close to my brain for my comfort, and the last thing I wanted was to give her information on the Anghellian.

Not if she wanted to be whole again. She might decide to take over my body and do something drastic herself if she realized how I'd transformed Pride, Michael, and their Grace from Purgatory into an Anghellian. After what I'd just learned from Envy's Halo, I was even more confused about the relationship between angels, demons, and their Graces in Purgatory. If Envy's Halo was its own entity separate from the Archdemon Leviathan, then what was an Anghellian?

Because Envy's comments sounded suspiciously like she might be a Beast...like Sanguina. Was that why Sanguina had left? Because I'd unknowingly brought home a new puppy and she felt left out?

I felt Envy growling unhappily, but she also seemed amused by my swift reaction since it basically confirmed her suspicion that I knew secrets that might benefit her. *Tick tock, stepsister*, she purred.

I shuddered, feigning exhaustion to get away from Fabrizio. "I think I might have overdone it," I mumbled woozily, letting my legs wobble.

Ryuu swept me off my feet and scooped me up in his arms, hugging me to his chest. "Let's get you back to bed." Fabrizio dipped his chin but I could see his brain clinking its rusty gears as he tried to work out why our conversation had taken such an abrupt detour.

Ryuu turned away and carried me back through the archway and into the Castle. I smelled the hulking bear before I saw him. Kenai winked at me, letting me know he'd delivered my message. Then he followed after us, lumbering down the steps with a steady grumble.

"We're fucked, Ryuu," I murmured, shaking my head. "How can I keep secrets when she's in my head?"

Ryuu looked down at me and I smiled at the flash of fire in his eyes. He looked so imposing and dominant carrying me in his arms. "I assume you have her locked away for the time being?" He asked.

I shrugged. "Yes, but just from my thoughts. She can still hear what I say."

Sure can, Envy chuckled, causing me to clench my teeth.

Ryuu pursed his lips thoughtfully. "Perhaps you truly do need to sit this one out," he said, knowing how angry it would make me and saying it anyway.

I glared at the world in general, hating the fact that he might be correct. I was now a liability. "I can't let her take over again," I said. I looked up at Ryuu. "And as fun as it sounds, I can't let you take me to my rooms."

He arched an eyebrow, staring ahead. "Let," he said, enunciating each letter as if he was tasting the word for the first time. Then he squeezed his fingers, pinching my ass.

I squawked vehemently but it was mixed with laughter. "Put me down, you brute!"

His smile faded and a protective mask slipped over his features, silently asking if I was sure without actually saying it out loud. He wasn't just asking about setting me down but also about my decision to not go rest. I nodded and he obeyed without a word of protest. Did I imagine the shimmer of approval in his eyes? He kept his arms close as I steadied my balance, ready to catch me if my legs truly did give out.

I did so easily and he scowled suspiciously, obviously amused. "You were faking it for Fabrizio."

I nodded primly and ripped open a Gateway to Solomon's Temple. "Of course." I glanced over my shoulder at Kenai and dipped my chin meaningfully. "Thank you, Kenai. Good luck on your hunt for Claire. I'll see if I can discover anything on my end and I'll talk to you later."

He nodded obediently, risking a glance through the Gateway. "Yes, Master Dracula." I wasn't sure when Dorian would make good on my command but Kenai would let me know.

I turned and stepped through the Gateway into an adjacent wing of one of the libraries everyone was working in. My Gateway didn't rip any of my allies in half, which was a good development for my day so far.

We started making our way towards the main area, keeping our eyes alert for allies or enemies since my safe spaces were apparently on open house status for Sins and Archangels lately.

In a soft voice so as not to give away our arrival, I caught Ryuu up to speed on my full conversation with Envy and how she had taken over my body to save me from the flying maw. Then I told him all about last night in the Garden of Eden since he had just witnessed my new houseguest taking over my body. He listened attentively, nodding along every now and then. My body felt alive with energy thanks to Envy's assistance, but that was dangerous in its own right. As we made our way down the rows of dusty books, his presence calmed me like a weighted blanket and I felt my shoulders relaxing.

I was a sucker for affection, and it had felt nice to let Ryuu carry me for a spell. I was unable to shake the thought of finally being strong enough to take my ninja out for a test drive back in my bedroom. Not now but soon. I licked my lips excitedly and then my thoughts shattered as the idea of Envy participating in our romance entered my mind. I grumbled angrily, clenching my fist.

"Are you all right?" Ryuu asked, sensing my abrupt anxiety.

I nodded stiffly. "I just realized the ultimate irony that I've been cock-blocked by Sin."

Ryuu burst out laughing, shaking his head. Envy echoed him with a laugh of her own, reminding me of her earlier comment that she wanted to take him out for a ride as well.

"You're a Halo Breaker," I said, studying his face. "Have you ever experienced something like this?" I asked, lifting my finger with the black ring.

Ryuu shook his head. "I immediately threw the Halo into a volcano. I smile every time I hear it's erupted, thinking of my old friend," he said with a grim smile. Envy grew abruptly silent in my mind. Ryuu saw me open my mouth and he shook his head. "No. I will not speak his name. Especially now that I know we may be tied together in some immaterial manner," he said. "Best not to tempt fate."

"I showed you mine," I pouted.

He arched an eyebrow and gave me a fiery look that undressed me with his eyes. "As a matter of fact, you have not," he grumbled, eyeing my chest.

I grinned, feeling my face heat up. "Envy would see," I reminded him. Hell, she might actually take over.

He pursed his lips. "Who cares? Let her envy what I *do* to you."

Agreed, Envy purred. *What's yours is mine and what's mine is yours. After all, what is family for, stepsister?*

I thought about it and flashed him a hesitant smile, ignoring Envy's chatter. "Soon," I promised him, resting my hand on his muscular chest. He nodded hungrily as we reached the library proper.

❧ 2 0 ❧

I strolled out of the confining rows to the circular balcony overlooking the rotunda. Thirty feet below, the reading area was decorated with equidistant braziers around the perimeter but a massive domed skylight provided enough illumination to see by, so the fire-bowls were mainly cosmetic. A long, sweeping staircase led downstairs but I grimaced at the idea of walking around the perimeter of the room to reach the bottom. Instead, I studied the male warriors turned academics in their unnatural habitat.

I froze to see Lucky staring at a ten-foot-tall painting of the Angel War outside the Garden of Eden. His face was distant and thoughtful and slightly...angry? I verified that my thoughts were secure so Envy would sense nothing interesting from him. Ryuu was glaring at Lucky with a wary expression, knowing he couldn't say anything with Envy in my head, but I knew he was alarmed because Lucky was supposed to be safely tucked away at Xuanwu's estate with the Divines. I let my eyes drift past him in an absent manner.

Roland Haviar's crimson-eyed glare was firmly fixed on Eae, the angel known as the Demon Thwarter.

I studied the angel thoughtfully, taking in the white wings tucked against his back, as I leaned on the bannister. Confident that my thoughts were masked, I let my mind wander. I wasn't sure what he was now, but he was no longer bound to Heaven. He could blaspheme and curse—although a life-time of good habits left him somewhat a prude in that regard. Still, he looked regal and majestic and I knew he was a good...man-angel.

Except he was mirroring Roland's glare perfectly and the tension was visible even from my vantage point. They were speaking in low tones but the passion in their argument was punctuated by clenched fists and angry hisses. I cocked my head thoughtfully.

A dozen tables were laid out in a ring with room to walk between them and the center featured a small fountain with couches surrounding it. Exotic plants in priceless vases were scattered about the room and I found myself wondering if any of them were extinct in the real world. It brought my thoughts to the Garden of Eden—the overgrown forest locked behind the wall and the warped gate. Envy had taken me there of her own volition, and she had spoken of a vow. That she needed my help.

Despite how I felt about it, she had helped me last night. She'd helped me save my nephilim and pick up a trail on Sanguina.

I took a deep breath and decided to ask her directly in my mind. *If you can take control of me, and you need my help, why haven't you just made me help you?*

Envy growled. *Now you wish to speak with me.* I waited in silence, still keeping my mind locked down from her intrusion. *It doesn't work like that. I made a vow. We are on a journey together now.*

I could tell she wasn't going to elaborate on her vow, so I tried a different tack. *Why did you take me to the Garden of Eden?* I asked Envy.

You needed to see what kind of man Uriel really is, she said carefully.

She hadn't mentioned Raphael. Interesting. *You made me kill angels.*

She snorted. *Pretty wings do not make for moral men. They were far from innocent.*

I blinked. *But why?* I demanded. *I didn't even know about you yet. Why did you help me?*

Envy was silent for so long that I thought she was ignoring me. *To save the man I love*, she finally said. *I am a hopeless romantic. Quite literally.*

I frowned. *Cliches? Really?* I asked, annoyed. *I thought you wanted to estab-lish trust?*

Envy growled warningly at me. *What would you do for love, stepsister?*

I shook my head. This had been pointless. *We are not having this conversation.*

But Envy disagreed. *What if Ryuu's life was in danger?* she asked me. *What if I told you that I could kill him with a single thought? Your thoughts, stepsister. Unless you did exactly what I said in the next three seconds.*

I froze, feeling my breath catch.

"What's wrong, Callie?" Ryuu asked in a concerned voice. "You just turned as pale as a ghost."

I tried opening my mouth to tell him to run away from me, but I couldn't control my voice. I felt Envy preventing me from warning him, instead telling him, "I'm just concerned about Sanguina, Ryuu. Don't worry."

I was unable to make my face look as panicked as I felt. I saw Ryuu nod, his concern fading away as he stared out at the library with a sigh. I could see his artery thumping beneath the thin flesh of his neck and I felt my fangs sliding out from my gums even as I felt my face smiling at him.

What is this, Envy? I demanded. *Extortion? This will definitely not earn my trust. What do you want?*

Envy replied in a resigned, committed tone. *To prove a point. What would you do for love?*

I stared at Ryuu's delicate throat, knowing I could kill him. *Anything!* I snapped at the Sin.

Prove it, stepsister. Jump over the balcony, Envy said in a strangely intense tone. It wasn't malicious but it was about as passionate as I'd ever heard anyone speak.

What? I hissed, feeling my hands grip the rail of the balcony in a white-knuckled grip.

When there is no time to negotiate and you are on the edge of a cliff, would you jump to save the life of the one you love, even when it terrifies you? Even when you do not know if jumping would actually save him or not, but it's the only answer you've been given? Is your love and faith that strong? she asked. *Three...*

Why? I demanded. *This is insane.*

Ryuu cleared his throat. "How about you get down from there, Callie," he said uneasily.

I hadn't realized I'd perched my ass atop the railing and I was nervously kicking my feet out over at least thirty-feet of open air.

Prove your love, White Rose, Envy purred in an icily calm tone. *Two...*

This is ridiculous! I already answered you! I would do anything! I hissed, panicking.

Easy words, stepsister. Prove it, Envy replied in a surprisingly morose tone. *One...*

I leapt off the balcony to prove my love. Or to prove I was an idiot. Two things could be true at once.

Ryuu belted out a loud curse as air whistled in my ears.

I fell like a fallen angel...with my new fallen angel headmate. She was strangely silent. Maybe she'd been bluffing and I'd startled the literal hell out of her with my recklessness.

Because she did not give me her super-strength or pain-blockers.

I missed the table with my feet but I nailed it with my tailbone instead.

I hit about as gracefully as a bag of wet sand, obliterating the table in an explosion of splinters and an electric shock of pain I oddly felt in both my molars and fingers. I slammed into the ground amidst the destroyed wood and found myself on my back, surprisingly not impaled, staring up at the giant skylight high overhead with very wide, startled eyes. I blinked slowly, panicking on the inside as I struggled to breathe.

Nailed it, I told Envy. *Does that answer your question? Did I pass the trust fall from Hell exercise with fallen colors?*

Wow, she murmured in my ears, sounding stunned. *I didn't think you'd actually do it the first time*, she said. *You must have had a very sheltered childhood.*

I felt my leg twitch but I couldn't lift it. *Did I pass your stupid test?* I repeated.

Silence answered me. *Yes*, she finally replied in a soft voice. *Shall I fix your tailbone?*

I couldn't move and I felt my pulse quickening in fear and anger. *You did this to me! Of course you shall fix it!* I snapped, imitating her voice.

Envy was silent and I felt my leg twitch again. Had I broken my freaking back?

I let out a short, panicked breath. *Sorry, Envy. Please heal me.*

Roland suddenly loomed over me with a panicked expression on his face. "Are you okay?" he asked, carefully pulling splintered wood out of the way so he could get to me.

"I think I broke my coccyx," I wheezed, feeling Envy's healing touch sliding down my ankles and tailbone. A few seconds later I felt an icy flash in my lower spine and I abruptly sat up.

Roland flinched in surprise, blinking rapidly. "Uh...what about your coccyx?"

I grunted. "I don't actually know where that is. I just always wanted to say it."

Ryuu appeared, having taken the long way down. He hoisted me to my feet with a stern glare. "I guess my blood is stronger than we both thought," he lied in a loud enough voice for everyone to hear, "otherwise that idiotic move would have killed you." His eyes were panicked and inquisitive and helpless, not knowing what he could do to aid me against Envy.

Translation: don't jump off a thirty-foot balcony onto an ancient library table. You moron.

"Yeah," I agreed, glancing up at the balcony I'd just abandoned. It was... at *least* thirty-feet high. "Great ninja blood, Ryuu." I leaned closer. "I called her bluff to earn her trust." He stared at me in complete silence, not remotely impressed. I finally averted my eyes, mumbling an apology. He glanced up sharply at the railing above and let out a grunt. Then he released me and walked away, looking like he wanted to murder a few dozen people. I followed him with my eyes and was surprised to see Alucard. The two of them shared a few quiet words, nodded, and then Alucard approached me with a big grin.

Ryuu remained behind, raking a hand through his hair and looking conflicted about...well, probably me.

"Oh. I almost forgot," Roland said, reaching behind his back. I'd completely forgotten his presence after Ryuu's arrival. "Thought you might want these back. I was going to bring them to your rooms, but here you are." He held out the two satchels Last Breath had given me—one that had been his and the one that had belonged to Solomon. My eyes widened in surprise, having completely forgotten about them during my recovery. I could feel Envy paying very close attention all of a sudden. Did they still have the Hellish cobras inside? I didn't dare open them with Envy peering through my eyeballs. I wasn't sure what to do with them or how to inspect their contents without spilling potential secrets to Envy, so I set them on the table beside me as if they were nothing too significant. "Thank you, Roland."

He nodded and glanced over his shoulder at Alucard's approach. He gave me a hesitant smile, frowned up at the railing, and then walked back over to Eae to resume their earlier argument. Unfortunately, Eae was staring at me with a very strange look on his face. I momentarily panicked, fearing that he might be able to sense Envy inside my head.

Relax, stepsister. He can't sense me. He's barely a foot-soldier, she said with a dismissive sniff. I hadn't realized I'd let my mental defenses down so I shored them back up. Or maybe she'd just seen the angel and read my obvious body language.

Once I was certain my thoughts were private, I diagnosed Envy as bipolar and myself as psychotic. What had she been trying to prove? Why had she been so adamant about love and then acted so strangely when I passed her suicidal test? I didn't have time to analyze it further as Alucard reached me.

I smiled at him but he was having none of it. He wrapped me up in a tight hug and buried his face in my hair, inhaling deeply. "You're insane," he said, chuckling. Then he pulled away, grinning at me. He glanced up at the balcony and let out a long whistle. "Did you forget you have wings?"

I blushed furiously. "Yeah. I'm a little out of focus," I lied. My embarrassment faded and I smiled deeply, remembering a green hand dragging me and Ryuu to safety from St. Peter's Square. "Thank you for saving us in Rome. Seriously."

He waved a hand and shook his head. "Don't mention it. Seriously. As far as anyone else knows, you strutted away from that fight with a smile on your face and one of Greed's claws as a souvenir."

I let out a breath, shaking my head. "Technically true. Any word on where she might be hiding?" I asked, thinking of both Greed and Claire. I wasn't as paranoid as Ryuu because Envy had said she wanted Greed dead for sending the flying maw and the venom in her voice when she'd said it had rung with truth.

Alucard shook his head sadly. "I'm off rotation for a bit, but the new team is in good hands."

"Paradise and Lost?" I asked, thinking of the alpha werewolves of Kansas City. They were working closely with the St. Louis werewolves Alucard had brought to my city.

He grunted. "And a hundred others. Armor and his bears, the ninjas, Phix," he waved a hand. "Too many generals can be a bad thing sometimes, and we've got a lot to figure out here," he said, gesturing at the library.

I nodded grimly. "And how is that going?" I asked.

"The look on your face accurately sums it up," he said with a resigned sigh. "Nothing on the Azrael Scrolls. Maybe they are in one of your other libraries?"

I frowned, recalling my last conversation with Last Breath. I managed to compartmentalize my pain over their murders and also my thirst for vengeance against the murderer in question who now lived in my head.

Last Breath had only mentioned a few titles: the Azrael Scrolls and a book called the *Sev'n Most Sinist'r*, but the book had been found with Solomon's body. He'd also spoken of the Watchers but admitted he hadn't read any of the books Solomon told him about.

What did the Watchers have to do with any of this, though? According to the Book of Enoch, the Watchers were the fathers of the original nephilim. In my opinion, the Watchers had many similarities with the Greek Prometheus story—the semi-fallen angels had taught mankind how to live better, easier lives. Unfortunately, they'd also boinked a few broads, and that had brought the wrath of God via the Great Flood.

The ultimate cold shower to separate horny energetic youths.

But according to Last Breath, the Book of Enoch had glossed over quite a bit, and the Azrael Scrolls told the unadulterated truth. Fun side note, the scrolls had also given Solomon horrific, debilitating nightmares for six hundred and sixty-six nights.

Maybe the Azrael Scrolls actually explained that the nephilim were really angel-sucking vampires. Was that why it had been deep-six-six-sixed? The public story about the Watchers had already been fairly grim, so what other truths could be too dangerous to let the world know about?

Inside my head, Envy piped up with a surprising little tidbit. *Azazel Scrolls not Azrael Scrolls. Leviathan lied.*

I blinked, feeling an icy shiver run down my veins. *Lied?* I asked her. Then it hit me. Leviathan-slash-Envy had been posing as Solomon and he had been the one to tell Last Breath to find the Azrael Scrolls. In fact, everything I thought I needed to research right now were...answers received from Leviathan rather than the real Solomon. Motherfucker. *Why did she lie and why are you telling me the truth?* I asked her, not knowing which claim to believe.

Envy sighed, sounding as if she was in pain and angry about it. *Azrael is the angel of death. He knows next to nothing about the Watchers or the nephilim. Some fathers are drinkers, but Our Father was a smiter. Azrael was the sibling who cleaned up the messes in the morning. Helped the other kids feel better. Azazel...was the sibling who ran away from home rather than putting up with it any longer. History was unjustly cruel to him.* She sounded strangely compassionate and almost...

loving. That was a topic I did not want to get into with Envy. A Sin's love life? No way.

Alucard was staring at me uneasily and I wondered if I had been speaking out loud or if my face just looked like I'd gone into shock. I flashed him a crooked smile. "Try searching for the *Azazel* Scrolls. I think I got the name wrong the first time." What if even that was pointless? How much time had we wasted relying on fake-Solomon's research recommendations?

He glanced at Ryuu, who was still pacing back and forth a short distance away, and then he turned back to me. "You...got the name wrong," he repeated in a flat tone. I nodded. "You sure you are feeling okay, Callie?" he asked, eyeing me up and down. "You seem remarkably strong and alert for almost dying a few days ago," he said, glancing back up at the balcony and then the destroyed table I'd used as a crash site.

I waved off his concern and flashed him a bright smile. "Good genes," I said with a smirk. "I don't know why I held back on drinking blood for so long."

Envy burst out into song in my mind, altering the words of a funny but inappropriate childhood jingle about baked beans. *Blood, blood, the magical juice. The more you drink, the stronger your roots. The stronger your roots, the deeper your will, so let's drink blood from every kill!* I managed not to bob my head to the catchy jingle and I also managed not to gag at the macabre yet strangely mouth-watering lyrics.

Alucard nodded slowly, not looking the least bit convinced. "Right. Well, did you *misremember* any other titles that we've spent the last few days trying to track down?"

I waited, hoping Envy would throw me a bone. She stubbornly refused to help so I shook my head. "Not that I can remember. Sorry about that."

He shrugged. "It's understandable after what you went through, Callie. That was a tough couple of days for everyone," he said, pursing his lips. He wasn't just talking about Solomon and Last Breath. Alucard and I had helped Nate Temple take on the Olympians and the two of us had executed Ares and Apollo.

Killing someone in a fight was one thing, but executing them while they knelt before you? That was a different thing entirely. I didn't feel guilty about it, but I did feel...something. A stain on my soul.

"I am telling her whether you like it or not!" Eae hissed, loud enough to echo through the library. Alucard and I looked over to see Eae storming our way. Roland's face was a picture of hard, resigned lines.

"Hey, Eae," I said hesitantly, trying to read Roland's face.

He bowed with a fist to his heart. "The Four Horsemen returned, but this time they came to Solomon's Temple," he growled, pointing at one of the nearby windows. "They're on the balcony out front. Right now."

"What?!" I hissed, suddenly panicking.

"They said if you don't turn yourself in, they will involve Nate Temple and it won't be pretty," Eae added with a grimace. "War said that last part, and he was smiling as he caressed the hilt of his sword."

21

Envy was uncharacteristically silent and I could sense a true flicker of fear from her. That was worse than if she would have simply laughed them off with a snide comment. If she was scared, I should be running.

Ryuu cursed. I hadn't even seen him approach. "I told them to wait until tomorrow," he snarled, looking torn between sticking by my side and going downstairs to throttle the Horsemen of the Apocalypse. "But if they want war, we will give them war," he vowed. "The Divines owe the White Rose at least two favors for rescuing Zoe and Bai." Despite the confidence of his voice, I saw his eyes flick past us towards Lucky with a hint of unease.

Alucard slowly turned to glare at Eae and Roland. "And neither of you two told me?" he snarled in a warning tone, and I saw that he was reaching into his pocket for his Horseman's Mask.

I snatched at his arm, terrified. "No! We can't resort to Masks. Mine backfired on me," I reminded him, although I didn't mention the fact that Envy had been the one to cause it to break.

Unless she'd been lying about that as well. The truth was, I had no idea what had happened to it, but we definitely couldn't risk two of the Dread Four's Masks out of commission.

Roland glared right back at Alucard. "Aphrodite is unsurprisingly adept at keeping men distracted, so we have time. And Pandora went down to assist Aphrodite. She has experience with them and Nate Temple, so I'm sure she can talk them down."

Alucard smirked smugly. "Nate wouldn't hesitate to defend Callie. Even from them. I say bring it on. Four on four, winner takes all."

I began pacing nervously, glad to hear that Pandora had come to the library like I'd asked her, but I wasn't nearly as optimistic as Alucard. Not with my Mask currently broken. I hadn't even dared summoning it to see if it still worked. It had abandoned me. If not for Ryuu, it would have gotten me killed. "Why are they so adamant about speaking with me? I'm not the one who picked the fight with Greed, and it's not like I have anything new to tell them. Why should I be under arrest?"

In unison, everyone turned to glance at Lucky. Before I considered the consequences, I glanced over as well. Envy hissed within my mind, but not out of anger. It sounded more stunned than anything. Or perhaps awed or terrified. Greed hadn't reacted like that, though.

Lucky was still staring at the massive painting but he apparently felt all the eyes on his back. He slowly turned to look at us and his face was unnaturally calm. When I said *us*, I meant that he did not look at anyone but *me*. And by that, I mean that his eyes bored into mine like arrows shot from a bow.

Envy began trembling inside me, sounding like she was praying.

Lucky cocked his head, blinked twice at me, and then winked out of view.

The library was utterly silent as we all stared at the empty space with bewildered expressions. "He's been staring at that painting for almost two hours," Roland murmured.

"He was supposed to be with Xuanwu," Ryuu growled angrily.

"He showed up about five minutes after he went to see Xuanwu, and he never said a word the whole time he was here," Alucard said, shaking his head. "Fucking weirdo."

Envy's praying had ceased but she was utterly silent.

I clapped my hands. "Four Horsemen. Balcony. Focus, people," I barked. "Somebody go tell Aphrodite to bust out her special occasion lingerie and pull out every trick or toy she has in her play chest, because I need more time before I confront the Four Horsemen! If they see me weakened, I don't know what will happen, but it won't be good," I said, even though I didn't feel remotely weak. I knew I looked just as battered as before but I couldn't feel pain. And they'd seen my failed super soldier leap from the upper balcony with hardly more consequence than needing to brush the splinters off my knees.

Alucard nodded grimly and sprinted for the doors to pass on the message to Aphrodite and Pandora.

Roland was staring down at my feet with a worried look and I bit back a curse. I'd completely forgotten about my shredded feet or even the fact that I didn't have shoes. He looked up at me, arching an eyebrow. "You simply must tell me who does your pedicures," he said in a monotone.

I grimaced. "Yeah. Ran into a flying maw at Castle Dracula."

Eae let out a hiss and his wings flared out, rattling dangerously. "A flying maw? Here?" he growled. "How in the blazes did you kill it? How did you even *see* it? They're practically invisible. Hell uses them to assassinate nephilim."

I maintained my composure and smiled. "I am a nephilim, but that is hardly the most dangerous thing about me, Eae," I said with an amused smile.

I was merely grateful he didn't ask where I'd heard the term before.

I turned to Roland. "I already told Alucard, but now he's busy. I was wrong about the Azrael Scrolls. It should have been the *Azazel* Scrolls. But if you find them, do not read them," I reminded him.

"I remember," he said with an amused smirk. Beneath his smile, I saw his concern about me getting the title wrong, but he didn't call me out on it.

Eae grimaced distastefully. "Azazel was a criminal and a liar. We should be careful putting too much stock in his scrolls."

Envy snarled viciously in my head and I flinched. I spoke quickly to cover my reaction. "Have you read them, or are you speaking from personal experience? Have you met Azazel?" I asked Eae curiously.

He shook his head with an amused snort. "I'm fairly close to the bottom of the midden heap we call a hierarchy, so no, I never met him. But you don't have to meet a man to know he's a bastard."

Envy snarled even fiercer and I felt pins and needles in my fingers. *Calm down*, I told her, *or the jig is up.* She grew silent and I felt her take a calming breath.

Roland smirked, pointedly glancing at Eae's angel wings. "Potty mouth."

Tell me how you broke him, Envy asked me curiously. *I love those sorts of stories.*

I sighed on the inside, refusing to answer her. "Just let me know if you find it, and keep looking for anything on...the other topics I mentioned," I said, cryptically, tapping my ear to signify stealth.

Eae cocked his head. "Why are you tapping your ear?"

Roland elbowed him in the gut and then used a tendril of magic to pinch Eae's wing, pulling him away forcefully like a father pulling a child by his ear. I bit back a laugh to see Eae dancing on his toes as Roland chastised the angel on discretion and not stepping over the line with me. Roland finally let go and folded his arms with a stern glare.

Eae hopped a safe pace away. "I need to go check on Quentin and Adrian anyway. Choke on the scrolls, vampire," he snarled. He disappeared in a twinkling of glitter and Roland started hacking and coughing, waving it away and cursing under his breath. Then he glanced over his shoulder at me, flung up his hands and stormed off, deeper into the library to search for the Azazel Scrolls on his own.

I looked over at Ryuu and then sighed to see him grimacing at the satchels Roland had given me. "Mind checking under the tables for monsters and doing a quick perimeter check?" I asked him. "I don't want the Horsemen deciding they can bully their way in to see me and catch me off guard."

He nodded, looking down at my ring. He could read between the lines, knowing I wanted a minute to myself in addition to the things I had asked for. "Of course. Let me know when you're ready to leave." He started to turn away and then paused. "We're not making much headway here. On multiple fronts," he said in a careful tone, referring to the research and the Horsemen downstairs. I nodded. "I have an idea but it will require me leaving the Castle for a few hours."

I nodded, trying to hide my sudden influx of joy as I thought of my plans with Dorian. Was that what had caused him to pace back and forth a few minutes ago? Debating this decision? I hated not telling him about Dorian, but he looked like he was on the verge of having his own breakdown. His concern for me was overwhelming him. So I would be extra careful and tell him about it after. "Tonight?"

He nodded. "Best keep it a surprise in case it doesn't pan out," he said carefully, obviously implying that Envy need not hear about it.

My curiosity was piqued but he was right. I nodded. "Okay."

"You will stay here." He glanced up at the railing. "And away from high places."

I sighed. "This job sucks," I muttered unhappily. He waited, staring into my eyes. "Fine!" He gave me a hollow smile and then bowed before making his way to the doors to do his security check. He'd trusted me up until the moment I'd leapt off the balcony, but I could tell he was now deeply troubled about my situation.

Had I traded his trust in me for Envy's?

22

The satchels from Last Breath sat on the table and I found myself wondering how I might get a look at them without Envy knowing. This whole Halo thing was becoming a real problem, but without her I was a crippled mess.

I walked over to the table and absently scanned the collected books and scrolls, sliding notepads and pens out of the way as I assessed what they had gathered. I absently hung the satchels over my shoulder as I murmured vague nothings, pretending to read the notes on the table for Envy's sake. Much of it was in Latin or read like passages taken directly from the Bible.

No flashing lights or colorful pictures that said *here are your answers, Master Dracula!*

The combined anxiety of the various storms swirling around me threatened to wear me down. I knew I needed to confront the Four Horsemen. Claire was still out there and I had no idea where to look. At least Envy had confirmed that Greed did actually have her, but I had no idea where Greed was either. If I could locate her, I could solve two problems at once—kill the Sin and save Claire. Thinking of taking Greed's Halo sent a shudder of panic through me. Two voices inside my head? No thanks. And there were no volcanos in the Kansas City area.

Then again, Envy could have been lying to me. She was a vindictive Sin.

Regardless, I needed to hunt Greed down before she had a chance to blab about Lucky or decide to try a second attack on Castle Dracula with her whole family.

And the wedding was tomorrow. If I was Greed, that would be the moment I'd target for a second attack. Maximum chaos. I knew my warriors were already preparing for that scenario and quadrupling security, but I would be next to useless in my current state—unless I relied on Envy's aid. Worse, Envy might decide to take control of my body all by herself.

Or she might even cut off my power to leave me helpless at the worst possible moment.

What if the Vatican chose this moment to make their move too? Or Uriel and Raphael?

I took a calming breath, forcing myself to calm down. I needed to find my own solution to Envy before I could be of any use to my allies. To suddenly be able to move my body without pain again had been a dream come true. So, to briefly have my mobility back thanks to Envy's help healing me had been—ironically—a Godsend.

But I did need a control to keep her in line. And in order to boink my ninja without her hopping into bed with us while figuratively wielding a video camera. What if she was subtly guiding my thoughts even now? I shuddered at that idea, especially when I didn't sense an amused laugh from her. The silence of the Sin was almost worse than knowing she was actively participating.

"The greatest trick the devil ever pulled was convincing the world that he didn't exist," I murmured. I was fairly certain the quote wasn't Biblical canon, actually coming from the film the *Usual Suspects*.

I felt Envy laugh. *Generous Gambler by Charles Baudelaire*, she whispered. *A truly devious quote by an inspiringly deviant man. One of Dorian Gray's associates, if I'm not mistaken—which I am not.*

I redoubled my lock on Envy's ability to read my thoughts and I felt her annoyance. I took a calming breath, knowing I needed to test just how good my lock actually was. *It was shockingly easy to rip your halo off and decapitate you*, I thought to myself rather than to her. *I've faced satanic human cultists who put up more of a fight than you, Envy.* I held my breath, waiting.

What are you thinking, stepsister? she demanded. *Why did your mind suddenly become so quiet? What are you doing?*

I carefully sent a response back to her while making sure that she couldn't read the rest of my mind. It was like managing a dam and using controlled spigots to lower the water level on one side. *Just thinking about how I figured out how to fuck Ryuu without you tagging along*, I lied, needing to know how good she was at reading me.

After a long pause, I heard her let out a dismissive laugh. *Perhaps you should let me give you advice if you want to make sure he sticks around. You are remarkably unskilled in the bedroom, judging by the memories I scanned.*

My eyes widened and my cheeks flushed bright red. She'd scanned some of my memories before I'd locked her up. What if she already knew dangerous things that I'd hoped to keep secret from her?

Granted, you performed admirably your first time with the ninja, but can you keep him begging for more or was that your best attempt? she teased cruelly.

A new suspicion came to mind and I smirked. What if...she was lying again? Maybe she hadn't scanned my memories, and was merely antagonizing me to hide her ignorance. Could it be so simple?

I walled her off, realizing she was entirely too good at provoking me, knowing exactly which buttons to press. I still held an awe factor for one of the Seven Sins whereas she saw me as just another human. More powerful than the rest but only impressive in a relative manner when compared to other mortals.

But knowing I now had a slight modicum of privacy boosted my confidence somewhat, so I kept up my mental barrier as I inspected Envy's Halo on my finger. I found my eyes drifting to the silver Seal of Solomon on my other finger and I frowned pensively.

The Seal of Solomon had been designed to trap demons—some of the most powerful demons in existence. I hadn't heard about my ancestor acquiring one of the Seven Sins, but he'd chained up some insanely powerful Dukes and Princes of Hell in order to build Solomon's Temple in the first place and learn the mystic arts.

A few days ago, when Envy had been disguised as Solomon, he'd implied that the Sins were tricky and slippery and couldn't be so easily caught. But Envy was a liar, as was Leviathan. What if that hadn't been strictly true? What if I held the answer to the Envy problem on my finger?

I took a nervous breath, wondering if it could be so simple.

I slowly lifted my hands vertically, palms facing each other. If I put my hands together in prayer, the two rings would touch. I almost laughed at the irony, or blasphemy, of that thought but I didn't want to give her any time to realize what I was doing. So, I closed my eyes and then clasped my hands in prayer, letting the rings click together with a pleasant chiming sound.

I felt a strange flushing sensation within my body, a sharp, furious scream in my mind, and then I felt Envy's Halo vanish from my finger, swallowed up by the Seal of Solomon with a bright flash.

Exactly zero-point-two seconds later, my body completely failed me and pain hit me like a dozen hammer-blows of frosted metal. In addition to my existing injuries from my fight with Greed, all the exhaustion from my walk through Castle Dracula, my unexpected fight with the flying maw, and my super table stomp hit me all at once.

It felt like I'd just set a new record racing one mile, and the moment I'd passed the finish line with my arms raised high in victory, the referee had rammed the front grill of his suburban into my gut at forty miles per hour.

Then it got *worse*.

My legs gave out and my forehead cracked against the wooden table on my way down, adding a fresh shade of agony to my palette of pain. The blow sent an explosion of stars blazing across my retinas and I folded to the ground in a boneless heap. I panted desperately as my muscles twitched and spasmed of their own accord. I thought I was having a seizure until I realized I was still more-or-less in control. My body was simply overwhelmed as my connection with Envy winked out, severing her ability to mask my pains.

My toe and feet burned like pure fire and my eyes flooded with tears.

I gritted my teeth, clenched my jaw, and rode the pain, hissing when I needed to and biting it down when I could. Within moments, I simply ached. I managed to lift my hand and check that I hadn't torn open any of my wounds. I felt more or less like I had when Ryuu had forced me out of bed earlier, except the parts of me that Envy had healed earlier were still intact. No broken coccyx or whatever it had been. Except my forehead was bleeding and I felt concussed on top of feeling exhausted and definitely-not-in-fighting shape.

I heard shouting from across the room as Ryuu leapt across tables, scattering books in his wake like an approaching tornado. He hit the floor beside me, landing on his knees and giving me a swift once-over rather than immediately grabbing me—a testament to his experience as a warrior. Moving an injured person could actually make everything worse. His eyes focused on my forehead the longest and I felt blood dripping down my temple, but

Ryuu seemed to dismiss it as non-threatening. "What happened?" he demanded.

I lifted my hands, not caring that they trembled and shook. "It worked," I croaked, showing him that Envy's Halo was gone and that Solomon's Seal seemed to be glowing brighter than usual.

His eyes widened in surprise but then he took stock of my battered body. He scooped me up and carefully laid me out on top of one of the library tables. "Are you okay? I'm going to go get Pandora if you are."

I nodded tiredly. "I'll be fine. I passed the worst of it while you were taking a leisurely walk," I teased, feeling my eyelids grow heavy. He clenched his jaw guiltily. "J-joke," I whispered, closing my eyes. "I'm...gonna...nap now," I mumbled. "Ni-night."

I heard Ryuu make a ruckus as he disappeared from view, shouting at someone in the library. I couldn't quite remember who was still here.

I saw a bright flare through my eyelids, making me squint as if someone was shining a flashlight into my eyes in an attempt to force me to remain awake. I felt myself reaching out for the light as I fell into a deep, exhausted sleep.

23

I stood on a perfectly manicured, rolling, grassy hill, facing a pool surrounded by tall marble columns. Elegant fountains with beautiful statues dotted the grounds, and the air vibrated with cheerful drum music. A mass of bodies around the pool danced in unison like it was the Burning Man festival—the country club edition. I heard laughing and splashing from the water and I gawked as someone flipped up thirty feet into the air. The stunningly beautiful naked woman seemed to weigh less than one hundred pounds as she performed a perfectly executed triple flip and then disappeared back out of view with a too-small splash. Cheers rose up from other voices in the pool.

"My turn, Morax!" a woman's voice laughed.

I shook my head dazedly, confused. I took a step to approach the party, but I hesitated, frowning as I noticed that all the revelers had strange runes tattooed on their backs. The tattoos were blue and red and they crackled with light like it was a rave under a blacklight party.

Except it was a perfect summer day.

I squinted at some of the runes, feeling like I could almost recognize them. Was this another trippy dream? Had Ryuu grabbed Starlight and his bag of drugs to experiment on me again?

A petite blonde woman wearing nothing but a breezy white sarong hung low around her hips danced up to me, giggling as she handed me a crystal goblet brimming with champagne. I accepted it on instinct, transfixed by the impossibly alluring woman. Her skin was entirely free of blemishes or moles or imperfections of any kind, like she was a marble statue brought to life. She was so beautiful that she literally took my breath away and I found myself unable to speak. I felt like a drowned cat in comparison. It took me a few moments of openly gawking at her to realize that her eyes were entirely black and, rather than pupils, there was only an endless loop of shooting stars zipping towards me like I was staring through the windshield of a space-ship in hyperdrive.

I stumbled back a step and she grinned, grasping my elbow to steady me. Her thin, delicate fingers were warm and gentle but ridiculously strong. I felt my knees shaking as I stammered, trying to find a single imperfection in her beauty. It didn't even seem strange that she was almost completely naked apart from the wispy sarong, because the whole effect seemed utterly natural on her. Like she'd been born this way.

"You must be the new guy...er...girl," she said in a chiming, sing-song tone. "Here. Let me show you around. You're in for a wild surprise," she clucked, wrapping an arm around my waist and guiding me towards the pool.

"You..." I mumbled, staring at more of the tattoos stretching from tail-bone to the base of the neck on the other frolicking dancers and pool-goers. The men wore what looked more like Greek war skirts rather than the flowing sarongs all the women wore. But plenty of dudes and dudettes were of the *suns up, buns out* persuasion, skipping about and laughing without a care in the world.

Others were lounging back on deck chairs, suntanning or huddled up at a tiki bar off to the side. I saw every shade of skin imaginable, and no matter how fat, skinny, tall, or short anyone was, they all looked like perfect creations from God. There was absolutely no denying that.

Even for me.

"What is this place?" I whispered, shaking my head. "Who *are* you?"

The vixen beside me let go of my waist with a jubilant laugh and lifted her fingers to her plump lips in an embarrassed gesture. She batted her starry eyes at me like a cosmically sad puppy. "Oh, gosh! How rude of me. We're used to the old man visiting us and we go back a long ways, so there are no strangers here. My name is Obyzouth, but everyone just calls me Obie." She used her non-drinking hand to hoist up the edges of her sarong and gave me an elegant curtsy that threatened to flash an indecent amount of skin. Then she wrapped her tiny arm back around my waist again and squeezed me affectionately, resting the side of her cheek against my arm because she was a head shorter than me. "Hugz power!" she giggled.

Her bubbly cheer made me feel like I was trapped in a bizarre crossover of Care Bears and My Little Pony. Her attitude was strangely contagious.

I glanced down at the top of her head with an amused smile and my cheeks abruptly caught fire as I realized that I was wearing the same exact outfit as Obie—my boobs on full display for all these strangers to see. I squawked, dropped my glass, and then covered up my bullseyes with my hands as my face turned fifty shades of red. "Where are my clothes?" I hissed, thankful to see that I at least wore the white sarong firmly wrapped around my hips, although it hung lower than I would have preferred. Did I have a freaking tattoo, too? I instinctively craned my neck but it was impossible to check for your own tramp stamp.

Those pieces of art were for the givers, not the takers.

Obie squeezed me reassuringly, still latching onto my waist like a magnetic, rainbows-and-hugz-fueled pygmy. "Oh, gosh. You really *are* new, aren't you? It's okay. Everyone here is incredibly polite. They'd probably stare at you harder if you *were* wearing clothes!" She laughed at her own joke. "What's your name, doll?"

"Callie," I mumbled, scanning the faces before me. Like Obie had said, most of them paid absolutely no attention to me. A few looked over at me with curious, anxious smiles, but their star-studded eyes were all latched firmly on my face. They lifted their glasses to me with warm, inviting smiles, and then resumed whatever they had been doing before making eye contact.

"Callie," Obie breathed, making my name sound strangely sexualized. "Beautiful Death," she murmured, and then she laughed lightly. I froze upon hearing her echo Pandora's nickname for me in that strange dreamscape with the pool of blood. Obie detached from me and set her drink down as she took a step forward, abandoning me.

"What are you doing?" I hissed nervously, feeling like I was in danger for some reason.

Obie clapped her hands loudly and the drums suddenly stopped, as did absolutely all conversation. "Hey, guys and gals! The new boss is here!" The gathered tramp-stamped nudist colony spun to stare at me with looks of genuine awe on their faces. Then they grinned and my shoulders hunched low under the onslaught of all those starry eyes. "Her name is

Callie Beautiful Death! Let's all give her a huge, Seal of Solomon welcome!"

My heart threatened to thunder out of my chest as I lowered my hands instinctively, preparing to summon up my claws as Obie's words hit me like a slap in the face. The Seal of Solomon. These people were...

The demons Solomon had trapped. "Oh, for crying out loud!" I growled, feeling my claws snap out and my fangs extend from my gums as I readied to defend myself. I searched the gathered faces, looking for the biggest, baddest demon so I could bitchslap them into submission and set an example for all the other would-be challengers. Prison rules, prison rewards.

Except...the beautiful demons clapped their hands together in unison and more magic than I had ever seen in my life suddenly bloomed around their hands—a dark, crimson, rippling power that almost took my breath away.

"CBD!" some of the demons screamed, while others howled "Callie!" or "Beautiful Death!" or "Solomon!"

The gathered power in the close to one hundred demons' hands suddenly erupted, shooting straight up into the blue, cloudless sky like comets. I sucked in a breath, marveling at the fiery beauty. The streaks of light promptly exploded like fireworks and I gasped to see my name spelled out across the expanse.

I lowered my hands uneasily, feeling decidedly foolish and more confused as the crowd screamed and cheered, chanting my name as the drums kicked back up even louder and livelier than before. My eyes threatened to pop out of their sockets and my jaw hung open as I stared at the mass of grinning, friendly, bubbly faces. They lifted their glasses to me in cheers and then waved as they took a drink.

"Come for a swim!" one gorgeous black demon hooted, looking like Mr. Universe. "I can throw you really high!"

A tan female demon smiled at me compassionately from her lawn chair. "Come kick your feet up and relax!" she laughed, patting the empty chair beside her. "I don't bite...anymore," she added with a grin.

"Come make some wishes, Beautiful Death," a trio of lithe women said in unison, laughing as they sat at the tiki bar and motioned me over.

Obie stepped in front of me defensively, waving off their invitations. "Give her a darned minute, sheesh!"

Everyone laughed back at Obie good-naturedly before bowing or curtsying and turning back to their party. I stared at the rune on Obie's back, committing it to memory. It...almost looked like Enochian script. It had enough similarities for me to guess what it was.

The demon's each had name tags branded into their backs. Their demonic seal.

Obie turned back to me with her brilliant, megawatt smile, her golden hair glistening in the sun. "I'd recommend leaving the djinn alone. They're tricksy," she explained, giggling as she discreetly pointed a thumb over her delicate bare shoulder at the three women at the tiki bar. I stared back at Obie, unable to formulate a response. Her smile faltered slightly. "Oh, gosh. Are you okay? Do you want to go inside or something?" she asked, glancing off into the near distance behind me.

I frowned in confusion, turning my head. I gasped to see Solomon's Temple towering over us. Except this one was much, much taller than the real thing. And it seemed to grow darker the taller it reached until I saw that the top of the building was completely black and surrounded by a ring of black storm clouds. The only clouds in the sky.

Obie wrapped her arm around my waist. "Oh," she said, sounding troubled as she followed my gaze. "You're here for the new girl."

I nodded numbly, having a pretty good idea who the new girl was. "Envy," I murmured, licking the tips of my fangs.

Obie shuddered nervously. "You sure you don't want to hang out and relax for a bit first? Poor love was kind of in a bad mood when she arrived." She paused. "We all are when we first come here, but then we quickly learn to appreciate the gift that was given to us."

I glanced down at her to find her looking up into my eyes with those haunting windows into the cosmos. "The gift?" I asked.

She nodded, smiling. "Solomon saved us from Hell. This is a second chance for us. A permanent paradise."

I swept my gaze over the partiers, shaking my head in disbelief. "But you are all prisoners."

She snorted. "Oh, gosh! If this is our prison, give me multiple life sentences and throw away the key!" She scrunched up her nose as if at a sudden thought. "Oh! Did you bring us new books to read? That vampire one about Sorin and the medicine man was freaking awesome. When he came back to New York, I was like 'yeah! Drink their hearts, boy!'" she cheered excitedly. "Give me some of that Shade of Devil, if you know what I mean!" she purred, swaying her hips salaciously.

I stared down at her, taken aback. I'd never heard of such a plot line, but it sounded like lazy writing. "Solomon brings you books?"

"Of course! But it's been a while." She glanced down at my hands, checking them for trashy fiction novels. She pouted briefly and then sighed. "Next time, you promise?" she asked in a stern tone that made my heart skip a beat, reminded of just how dangerous she probably was. Then she laughed again and I realized she'd been trying to sound tough. "Got ya!"

"I...um, really need to take a walk or something," I told her, wondering if this was a dream. I had been thinking about the Seal of Solomon when I passed out, so it would make sense. I glanced back up at the dark penthouse high above. "Does this place have an elevator or something?" I asked dubiously, feeling like my legs wouldn't be up for that many stairs. Memories of my injuries struck me and I gasped. My legs! My stomach!

I glanced down sharply and saw that my wounds were completely gone. And...I felt perfectly fine.

Obie noticed my anxiety and squeezed my waist comfortingly. "Alright, Beautiful Death. I'll take you to her." She eyed my claws thoughtfully, touching them with her fingers. "Don't worry. She can't hurt you here. No one can. That's why she was so grouchy," Obie explained, chuckling. "Threw everything she had at us but we just kept on living life, ya' know? Sometimes that's all you can do."

I nodded numbly, not knowing if I could believe a word she said. "Right."

Obie abruptly slammed her palm over the tips of my claws and they ripped through her skin like kabobs. I gasped, jerking my hand back. She laughed, lifting up her perfectly unbroken hand. "See?" She laughed. "You can't hurt us, and we can't hurt you!"

Then she called up black claws of her own from one hand, each as long as swords, and shoved them into my gut, laughing maniacally.

24

I let out a shout, dancing back even though it was already too late. I felt her claws rip through me and then slide out as she recalled them even before I'd fully leapt back. I stared down at my stomach to find absolutely no wound at all. No pain. Nothing.

My eyes widened as I looked back up at Obie. Her eyes had turned a fiery red but I watched as her black claws disappeared and her eyes returned to windows into space. "See?" She laughed delightedly. Then she lifted her glass, clinked it against mine—which I was somehow holding again even though I had hurled it at the ground—and then she wrapped her arm back around my waist, ushering me towards the entrance to Solomon's Temple. I rolled with it, not knowing what else to do. I let my claws slip back into my knuckles and my fangs retract.

I stared up at the balcony overhead, recognizing it as where I had often hung out with Solomon and Last Breath as they overlooked the infamous gardens in the real world.

I frowned, wondering if Solomon had somehow been able to see all of this revelry when he looked out at the gardens from the real Solomon's Temple. Or had he simply liked suntanning there? And he *had* loved to strut around in the nude. I shook my head in disbelief. The old king held a never-ending rave party on his finger and hadn't mentioned a word of it to me.

"Hold onto your hoo-ha," Obie chimed, pointing down at a blackened ring burned into the ground. "This is going to get tickly in your naughty place," she warned.

Before I could respond, my soul was sucked up into the sky and my naughty bits tickled. I burst out laughing, glancing over at a beam of rainbow-colored light beside me. It was no longer humanoid, but I could tell it was Obie, judging by the familiar sound of her own laughter at the tickling sensation.

We came to an abrupt stop and I felt my body return to normal. I realized we were standing on the open balcony of the top penthouse at Solomon's prison. The windows were tinted black and the dark storm clouds flickered with crimson lightning all around us, close enough for me to almost reach out and touch with my fingers.

A tall, curvaceous red-head stormed out of the penthouse, glaring at the both of us. She also wore the prison uniform of white sarong and no top. Her olive skin glistened, reflecting the crimson storm behind me and I felt my breath catch in my throat as I marveled at her raw power and beauty

"Get me out of here, White Rose. Now!" she demanded, glaring at me with blood-red eyes.

"Oh, gosh!" Obie tittered, pouting her lower lip out. "I hoped you might have calmed down a bit—"

A bolt of crimson lightning struck Obie in the face and the concussive boom threatened to shatter the balcony. I shouted, blinking away the afterimage of the blinding flash.

Obie stood there with a disappointed frown, her hands on her hips as she scrunched her nose up at Envy. "That," she said in a stern tone, "was very rude. I respect you, Envy, but what you knew out there doesn't apply here, so put a smile on your face or keep throwing your temper tantrums. We look forward to welcoming our sister out by the pool once you've cooled off."

Envy sputtered indignantly. "I am one of the Seven Sins, you insolent little sh—" Her curse word cut off abruptly and a string of bubbles floated out of her mouth.

"Naughty language is not permitted when used in anger," Obie said, all-too-merrily. "Only for fun stuff," she said, turning to me with a toothy grin. "I want to fucking hugz you, Beautiful Death!" And then she hit me with her fucking hugz, wrapping her arm around my waist again.

I burst out laughing, unable to restrain myself. "Well. Ain't that some shit." No bubbles slipped out of my mouth, and I started laughing even harder, blinking away sudden tears of joy.

Envy began cursing up a storm, hurling blasts of crimson lightning all around the balcony in an attempt to destroy the firehouse of bubbles spewing out of her mouth, which only caused her to curse more.

Knowing that the lightning could not actually harm me, I strolled towards a comfortable looking white couch with Obie. We sat down and crossed our legs like ladies, straightening our sarongs as Envy let loose a tirade the likes of which I had never seen before.

Obie winked at me and then clinked her glass of champagne against mine. I smiled, eyed the champagne, and then shrugged. I took my first sip and immediately gasped at how delicious it was—like the smell of fresh fruit and flowers hitting my tongue.

We watched Envy hurl lawn chairs out over the balcony, only for them to reappear where they'd been moments before. Obie sighed wistfully. "My first day was crazier than that. Took me *years* to calm down."

I grinned, finding it strangely, sadistically satisfying to watch Envy lose her freaking mind.

"Know any of our brothers and sisters on the outside?" Obie asked curiously, settling her crystal glass on her knee as she bounced her perfectly manicured toes up and down in an absent, restless motion.

I considered her question, curious to know how safe it was to answer. I hadn't heard of a demon named...Obyzouth? Was that what she'd said?

I chose the path of least resistance rather than mentioning the other Sins. "My godparents are Samael and Lilith."

Obie smiled nostalgically and let out a wistful sigh. "I haven't seen Lilith in forever, obviously, but we were close." She frowned thoughtfully. "Wait. I thought she got locked up at Castle Dracula? I could swear Solomon told me that," she said.

I nodded. "I rescued her and accidentally became the new Master Dracula."

Obie grew still and slowly turned to look at me with the first hint of anxiety. "Gosh," she said lamely. "No wonder Envy's so upset."

I frowned. "What? Why?"

She leaned forward, whispering conspiratorially. "You're part of Azazel's trap, aren't you?"

I blinked, having no idea what she was talking about, but her mention of

Azazel made my stomach flutter nervously, recalling the Azazel Scrolls Roland was trying to find for me. I had no idea what that had to do with Envy, but I'd apparently just caught her in another lie. Then again, Envy had corrected Leviathan's lie about the Azrael Scrolls, so...

Not wanting to ruin an opportunity, I took a gamble. "Yes." I eyed her thoughtfully, appearing as if I was assessing her for trustworthiness. "Solomon should not have spoken about that with you," I said carefully. "He must have really trusted you..."

Obie nodded. "Yupz."

"What exactly did he tell you?" I asked.

She glanced over at me. "What's the password?"

I stared at her, my face frozen. "Um. He never mentioned a password," I said carefully. "We just talked because I'm his last-living descendent."

"Oh, gosh. I'm surprised he still remembered anything to tell you," Obie said, scrunching up her cute little nose again. "He was starting to forget things. That's why he gave me his journals but made me promise to require the password before discussing it."

I stared at her, feeling the hair on the back of my neck stand on end. Was this what Solomon had been hiding? What Envy had been searching for? The answers to my questions were right here, locked up in this friendly demon's mind. I scooted closer and leaned forward to whisper so Envy couldn't overhear, although she was still stomping around and spewing profanity bubbles.

I pointed a discreet thumb over my shoulder at Envy. Obie frowned pensively, turning her ear towards me. "Before he could give me the journals, she—or Leviathan—killed Solomon and Last Breath—"

"MOTHERFU—" Obie screamed in outrage and abruptly took off into the skies like a rocket, spewing bubbles the whole way. Her crystal glass crashed to the floor at my feet and shattered.

Envy even paused her tirade, turning to glare at me suspiciously. She glanced up at Obie with a thoughtful frown and then back to me. She took a calming breath and straightened her sarong. She reached up to pet her perfect breasts like she was straightening her blouse, and then sashayed over to me, staring into my eyes.

She took Obie's seat directly beside me and she was suddenly holding a crystal glass full of blood. She smelled of cinnamon and sulfur and her eyes burned with crimson fire that matched her thick, wavy red hair.

"Callie, Callie, Callie," she purred. "I think we got off on the wrong foot."

✣ 25 ✣

I stared back at her with a stoic face, masking my emotions. Then I clinked my glass to hers and gave her a single nod. "You threatened to destroy me when I mentioned sending you here. And you threw me off a balcony."

She smiled faintly. "Technically, you threw yourself off the balcony. For love."

I glared back at her. "There was supposed to be a point to that exercise," I reminded her.

She lifted her head and stared out at the blue sky below. "This place is... not what I expected, but it is still an abomination," she said firmly. "And you did draw a..." she pursed her lips at some still-floating bubbles overhead, "penis on my severed head."

I snorted, trying not to burst out laughing at the memory. I hadn't realized she'd been aware of that, so I felt my moral high ground eroding rapidly. She seemed averse to meeting my eyes for some reason, so I drilled her with my gaze, refusing to look away. "You've been lying to me. Or at least holding back a lot and misleading me," I said.

"I also healed you," she reminded me in a defensive plea. "And I saved you from the flying maw."

I gave her the faintest of nods, refusing to break eye contact. "After you killed my only blood relative and Last Breath. Because you wanted to destroy everything I loved. Ring a bell?"

She stiffened as if she'd been stabbed, and I thought I saw a flash of fear in her eyes. Strange...

"You mentioned trust. A vow. A lover."

She dipped her chin sadly. "He was wrong," she said, sounding helpless. As if she was chastising herself. If I found out she had her own inner voice, I was going to quit everything. "You will not believe the truth."

I considered her words, reading her body language. Her spirit looked frail and broken. "If you expect me to believe Leviathan did those things, not you, then it's going to be a hard sell, Envy. You have given me zero reason to believe you."

"Even a Sin can suffer fear," she whispered, "despair, hope, rage, pity..."

I frowned, staring at her. "Unless you explain, this is the end of the road, Envy. I leapt off the balcony and now it's your turn."

She took a deep breath and nodded. Then she leaned forward and tipped her glass into mine, refilling my empty glass with blood rather than champagne. I pursed my lips and Envy smiled. "I think we could be very, very good friends, Callie Penrose. We both want blood. We just need to scratch each other's backs."

I arched a cool eyebrow at her. "I need to *trust* you. I need the truth." She nodded, looking suddenly smaller. "I'm willing to leave you here until you're ready to talk sense."

She shuddered at the thought, staring into her crystal glass in silence.

I kept my composure and took a sip of the blood. It hit my tongue like honey and I felt myself greedily lapping it up. I hoped it wasn't demon blood, but it tasted too good to ignore. The truth was, I needed her power to step back into the fight, but I couldn't do so blindly. "I hold the cards, Envy. I'm willing to hear out your request because you know time is not currently on my side. But there will be terms to any potential parole I grant you, and one misstep will land you here in Hugztopia for eternity."

Envy's lips tightened into a thin line and she let out a resigned sigh. "Of course."

I sipped my blood again and then nodded. "If I catch you in a single lie, you're done. Period."

She shot me a helpless look. "I've been with Leviathan since as long as I can remember. I can't just flip a switch and be something else!" she whispered hoarsely. "I'm trying, but I don't know *how!*"

I considered her words, realizing she had a fair point. "I can forgive slip-ups, but you will vow to be obedient and loyal to me. You will swear an oath right here and now that your only purpose is to serve me and act in my best interests. No lies. Or this will be your home forever. Soaking up the sun and singing show tunes."

I forced myself not to laugh at how ridiculous my threat was—forcing paradise upon her if she disobeyed. But I needed her power with my Horseman's Mask broken and my collection of injuries. She needed me to keep on living or else she would be trapped here for good. I was the last Solomon, so no one else would ever be able to release her.

She shuddered, looking around in a panicked manner at her posh surroundings as if they were a dungeon with blades and burning brands and mad scientists. "I swear to serve your every desire and to always act in your best interests."

"Say my name, Envy."

She licked her lips, glancing up at me hesitantly. "Callie Penrose?"

I shook my head. "Master."

She nodded nervously, her eyes darting out to the horde of demons I so easily controlled. She'd already seen how impotent she was here. I held a figurative blade to her throat. I had dozens of important questions for her but I didn't trust her yet. Even with her oath. She would need to earn that from me.

"Master," she finally whispered.

The dark clouds surrounding the penthouse slowly dispersed and drifted away as I felt something click inside my chest. I tried not to read too much into that, but it was impossible to deny that it had felt and sounded like a pair of handcuffs firmly latching onto my soul.

Here's to hoping I hadn't just become the new stepsister to the Sin family dynasty.

"Tell me what Greed meant about you being a martyr, and why you were so insistent about doing terrible things for love," I said.

Her face flashed with an inner pain. "You won't believe me," she whispered. The tiny tear that rolled down her cheek was genuine. Her lip trembled and her forearms were pebbled with gooseflesh.

"I might not, but you're going to tell me anyway," I said. "Trust me like I trusted you." I glanced at the railing of the penthouse balcony. "We could switch roles and do another trust fall but it seems rather pointless in a padded wall prison."

Her lip barely twitched into a ghost of a smile and she nodded. She let out a forced breath and spoke in a rush. "I...did not kill Solomon."

My heart froze and I stared at her. My hand trembled and shook, disturbing the blood in my glass. I had seen her kill Last Breath with my own eyes. But Solomon...

She had to be lying. Then another thought hit me and I frowned. "If you are trying to pin his murder on Leviathan, that's just not going to cut it for me," I whispered, biting back my inner rage.

She shook her head stiffly. "No. Not Leviathan either."

My eyes narrowed. "Then who killed Solomon?"

She met my eyes then, reading me soberly, trying to see if I could handle what she was about to say. I nodded encouragingly even though a large part of me wanted to slap her in the face for even the potential of such a lie. The audacity.

"You understand that there will be no mending our relationship if you are lying about this."

She nodded stiffly. "This is my trust fall," she whispered. "My second one. The first was with...him."

"Who?" I hissed, leaning forward.

She closed her eyes for a moment. "Solomon. He promised me a second chance and I chose to trust him. I vowed to help him. I had nothing else to lose after you killed Pride and the others. It was the only way to have my revenge."

I frowned. "What are you saying, Envy?" I demanded, confused.

"Solomon found me in the halls of Solomon's Temple. Even though I was disguised as Claire, he knew me and trapped me," she said with a hollow smile, amused by the memory. "He put Leviathan to sleep and spoke directly to me," she whispered, blinking away another tear. "He said he knew why I was there but that he knew a better way for me to get what I want. All I had to do was trust him."

I stared at her, dumbfounded. If she was lying, she was the best liar to have ever walked the planet. Now, being an Archdemon, that kind of went with the job description, but this seemed something...more. Raw. Primal. This was the most important topic she had ever discussed, and it had little to do with Solomon. It had to do with whatever he'd promised her.

"Who. Killed. Solomon?" I asked in a cold, hoarse tone.

She blinked up at me, looked to murmur a silent prayer, and then sighed. "Uriel. Lord Uriel tortured Solomon to death to hide the shame of his crime. And to get his missing armor back. That's why he told you to find the Azrael Scrolls. To throw you off track."

My heart fluttered anxiously and I blinked rapidly, struggling to process it all. "What crime?" I rasped.

"Uriel secretly abducted all the nephilim before the Great Flood, bonding them in cuffs to hide their abilities and use as his own secret army. He executed all but two of the Watchers, pinning all blame on them, and chained the two men up together in a wasteland where they would remain until the Last Days when Uriel returned to gloat and execute them. Uriel cannot kill them until then, so the risk of his crime being discovered has hung over his head like an axe ever since. Solomon discovered it somehow."

I stared at her, blinking slowly. I had no way to know the truth of her claim but her body language was undeniable. Right or wrong, she believed this story.

"Azazel," I murmured, connecting some dots. She flinched and let out a soft sob. "Azazel was one of the two scapegoats. The Azazel Scrolls tell his side of the story."

She nodded, smiling wistfully, looking broken. "And Azazel was the man I loved. I have wanted to kill Uriel ever since his betrayal but he is a snake, hiding behind Gabriel at every opportunity. Until you did something to scare Gabriel into hiding and I saw my chance." She looked to me. "Until Solomon caught me, I did not know that you would provide an even better chance to save my lover and get revenge on his jailor."

"Me?" I hissed. "I don't know a thing about any of this. I might be ready willing and able to kill the asshole Uriel, but this is the first I'm hearing about Azazel. You think we can bully Uriel into telling us where he imprisoned Azazel and his brother Watcher—"

"Samzaya," Envy said with an abrupt snort and amused smile. "He is an asshole, but he's one of my favorite brothers," she whispered. "Even though he is the father of fangs and blood vampires—scourge of demonkind."

My eyes widened incredulously, thinking back on my first real conversation with Sanguina. How she had accidentally made vampires. I kept it to myself. "Which makes Azazel the father of...claws? Angel vampires?"

She nodded. "Yes."

Silence stretched between us. "So, Solomon's plan was for us to beat on Uriel until he tells us where Azazel and Samzaya are? That was his big secret?" I asked dubiously. She nodded. I shook my head. "That can't be the full story. Solomon obviously knew more because Uriel killed him to hide something."

Envy shrugged uncertainly. "He told me you need only think on memories of your parents to find what you need." She looked up at me hopefully. "Does that mean anything to you?"

My breath had caught at mention of my parents. Not memories. *Mem or E's*. The marbles my mother had left me in her laboratory. I nodded slowly, meeting Envy's eyes. "Yeah...I think it does, Envy." I leaned back in my chair, feeling overwhelmed and frustrated by the numerous gaps in the story. "Why wouldn't Solomon tell me any of this himself? No offense, but why rely on you and not me directly?"

Envy nodded. "He said he knew it was time for him to die by Uriel's hand the moment he saw you reveal the truth about the nephilim vampires. It was the first domino to fall in a plan he had set in place long ago. That is why he sent Sanguina away. To search for Azazel and Samzaya in case I failed my part of the agreement."

My eyes widened. "You and Sanguina were both in on Solomon's gambit?"

She nodded. "Yes. Where do you think Sanguina first learned how to consume blood to stay alive? Azazel and Samzaya nurtured and cared for the baby Beast. Sanguina belonged to Azazel. To...us," she said softly with a distant, wistful smile.

My eyes bulged, recalling Sanguina's version of the story about how she'd come to form Castle Dracula by accident in order to survive, not knowing that teaching the vampires to suck blood would be contagious.

"You're saying my fox is actually the first pet you, an Archdemon, and Azazel, a Watcher, owned as a couple? I adopted your dog," I said flatly.

Envy smirked at the ridiculousness of it all. "You inherited her and made her your own, but yes. You took my dog and Uriel took my man. Now, can we go kill the bastard and drink all his blood? Maybe we'll find out more about his armor," she said, glancing down at my hands meaningfully. "And it's the only way to take the nephilim back from Uriel."

I stared back at her and then I burst out laughing.

26

My eyes tiredly fluttered open and I sucked in a breath, momentarily confused to find Pandora staring at me from a few inches away. My heart started to race, fearing I was in another dreamscape with her. But then I realized we were both sprawled out on adjoining couches in the library. I saw fresh bandages on her forearm and I swiftly lifted a finger to my lips. It came away pink, proving the obvious. The warmth resonating from my throat and stomach confirmed it as well.

"Out with the old and in with the new," Pandora said sleepily, a faint smile on her face as she pointed at an IV stand beside her couch. Tubes hooked it to her other arm.

I grimaced and slowly sat up. "I'm better," I mumbled, feeling Envy's strength pouring into me. I also felt the weight of burdens she'd inadvertently placed on my shoulders. I wanted to trust her, but she'd given me a real doozy of a story to verify. Uriel was not only an asshole who wanted me dead to get his precious armor pieces back, but he was also the asshole who had brutally tortured Solomon to death and then fled to pin it on Envy. But her story did check a lot of boxes on my list of mysteries.

I would need to go to my mother's laboratory and check the Mem or E's —something I had avoided since I first learned about them. I shuddered at the thought of hearing my mother's or father's voice speaking directly to me.

Some marbles were memories of theirs but some would be direct messages from beyond the grave.

Pandora set a delicate hand on my forearm and I flinched on reflex. She met my eyes. "I know you are better, Beautiful Death," she said with a wink. Then her eyes settled on the black ring on my finger. I stopped breathing, again connecting the nickname she'd first used in our shared dream with the nickname Obie had given me at Solomon's Prison. Had she known about Envy even then? Pandora looked back up at me with a smirk. "I hope you know what you're doing. Deals can be dangerous." She glanced at the destroyed table behind us and snorted, shaking her head. "And even wise old men can make poor decisions."

I stared at her, stunned. I opened my mouth but she shook her head, obviously refusing to elaborate. She lifted her hand from my forearm and I heard Envy growl. *What just happened? Everything went quiet for a few moments.*

I blinked a few times, realizing that Pandora had put Envy on mute.

"What happened with the Four Horsemen?" I whispered instead of answering Envy.

Pandora sighed. "They left empty-handed, but they said next time that will not be an option. Unfortunately, they didn't specify when that next time will be," she added, sounding troubled.

I let out a frustrated sigh. "I'm going to have to confront them, but on my terms, not theirs."

Pandora nodded, looking thoughtful as she stared up at her IV and then back at me, as if to remind me that I was in no shape to confront them on any terms whatsoever. Without Envy's Halo, at least, because she looked down at that next.

I shot her a guilty smile, nodding. "Thank you, Pandora," I said, pursing my lips at her bandaged arm and the IV replenishing her. Envy wasn't actually healing me—except for the table incident earlier—so I did need Pandora's blood to get physically better. "Is all this really because Sanguina left?" I asked in a soft, fearful tone, gesturing at her bandage and thinking back on what Envy had told me.

Pandora hesitated, considering my question. Finally, she nodded. "I believe so."

"Why? I'm at Castle Dracula so why would her proximity, or lack thereof, diminish my blood-healing abilities?"

Pandora sighed, lifting her gaze to stare up at the arched ceiling high overhead. It was painted with beautiful murals like many of the Renaissance churches in Italy. "She is devoting all of her attention to something beyond Castle Dracula, and it is weakening both you and the Castle."

I felt an icy shiver run down the back of my neck. "It's not just me growing weaker?" I asked nervously.

Pandora shook her head. "If not for Solomon's Temple, this place might be flickering in and out of the real world even as we speak. The power of the Temple is keeping it alive. My father is having a hell of a time forging the Eternal Metal. He says it doesn't want to cooperate like it should. It's still working, but for how long?"

I bumped the back of my head against the armrest of the couch. And I'd thought I had enough problems to deal with already. "I need to *do* something, Pandora!" I hissed angrily. "But I don't know what! Which fucking target do I aim at? Do I go to war with the Four Horsemen? Take on the Conclave? The Sins are playing whack-a-mole with me and I'm about ready to pull my hair out."

She glanced over at me, smiling sadly. "Unfortunately, I have no expertise to give, only blood to donate and a shoulder to lean on," she said, patting my forearm again. Her fingertips felt cooler than they should, letting me know she was giving me entirely too much blood. "I'm fine, Callie. I'm not tired from donating blood," she said with a faint smile. "That just added to it."

I frowned, watching as she sat up. She actually looked rosy-cheeked and chipper in spite of the exhaustion in her eyes. "Get some rest," I told her.

She smiled and stood from the couch. "Ryuu and Alucard left." I nodded, wondering what his mysterious plan was and why it involved Alucard. Then she shuffled away, humming to herself as she pushed her rolling IV drip across the floor.

I realized Eae had returned and he was speaking passionately with Roland in low tones a safe distance away from me. I frowned, not liking their body language. The two didn't seem to get along but I always saw them together. What had Eae learned from his meeting with Quentin and Adrian? I needed to clear my head before I added that new problem to my plate—

Dorian rolled out from under my couch, grinning up at me. "Giggity."

I kicked him in the forehead on instinct and he let out a curse while managing to laugh. "How long were you down there?" I demanded.

"An hour?" he mused, rubbing at his forehead. "Kenai made it sound urgent and you're always hopping about so I didn't want to chase you."

I frowned, wondering what incriminating information I might have said to Pandora that he didn't need to know. Instead of revealing any concerns, I flipped my hair out over my shoulders and then pulled on my new hooded cloak from Ryuu. I stared down at my white clothes and my bright red cloak with a frown. Not very conspicuous. "Where's the meet? Your house? How armed do I need to be?" I asked warily.

He shook his head. "Not my house. The Sins all know about it. We're going to the safest place I know." I frowned at him, waiting. "The Strip Club," he said in a reverent tone, licking his lips eagerly.

I snorted, laughing to myself. Silence answered me. I frowned, turning to face him as I realized he was serious. "No."

He shrugged. "Then you don't get to meet with the Toymaker." He rose up from the floor and extended his elbow like a gentleman. "We are already cutting it close, so if you wish to move forward, we must be on our way. You already missed the first meeting and second chances aren't often entertained these days. I had to call in some favors."

I narrowed my eyes and sighed. Doing something was better than sitting here like a caged bird. I felt helpless here. Trapped. "Fine. But the last time I went to a strip club on your recommendation, I ended up fighting leprechauns with mob ties and watching as a rainbow ripped a shifter stripper in half."

He smirked. "What happens in Vegas stays in Vegas," he said solemnly. "But this is a very...different kind of strip club."

I sighed, shaking my head. "That doesn't make me feel better. You know what? I don't even want to know. But I do need to get changed first," I said, deciding that I wanted to put on my mother's black monster-slaying outfit. It also had a dark hood to hide my hair. Strip clubs had neon and black lights so I would stand out like a glow stick if I didn't cover up my white hair.

He grinned roguishly. "I can either help you get changed or I can wait here." I shot him a silent glare and he chuckled, lifting up his hands in surrender. "Never hurts to ask."

I saw Lucky standing at the same painting from earlier and I frowned. He was back again? "Just wait here, Dorian. I have a few things to wrap up and then I'll get changed."

He shrugged and sat down on the couch with a resigned sigh.

I turned back to Lucky, studying both him and the painting. Why was he so infatuated with it, and why wasn't he staying at Xuanwu's estate where it was safe? I strolled up behind him, choosing to adopt Dorian's advice. Never hurts to ask. "You okay, Lucky?"

He continued staring at the painting, completely motionless. I grimaced at the macabre scene of angel killing angel. I saw Michael in his elegant armor stabbing one of his brothers in the chest. Was Lucky feeling remorse? Was that why he had been so distant and cold to everyone lately?

"Why do you keep staring at this—"

"I'm going out," he replied, practically cutting me off.

I grabbed his arm nervously, shaking my head. He turned his cool, eternally wise eyes on me and I instinctively released his arm, murmuring an apology. "Is that wise? Greed will be looking for you."

"Are you implying that I am not permitted to leave, Halo Breaker?" he asked in a chillingly calm tone.

"I..." words failed me as I studied his face, realizing that Lucky had most definitely changed in the last few days. Had he been like this before the attack at the Coliseum? Had I missed the subtle changes or had they happened all at once like people kept saying?

What—exactly—had I done in creating an Anghellian?

27

I took a calming breath and met his eyes. "I'm sorry for hitting you at the Coliseum. I didn't want you to kill her there because it would have just sent her home." Lucky gave me a blank inhuman stare, reminding me of the first time I had met Michael. No anger and no forgiveness, just a cold, merciless finality. If not for that, I might have asked him about Uriel's armor, but I was picking up very concerning, murderous, slightly insane vibes from the Anghellian. "I...just want to make sure you're safe, Lucky, and I'm not back at full-strength to support you."

He smiled in amusement and absently patted me on the head like I was a cute puppy. "Support," he repeated to himself with an amused, entirely condescending chuckle. "Tell me where Sanguina went, Halo Breaker," he said, leveling those damning eyes on me.

"I...don't know," I mumbled, biting down the fear creeping up my neck. Did he know? Why would that make him upset with me? Whose side was Lucky really on? "Where are you going?"

"The Garden of Eden."

My eyes widened in surprise. "Why?"

"Nostalgia," he said drily. "And because I can."

Envy began whimpering in my mind but I tuned her out. "The Garden is locked up, Lucky," I said with more confidence than I felt. Hadn't Michael told me that long ago?

He smiled and leaned closer to whisper softly. "So are Azazel and Samza-ya." Then he pulled back, studying my face for a reaction. I stared at him, feeling suddenly cold. How...did he know about that? Lucky chuckled. "And I am the key to both."

My heart skipped a beat and his smile stretched wider as if sensing it. "Why?" I asked.

"To beat everyone else to the treasure, naturally," he said, sounding bored.

Treasure? What treasure was he talking about? "Why not work together, Lucky? Why have you changed?" I asked, frustrated and confused.

"You changed me, remember?" he asked in a dangerous tone. "You made me, and now I think it's time I spread my wings and leave the nest, mother. I no longer need you."

I felt my fists clenching in both anger and pain at his harsh, cruel words, but the resolve in his eyes was undeniable. I shook my head, not knowing what treasure he was talking about but knowing that it couldn't be good in an unstable Anghellian's hands. "I can't let you do that, Lucky. Not without more information. Tell me what is locked inside the Garden of Eden. Please."

He cocked his head and glanced down at my chest. "The only way you will stop us from getting to the Garden is if you are willing to use your precious Spear on me."

My heart was racing, knowing he was probably right. I couldn't take on an Anghellian. But he had said *us*. He...was speaking of the Divines! That was the only thing that made sense. He had no other friends and they had been strangely subservient to him lately. Everyone wanted the Divines, and he'd just said he was the key to unlocking the Garden of Eden—something everyone would want for themselves. "Are you the fifth Divine?" I whispered, not sure whether that was something to fear or something to celebrate.

He scoffed dismissively. "No. I am an Anghellian, *mother*," he said, reminding me of what he now saw as my crime. "But the Divines serve me now because they know I am the only one who can protect them from my siblings, as they learned from your failure at the Coliseum."

I flinched as if he'd struck me in the face. "We are on the same *side*, Lucky," I said, shaking my head. "Why are you suddenly treating me like your enemy?"

He pointedly glanced down at my black ring with a sneer. "Are we, Callie?" he asked, shifting his attention to squint directly into my eyes. My breath caught and I knew with complete certainty that he had noticed Envy lurking within me. He winked, seemingly at her rather than me. "Why don't you take care of your own problems, White Rose. I will see to mine. Maybe we will meet back in the middle, staring at each other over a thin line in the sand." He glanced back at the painting over his shoulder with a committed nod. "The pathway to hell is paved with good intentions, Halo Taker. Maybe even a white rose or a burning bush. Safe travels and..." He laughed harshly. "Godspeed."

With that, he simply winked out of existence.

I stared at the empty space, licking my lips nervously. He'd said Halo Taker, not Halo Breaker. He *knew*.

That...was an Anghellian? Envy whispered, sounding as if she wanted to claw her own eyes out or fall to her knees in worship. *I didn't think they were real. He is deranged and must be put down.*

"I told you he had changed," a familiar voice murmured from behind me, causing me to jump in fright, swinging my elbow on reflex. Roland's steady hands caught it and then gripped my upper arms in a reassuring gesture. "Easy, Callie, easy," he said in a calming tone, slowly turning me around. I stared at my old mentor's crimson eyes and forced on a smile that I knew he could easily see through. "You sure you should be up yet?" he asked gently. "I know you will work yourself to death, so it's not a question of your resolve but more a question of what we'll be left with when you burn yourself out. A lot of people lost a lot of sleep the last few days, fretting over you."

A defensive retort had been on the tip of my tongue before he'd murdered it with the guilt trip. My teeth clicked together and I closed my eyes, letting out a long sigh, shoving down my newfound fears of Lucky since there really wasn't anything I could do to stop him. He really did think I was in Envy's back pocket, so I couldn't blame him. How could I prove to him that we were still on the same side?

"Cantankerous old bastard," I mumbled to Roland, pulling him close and resting my cheek on his shoulder. "You scared the bubbles out of me."

"What?" he asked, laughing. "Bubbles?"

I blushed, shaking my head at thoughts of Obie. "Never mind."

He laughed softly and wrapped an arm around my waist in a fatherly manner as we studied the library and the stacks upon stacks of books.

"How long was I asleep?" I asked.

He was silent for a few moments. "Oh, a while. It's evening," he said absently. I grunted, surprised to hear it had been so long. "It's not going well, Callie," he admitted. "Eae said Quentin and Adrian didn't show up for their prearranged meeting. He went back to see if they were simply running late. Really late."

I grimaced, shaking my head. "Damn it." If those two morons got themselves caught again, I would flay them alive.

He grunted in agreement. "And the next time the Four Horsemen return, they will not leave without you in custody...or without their heads," he added in a grim tone. "We have exactly zero leads, so the only thing I can think to do is start swinging until someone swings back."

I nodded, grimacing. He had no idea about Lucky going rogue, which would only give the poor man a heart attack. He needed an appetizer before I shared that tidbit. "I have one of the Sins inside my head," I said. I wouldn't tell him the rest of the details Envy had divulged until I had a chance to verify at least some of them.

He tensed, frowning down at me for about five long and silent seconds. He didn't ask the obvious or freak out like everyone else would have. He just...squeezed me closer. "I think I tweaked my back twice while you slept all afternoon, but you don't hear me whining about it."

I blinked, caught entirely off guard. Then I burst out laughing. "How did you pull a muscle in your back? You're a *vampire*."

He was silent for a few more moments and I realized he was studying Pandora on the other side of the fountain. "Library work is hard," he said absently. "Reaching for that topmost shelf..." he murmured. "So hard."

I swatted him on the shoulder as I started laughing even harder. "You... dog! *Twice?*" He smiled smugly and Pandora winked at him, confirming their dirty secret. Pandora had claimed her treat after all. "Oh, gross!" I hissed, shoving him away and wiping my sleeve on his shoulder. "Old man swext. Get it off."

He shot me an amused but puzzled look. "Swext?"

I nodded. "Sex sweat. Ick!" I said, firmly wiping my hand on his shoulder for emphasis.

He chuckled, shaking his head. "I'm not old," he grumbled defensively. We stood in silence for a few moments and he finally let out a long sigh. "What do you need, Callie?" he asked in a serious tone.

I smiled, breathing in his familiar, reassuring scent. "I need what all women need—an ocean of blood."

He nodded. "I'll go get Pandora. Wait here—"

I grabbed him firmly, not letting him leave. "Not for feeding, Roland. I need an ocean of my enemies' blood to decorate the fountain at the entrance to Solomon's Temple. That is what I need. Then I will be able to rest easy. When everyone is too scared of me to cause me problems."

He shot me a look of understanding and nodded. "I see." We stood in silence for a few moments. "Ryuu seemed to think you were laying low this evening," he said carefully. "What are you really going to do?"

I smiled and nudged him with my hip. "I'm sure glad he's not as observant as you."

Roland snorted. "He's far more observant than me. He knows, I'm sure. I think that is why he left."

I nodded. "Take care of that back, Roland," I said with a faint smile. "She has a pretty sweet hot tub, by the way. I need to go get changed."

He chuckled and left, either to seek out Pandora for a hat-trick or to find my scrolls. I didn't have the heart to discourage him from seeking a little joy. I ripped open a Gateway to my bedroom at Castle Dracula and hurriedly dressed in my mother's black slaying outfit, not even bothering to close the portal behind me. I grabbed a few necessities from the closet and then grimaced at myself in the tall standing mirror.

Can you heal my entire body like you did my tailbone? Not just block the pain but actually heal me? I asked Envy.

Of course, but people will ask questions...

I nodded. *Just the major wounds.*

I felt a rush of cold ice spread through me and I gasped, my eyes widening as I trembled and felt my fingers go numb. I shivered as she finished and then I lifted up my shirt to check my stomach. It wasn't perfectly healed on the outside but I could take deep breaths and no longer felt the sharp pains from my severe injuries.

Thank you, Envy.

I tried not to think of Lucky's warning about good intentions but I failed. Then I hopped back through and grabbed Dorian by the elbow, releasing my Gateway.

"Let's hit the strip club," I told him.

He grinned, rubbing his hands together greedily. "Goody." Then he reached into his pocket and withdrew a small black jar. "Smear this on your eyes like warpaint," he said. "It will distort your features and mask your scent." I didn't even question him as I unscrewed the lid and followed his advice, smearing a greasy black paste from the corner of my eyes to my temples like I was making raven wings.

If it got me out of this cursed prison, I would have done almost anything. I was feeling stir crazy and Dorian Gray was always the solution to boredom. For better or worse, you could never be bored on a night out with the world's most deviant bachelor.

⚘ 28 ⚘

I strolled down the dark, damp streets of the Power and Light district in Kansas City, careful to keep my black hood up and conceal my shockingly white hair. The black warpaint made me feel like a Viking warrior but I couldn't take any chances with my hair. Dorian strolled beside me, humming faintly under his breath as he did a little dance shuffle mid-step in time with his humming. Groups of drunk college kids lingered here and there, waiting outside bars and clubs with bright flashing lights. Girls wore sparkly tight dresses and boys wore pristinely pressed dress shirts with skinny jeans. The amount of perfume and cologne in the air was an arsonist's wet dream, even from across the street.

"Smells like a French whorehouse," I muttered, rubbing my nose.

Dorian cocked his head pensively, sniffing at the air. "Not at all, actually," he said matter-of-factly, not even trying to make a joke. Just correcting the academic record.

Dorian gently grasped my elbow and guided me down a dark side street. I let out an annoyed sigh, shaking his hand off with a warning growl. A thought from Envy hit me as I followed after him. "How long were you friends with Charles Baudelaire?"

He flinched as if I'd goosed him. "How the hell did you know *that?*" he blurted.

Told you, Envy purred in a satisfied tone.

I smiled and gave him a mysterious shrug. "How long until we get there?" I asked, scanning the street warily. "There're a whole lot of people who want me dead these days."

Some of them were even friends. What the hell was Lucky up to?

"Not long." He was silent for a few steps, pulling out his phone and lifting it up before him. I realized he had the camera app open and I scowled, assuming he was making a live video for social media. I checked to make sure my hood was up and my face hidden in the shadow of the fabric. He swept it across the walls of the buildings until a bright pink image appeared on one of the damp brick walls. I frowned, looking from the phone to the actual wall. There was no pink design in the real world, but his phone showed it clearly. A neon rose.

He nodded matter-of-factly, glanced over his shoulder behind us, and then placed his palm on the brick wall where the digital rose was on his phone. The brick wall rippled and then disappeared, revealing a brand-new cobblestone street that shouldn't exist. I blinked, surprised. It was a hidden street right here in Kansas City. Not only that, but it was in the middle of the Power and Light District—a highly-trafficked part of town.

Dorian glanced over at me with a smirk. "This way, my lady."

I followed him through the new opening and flinched as the brick wall reappeared behind me, rebuilding from the ground up. I shuddered, turning to study the signs of the various shoppes down this magical side street. I saw flame lanterns up ahead and realized that the street was actually quite busy fifty feet away. It was like a street fair. Flickering lanterns hung from awnings and braziers lined the street, casting everything in a warm glow like we'd stepped back in time to a world before electricity.

Except with shifters and fairies and leprechauns and witches and other mysterious creatures unafraid to live out in the open. Much like Castle Dracula, actually. Many of them drank raucously, laughing and chatting back and forth with other store owners or jeering at pedestrians walking down the street. I grunted in surprise to see a couple of fairy children talking trash to a trio of massive shifter bears as they lumbered down the street, chuckling rather than murdering the offensive fairy kids. "How long has this been here?" I asked, unable to dismiss the parallels of Diagon Alley from the Harry Potter books.

Dorian smiled. "Long time. Hellfire Club and the Chancery moved here to stay off the radar as best they could. Neutral territory. It's where I found your pops. Welcome to White Rose Lane," he said, spreading his arms wide as his eyes settled on a cute, painted wooden sign hanging on the brick wall.

I blinked, caught off guard as I read the decorative script. "They...named this place after *me*?" I whispered, unable to shake the overwhelming rush of emotion that hit me in the heart. Dorian nodded. Then the rest of his comment hit me and I frowned over at him. "Wait. My dad was *living* here?" I asked, feeling a surge of guilt. Dorian nodded distantly, apparently more focused on assessing the other Freaks in the street than answering my question. I absently checked the throwing knives up my sleeve, even though I didn't see any danger.

A violin played a haunting yet merry jig, and Freaks from all walks of life were carrying baskets from shop to shop, buying goods or pausing in the middle of the street to chat with neighboring werewolves and witches. I even saw a few more bears arm wrestling over a rickety table outside a tavern. A crowd of men were cheering them on, hoisting wooden and ivory mugs of ale. I glanced over to see several humans with painted candy skulls on their faces. My eyes momentarily widened, fearing they were actual Candy Skulls from Hell, but I let out a breath of relief to see it was just witches and wizards.

"It is neutral territory, but no one here has the strength to really defend themselves against the big dogs coming to town, so these people prefer to hide. Angels and demons occasionally visit but they seem to respect the sanctity of the place better than the Freaks," he said with a bemused shake of his head. If he hadn't said that, I might have instantly tried to kill the pair of demons I picked out of the crowd. They were crouched down in an alley throwing dice against the brick wall and grinning horrific smiles. Their pitchforks were propped up against the wall and they looked...to be having fun. I saw an angel striding down the street with tense shoulders, looking like a patrolling officer of the law. No one hassled him and he didn't disturb the mellow revelry. I shook my head in disbelief.

My father had been living here on White Rose Lane. The thought gave me a regretful smile—that he'd had to accept a lifeless street name rather than the real White Rose keeping him safe. I hoped he was safe at Castle Dracula right now, but I was sure Samael and Lilith were keeping a close eye on him, not to mention the personal guard of shifter bears he'd acquired. It was safer for him if I didn't get too close to him.

"Take me to the strip club," I told Dorian, grabbing him by the elbow and tugging him sharply down the street to get him started. I kept my hood up and my face angled down, but I felt a few pairs of eyes taking note of us. None of them seemed hostile, or even remotely aware of who I really was; they simply watched with idle curiosity. We passed several more taverns that had spilled their patrons out onto the streets to sit at rickety tables as they were full of men and women singing loud and bawdy drinking songs and raising their mugs in cheers at every little comment or joke.

It was like a punch to the gut to realize that I felt anxious and suspicious of people simply having fun and living their lives. It was like the KC Ren Fest but completely authentic.

We slipped through a gathering crowd that was watching a street performer juggle fire and live snakes. No, the snakes turned to fire at the apex of their arcs, then back to serpents in time for the juggler to catch them. I smiled delightedly at the obvious joy and festive looks on everyone's faces. Freaks having innocent fun in any way they could. Not being monsters, but just trying to get their slice of life out of a world gone mad.

Dorian pulled me through a crowd of goblins who were smoking cigars and playing quarters on a stained wooden table outside a bar that was blasting a familiar song. The windows were blacked out so I couldn't see inside. "Welcome to the KC Strip Club of White Rose Lane," Dorian said with a twinkle in his eyes. "Keep your hood up," he reminded me.

My boots started to tingle and I felt a flicker of anxiety rush through me. "Demons inside," I murmured.

Dorian nodded. "Probably a few angels as well. Nothing to be concerned about. They come here to relax and socialize." Then he shoved open a thick wooden door and we entered a gloomy, smoky bar with loud music blaring. But it wasn't techno or any fast-paced dance music.

Instead, it was *White Rabbit* by Jefferson Airplane.

I froze, staring in disbelief as my eyes settled on the bar. A woman, who was maybe a few inches taller than me, stood atop the wooden counter, twirling and dancing with hypnotic grace to the song as if she'd recently taken a hit of acid and was becoming one with the universe. Except...she wasn't a human.

She was a cute, velvety white rabbit with big blue eyes and tall pointed ears.

Dorian stiffened in alarm upon seeing her. "Shit," he muttered.

Tight black pants emphasized her curves and featured lacing down the sides that revealed the white fur beneath. She even had a cutout on her ass to show off her fluffy white tail. She wore a black leather halter top that seemed to hold an armament of black throwing knives. She was remarkably drunk or high, exceptionally good at scandalous dancing, and her little bunny tail got screams of surprise when she...

"She just twerked," I blurted out in disbelief.

Dorian swatted my hand down with a hiss. I hadn't even realized I'd been pointing at the twerking rabbit. "Best leave her alone. She's a killer."

I snorted. "She's a dancing rabbit. Cute and fluffy."

Dorian gave me a flat look and shook his head. "No. See those tattoos?" he asked. I glanced back at the dancing bunny and saw a tribal design of some kind marking one of her tall, pointed ears and part of her soft fluffy cheek. Her eyes were sapphire blue with black pupils, but there was absolutely no white to the sclera. I thought I spotted a scar crossing one of her eyes but it was hard to tell with her white fur and her continuous dancing. Half a dozen or so silver hooped earrings pierced her tall white ears. Her arm also sported several familiar looking designs that tickled the back of my mind for some reason. "She gets a new one for every one-hundred confirmed kills," Dorian said in a solemn tone.

My eyes bulged open in disbelief. I did a swift count of the tattoos I could see and felt my stomach lurching. She'd killed close to one-thousand people if he was right. "What the fuck? A wererabbit assassin?"

Dorian looked back at me as if I was daft. "That's the fucking Easter Bunny, Callie."

❧ 29 ❧

I stared at the twerking, sultry, seductress rabbit, unable to formulate any response whatsoever. Then I realized why her tattoos looked familiar. They were the same geometric shapes as those used to paint Easter eggs, although hers looked somehow more dangerous and foreboding. A crowd of people were cheering her on as she did a Coyote Ugly impersonation atop the bar, spinning bottles of liquor in her paws, guzzling a drink every now and then before squatting down to pour liquor down on the crowd. It should tell you something that she was so distracting that it wasn't until that moment that I realized the crowd featured quite a few lesser demons who seemed to be having the time of their lives. I even saw a pair of angels at a table in the back corner of the room. They were pretending not to stare at the rabbit and failing miserably.

"You're shitting me," I breathed, turning back to the Easter Bunny. "She's...amazing."

Dorian shrugged. "As long as you're not on her list. She's got a vicious streak a mile wide. She's a killer. Keep your hood up and stop staring before she notices."

I scoffed. I'd met plenty of dangerous killers. "Stop being so dramatic. She looks *fun*."

He stared at me for about three long seconds and then clenched his jaw. "I'll show you." Then he grabbed me by the elbow and guided me to a high table near the edge of the room. Unfortunately, it was occupied by two large men. The smell of their blood told me they were werewolves, but I didn't know whether they were of the Kansas City or St. Louis variety. I kept my distance and hung my head low enough to conceal my face from them but still watch. Dorian tapped them on the shoulders. They turned, annoyed to be pulled away from ogling the stripping murder bunny. "You two need to leave before it's too late."

The blonde werewolf looked to be in his mid-thirties, scrappy, and reckless. His pal was much larger, rougher around the edges, like he was in a biker gang, had a buzzcut, and a gnarly beard that touched his chest. The bearded brute arched an eyebrow incredulously but the other narrowed his eyes at Dorian for a moment before sucking in a sharp breath through his nostrils. "That's Dorian Gray," he urged his friend, swiftly grabbing his hairy forearm before the biker wolf could make a scene.

Big bad wolf hesitated, eyeing Dorian up and down. He glanced at me but my face was still shrouded beneath my hood. He turned back to Dorian. "I paid for this drink, and I'm going to finish it. No disrespect, but I don't get paid enough to throw it away because you can't bother standing up for thirty minutes."

His blonde friend swallowed audibly.

Dorian shrugged. "I don't mind standing, but I wasn't talking about my comfort." He pointed a thumb over his shoulder at the dancing Easter bunny. "You're on her list. She came here specifically for you, brother. Choice is yours. Drink and die, or run before this song ends." He shrugged and turned away nonchalantly.

The two werewolves looked like Dorian had just fatally stabbed them in the gut and then promised to burn their grieving mothers alive when they came to pay respects at their sons' funerals. The big bad wolf downed his beer, spilling most of it over his beard in panic, but the other had already taken off for the door with a whimpered yelp, ducking down low as he raced for the exit. His friend was only a few seconds behind him as the wolves fled for their lives from the Easter Bunny.

Dorian turned to look at me and gave me a slow nod as if to say *I told you so*.

"Jesus," I murmured, hopping up onto the barstool as I turned to watch the assassin rabbit finish up her dance routine. She looked hammered but as fluid as a ribbon—completely in control of her inebriation.

A grumpy green sprite zipped over to us, flying over the busy crowd and then dropping down to the center of our high table. He was a horrid-looking bastard with dirty green skin and warped claws on his feet. I spotted a few rashes on his arms and chest that looked suspiciously like tree bark. I winced, betting he didn't have any female prospects with rashes like that. Maybe he hadn't ever heard of moisturizing.

Hydration makes the girls go down.

"Welcome to the Strip Club. What the fuck do you want?" he snapped, pulling out a tiny notepad and a feather quill.

"Hey, Graves," Dorian replied in a polite tone. "She here for business or pleasure?" he asked, indicating the Easter Bunny with a slight shift of his chin.

Graves narrowed his eyes. "You think I'm stupid enough to ask? What the fuck do you want?"

Dorian sighed and plastered a bright smile on his face. "Sixth Horseman. Two. Make them doubles."

The grumpy sprite stared at him with a menacing glare. "The only thing you can get for free here is werephilis or a broken jaw." He scratched his green ass with a gnarly claw and then lifted it for a quick sniff that made him —and me—gag. "Scratch that. Werephilis isn't free either. You actually pay for it twice."

I leaned away with a grimace. Well, that might explain the tree-bark rashes.

Dorian chuckled and slapped a golden coin down on the table. Then he pulled out another golden coin. "This one is for your discretion, Graves. We're meeting someone."

The sprite growled greedily and scooped up the two coins. He tossed them into a satchel on his hip that looked to be made of spiderwebs. He shot me a brief, hostile glare. "This is neutral territory." I nodded. Over his shoulder, I noticed that the Easter Bunny had ended her routine and had hopped down from the bar but I didn't see her ears swimming through the crowd. The green-skinned sprite grunted at me suspiciously, but I must have passed his appraisal. Then he promptly stabbed himself in the thigh with the quill pen, dipped the pointed tip in his blood, and then jotted down the order. "I'll send them over promptly." He sheathed his quill and his face went blank as he stood in the center of our table like a zombie. He scratched his ass again, but this time he tasted what he dug up and I cringed.

"I'm not thirsty anymore," I muttered, shaking my head.

Graves glanced up at me and cocked his head. Then he held his stanky hand up to me. "Want some?" He chuckled wickedly at the look on my face and lowered his hand. "Your loss." Then he abruptly snapped his fingers and two silver cups appeared before us. My eyes widened in surprise and I glanced down at our magic drinks. He hadn't touched them, thankfully. Frosty air rose up from the cups like dry ice and I caught the strong scent of mint alcohol, and something else that made my mouth water. *Angel blood*, Envy mused, sounding pleased. I stared down into the cup to see a single red drop suspended in the center of the drink. The nasty sprite left without fanfare and I glanced over at Dorian with an arched eyebrow.

"Did he really say werephilis?" I asked, grimacing.

Dorian nodded absently, his eyes scanning the crowd with a nervous wariness. He must have noticed the Easter Bunny's disappearance as well. "Like syphilis but from a were-creature. Not as bad as it sounds. I know a cauldron shop who keeps the antidote on hand. Especially during the full moon." He frowned to himself. "Wait. That's tonight, right? I should probably restock my supply."

I scrunched up my nose, shaking my head. "Yeah. That's just nasty—"

"Kink-shaming will earn you no friends here," he interrupted swiftly. "Where *is* she?" he murmured in a troubled tone, anxiously looking for the Toymaker in the dark sea of dancing, drinking monsters as the music changed to an old punk rock anthem that instantly made me feel old.

I scanned the crowd of Freaks as they chatted, laughed, and bobbed their heads to the song. Even the demons seemed light-hearted and chill. I wasn't dumb enough to ask Dorian about the angel's blood in my cup, not with how close the dancing Freaks and demons were to our table. I even saw a trio of witches playing limbo beneath a demon's tail as a werewolf held it up and laughed. No one recognized me or even seemed to care who I might be, but I wasn't the only hooded person in the room. Strangely enough, I saw no actual strippers. I frowned, realizing I was actually disappointed after all the build-up. "Where are the boobs?"

Dorian glanced over at me, but only briefly, before resuming his search. "This is a restaurant. The Kansas City Strip Club," he said with an amused smile. "Steaks, not tits."

I narrowed my eyes, realizing he'd been stringing me along this whole time. Then I thought of Graves and shuddered. "I would *never* eat here."

Dorian chuckled. "Best steak I've ever had. Graves is the bartender not the cook—" He cut off abruptly, squinting over my shoulder. "Someone's coming."

I looked up to see the crowd parting for someone. Then two tall bunny ears abruptly flicked up over the assorted heads, swiveling our way like periscopes. Or shark fins.

Dorian cursed. "Oh, shit," he whispered. "I knew she would bring backup, but not *her*! We should leave."

My pulse jumped in alarm. "The Toymaker needs a bodyguard?"

"KC is a dangerous place these days, and everyone has heard about what happened in Rome. Can you blame her? Let's just go," he said, rising to his feet.

"Did you tell her *I* would be here?" I hissed, glaring at the velvety ears of death. Was this a hit on the White Rose?

Dorian paused and cocked his head thoughtfully, looking suddenly thoughtful. "No, actually. I said I was bringing one of my trusted associates." He glanced at me, scrutinizing my face paint. "Just sit there and look ominous. Nod occasionally, but let me do the talking. Your disguise should hold up."

"Should?" I hissed in a furious hiss.

"It's the fucking Easter Bunny," he reminded me in a nervously reverent whisper. "Who knows which vicious legends about her are true?" The crowd parted around the Easter Bunny in a mixture of fear and awe as they nervously congratulated her on her earlier dance routine or ducked their heads in respect of her death tally. "Maybe she's not with the Toymaker and she just saw me from across the room," he said, dubiously. "Be ready to Shadow Walk if this goes south and she kills me," he whispered. "I'll shake it off and we'll regroup after."

Because Dorian Gray couldn't die unless you destroyed his painting. Yet he was still terrified of the apparent Killer of Caerbannog.

❧ 30 ❧

Before I could respond, a furry paw darted out from the crowd and slammed a liquor bottle onto our table like it was the climbing spike of a mountaineer reaching the peak of her greatest challenge. Then she released the bottle with a laugh and fell, bowling over close to a dozen Freaks who promptly buried her in a pile. The white paw and fluffy ears disappeared and I heard a drunken "Oof!" followed by another bubbly laugh from somewhere within the pile.

I snatched up two daggers on instinct, fearing I had become the target of the Easter Bunny and that Dorian had unintentionally gotten me killed in a chance storm of ultimate irony—on a street already named after me. Less work for my survivors.

Dorian shot me a reassuring look, hopped down off his barstool, and then crouched down low, reaching into the swarm of people. Like a magician pulling a rabbit out of a hat, he found a furry white paw and pulled. A moment later, the highly intoxicated Easter bunny stood before him, giggling and laughing as she released his hand and used her paw to shift her breasts back into her top since they were in danger of falling free entirely. She hiccupped loudly and then plopped herself down on one of the free stools across from me. She set a gilded wicker basket down onto our table, almost fell off her stool, and then caught her balance with deft paws. When she removed them, my eyes took note of the deep gouges left in the wood from her claws.

I hadn't even seen them through all the fluffy fur. I surreptitiously eyed the wicker…Easter basket. Really? Dorian sat down beside her and politely slid her liquor bottle towards her. It was Don Julio 1942. Couple hundred bucks a bottle.

"Finding Dory!" she giggled at him in a sultry, singsong voice, scrunching up her nose and wiggling her whiskers in that cute way bunnies did. I stared at her from within my hood, doing my best not to openly gawk. Up close, I realized the tribal designs on her ears, cheek, and arms were actually branded into her flesh, leaving her fur to grow out from the undamaged skin so that it looked like a barber had simply cut the designs into her fur. I counted numerous black throwing knives sheathed on her halter vest and I saw two much longer, sinuous kukri blades hanging on her hips. Judging by the daggers I could see, she probably had a whole lot more tucked away on her person. Her basket was closed and I desperately wanted a look inside to see if she really carried Easter eggs around with her. Maybe it was just her version of a purse.

"You found me," Dorian replied with a nervous chuckle. "It's always a pleasant surprise to see you, Grace. I've missed you at my parties."

Grace—apparently—chuckled, squinting down at her liquor bottle as if needing to devote her full attention to working the complicated device. Rather than twisting off the cap, an insanely sharp claw suddenly extended from one of her paws and she sliced through the glass neck with perfect precision. She blindly flicked the top out into the crowd, hoisted her bottle in the air—eliciting a round of uneasy cheers from the crowd around us—and then guzzled a healthy dose of the expensive tequila.

She thumped the bottle down and squinted at Dorian with one eye as if trying to pierce through her double vision. "You're not on my list, are you? I've got a backlog ever since I spent a few weeks in Boston and St. Louis. Damned Valkyries in both towns messed up my contracts, but then took me drinking and filled my pockets with coin, so I can't complain." She eyed me suspiciously. "You ain't a Valkyrie, are you?" I shook my head and her frown evaporated, replaced by a relieved grin. Was she talking about Kára? I didn't know anyone in Boston other than Quinn MacKenna, but she wasn't a Valkyrie.

Was she? I mean, I hadn't been Master Dracula the last time we hung out, so it could be possible.

Grace turned back to Dorian and I took the opportunity to sheath at least one of my knives below the table. "Couldn't find the time to drag my cottontail ass down here. The shit I've seen over the last few days," she slurred, shaking her head and seeming to completely forget about her idle threat against his life.

Dorian shook his head. "Well, if I am on your list, I'll pay you double not to follow through—"

"Booooooooring!" Grace interrupted, rolling her eyes. Her ears constantly twitched and twisted, tracking the sounds of the bar as if always alert to danger, even when she was smashed. "People always offer more *money*. Be more creative for fuck's sake. Knives. I could *always* use more knives. I leave them around everywhere. Usually in people's skulls, but still." She laughed and took another drink.

"We're actually expecting someone. Maybe we could share a drink after—"

"You hear about that shit in Rome a few days ago?" she asked bluntly, cutting him off. Dorian nodded with a crooked smile. Sweat beaded on his temple and I did my best to look relaxed. "I laughed my tail off. Serves those pious pricks right." Her nose scrunched up again and her whiskers wiggled merrily. I found myself smiling at her, unable to see anything other than a highly intoxicated Easter Bunny even though she was calmly discussing assassination contracts and terrorist attacks. She patted her gilded basket with an affectionate purr. "Almost got me caught, but it ended up being a great diversion."

She made as if to peel back the lid and I leaned forward reflexively.

Her ears swiveled to me and she grew abruptly still. She stared into the depths of my hood with a suspicious look. Then she removed her hand from the basket, lifted her bottle and took another drink, not breaking eye contact. "And what might you be, cutie-pie? Shy or dumb?"

I smirked, discreetly checking my knife under the table. "Mysterious," I replied, deciding it was the cleverest answer to press her buttons. I lifted my drink to her with my other hand and then took a healthy sip. "What's in the basket, bunny?" I asked in a soft tone, ready to defend myself if I'd read her wrong.

She cocked her head. "What?" she asked in a cool warning tone.

I gestured my cup at her basket. "Curiosity killed the cat," I said with a devil-may-care shrug.

Dorian froze, looking like he'd just shit an egg.

Grace stared at me in complete silence, suddenly looking entirely sober. Then she burst out laughing in a chittering, giggling roar. "Damn, woman! You know how long it's been since someone showed any spine to me?" she hooted. Then she lifted her bottle to me and we clinked glasses. "Cheers!"

"Cheers!" I replied, letting out a breath of relief. I kept my face hooded to hide my hair because while Dorian had been helping Grace to her feet, I'd counted no less than six demons in the pile of bodies she'd bowled over. My boots were steadily buzzing like they were full of bees. If they recognized me, all Hell would break loose. Literally.

Grace leaned towards me over the table and set her paw on the lid of the basket. "Can you keep a secret?"

"Only if I can't capitalize on it," I admitted with a chuckle.

Grace grinned toothily, glancing over at Dorian. "I like her." Then she lifted the lid a few inches. I leaned forward and my heart jumped into my throat. Three priceless jeweled eggs were nestled in a bed of vibrant green grass, and they glittered with blue, red, and yellow sparkles even in the dim bar. She closed it with a soft click and stared into the depths of my hood. I took a calming breath and leaned back in my seat with a grunt. I lifted a shaking cup to my mouth and took a drink. The angel blood hit my tongue and I almost guzzled the rest of the drink down in one greedy pull. I managed to control myself and slowly lowered the cup to the table, refusing to look at it. Grace took my response as a compliment to her thievery skills.

Faberge Eggs. She had three of the rarest treasures in the world tucked into a cheap basket in a shitty tavern in Kansas City.

"Wow." I had unknowingly helped the Easter Bunny rob the Vatican when I'd attacked St. Peter's Square. Talk about unintended consequences. "I don't know whether to clap or curtsy."

I wasn't sure which eggs they were, but most Faberge eggs had been crafted for Russian emperors to give to their wives as Easter presents in the late 1800's. The Easter Bunny was not merely a reputable—legendary— assassin, she was also a white-collar criminal.

She grinned proudly. "On loan for an exhibit at the Vatican. I decided I gotta get 'em all like Pokemon. They want to appropriate the Easter Bunny's special day, then I'm gonna take my eggs and go home."

"More power to you," I said, laughing as I raised my cup. "Your secret is safe with me."

She preened and then seemed to take notice of Dorian's awkward fidgeting. "Oh, right. You're waiting for Carla," she said with a wiggle of her nose. "Poor girl would lose her head if I didn't keep an eye out for her. Told me all about the...big brothers from downstairs possibly hunting her," she said cryptically, reaching a furry paw below the table. "Let me just check that you two aren't on my list and then we'll talk about the Toymaker."

Dorian let out a sharp breath, his shoulders deflating. "Oh! *You're* Carla's friend. I thought she may have stood us up," he said with a light laugh that was definitely concerned.

"I was already in the neighborhood on business of my own," Grace murmured absently, whipping out a forearm length dagger in her paw. She deftly spun it over her furry knuckles, snorted, and then flipped it into the air to then catch it by the tip of her other paw. "Hold that for a minute, toots," she mumbled, blindly extending the hilt my way as she looked down and reached back into her pocket with a frown.

I accepted it, aiming a grim look at Dorian while she wasn't looking.

"Ah. Here it is," she said, pulling out a folded piece of parchment. It had a ringed coffee stain on it and was torn at the edges. Very professional.

She set it down before her and squinted her eyes. Then she let out a chuckle. "Upside down. Thought I was drunk for a minute there." She spun the paper right side up and started reading.

The air grew tense as Grace continued reading, casually sipping from her bottle of tequila. She frowned suddenly and lowered the bottle. She looked up at me for a few seconds and then turned to Dorian. She saw the grim look on his face and let out a soft laugh, placing her soft paw on his arm. "Oh, no. You're fine. Just saw a new name on my list." She winked at him and folded up her letter, shoving it back into her pocket. Then she drew another of her daggers, leaned back and started cleaning her claws with the tip.

Dorian's shoulders sagged and he let out a sigh of relief. "The Toymaker?" he reminded her.

"Yeah...she's not coming," Grace said, drawing out the words as she frowned down at her claws.

I narrowed my eyes, gripping the dagger she'd handed me moments before as I steadied my breathing.

Grace finally glanced up at me and her eyes were entirely sober. She palmed the dagger and blindly sheathed it in her shirt in a blur so fast that I almost missed it. "You know where I can find the White Rose? I've got a few daggers with her name on them."

"Fuck," Dorian groaned.

❧ 31 ❧

I stared back at Grace from within my hood. Then I spun her dagger effortlessly across my palm and over the backs of my knuckles— nowhere near as swift and agile as her abilities, but revealing my mastery of the perfectly balanced blade—before I slammed the tip down at her paw.

The blade stabbed down between her knuckles and buried into the wood.

She didn't move and she didn't blink as she stared into my eyes with an amused smirk.

Dorian was panting and stammering. "Easy, girls. This is neutral—"

"How long have you known?" I asked her, releasing the hilt and leaning back on my stool.

Grace shrugged and finally withdrew her paw from the blade, revealing that I hadn't even nicked her flesh. "Since Ryuu hired me to be your body-guard two hours ago. Paid with three of these beautiful knives." She tapped the blade with a sharp claw. "See? Your name," she said, pointing at a rose etched into the blade. Dorian sputtered in confusion but neither of us acknowledged him so he resorted to downing his drink.

I glanced down at the familiar blade, nodding. I'd recognized it the moment she had handed it to me—which had been her point, of course. I wasn't sure why she'd chosen to play games but I knew Ryuu didn't give these particular knives away—because he had made them specifically for *me*. A rose was engraved at the base of the blades. No one else could have given them to her because Ryuu had hidden them even from me, telling me I had to earn them by besting him in my training.

Yet he had given them to Grace to keep me safe, which meant she was even more dangerous than Dorian had believed. Ryuu was not easily impressed. At all.

I saw three men in the crowd staring at me. They blended into the crowd easily, and I hadn't noticed them before this moment. They simultaneously glanced at Grace—and I saw her ears swivel their way, tracking them—and then the men turned their attention back to me before giving me a subtle bow of the chin. Ryuu's shinobi. They disappeared from sight between one moment and the next. Reassuring me of her claim.

It wasn't just that she was a stranger, but that the Sins and Archangels could disguise themselves as anyone they wanted, and it was impossible to detect them.

And Grace had noted their presence without saying a word.

"How did he know about the Toymaker?" Dorian demanded. "I didn't tell anyone."

Grace shrugged. "No clue. Carla's already started work at Castle Dracula, by the way," she said, glancing at Dorian with a smug grin. "Ryuu told me there was no point in both of us sitting here all day until you arrived, and I'm a big fan of drinking alone," she said, glancing at the bar.

I leaned forward, keeping my hood up for the benefit of everyone else at the bar. Ryuu had mentioned a plan up his sleeve, but I hadn't anticipated him hiring me a bodyguard and a security consultant. "Did he hire you because of the Toymaker or for another reason?"

Grace smiled. "He said you needed the Halo Breaker right now, not an overprotective lover." She pulled the dagger out of the wood and inspected it in the lantern light. "Said you still needed a blade in the shadows. Weddings are known for all sorts of backstabbery," she mused, wiggling her nose and whiskers again.

I wanted to punch him in the throat and kiss him, but neither of those were options at the moment. "Where is he now?"

"Recruiting was all he told me." She glanced down at the basket between us and smiled faintly. "Figured three knives and three eggs were worth my time. Thanks for that, by the way." I dipped my chin. "But to stick it to the

Vatican, I might have helped you for free." She lifted her bottle of tequila to me and waited.

I found myself smiling as I lifted my own cup and clinked it against hers. "To the End of Days," I said.

Her ears twitched and she squinted thoughtfully. Then she nodded. "To the End of Days."

We drank and then Dorian leaned forward. "Well, I'm glad I could be of service," he muttered moodily.

"Thank you, Dorian. We've got it from here," I said. "It's time for girl talk."

He huffed and got up from his stool. "Well, I'll see you back...home," he said, remembering to keep said home from touching his lips where others might overhear. Then he was shoving his way through the crowd towards the door. It opened, letting in the loud sounds of festivity from outside, and then closed behind him.

I turned to Grace with a pensive look. "How do you know Ryuu?"

"I was a student of his before you."

I frowned. I had thought Ryuu never accepted students. Hadn't he told me that before? What was he up to and why was he being so secretive about it? It couldn't be a concern for Envy or he would have chosen to personally remain by my side. Was this because of the Four Horsemen?

"Did he tell you exactly who you're supposed to protect me from?"

She grinned, leaning closer. "No. But if you don't know the answer either, I can only assume he wants me to protect you from yourself—"

The front door exploded inwards and a body flew into the Strip Club. The door knocked back the crowd in a domino effect and the body slammed into the counter with a bone-breaking snap before crumpling to the ground. I climbed up on my stool to see that the dead body—not Dorian, thankfully —had a gaping hole in his chest. The now open doorway showed a war zone of milling, screaming people accompanied by the sounds of violent battle.

A hooded man I hadn't noticed was hunched over in the entryway with both hands on his knees, struggling to catch his breath as if he'd just finished a race. The tangle of people on the ground were growling and arguing with each other as they fought to get back to their feet but they kept their distance from the gasping hooded man. He finally straightened and placed his bloody hands on top of his head, sucking down great lungfuls of air.

"Okay," a familiar voice finally wheezed, flipping his hood back. My eyes widened. What the hell was Alucard doing here? "I'm here for the Killer of Caerbannog!" Alucard said in a horrendous Scottish accent. "Oh, aye! The most foul, cruel, and bad-tempered rodent you've ever set eyes on," he declared, really enunciating the adjectives.

I grinned. I knew I loved Alucard for a good reason. I'd been wanting to say those Monty Python quotes about the white murder rabbit to Grace this whole time.

Grace growled murderously, as if personally offended, brandishing a knife but I swatted at her hand and shook my head no. Was it really him or an imposter Sin or Archangel? Because I saw angels and demons going at it behind him through the open doorway, destroying the once pleasant aura of White Rose Lane.

"Who?" a demon growled.

Alucard swiftly punched him in the face, sending him flying over the bar with a cry. "The Easter Bunny," Alucard drawled. "Does no one watch Monty Python around here?" he demanded, scanning the faces before him.

The green bartender sprite zipped out from behind the bar, hovering in the air before Alucard. "This is supposed to be neutral territory!"

"It's also supposed to be a strip club but you don't see me complaining," Alucard grumbled. "And technically, I just helped him open the door with his face," Alucard added, pointing at the dead body. Then he pointed back over his shoulder. "If you have a complaint, take it up with the mobs outside." I heard the clang of metal on metal, screams and shouts, roars of flame, and flashes of light. Grace shot me a meaningful look, urging me to follow her out the back.

"Who *are* you?" one demon demanded, panting furiously as he squared off against Alucard. Several of his buddies stood behind him and were looking from us to Alucard as if debating which one to go after.

He puffed up his chest proudly and grinned. "I am Alucard—"

An angel slammed into his back from the open doorway, cutting him off short. The two went crashing into one of the supporting pillars and that portion of the ceiling abruptly dropped a good foot in a shower of dust and splinters as the two tumbled and rolled across the bar, destroying tables and chairs and sending drinks flying into the air. Lanterns flew and toppled, spilling oil and flame across the floorboards and furniture.

32

A black rhino demon stormed into the bar with a snarl, holding a glowing red battle axe and sweeping his beady eyes from left to right. He saw Grace's tall white ears and let out a shout. "Get her!" Then he started swinging his axe wildly, destroying everything in his wake with eruptions of sparks that swiftly increased the number of fires spreading through the room. Everyone started screaming and running in every direction—either outside into the raging battle or deeper into the bar's kitchen and storage rooms.

Fire swiftly began climbing up the rafters and I knew we were on borrowed time.

"I said get her!" The berserker rhino demon screamed at the demons in the bar.

Three demons near our table spun around to stare at us with miserable looks on their faces, knowing things would not end well for them. Grace scooped up her wicker basket and abruptly disappeared, leaving me all alone to face the demons.

Some bodyguard, Envy murmured, sounding amused. *Want me to drive?*

No. I don't want stories spreading about me using crazy Hell magic in downtown. You're my dirty little side chick.

She laughed at that.

I flung back my hood and summoned up my claws just as two of the demons rushed to attack me. The black grease Dorian had given me still distorted my appearance, but my silver claws and white hair were infamous and feared in Kansas City from my brief stint as a homicidal vigilante. They took one hesitant step in my direction before a white blur zipped in front of them and a shower of blood sprayed all over my face. I furiously wiped my eyes on the inside of my elbow and saw Grace standing by my side, lazily flipping a bloody dagger in her paws. The remaining demon turned to run away and Grace zipped ahead of him in another blur, calmly holding her dagger out in front of his face so that he impaled himself on it with his own momentum.

Okay. Yeah. Killer of Caerbannog. Check.

"I'm fast," Grace said, slowly shoving the demon off her dagger with one furry finger to his forehead so that he crashed back to the floor with a bone-less thud.

"Where's your basket?" I asked anxiously, fearing that the priceless treasures had fallen to the ground or been stolen while we were distracted.

She smirked. "I hid them," she said, drawing another dagger with her free hand. "Kind of my thing."

And then I saw Mr. Rhino barreling my way in a smashing, splintering, burning charge, and a handful of other demons jumped the rabbit from behind, dog piling her.

I summoned up a whip of white fire, lassoed it around the rhino demon's horn, and then I sprinted towards him, dropped to my ass and slid through his legs just as he was swinging his axe for my face. The axe destroyed our table in an explosion of flame as the blade sunk into the floorboards, but me yanking the whip down and through his legs caused him to slam face-first into the ground and do a headstand.

While he was stuck like that, I worked his body like a heavy punching bag.

Except I still had my claws out. He squealed and screamed before toppling into his own fiery mess and thrashing about in agony. I turned to see Grace arching an eyebrow at me and my claws. The demons who had dogpiled her were dead and twitching at her feet, creating a slowly spreading pool of blood. Her pretty white fur was soaked with crimson stains and she held the two kukri knives at her sides.

The ivory hilts had emerald leather strips hanging from the pommels so that they actually looked like carrots. Alucard trotted over to me with a grin, his face covered in blood, soot, and feathers as fires raged throughout the bar behind him. "I got one," he said, proudly pointing a thumb over his shoulder as he coughed into his elbow from the smoke.

Grace burst out laughing, eyeing her own pile of bodies.

Alucard glanced back at her and did a double-take. "No shit! You're *real*? I thought Ryuu was pranking me!" he said, reaching out to rub her forehead and laughing delightedly, even though she still held her bloody knives. "Big fan. I'm Alucard."

"Yeah," Grace said, drawing out the word a few syllables as she shot me a desperate look, silently asking me to get the crazy guy away from her before she killed him, "I heard that part right before the angel whooped your ass."

"So cool," Alucard said, grinning and obviously not hearing a word she'd said. "Easter Bunny," he chuckled, shaking his head as he patted her forehead again. "We need to get out of here before this place burns down and there's no one left to kill out there," he said to me, glancing outside. "Don't worry. I'll keep you safe. Follow me, Easter Bunny," he said in a chivalrous voice as he turned to face the door.

I grabbed Grace's wrist as she silently lifted her kukri overhead to stab down into the base of Alucard's skull. "Lead the way and tell me what's going on," I told Alucard, shoving him forward and out of Grace's reach with my other hand.

Grace narrowed her eyes at Alucard's back and gave me a short, stiff nod. "He touches my forehead again and I'm chopping off a lucky Alucard's foot," she grumbled, lowering her blades.

I bit back a smirk and we followed the Daywalker vampire through the growing flames. Grace's ears swiveled and twitched at every little sound and I heard a few bloodcurdling gurgles when I let my eyes wander off her. When I would look back, I would simply see her milking the cute, big-eyed, dumb bunny face, batting her long eyelashes at me and wiggling her nose. I grinned and turned back to Alucard.

"We were ambushed by both sides like they were reenacting West Side Story," Alucard said as we reached the front door. He pointed and I gasped to see fire everywhere and White Rose Lane pretty much destroyed.

Witches were hiding behind smoldering crates or broken windows, rising up to hurl glass vials at demons and angels alike as they swept through the alley, rioting and pillaging without any specific target. The bottles exploded in bright flames of a dozen different colors and the air was thick with colored smoke.

Werewolves howled and snarled, loping through the streets and leaping up into the air to try and snatch low-flying angels as a few bears fought back-to-back against a mass of red demons with pitchforks.

"Holy shit," Grace breathed, lowering her daggers to her sides with very wide eyes. "Why?"

I stared at the burning, battered sign for White Rose Lane as the KC Strip Club behind us abruptly collapsed, sending a blast of flame, bricks, embers, and smoke at our backs. I flung up a shield without looking as the chaos whipped around us, murdering a dozen demons and sending a few werewolves tumbling across the cobblestones with angry yelps and snarls. I ignored the agonized screams from within the Strip Club. There was no helping them, because I was entirely sure this was a trap intended to net me.

"I don't think they like me very much," I said in a cold tone.

"They came out of nowhere," Alucard said. "I think someone is sending them here because, between one minute and the next, it was mayhem." He pointed further down the street where it was completely full of Freaks, demons, and angels tearing into each other. Here, we were in no immediate danger for the next few seconds, despite the mob of shifters, angels, and demons brawling in the center of the street ten feet away. "Ryuu is down there with his ninjas, chasing the larger group of foes."

I almost took a step in that direction before I hesitated, remembering Grace's presence. Ryuu had hired her to watch my back so that he wouldn't have to. So that he could do his job as a general rather than play nursemaid. I...needed to let him do that.

In a way, that thought hurt.

That hurt rapidly morphed to anger as I assessed the pointless destruction of this once quiet, peaceful, neutral street.

That anger roared into rage.

I gathered my magic around me, ready to unleash a storm of destruction that would make Heaven and Hell learn who was the biggest thug in this particular prison yard. For whatever reason, the angels and demons were targeting my ally shifters and witches just as often as their natural foes, sometimes even briefly allying with their brothers to take on one of the shifter bears. My skin tingled and air rushed over my lips like cold ice as I sought out targets to utterly vaporize and I felt a smile creeping over my face as—

I froze.

Envy? I asked in my head. *Stop.*

That was all you, she said with an amused smile. *I just cleaned the car's interior and checked the engine. Enjoy the new air freshener.*

Oh. Thank you. With the oath she had made in Solomon's Prison, I trusted her. There was no wiggle room for her if she wanted me to help with Azazel and avoid an eternity of hugz with Obie.

I let out a breath—not convinced that I should feel better that the desire to punish had been all me—and then I unleashed my power, acting on instinct rather than consciously summoning anything.

A forest of glossy black thorns abruptly erupted out from the cobblestones, crackling and hissing as they screamed into existence beneath angels and demons alike. The thorns impaled wings, arms, throats, tails, mouths, eyes, and limbs, ripping every angel and demon to pieces as the hedge grew taller. Only when the hedge was creeping up on basketball rim territory did I release my power.

"What about your allies?" Grace whispered in a very soft, nervous voice at my side, staring wide-eyed at the lattice of body parts and gore.

33

I snapped my fingers and my hedge of thorns crumbled to ash, revealing about ten very startled werewolves with their tails tucked between their legs, and two wide-eyed shifter bears. They turned to look at me with frightened gratitude and then helped a third bear back to his feet. I gave them a hollow smile and pointed deeper down the street towards Ryuu's forces where the fighting still raged hot.

The shifters tore away as if their lives depended on it, glancing back at me nervously.

My legs buckled and Grace caught me before they even had time to fully bend. "Easy, girl. Easy."

I nodded woodenly, feeling lightheaded at the sudden expense of magic after days of practically no use. Even in tip-top shape that would have been a doozy. I had no idea where it had come from and I could tell that Envy was just as startled—and impressed—as me. I felt my body rapidly recovering from the spell and I could tell that it wasn't Envy feeding me performance Hellhancement drugs.

That...had been mildly excessive. The bar behind me continued to burn and I narrowed my eyes, thinking about all the murdered innocent Freaks who had been celebrating within. Okay. Maybe not that excessive. Still, I took a moment to clear my head by closing my eyes and taking a deep breath.

I felt a blanket of calm settle over my shoulders and I forced my brain to take the reins rather than my emotions. Angels and demons attacking a quaint little street of magical refugees that I just happened to be visiting when no one should have known I was here—other than Dorian, Ryuu, the Toymaker, and Roland.

It wasn't that I thought they may have alerted my enemies, but who else knew I was here? There had been plenty of demons in the bar who may have assumed I was Dorian's hooded friend. The attack could also have been designed to simply attract my attention or those of my forces.

"You see Dorian out here?" I asked Alucard.

He nodded. "Stepped out of the bar right as the chaos started. I saw him kill a pair of angels before running down the street to help Ryuu." So, not Dorian.

"This is a trick," I murmured, surprising myself with my own thought as I swept my gaze down the street towards the chaos. "Just like the Coliseum. Someone wants me to overreact and wear myself out. To look where they want me to look when the real danger is elsewhere."

Alucard grunted. "Makes sense, but who?"

"Let me think on it," I murmured. "Go kill things with Ryuu. I have a Grace," I said, pointing at the bloody rabbit. Alucard made as if to leave and I abruptly lashed out to grab his arm as a sudden thought came to mind. "Oh. And no Mask," I said meaningfully. "Not against angels or demons."

He frowned, reading the seriousness in my eyes. "It wasn't a problem at the Coliseum. Or here for that matter," he said, pointing at a few dead bodies—angels and demons both—smoldering with green flame.

I considered his point and sighed. "You fought the wendigo at the Coliseum, not Greed. Maybe it only matters against the big ones," I admitted. "Use it as a last resort because we can't risk another Mask—"

A mob of angels darted out from the flower shop in front of us, holding bloody swords. Their eyes settled on our party and I grinned, lifting my palm towards them.

A giant white werewolf fell from the sky with a bone chilling howl, wielding a heavy hammer crackling with lightning. He slammed the hammer down on top of the gang of angels—and the sheltered overhang of the flower shop—and struck the ground with the sound of a massive bell toll. The front of the business exploded in a shower of broken glass and splinters and the ground cracked outwards, creating a perfect crater. The angels who weren't pulverized to goo and bone chips and feathers were immediately electrified by living arcs of crackling light that connected one angel to another, freezing them in place and frying them in less than three seconds. The electricity winked out and the blackened angels thumped lifelessly to the ground.

Alucard glanced back at me with a smug grin. "Did I forget to mention Ryuu and I picked up a stray?"

"What. The. Fuck?" Grace demanded, crouching and drawing both of her huge ass kukri as she stared, wild-eyed at the colossal werewolf rising up from the smoke and rubble.

The seven-foot-tall white werewolf turned to me and started panting happily, letting his tongue hang out the side of his mouth as his massive wagging tail destroyed more of the flower shop's entrance, causing the remaining pieces of broken roof to fall down and conk him on the head and back. He batted it aside with an absent swipe of his claw and stepped clear of the carnage. His long fur coat was braided into dreads at the neck so that it looked like a mane, and I saw bones woven into some of the braids. He looked like a prehistoric monster compared to his fellow werewolves.

Gunnar Randulf, the alpha werewolf of St. Louis, had come to play in my city, thanks to Alucard and Ryuu. The Four Horsemen wanted me arrested and Ryuu had gone collecting my own fellow Horsemen to back me up.

Was Nate Temple here too? I shuddered at the thought. Kansas City itself would never recover if Horsemen fought Horsemen in the streets. We would never be able to hide that from the Regulars. I studied the destruction around me. Even though this was a hidden street, I had a hard time believing that hiding magic from the world forever was still an option.

Gunnar was probably the biggest and scariest werewolf I had ever seen thanks to an upgrade he'd received after Nate Temple took him to Fae for a mancation several years ago. He had claimed Mjolnir after killing Thor, and he was also the Horseman of Justice. Thankfully, he wasn't wearing his Mask now.

His quartz eyepatch reflected the numerous fires in the street as he turned to look at me. "Hey, Callie!" he growled, tossing Mjolnir from one paw to the other. He saw Grace and his entire posture changed, like a hunting dog on point. "Murder rabbit," he growled, licking his lips and pointing the hammer at her.

"Easy, Fido, or I'll show you firsthand what happened to John Wick's dog," she growled back, twirling her kukri to limber up her wrists.

Alucard stepped between them, holding out a hand to calm the Horseman of Justice down. "Easter Bunny meet Gunnar. Gunnar meet Easter Bunny. Friends," he said, drawing out the word and swaying one hand through the air like he was painting a rainbow of love between them. No, wait. He *did* actually create some kind of hazy rainbow in the air with his hand. What the hell? He winked at me, sensing my attention.

Grace and Gunnar both turned their noses up at the rainbow and mumbled vague greetings, but they didn't look pleased about it.

Grace abruptly hefted her arms up and sprinted down the street.

Gunnar reflexively lunged after her with an excited growl and promptly ran right into a straggler, low flying angel—who instinctively kicked the werewolf in his one good eye before frantically flapping his wings to get away. Grace—who had only actually taken two strides before coming to an abrupt halt—burst out laughing at the successful pump-fake. She began shadowboxing the air, grinning wickedly in triumph.

The rabbit fucking with the dog's chase instincts.

Gunnar snarled furiously, leapt into the air to snatch the fleeing angel in his massive claws, and then tore his body in half before his paws even hit the ground. He slowly turned to glare at Grace and blindly flung the two angel halves into opposite walls of the street with sickening splats. They slid down to the cobblestones, leaving smears of blood on the brick.

Grace clapped delightedly.

34

I heard low but ominous thunder in the distance and I glanced up at the sky to see pregnant black clouds drifting overhead. They weren't magical or apocalyptic. Just a typical Missouri thunderstorm—epic and dangerous but not a portent of the end of the world.

Grace lifted her head to the sky with a big grin and a contented sigh, closing her eyes for a long blink. "Ishtar, bless your daughter this day. Make it rain blood and hail bones."

"You worship Ishtar?" I asked. "That meme was debunked," I blurted, thinking about the conspiracy theory claiming that Ishtar was actually the origin of Easter and the Easter Bunny traditions adopted by Christianity.

Grace arched a cool eyebrow at me. "Ishtar is the goddess of fertility, storms, and war, and she's practically the patron saint of alehouses and whorehouses." She pointed at the burning Strip Club. "I worship whoever wants to throw some luck my way. Today, it's Ishtar."

I nodded at her pragmatism. I still had plenty of questions about the Easter Bunny myth, but now wasn't the time. I glanced back to see Gunnar glaring at Grace with his one good eye and his lip curled back in an idle snarl, but he looked slightly more hesitant after her short prayer for death and destruction to rain down from the black clouds.

Alucard stepped towards Gunnar, holding his palm up in front of him in a soothing manner. "Moon's getting real low—" Gunnar lashed out with a claw to grab Alucard but the vampire leaned just out of reach, cackling at his own Hulk reference joke.

"I'm not a mindless brute," Gunnar growled. Alucard pointedly glanced at the destroyed flower shop, then Grace, and then the two half-angel splatters on the brick walls. Gunnar sat down on his haunches with a resigned grumble.

"Gunnar," I said, pulling his glare away from Grace and Alucard. "She's my bodyguard." He cocked his head curiously and then his shoulders visibly relaxed as he turned back to me. "What are you doing here?"

"I'm here for war," he said, looking confused. "And a wedding tomorrow." I stared at him with a blank expression. He turned to Alucard. "You told me she knew."

Alucard held up a finger. "Ah. Semantics. I *implied* it but I didn't actually *say* it."

"What war?" I asked, folding my arms at both of them. I hoped he hadn't meant that he was here for *War*, one of the Four Horsemen of the Apocalypse. My eyes continued to dart towards our surroundings, checking for more surprise visitors.

Gunnar and Alucard shared an even more confused look. "Um. This one?" Alucard said, gesturing vaguely in every direction. "Ryuu seemed absolutely certain that it was about to kick off any minute. We hadn't even finished our beers before everything went to shit," he said, pointing at one of the taverns I'd walked past on the way here.

My eyes widened. "You were here the whole time?" I demanded.

Gunnar nodded. "You walked right past us but Ryuu told us to leave you alone. He mentioned something about the Easter Bunny and that's when I began to think the whole war thing was some kind of prank. Then..." he trailed off, gesturing with a claw.

I felt the hair on the back of my neck rising at a new thought. "Which side showed up first?" I asked, glancing up and down the street nervously. Because it wasn't just angels and demons here. They had both arrived to target the Freaks and had seemed either surprised or indifferent to each other.

Alucard shrugged. "Kind of like a chicken and the egg question—"

"Egg, morons," Grace snapped, lifting her blades warningly. "It's always the eggs."

Alucard smirked. "Right. They both attacked at pretty much the same time," he said, turning back to me. "Does that mean something?"

I nodded. "Yeah. I think it does. It means you guys need to go help Ryuu. Now." They shared a long look, frowning at the sudden anxiety in my tone. "NOW!" I snapped. "And no Masks!"

Gunnar and Alucard hopped to comply and sprinted towards the distant sounds of fighting. They glanced over their shoulders at me and Grace but I turned away, thinking furiously about the situation and trying to connect the order of events into some logical sequence or purpose. Grace watched me curiously, but she was also sweeping her gaze across the destroyed street in case more visitors arrived.

If angels and demons had both arrived at the same time to attack the same target, it meant the two forces—or whoever led them—were working together.

Which likely ruled out everyone I had encountered so far. Uriel and Raphael definitely hadn't seemed like fans of the Sins. Likewise, Greed and Lust hadn't seemed amicable with the Archangels. But I knew two long lost brothers who seemed to be doing swell at reconnecting.

Were Wrath and Gabriel behind this? Had they finally made a move? To send my location and my allies into chaos so they could wear me out and then take me? But I couldn't just leave my people to fight alone. If it was a trap and I left, it would all fall apart and piss off Wrath and Gabriel for having wasted their time.

I hung my head and lifted my hand to my face in a frustrated gesture. As I did so, I spoke out the side of my mouth where no one but Grace could see my lips move or hear my voice. "Stand absolutely still and follow my lead no matter what you hear. When I let your hand go, follow the screams. Wiggle your whiskers, so I know you heard." She did and I slowly straightened, turning back to the burning bar.

Then, recalling my strange dream, I froze time—or sped up my perception of it. Then I hurriedly swamped us with magic, making illusions of our bodies exactly where we stood. Then I slowly stepped out of my illusion, carefully grabbed Grace's paw, and gently pulled her out of her own illusion so as not to let it ripple to anyone watching. Her eyes slowly began to widen as she stared at me and I recalled her ability to move swiftly. Her perception of time was probably heightened as well so she could notice the strange anomaly where others would miss it.

I pulled her over to the adjacent building and ducked behind a bench that had been knocked on its side. I cast another illusion over our real bodies to make us invisible, and then I let time return to normal. Grace's eyes bulged as she turned from our new surroundings, to my face only inches away, and finally to our illusion doppelgängers still standing in the middle of the street. I held a finger to my lips and kept a tight hold of her paw as I turned to our look-alikes for one last trick.

"What are you looking at?" Grace's doppelgänger asked mine, frowning warily.

"I left the Seal of Solomon in there," my voice said, sounding frustrated as I stared into the Strip Club.

The Easter Bunny's double cocked her head. "Is that why you told them to go on ahead without us?"

My double nodded with a faint flush of embarrassment. "The whole thing will come down if I try to move the rubble or put it out."

"I think I can wiggle through and get it," Grace's illusion said, peering at an opening that wasn't entirely on fire yet.

My doppelgänger shot her a relieved look and nodded. "Okay. Go. I'll keep watch on the streets. But hurry. I think Ryuu needs our help down there." The fake Easter Bunny hopped along towards the burning building and then slipped inside through the tiniest opening.

The real Grace grinned savagely and squeezed my hand back, fingering her dagger with her free hand as her eyes scanned the supposedly abandoned street. She knew what she was seeing. A trap with me as bait. Well, my doppelgänger as bait. I kept my eyes to the rooftops since Grace seemed to be focusing on the street.

Thunder began rumbling ominously, drawing closer at a rapid pace as the clouds flashed with cracks of lightning. My look-alike began to nervously pace back and forth, peering into the destroyed buildings at every suspicious creak and groan. She also stared down the street towards the fighting and clenched her jaw before turning back to the burning building, waiting impatiently for fake Grace.

"You're very good at looking neurotic," Grace breathed, trying not to smile and failing miserably. I squeezed her paw hard and let a breathy warning growl escape my throat.

And that's when a sword as long as I was tall flew down from the opposite rooftop and impaled my doppelgänger in the thigh. I made sure to let my illusion show an eruption of blood, but I half-assed it as I let go of Grace's paw and Shadow Walked to the angel I had seen on the roof.

I kept my invisibility up, deciding it couldn't hurt to wear protection during my brief but passionate one night stand with the angel.

35

I appeared directly behind the tall angel right before a flash of lightning cracked across the sky with an immediate explosion of thunder that made my ears pop and left a purple afterglow in my eyes, outlining where the angel had been standing on the edge of the roof. The lightning disappeared, and without the ambient light from the fires or lanterns, the rooftop became dark and treacherous. Fat raindrops and even hail started to fall, pinging off the metal flashing and aluminum vents on the roof. The crack of lightning had perfectly concealed my arrival, and the abrupt darkness forced me to rely on the angel's silhouette now burned into my eyes.

Knowing I couldn't use Envy's powers or my Horseman's Mask without alerting him, I darted forward and lashed out with my silver claws, severing his wings at the shoulder blades.

Like my sleepwalking episode, I caught a wing in each hand as he let out a scream that made my bones vibrate. I lifted the wings high to either side as he awkwardly spun to face me. Another explosion of lightning actually struck the roof somewhere behind me, making my hair stand straight up on edge like it had been a warning shot from God. Uriel's eyes bulged in pain, horror, and confusion to see me. I was just as startled to see him rather than Wrath or Gabriel, but I hid it better because I'm a woman, and the fairer sex doesn't puss out over intense emotional shock.

"THIS. IS. KANSAS CITY!" I screamed in my best King Leonidas roar as I lifted my—Uriel's—angelic armored boot and kicked him square in the chest and out into open air.

I rushed up to the edge and leaned out so he could get a clear look at me holding his wings high as more lightning crackled across the sky above me in a continuous network of living power, hopping from one black cloud to another. He screamed as he fell, spinning and cartwheeling wildly without his wings to catch him.

At the last second, he tore open a Gateway of some kind, and I got the faintest glimpse of his destination before he fell through and it winked shut. My eyes widened in confusion at what I saw.

I heard a sound behind me, and I abruptly spun, snarling as my silver fangs ripped out from my gums and my own angel wings exploded out of my back, glowing with blue light. I wasn't going to let Uriel's mystery sibling kill me with poetic justice.

Grace stared at me from a safe distance away, soaked and matted with blood and rain as her eyes took in my glowing wings in addition to the severed feathered pair in my hands. A four-winged monster with claws—her supposedly defenseless new client.

She glanced at my hands and feet with a pensive frown, and I realized I wore the gauntlets and both boots now. She sheathed her blades with a huff and scowled at me. "I can't protect you if you keep disappearing on me."

I lowered the wings and gave her a grim smile. "Then keep up, Speedy."

She hopped over to the ledge and peered down, frowning. "Damn. Who was it?"

"Uriel," I growled, sweeping my glare across the other rooftops in search of whomever had sent the demons. Seeing nothing, I let out a curse. "You ready to continue the fight or do you need a breather?" I wasn't entirely sure I wanted her along because I doubted her knives would do anything against an Archangel, which meant she would only become a liability if Uriel tried to use her as leverage against me.

She narrowed her eyes at me, but I could tell Uriel's name had shaken her slightly. "Uriel..." she mused, scratching at her plump cheek. "We aren't going to be able to turn the other cheek on this one. No forgiving and forgetting, right?" she asked, pointedly staring at the Archangel's wings in my hands.

"Absolution is Alucard's shtick. Mine is Despair," I growled.

Not wanting to bring his precious wings with me, I ripped open a

Gateway to Castle Dracula and tossed the wings through to a dim, musky, leather maker's shop. A fireplace crackled in the corner and I heard loud, German hard rock blasting through the room. Rammstein? Two familiar faces looked up at me and they both had ball gags in their mouths. Dear was hanging upside down from a chain in the ceiling and Darling was tied up with thick knots of glossy rope on some kind of reclining dental chair.

Aphrodite sauntered in, holding her infamously mysterious yellow rubber Duckie, Alfred.

She sensed Darling and Dear's wandering attention and glanced back at me through the open Gateway. Her eyes widened slightly and then she slipped the duck behind her back and curtsied. "I'm on break, Master Dracula. I already did what you asked."

Grace burst out laughing. "You literally have a sex dungeon!" she hooted.

I sighed and pointed at the severed wings on the ground of the shop. "Mail delivery. Ingredients for new weapons or armor—not personal toys," I warned, waggling a finger at them. "From Uriel, with love." Darling and Dear both stared at the wings with greedy, lustful eyes.

Aphrodite opened her mouth to say something, but I closed the Gateway on her.

"I am so happy to be working for you," Grace said, grinning.

"The day isn't over," I said. "Can you tell Ryuu that I've got somewhere else to be and that they need to handle the rest of that fight on their own?" I asked, already pacing back and forth.

"Sure thing," Grace said, and abruptly disappeared in a blur of motion I could hardly track.

The moment she left, I ripped open a Gateway to hunt down Uriel on my own.

Because he'd sent himself to Abundant Angel Catholic Church, of all places.

I slipped through. It was raining even harder here, and the thunder and lightning seemed to be an unending display across the night sky. I let the Gateway close behind me and crouched behind a tombstone. I fought back the wave of anxiety that rippled through me to see the exact scene from nightmares that had plagued me for most of my life—back when I'd been abandoned by my parents on the steps of this very church on a night exactly like this one.

A2C2 loomed like a gothic monster, unshakable and immovable. Stoic—

"What's the play?" a voice whispered beside me, making me jump. Grace was casually slipping a long, knitted stocking cap over her head, forcing her sodden ears to hang back and down like dreadlocks. She looked like an angry drowned rat as she flashed me a mischievous smile with her big blue rabbit eyes.

I wasn't falling for it. "How did you—"

"Hopped through your ring of fire. I'm fast, remember? I can't guard you from across the city," she said smugly as her gaze shifted to the church. "From a bar to a church. I love Catholics."

"You were supposed to alert Ryuu, so he doesn't come looking for me."

She shrugged. "He told me you would occasionally come up with stupid orders to try and bypass red-tape or to keep people safe and put yourself directly in harm's way." She glanced up at me pointedly. "Like trying to trick the Easter Hare into getting out of your hair," she said drily. "He knows his job without me playing messenger, and he said you would know yours as well. Different paths in the forest, same destination."

I grimaced, resigning myself to my new shadow as I wiped water from my eyes and tied my own hair back in a ponytail. Then I flung my hood up to conceal my noticeable white hair. "Uriel came here," I breathed, peeking my head out from behind the tombstone to assess the quiet building. I saw a few lights on within and the front door was illuminated by an exterior light, but it was too late for any kind of service, which meant we should be able to get in without a problem. I'd learned every possible way to break into this building as a young teen, even though it had infuriated Roland to no end that his student continued to feed her criminal desires.

Now, Roland worked for me. There was a lesson there, somewhere. Probably not a good one.

Why had Uriel come here? The Shepherds weren't here since Roland and Fabrizio had been excommunicated. Unless someone new had moved in and I hadn't heard about it. Even then, why would Uriel be working with the Vatican? They had nothing to offer him.

Uriel wanted my—his—armor back from me. The Vatican just didn't seem worth Uriel's time and effort because I'd already proven them feckless time and time again. Unless they had a lot more shifters than I thought in their new army. Even still, Kansas City had to have more—especially with Gunnar and his pack helping us—than the Vatican could ever muster to their flag.

I shook my head, knowing I was only wasting time and there was only one real way to get answers.

"We're going to kidnap him or beat him to death. I'm not very picky right now," I told Grace.

I ducked down low as I saw a figure looking out the window of Father David's office. A flash of lightning partially illuminated his face, confirming it was him. He looked nervous and his arm shook as he awkwardly tugged the curtain closed. My breath caught in my throat. "He's injured," I said, my eyes narrowing. "Uriel took my friend's face." I forced myself to take a calming breath, eyeing the church angrily. I knew this was a trap, but I had Grace to help me. And even if it was a trap, Father David would become a casualty with Uriel in the church. And if he'd already been killed, I needed to see it for myself. "We're going in."

I would spring the trap on him. *Different paths, same destination.*

Ryuu believed in me, even after my loss at the Coliseum. I was only just beginning to realize how much that had messed with my psyche. I was acting more emotionally rather than calculating. My confidence had waned and it was time to get it back.

"If you want someone dead, put me in, coach. Just give me a name and I'll put it on my list."

I glanced at her, considering. "Can you kill an Archangel?"

She scrunched up her nose, thinking. "Technically, the answer to *can you kill this person* is always yes. I just need to find the right tool." She glanced down at my hands, likely looking for my claws. "Any chance you can lend me an extra set of those?"

I shook my head. "Not here. Maybe at Castle Dracula, but I'll have to have them forged by Hephaestus," I said absently, my mind racing with questions. Why Father David? Why here? Beneath the church was the Shepherds' secret Vatcave, consisting of my old training rooms, an armory of weapons and artifacts that Roland had accumulated over the last decade plus change, and even powerfully warded prison cells that could hold all sorts of supernatural beings. Could they hold angels or demons? Archangels and Archdemons? As far as I knew, they were as empty as they'd been when I'd had access to the secret levels beneath the church. There were also levels beneath the armory that I had never been permitted to see or learn about.

Was that why Uriel was here posing as Father David, and why Fabrizio had been banished? That might make sense. Only one way to find out—

My phone vibrated and I frowned down at my pocket, having forgotten that I even had it on me. I concealed the bright screen as I risked a quick glance to see who was calling. *Say the devil's name*, I thought to myself as I read *Fabrizio* on the screen. I silenced it and turned on airplane mode before slipping it back into my pocket. He had probably heard about the attack on White Rose Lane and wanted to know if I was safe—and our current situation would not pass that standard in his eyes.

And answering phone calls wasn't conducive to sneaking into churches undetected.

Grace eyed me and then the church. "How do you kill an Archangel?" she asked, picking right back up on our earlier topic.

"Slowly, Grace. Very, very slowly."

"Someone was bringing demons to the fight," she reminded me, eyeing the church. "What if Uriel has one of the Sins here?"

I had been wondering the same thing, but I shook my head. "Uriel got hurt and fled. No way would he want one of the Sins to see that I'd just ripped his wings off. Not only would it be humiliating, but it would also show weakness and this family isn't big on trust."

Envy murmured her agreement with my assessment, but she no longer rattled on in my ears after our long talk in Solomon's Prison. She respected the boundaries I'd established yet she also knew that too much of her influence might attract the attention of the Archangels or Sins, so other than healing me, it was wisest for her to sit back and enjoy the ride until I specifically asked for her.

I still had no idea how I would help her with Solomon's gambit, but I wasn't going to get answers by heading back to Castle Dracula so some well-intentioned friend could toss me into a bed for my own good.

I stared at the imposing church as it seemingly flickered in and out of view from the brighter flashes of lightning. "Uriel's grounded and all alone," I said, licking my lips hungrily. He had tried to kill me with his sword in the street. He was no longer willing to discuss the topic of my armor; he wanted to pry it off my cold corpse. Diplomacy was no longer an option for me. Live and let live, kill or be killed.

I cast a veil around us since Uriel hadn't been able to see through my illusions the first time. "Stay close and follow me."

36

Ileaned out from behind the parked car and stared at the backdoor to the church. The heavy downpour pattered against my hood but, strangely, it didn't soak up water. Some kind of rain-slick coating? Grace, on the other hand, was a sodden, miserable wretch, frequently shaking off her legs and fur with angry growls. I'd tried making a Gateway directly inside the doorway, but it had fizzled out with a hiss. Uriel had some kind of ward up, obviously. "What's wrong this time?" Grace whispered, reminding me of the failed Gateway.

"Door is probably locked, and I don't want to alert anyone if they happen to be walking down the hall."

Grace held up a pair of lock picks with a smirk. "Ready when you are."

I grinned, nodding. Then I dashed up to the door, ducking low against the frame.

"Oof!" Grace grunted from behind me, followed by a heavy thud. I glanced back, panicking as my eyes searched for threats, fearing someone had attacked her. I only saw Grace laying in a puddle and blinking dazedly. Between us was a rippling dome of light that swiftly faded away as if I'd only imagined it. Grace sat up, rubbing her forehead. "Ward," she muttered, glaring at the air between us.

I grimaced, knowing I didn't have time to figure out what kind of ward it was or how to break it. But I'd passed through it fine. I frowned as I noticed that my angelic gauntlets were vaguely visible, as were my boots. I scuttled down the steps and put my hand through the space where I'd seen the ward. "Grab my hand," I whispered anxiously.

Grace grabbed onto my gauntlet with a wary grimace, and I pulled her towards the door. She passed through the empty space as if we had only imagined it. My gauntlets hadn't even flared to signify their power helping unlock it for me. If angelic armor was the key, then how had Uriel gotten inside? And why hadn't Envy's Halo neutralized my key?

Thoughts? I asked her.

I do not know, she replied in a troubled tone. *I would swear it was to ward against Hell, but the hare is not a demon and...well, YOU kind of are a demon right now, technically speaking.* The black ring throbbed warmer to emphasize her point.

The last time I had come here with Fabrizio there had been a ward that knocked me back on my ass, but that one seemed to have been for vampires. I hoped we hadn't bypassed one ward only for me to go flying into the parking lot as soon as we hit the vampire ward on the interior threshold. I pulled a very baffled looking Grace up the stairs and all the way to the door.

I reached for the handle and was surprised to find it unlocked. I held my breath, still holding Grace's hand, as I once again established our invisibility and we entered the church. No rune flared to life to figuratively hit me in the head with a ballpeen hammer or anything like that and I let out a soft breath of relief.

When Fabrizio had left, he must have disarmed his wards, so they didn't actually harm anyone. Wizards were courteous like that—don't leave bombs behind when you move out.

Grace closed the door behind me with a soft click and then let go of my hand. Nothing happened and we grinned at each other like thieves. I lifted my finger to my lips and we nefariously skulked through the church to kill the imposter pastor—

The impastor. Heh.

The church was blessedly quiet, as if holding its breath. The heavy rain continued to patter against the windows outside, hopefully masking any sounds we might make. I'd wanted to keep my magic to a minimum in case Uriel was able to sense it. I still had the greasy paint from Dorian over my eyes, but Uriel had already seen me with that, so I doubted he would fall for it again. The invisibility spell was my only consolation, but I kept that light and faint since the hallways were already dark enough to hide in without being seen. We slipped down the hall like wraiths. I paused beside the hidden door leading downstairs to the Shepherds training area, but I kept my eyes on the corridor as I touched it with my fingertips, not wanting to let Grace know about it just yet.

You have any way of knowing whether the bunny is a Sin or Archangel? I asked Envy, trying to keep my face calm at the sudden thought. The ward had kicked Grace back, after all, but I'd been too focused on chasing Uriel to consider the danger at the time. With her frequent disappearing acts, anything was possible.

Definitely not, Envy replied without hesitation.

Absolutely sure? I pressed.

She paused and I felt my ring grow warmer. *Solid eighty-percent*, Envy finally said. Another long pause. *Let's call it seventy-five, but I'm sure it will be fine.*

I stared down at my ring and blinked. Then I clenched my jaw and pressed on. Nothing to it but to do it. If Grace tried to kill me, I'd kill her back faster. We reached the stairs leading up to Father David's office, but the lights were no longer on up there. Had he left? I heard a soft chanting in the chapel, but the main doors were closed. I groaned inwardly and made my way to one of the side doors that would let us slip in without notice.

Thankfully, the door didn't creak, and we duck-walked over to the back pew, staying low as the chanting grew louder. I recognized the singer as Greta, my arch nemesis. She was seated in one of the front rows, facing two candelabras burning near the pulpit. I waited a few seconds, recognizing the song the woman was singing as the popular hymn, *Hark the Herald Angels Sing*.

Envy scoffed disgustedly. *Ours are way better*, she grumbled unhappily.

Yeah, hard pass on that, I thought to myself, making sure Envy couldn't hear it.

Greta didn't look injured, so I doubted it was Uriel in a new disguise. Then again, it was easy to hide an injury while sitting down. Grace watched me, waiting to follow my lead. I was about to rise up when the side door we had used clicked closed. I glared at Grace, thinking she had closed it. She winced and mouthed *sorry*, but the damage was done because Greta's song immediately stopped, and I heard the pew creak as she turned to look.

"Father David?" she asked softly, sounding concerned. "Have you returned?"

Silence answered her. I couldn't really blame her. The chapel was rather dark and sinister this late at night, but it was going to get a whole lot more dangerous if Uriel and I started duking it out. We just had to find him first. I held up a finger to Grace, sweeping my gaze down the rest of the room to see if Uriel was lurking anywhere as Father David, about to make an appearance. In that case, Greta would see me murder him and that would do nothing for her opinion of me because she thought he was the real Father David.

And she would definitely tell the cops everything she knew—and plenty of things she merely suspected.

"Wendy?" Greta asked instead. "Is that you, child? Have you finished cleaning, dear?"

I shared a long look with Grace, shaking my head. Old churches made all sorts of noises.

"I must be losing what little sense I have left," she murmured. "I blame it on that rapscallion, Nate Temple. Stole my patience and then my grandson from me—" she sighed abruptly, cutting herself off and turning back to the altar judging by the squeal of creaking wood. "Forgive me Father, for I have sinned," she prayed.

I thought about leaving her there. Gretas, in my opinion, were like cockroaches—they could survive nuclear winters. And if she did become an accidental casualty of me fighting an Archangel, at least she would die praying to the only person in the universe who actually liked her. A mural of Jesus on the wall glared at me but I ignored him.

He didn't know Greta.

She was evil, vindictive, hypocritical, and...innocent.

Goshdarnit.

So, the woman she hated—who was planning to brutally murder one of her JV team heroes, Uriel—decided to save her life. I needed to stack up enough goodwill points as possible because killing Uriel was going to cost me. My own hypocrisy was very, very loud in my head, and that didn't even include Envy's stunned laughter.

I ignored both voices and approached the horrid old woman on silent feet, closing the distance so she would be able to see me when I spoke. Calling her name from the shadows of the back of the chapel sounded appealing but counterproductive. Grace and I slipped from pew to pew, keeping low so as not to be seen since...well, she was a giant, talking, rabbit assassin who also had a seventy-five percent chance of actually being one of my other enemies in disguise and I was...me.

When I was three pews away, I lowered my hood and dropped my invisibility spell. "Greta?" I called out in a soft voice so as not to startle—

She spun and flung a hymnal at me, hitting me directly in the nose. "Get back, devil! The power of Christ compels thee!" she shrieked, brandishing another hymnal in her geriatric claw.

"Motherfucker!" I hissed, grabbing at my face.

My eyes watered and I wondered if one could get paper cuts in their eyeballs. With that goldfoil-edged paper, I might be in real trouble.

"Language, beast!" Greta hissed, squinting her beady eyes at me.

"Is she for real?" Grace blurted from behind a pew, biting back a grin as I blinked back tears.

"Who said that?" Greta gasped, her eyes wide as she craned her hunch-backed frame left and right.

"It's *me*, Greta," I growled, pinching my nose as I slowly advanced with one hand out in a peaceful—and defensive—gesture. "Callie Penrose." One more hymnal to the face and I was letting God roll the dice on her wrinkly ass. Period.

Greta still seemed terrified of the mysterious second voice, but she looked downright furious upon recognizing me. "How did *you* get in here, *Jezebel?*" she slurred, confirming our special, loving relationship. "I will tell Father David!" she snarled, hunching low as if she thought I would actually strike her. Drama Queen.

"Greta," I whispered in a much gentler tone than I felt like using. "Get up. This place isn't safe. I saw a thief break in, and I wanted to make sure everyone was safe. Is anyone else here?" I asked, wondering who Wendy was. A cleaning lady or a friend of Greta's perhaps.

"So, you creep up on an old woman!" she accused, upgrading her arsenal to a glossy black, single action assault Bible chambered in metal holy-tipped points at the corners.

Grace shot me a meaningful look and then abruptly disappeared. My eyes widened in alarm but then she reappeared directly behind Greta, ready to put her in a sleeper hold the moment I gave her some kind of affirmative signal. No, no, no. If anyone was going to choke the bitch out, it was me. I needed to find out where the cleaning lady was before we resolved the Greta situation, but she was being entirely too loud, and she was going to alert Uriel or the cleaning lady. "Let's get you outside, Greta," I said with a smile that I hoped looked sincere rather than hungry and malicious.

Her eyes slipped over my shoulder and she cried out in relief. "Father David! Help! Callie is drunk! *Again!*"

I spun, crouching and almost summoning my claws when I realized that no one was behind me. I narrowed my eyes as a film of red settled over my surroundings. That was it. I was choking Greta out. I slowly turned back to her with a fiery glare.

And I discovered that the nasty woman was packing. She smirked smugly as she leveled a .38 revolver at my chest. The gun shook in her liver-spotted hands, but she was close enough to kill me unless I used magic directly in front of her. "That did not look like concern for Father David," she said smugly.

"Okay," Grace said from directly behind her. Greta's eyes bulged and she spun, firing blindly, but Grace deftly disarmed her and secured Greta in a sleeper hold and then firmly but gently started to apply pressure. The gunshot echoed through the chapel and I prepared for the worst, spinning in a slow circle in order to anticipate Uriel's arrival. This wouldn't be the first epic battle I'd had in a church chapel, but it would definitely be the *most* epic. Behind me, I heard Grace speaking to the choking old hag in a soothing tone. "We're only trying to help—"

I heard a startled grunt and then the sound of shattering wood. I spun, prepared to save both Greta and Grace from Uriel's surprise attack—

Greta had body-slammed Grace into the pew, destroying it and possibly killing the Easter Bunny. Greta picked up the limp rabbit with one incredibly strong arm and hurled her at one of the stained-glass windows over the altar. Grace exploded through a depiction of Jesus, decapitating that portion of the window but leaving the body intact. Then she was gone, leaving me alone with the woman I had always known I would one day murder.

"Greta," I growled, summoning my claws. "I somehow always knew it would come down to me and you. I think I actually hate her more than you, Uriel."

Greta started laughing maniacally as her form rippled ominously. "WEEEENDY!" Her voice boomed through the chapel, making dust rain down from the ceiling as Greta's disguise slowly smoldered away like burning paper to reveal the true form beneath.

Greed, not Uriel.

And that meant Wendy was actually a *he*—the wendigo.

I hurled a blast of magic at Greed, cursing at the top of my lungs, "Oh, for fuck's sake!" Greed deflected the attack with a snarl, and I felt a flash of pride to see her forehead was still a shattered mess and she wasn't currently on her *A* game.

Then a giant skeletal claw erupted from the floor beneath me, sending pews and shattered tile flying in every direction before it grabbed me around the waist and yanked me down into infernal darkness. I summoned my angel wings and wrapped them around me like a shield as I was pulled further and further down. Greed's laughter followed me three floors down to the agility training area where I'd spent ten years mastering moves with Roland, and I knew that neither of us had ever anticipated the shit-show I'd just brought to Abundant Angel Catholic Church.

I was coughing at all the dust and debris falling down from high above as my momentum finally slowed. I lashed out with my claws and sliced entirely through the wendigo's arm, eliciting a pained honking sound that echoed throughout the rubble of the once beautiful training room as I fell to the ground. I broke free of the severed claw and summoned my angelic boots and gauntlets as I jumped to my feet and cloaked myself in magic so I was invisible again. I started running through the dust and smoke, disappearing into the comforts of my old home. If I hadn't known the place so well, I would have been panicking because I couldn't see more than a few feet in any direction from the massive amount of destruction caused by the wendigo somehow breaking through the floor of the chapel. Had he been waiting directly below Greed the whole time?

Was Grace dead? Where was Uriel? Or the real Father David and Greta?

Despite the insanity, I felt a sense of comfort from the Shepherd's quarters. It had been my crucible, my testing ground. It had broken me, shattered me, humbled me, and then reformed me into something stronger and better.

And I knew plenty of her dirty little secrets. While Greed and Wendy argued and shouted in search of me in the wreckage of the agility room, I slipped through the next two areas on invisible, silent feet, hopping over three unfamiliar bodies, who had been partially gnawed on, and skirting a heap of skeletons bunched up against the wall.

I hoped none of them had belonged to Father David or Greta. Well, maybe Greta...

I silently armed myself with an arsenal of swords, hatchets, and one of my old, bladed, dragon chain swords. I even sent up a silent prayer upon seeing them still here rather than reclaimed by the previous Shepherds—myself, Roland, and Fabrizio—or even the Conclave themselves after our banishment.

Armed to the teeth, I cocked my head to check the distance between myself and my foes. I could hear Greed shouting at Wendy to check the rubble of the now destroyed platforms in the training room. I smiled as a plan began to form in my mind. Back to basics. Teach them how to be a Shepherd.

The hard way.

It was training day for the newest SHITs in Kansas City.

Why didn't you sense Greed? I asked Envy.

I...don't know. I couldn't sense a thing from her. And I didn't sense Uriel either.

I grimaced. Well, that was entirely unhelpful. *You are allowed to help if things go poorly*, I murmured to Envy, *but I need to do this one for myself. They took my home, and now I'm going to take it back.*

She purred excitedly. *What's the game?*

Break them. Utterly.

I sped up my perception of time and then knelt down on the mat. I closed my eyes and sought my happy place, envisioning a field of black and drowning out all sensory input. I created a pedestal in the center of my silence, and then I created a ball of white fire to hover over that pedestal.

And then I gave the white fire my angel wings.

Next, I played judge, jury, and executioner with the emotions plaguing my mind: Panic. Anticipation. Fear. Joy. Haste. Anger. Hate. Pleasure.

I summoned them each to the altar of the White Rose, and then I beheaded them, one after another, until only the goddess of this realm remained. Her and the silver blood of her criminal emotions.

And then the goddess was alone with her throne of blood.

I opened my glowing white eyes and smiled, feeling my fangs slowly extend from my gums. I bowed and then silently rose to my feet as I released my grip on time. I darted to the opposite side of the room to snatch up a few familiar vials I saw on a wooden shelf and then I pressed my back against the cool wall and took a single breath. I softly slapped my palm down on the correct tile and the section of wall spun one-hundred-eighty-degrees, delivering me to a secret hallway that was black as pitch. I tapped into my strangest of powers—the Silvers from Sanguina, which thankfully still worked—and my vision shifted to a chromatic scheme that permitted me to see in the darkness.

I'd been played for a sucker by Greed or Uriel or both, and now I had the wendigo to deal with on top of it all. A slew of heroes, the Minotaur, shifter bears, a Horseman, two Divines, and two Greater Demons hadn't been able to take the bastard down back in the Coliseum.

But I was the White Rose, and I felt like Kevin in *Home Alone*.

The Wet Bandits were about to take it up the ass and beg for escape.

But it was more than that. For the first time since the Coliseum, I felt like myself again. More thoughtful and proactive. Being stuck in bed hadn't been good for me.

This...this was my element. Order. Work. Scheming.

At least I was almost certain that Grace was trustworthy since Greed had tossed the rabbit out the window where she wouldn't be able to interfere with our fight, and the ward would prevent her from reentering to help me, so I was fairly certain she was trustworthy.

Like...eighty-percent certain.

38

I ran down the narrow corridor, counting my steps and keeping my ears open in an attempt to track Greed and Wendy on the other side. I grinned, realizing they were still wasting time in the agility room.

I also kept my eyes open for Uriel. He had set this trap for me.

I reached the end of the hall and turned away from the wall of my secret corridor that was shared with the room Wendy and Greed were still searching. I saw an array of buttons and a flatscreen mounted to the wall. I hit the power button and grinned to find it not destroyed from the wreckage in the adjacent room. I got my first look at my enemies and I watched for a few moments, searching for Uriel. He hadn't joined the party. Greed was limping back and forth in her black armor, looking only slightly better than when I had last fought her in St. Peter's Square. Why hadn't she been able to heal herself like Envy had healed me?

Envy had no answer in my mind.

The wendigo continued honking as he easily lifted up slabs of stone and flung them to the side with resounding crashes that caused more stones to fall from above and fill their space with even more dust. One of his massive antlers hung listlessly off his skull.

"I know you're hungry!" Greed snapped. "But it won't do us any good if you bring the entire church down on top of our heads! The ward won't go down and then we'll be trapped in rubble! Uriel promised us a truce if we got him the Divines, so that's what we're going to do."

My heart skipped a beat, and I felt my rage roaring up within me. Uriel... had made a deal with Greed. The only reason anyone might want the Divines was to break into the Garden of Eden, like Lucky had told me.

What the fuck was in the Garden that was so enticing it convinced Archangels and Sins to work together in harmony for the first time since the Angel Wars?

Greed snapped me out of my daze by barking at the complaining wendigo again, "She's trapped in here with us, so calm down."

But Greed didn't sound remotely calm. She sounded desperate and uncertain. Maybe she realized how fragile her deal with Uriel really was.

I hit a button on the control board. "I'm not trapped in here with you," I said with a sinister laugh, using one of their room's various speakers to project my voice. They both flinched, tracking the sound. "You're trapped in here with *me*!"

I released the speaker button, grinning from ear-to-ear as both Greed and Wendy raced over the rubble to snatch me up from the wreckage where they'd heard my voice. Was this how much fun it had been for Roland to control the room while I was training? Every display of my cockiness only serving to challenge his desire to humble me with this devilish control board?

"Too easy," I whispered as I hit another button. A geyser of flames erupted from the floor just as Wendy reached the target zone. We must have damaged the device in our fall because it exploded about two seconds later, sending the flaming wendigo cartwheeling into Greed and slamming her into one of the shorter, still-standing platforms.

I hit another button and spikes erupted from the base of the platform, ripping through their stomachs and torsos, pinning them to the wall. One of Wendy's arms actually went flying across the room, sheared off by one of the spikes. Because everything in this place was blessed or regularly washed with Holy Water, it was apparently able to break through Greed's armor. It actually boggled the mind to realize that Greed had chosen such a poisonous place to make her lair.

"Houston, we have liftoff," I breathed as I hit another button. Their platform abruptly lifted twenty feet into the air. I hit another button and started toggling them off and on, turning the platform into one of those amusement park rides that shoot up and down at unpredictable intervals.

I was a spider toying with the flies trapped in her web.

They screamed and honked as the iron spears through their chests jostled them up and down, up and down, up and down, even as Wendy's flames continued to burn both of them. The inferno actually increased in size and heat from the constant rushes of air created by my mad carnival ride. Greed finally managed to shove Wendy off, and I watched with glee as the blackened, burning wendigo crashed to the ground with a cracking sound and an agonized honk. I grinned to see that the Sin's armor was a broken, bloody, smoldering wreck. Still, she pulled herself off the spear and fell towards the ground.

I hit another button and a second platform directly below her shot up like a piston. It slammed into her—with a crunching, cracking sound—and pounded her straight into the ceiling, crushing her like a pancake. It slowly started to descend, and I hit the button again, but a spark of electricity and the smell of burnt wiring told me the system was beginning to crap out after the damage Wendy had caused.

I saw Wendy rise up from the rubble with a honking growl. His shoulders were burned and smoldering, he was missing one whole arm, and only one of his legs worked properly. One of his massive antlers hung loose, and the other half of his deer skull was broken off, letting me see the inside of his...well, skull. There was no brain or eyes or anything, just an empty skull, yet he shambled out of the room with a honking cry.

I realized he was going for the three bodies I had seen in the sparring room. "Oh, no you don't, Wendy."

I hit a new button on the controls and let out a sigh of relief to see the smoke machines still worked. The room began to fill with a dense, opaque white fog, and I saw that Greed lay motionless on her pedestal, spasming infrequently as it slowly lowered into the smoke. I didn't want to leave her, but I couldn't let the wendigo replenish himself and power back up. I hit a few more buttons to send the room into random chaos mode, hoping they might work to buy me more time by beating the hell out of Greed while I finished the wendigo once and for all. Then I raced back down the corridor, heading for the sparring room to beat Wendy to his snacks.

I eyed one of the vials I had pocketed and considered throwing it on the ground ahead of me. It would throw up a cloud of wet white fog that would color my entire body white if I ran through it. Like I had taken a dip in a bathtub of paint.

It wasn't really paint and it would wash out easily, but it had been one of Roland's favorites. We would enter an adjoining sparring room that was painted entirely white and brightly lit, and we would both enter covered in the substance. The absolute lack of color and the white lights made our sparring match strangely disorienting, causing our eyes to play tricks on us since the only color came from the eyes, nostrils, and open mouth of your opponent.

Sensory deprivation sparring.

I decided to hold off on using it for now. It would only camouflage me if I made it to that room or the smoke-filled agility room.

We had a blackout training room as well, but I hadn't seen any of the black paint vials on the shelf when I'd added the projectiles to my arsenal.

As Roland's student, I'd found the blackout sparring room even more disorienting and terrible to master, because my mind would keep screaming at me that I was about to fall off a cliff and into a bottomless dark void, or that I was floating in nothingness with Roland's damning white eyes and teeth haunting me like a specter of death.

That fear of the blackout room was actually the reason I'd chosen a dark endless background in my meditation visual—because that room had so frightened and unnerved me that I had committed myself to facing it and mastering it.

I reached the revolving door and pressed my ear to the wall to make sure I'd outpaced the limping wendigo. I heard him crashing through one of the rooms I'd already passed, and I grinned. He was too large—and too injured —to easily navigate the rooms, forcing him to crouch and lurch lower or tear his way through supporting walls to get to his food.

I pressed my back to the wall and hit the pressure plate. It spun, but only halfway as something lodged in the mechanism on the other side. I gasped to see the wendigo glaring at me with one fiery eye as it shoved a human leg down its throat, swallowing it whole. I lashed out with my hatchet, burying it into the hunk of meat like a hook. Then I yanked it back out of the wendigo's mouth and hurled the hatchet and leg down the secret corridor behind me where he couldn't get to it.

The look of pure horror and anguish on his face let me know that the wendigo had *never* had his food taken away before, and he didn't quite know what to do about it.

The wendigo honked pitifully, and I felt my hair blow back from the blast of rotten breath. He grabbed me and pulled me into the room before flinging me back exactly as I had done with his food using the hatchet. It started tearing at the revolving door with fervor, honking and clawing at the stone in a desperate attempt to retrieve his meat.

I hit the wall and fell to the ground, somehow still gripping my dragon-chain sword. I stumbled to my feet and shook my head. I saw two of the dead bodies still remained and I grimaced. He had only eaten one before yanking me out of the corridor.

The crashing sounds from the other room told me my mistake. It hadn't been the wendigo I'd heard moving slowly through the other rooms. Greed had escaped the agility room of death. I saw her silhouette lurching through the next room, making her slow but sure way towards us.

"Eat the other ones, you fool!" Greed shouted at the wendigo. He stopped digging through my secret tunnel and turned to look at the bodies. He turned further to look at me, hissed as if he'd momentarily forgotten all about me, and then he lurched for the bodies with a starving honk.

My eyes latched onto the bodies and I said a silent prayer. Then I hurled a blast of the hottest fire I'd ever called at the remaining bodies. I had to close my eyes against the blazing light, and I heard the wendigo scream in outrage as the smell of burning charcoal filled the air. I squinted one eye open as I shifted my fire to the wendigo, feeling my magic draining at an alarming rate from the serious use of power.

He screamed louder as my white fire washed over his chest, but I ignored him, checking on the bodies. They were now piles of burning coals and I saw nothing that might be even passably counted as meat. I released my fire with a gasp that made my knees momentarily buckle. Greed shrieked in outrage and I gathered my resolve to hurl every blade I had at the wendigo, turning him into a pincushion. Lastly, I lashed out with the dragon-chain sword and the blade extended like a whip of interconnected, razor sharp scales, wrapping around his neck. I heaved back and let out a shout of joy to see his skull go whipping across the room. The wendigo's body crashed to the ground and I let out an exhausted wheeze.

Greed stared at me from the other room, her eyes twin stars of fiery red.

I grinned and wiggled my fingers at her in a playful hello. "Just you and me, babe. Need some Tylenol? That thing looks brutal," I said, tapping my forehead with a vicious grin.

And then I sped up my perception of time. I sprinted towards her as fast as I could in order to gain as much momentum as possible. Uriel's gauntlets and boots crackled with power and my wings whistled behind me, flapping with hazy mist as they pushed me forward in a blur. I hit Greed like an armored truck as I let time return to normal.

39

I'd been intending to tackle her into the white-smoke-filled agility room where my white body paint would turn me into a ghost, but Greed had heaved her legs at the last second, altering our course into the adjacent wall. We blew through it and entered the blackout room. The wall caved in behind us as we tumbled across the floor and into the bedrock of the opposite wall.

We scrambled woozily to our feet in total darkness and backed away from each other. In the absolute darkness, I could see only her glowing red eyes.

Unfortunately, I was glowing like a lightning bug from my wings and Uriel's armor. The spells Roland had cast on this room prevented the opponents from summoning light to aid in the fight. So, although parts of me were glowing, they cast absolutely no light into the room. In other words, they didn't make Greed any easier for me to see.

But they did make it easier for Greed to see *me*.

"Welcome to my world, child," Greed taunted in a pained but amused rasp. I couldn't fight her without armor, and I only had my claws for weapons, so abandoning them to hide in the darkness wouldn't help me actually beat or survive her. It would just prolong the beating headed my way. Then again, she was wounded. She closed her eyes and I tensed, unable to see her or anything else but my own glowing gauntlets and boots and wings.

The room smelled of sulfur, making my eyes water, and I felt a wave of vertigo as she rustled back and forth from one corner to the other. Panic began to invade my mind and I sucked in a deep breath. Greed hit me in the stomach—the same spot she'd gored at the Coliseum—but I had luckily been turning away, so it only grazed me and sent a flash of fire across my skin.

You can do this, Callie, Envy purred in my ears. *Let go of your childhood fear. Trustfall!*

The room spun in my mind's eye and I knew I was my own worst enemy. I banished my wings and Uriel's armor, plunging us into total darkness. Greed cursed furiously but I felt a reassuring presence steady my core.

Envy.

"You have no protection from my might," the darkness taunted, scuttling back and forth across the room like a chitinous crab, Greed's voice echoing off the walls too loudly for me to pinpoint her actual location. "Call your Horseman's Mask again, child. Please. Summon your light so that I may feast—"

Move to the right, Envy said calmly. I obeyed without question and heard Greed's claws slam into the ground where I'd just been standing. I held my breath, fighting back my vicious panic and relief.

Greed cursed, swinging wildly now in every direction.

Left. Back. Duck. Lunge. Envy's voice was a calm, emotionless tutor, and I felt my body responding like an obedient student, reminded of my time in this room as Roland's student all those years ago. Calmness soon settled within my chest at the familiarity of following orders from someone I trusted—Roland and now Envy—and I had to stop myself from smiling so I didn't show off my fangs.

But I had no weapons and I feared pitting Envy's abilities against Greed. Letting two Sins go at it in a pitch-black room sounded like a good way for an unexpected consequence to happen and accidentally break the world. Two wrongs didn't make a right, after all. I knew how to fight but summoning my claws would tell Greed exactly where I was, and using my bare fists wouldn't help either. My magic was equally unhelpful because it was bright and might not even be strong enough to break through her armor. Even the black thorns I'd summoned felt like the wrong idea—like they might be tied to some Hellish power my mother had slipped into my milk bottle as a baby.

Do you trust me? Envy murmured. *Step back twice,* she promptly barked, forced to interrupt herself to save me from Greed's furious claws.

Yes, I replied, but I also let her see the concerns in my mind of letting Envy take control or how giving me too much help might be a bad idea.

I felt her murmur uneasily. *You may be right. Something is off about her. Something different. Step to the right. Roll forward!*

I did, but not as swiftly as I should have, and I felt her claws tug on my flowing hood. *Ideas? Because I'm about to blast a hole in the wall and hope she doesn't impale me from behind while I try to escape.*

Face your fear, Callie. Cowards die with wounds in their back and terror in their eyes. Heroes die with smiles on their faces as they hold in their own guts.

...um, I replied. *Door number three?*

Do you trust me? she repeated intensely.

I nodded. *Yes, Envy.*

Then let darkness be yours. And I felt a rush of ice water pour over me. I cried out at the sudden frigid temperature, and a puff of icy vapor escaped my lips, so cold that I could see it in the darkness.

Greed shouted triumphantly and raked her claws across my chest in a killing blow.

Crimson sparks erupted into the air, impossibly illuminating her bloody, shocked face. Her forehead was a crater, resembling cracked china, and her ruby red eyes shot wide open in disbelief as her claws slashed across my chest with a metallic shriek.

I glanced down to see black armor identical to Greed's broken set now covering my body. I wore Hellish black gauntlets, boots, and greaves, and I had an obnoxious shielded shoulder plate protecting my non-dominant arm. Other than that, my body looked like I was simply naked and formed from black sand. I glanced down to see the armor hadn't turned my breasts into a spitting image of Greed's saggy rotten melons.

Greed stumbled back a step in horror. "What the heaven?"

I grinned, no longer afraid.

Let the darkness be yours, Envy had said. She purred approvingly in my ears.

I held my arms wide, indicating the compound surrounding us. "I was reborn in this darkness, Greed," I said in a calm voice. "My childhood was spent here, facing my fears and learning to toy with the monsters so they couldn't toy with me. Welcome to my playhouse, Greed. I think I want you to stay here. Forever."

Greed snarled and swung her claw at my throat. I swatted her hand aside with a resounding *crack* that snapped her wrist. Her eyes bulged in disbelief and horror, and I let out a laugh of glee. "That...is not possible, unless she took you over!" Greed cried, actually sobbing in horror. "What have you *done?*" she roared as she took another swing directly at my face.

Instead of dodging or blocking this one, I called up my inner Johnny Cage from Mortal Kombat—I dropped down into the splits and let loose a full-forced, Hellish fist to her Mary-Ellen.

Her Minky. Foof. Bajingo. Fandango. Whatever lady demons called their vajayjays.

My fist broke her naughty place with a horrible crunching sound. Every molecule of air or sulfur she needed to breathe left her in an explosive wheeze as she doubled over and flew back into the rock wall with another terrible shattering sound. She crumpled to the ground like wet laundry and reflexively started rolling from side-to-side, whimpering and sobbing as she clutched at her now shattered Pink Panther.

"Muffality," I intoned in a perfect basso Mortal Kombat voice. "White Rose *WINS!*"

Greed did not get back up. She could hardly breathe as I rose to my feet and brushed my new gauntlets together. "I'm going to need to wash these," I said with a grimace. I called up a ball of red flame to hover over my new gauntlet and then I crouched down over her. "Before I kill you, would it be terribly impolite for me to ask your real name?" I asked kindly.

Greed glared up at me with pure hatred. "Mammon. May you choke on Greed's Halo just like my wendigo choked on Claire Stone," she said with a bloody smile.

My heart stopped. "She's *here?*" I demanded, grabbing her by the throat. I didn't believe for one second that she would have let the wendigo feed on Claire. It had been her only leverage and she'd been just as wounded as me from our first fight. She would have held onto Claire Stone as insurance if things went south. "Where are Father David and Greta?" I demanded.

Greed laughed at me. "Uriel may have betrayed me, but your nightmares are only just beginning. I will say no more." I felt my hand reaching for her Halo as I clenched my jaw.

No! Envy screamed in my ears. *Not with my armor or we are both doomed!*

I froze, sensing genuine panic in her plea. *I can't just leave it here. Could I use Uriel's gauntlets or will I wind up with her voice in my head as well?*

I...do not know, Envy said anxiously. *If you do not put it on your finger, you should be safe.*

Should? I demanded, keeping my eyes on Greed. She was staring up at me with a strange look, her arrogant smile fading to wary anxiety. Did she know I was talking to her sister? Even afraid, I knew she had nothing left to say. Sins knew torture unlike anything I could ever formulate in my darkest dreams.

Ninety-percent certain, Envy guessed.

I smirked. *I'll take those odds.* I glanced down at my hand and watched as one of her gauntlets faded away like black smoke. I let my crimson ball of fire hover over us as I took a breath and summoned Uriel's gauntlet over my bare hand. It winked into view, brighter than before, and I watched as tendrils of black smoke from my armored skin and vapors of blue smoke from Uriel's armor danced with each other over my wrist, sniffing at each other like curious dogs in a park.

My hand didn't explode or anything and I let out a sigh of relief. Greed was staring at my hand in stunned disbelief, but she clamped her lips defiantly. I smiled down at her. "This is really going to hurt, Mammon," I told her, pressing a finger down on the fractured crater of her forehead. And then I drew the same Omegabet rune I'd used on Leviathan when I'd ripped off Envy's Halo. She screamed loud enough to make my ears pop as green fire burned into her flesh and her Halo flickered into view.

I grabbed it with Uriel's gauntlet and tore it away like a vine in the garden.

Mammon screamed as if I'd just scalped her, panting and whimpering frantically. I lifted the Halo, noticing red sparkles within the black thorns. I hadn't noticed that with Envy's Halo. I would have guessed Envy to have the glam rather than Greed.

With my other hand, I brushed Mammon's forehead with the backs of my black gauntlet so I could inspect the Omegabet rune. I polished it rigorously and she squealed in agony at the pressure on her already shattered skull, her leg spasming uncontrollably like a puppy when you scratched just the right spot. I smiled down at her. "May you rest in Despair." I extended my silver claws through the Omegabet rune without waiting for a response, crushing her skull and impaling her brain. I was relieved to see that my claws still worked through Envy's gauntlet. Mammon's eyes flickered out and I rose to my feet as her body deflated in on itself to reveal a wretched, gaunt serpentine creature.

Do you really think your friend is still alive? Envy asked warily.

I shrugged, turning away from Greed's body. *If she is, she will be in the cells down below.* I blasted through the wall with a ball of condensed air, sending dust and rubble out into the main rooms. The roof groaned ominously and dropped a foot. My eyes widened and I leapt through the hole, glancing upwards. More of the roof dropped, but several of the pillars in the agility room were stuck in the upmost position and caught the falling roof. "Shit," I breathed, assessing the giant hole in the ceiling that led up to the church proper. "The whole thing is going to collapse."

I heard a furious honking sound from deeper within the sub levels and I cursed. "How the *hell* is it still alive?" I demanded, racing deeper into the compound. I skidded to a halt as I saw the wendigo's head sitting on the ground where I'd left it, but the wendigo's body was gone.

A gaping hole had been torn through the back wall and I raced over to it, confused. The hole opened up into a shaft that plunged far deeper into the earth. "The elevator," I cursed, remembering the time I had ridden it to the lower jail cells. The cables that had supported it were shredded and I realized the headless wendigo had cut them to take the quickest way down to the last possible source of food in the subbasement.

Claire.

Feed the wendigo its own head, Envy suggested. *I'm certain I read that somewhere.*

I grunted and scooped up the broken skull. "I have no better ideas," I said. The wall to my left cracked and split as the roof let out another alarming groan.

I don't think we have time to make it down and back, Envy said in a very careful tone. *We could wind up trapped with her...*

I nodded, considering. *Does this thing have wings?* I asked, tapping her armor.

Yes, but—

I jumped into the elevator shaft with a wendigo skull in one hand and Greed's Halo in the other. "TRUSTFALL!" I hooted, my voice echoing all around me as I fell through empty space.

❦ 40 ❦

Envy didn't bother asking my permission, taking my suicidal jump as all the invitation she needed. Black wings erupted out from my armor—not my actual shoulders like my own wings, thankfully—and my descent slowed slightly as the base of the shaft came into view. The broken elevator was a mess of flattened metal, severed wires, and shattered stone. I saw serious cracks arcing up the walls, furthering the structural problems of the crumbling church high, high above.

Through the rubble, I saw the headless wendigo painfully army crawling towards the row of prison cells. I rushed up to him and frowned, shaking my head at the gruesome monstrosity. "You're acting like a diva," I told him, crouching down. "Eat this."

And I shoved the broken skull down his open neck hole. The wendigo spasmed violently and I watched the skull vaporize to smoke through its open ribs. The wendigo went limp with one final pathetic honk and I let out a sigh of relief.

"H-hello?" a hoarse voice croaked from one of the cells.

My heart dropped in my chest and I raced towards the sound. "Claire!" I shouted. I quested out with my vampire senses, checking for heartbeats in the rest of the cells, but I found only one and it was very weak. I skidded to a halt to see a filthy woman in rags who looked like she hadn't eaten in weeks. She was huddled in the back corner of her cell and her head bobbed drunkenly. "You're alive!" I gasped. "Where is Father David and Greta?"

She blinked blearily. "I...w-won't fall for it, G-greed," she mumbled. "C-callie doesn't...have f-fangs."

I retracted my fangs and gripped the door before I hesitated. What if this was a trick and not really Claire at all?

Can you see if it's really her? I asked Envy. *Is there a way to tell?*

I doubt Uriel's clever master plan is to hide in the collapsing sublevels of a crumbling church, she said drily. I glared at her with my brain and she huffed. *If this was an imposter, their pulse would not be that weak.*

That actually made a lot of sense and gave me a few ideas for later. I tore open the door to her cell with Envy's gauntlet and flung it to the side, marveling at the power of her demonic armor. "Claire, it really is me. But we have to leave right now. The whole place is coming down," I urged, torn between haste and compassion. My words were punctuated by a sharp crack in the roof of Claire's cell, followed by a concussive thud as something very large and heavy fell through the roof of an adjacent cell. The back wall of Claire's cell let out an ominous crack of its own as a result.

Claire's head lolled to the side and she whimpered. "G-go away or feed me to W-wendy." Then she promptly passed out.

Blessings in disguise, Envy growled. *WE. NEED. TO. GO!*

"Right." I scooped up the unconscious Claire with my happy hand while keeping my naughty hand with Greed's Halo as far away from Claire as I could. I slung her over my shoulders in a fireman's carry and then sprinted for the elevator shaft. Envy's armored wings unfurled from my back and I took a heroic leap into the air.

My boots hit the ground in the world's most pathetic landing and Claire let out a groan of discomfort as she was jostled up and down.

Okay, Envy. Why don't you drive again, I said, having no idea how to use her wings. She chuckled and I leapt into the air of the shaft. There was a persistent rumbling sound from all around and above, and I clenched my jaw as grit and rocks began raining down on us. Envy dodged most of it, but it was impossible to dodge all of it. And Claire had absolutely no protection at all. I saw a rock clip her cheek, biting into her skin with a trickle of deep red blood, and I did my best to lean my head over hers, protecting it like an umbrella as Envy zipped left and right, back and forth, dodging even larger pieces now.

I saw a huge, impossible-to-dodge chunk coming straight for us and I heard Envy laughing excitedly as she poured on the speed. We hurtled directly at the falling vehicle-sized slab of stone in the ultimate game of chicken. Envy zipped out the seemingly tiny opening just as the stone block clipped my ankles, coming dangerously close to snapping them between the ledge and the boulder.

We hit the ground hard, but Envy wrapped her wings around us in a cocoon, and we rolled across the training mat, bumping to a stop against a giant boulder that hadn't been there when I jumped down the shaft. Envy's wings unrolled and I let out a breath of relief to see Claire breathing and relatively uninjured—

I gasped, staring at Greed's Halo pressed against Claire's palm. I yanked it back with a hiss, staring at Claire as if I expected her to suddenly sprout horns. She was still unconscious and seemed unchanged.

But Greed's Halo no longer held the faint thrum of power I'd been feeling through Uriel's gauntlet.

"Talk to me, Envy," I whispered, panicking.

I...don't know, she whispered.

"Give me a percentage," I rasped. The roof groaned and squealed, dropping a foot. We were out of time.

A slightly better chance than we have at escaping this place, she said. *Even my armor can't withstand all of this, and it definitely couldn't protect her as well as you.*

With nothing else to do for it, I slung Greed's Halo around my forearm and scooped Claire up in my arms. I definitely wasn't turning it into a ring and accidentally fingering it—

Damn it. My subconscious mind was a dirty, dark, twisted alley.

"Let's go, Envy," I said, forcing myself not to give up. "Fly us out of here—"

The walls crumbled and the roof completely caved between our room and the next, sending a wave of dust and debris into my face. I coughed violently.

Envy moaned in my ears. *You promised to get me back to Azazel! Everything you've asked, I have done!*

"I know!" I snapped, panting wildly. "But if I'm the type of woman who would abandon a friend then I'm not the right woman to free Azazel!"

She grew silent upon my reprimand, but I could hear her sobbing softly.

I stared at the wall of stone blocking us from escape. "Think, Callie.

THINK!" I growled. I tried making a Gateway to the parking lot outside the church, but it fizzled out with a sharp pop, still blocked by Uriel's ward around the compound. Which likely meant I couldn't Shadow Walk either.

Could I claw through the rubble? That sounded like a guaranteed way to expedite the rest of the roof collapsing. Alarming groans and thunderous crashes sounded from the rooms beyond ours and I heard water rushing through the walls, lubricating the already struggling foundation as if encouraging its collapse.

I smelled strange, acrid smoke nearby and I cringed warily. For me to smell the chapel burning from up here meant the fire had to be fierce or inhuman. I'd give two guesses which one it was. I closed my eyes and took a calming breath, assessing the situation. I couldn't make a Gateway out of the church...

But maybe I could make one *within* the church!

I called up my magic and ripped open a Gateway to the back of the chapel. It screamed to life and I let out a laugh as I hopped through. My laughter cut short to find the entire chapel in otherworldly flames. Sections of the roof were simply missing, and more were falling with every second. Rain poured through the holes above, but the heavy rain did nothing to douse the flames, only seeming to fuel them to greater heights, like gasoline. There was no way Uriel was still inside the church—if he'd ever truly been here. The man I had seen in the window had definitely been a lure to drag me here and had likely fled long since.

He might even be waiting outside for me right now. I shook off the thought.

That fire is from Heaven and Hell, Envy told me, stunned. They did look alive, burning hungrily and fiercely despite the pouring rain. The door to the chapel growled and roared with unnatural blue and green flames mixing with the usual warm colors. *You might survive them, but she would not.*

"I can blast it down with magic and then run through," I argued, even though I knew it was a lie.

I could draw power from the Spear, Envy suggested in a wary tone. *Or you could leave her here. You tried your best, Callie Penrose, but the Spear is the only solution I can think of.*

I clenched my jaw. "How much?" I rasped, knowing she was right. The smoke was getting too thick for me to breathe properly, which meant Claire would suffocate any moment. "Could you do it without breaking it?"

Yes, she said in a firm tone. *But it will bind us closer together*, she admitted. *I don't want you to think I held back information. The decision is yours*, she whispered.

Remember your vow, Envy, I reminded her. *A lie about something like this and I will kill myself to see you punished*, I vowed, meaning every word of it.

I swear it, Callie Penrose.

I felt the Halo warm around my finger and I glared at the door. Then I summoned up the Spear of Destiny. It blazed to life in my fist. "Get us out of here, Envy."

I gasped as cold power washed through me again, exactly like when she'd given me the armor. Except it leached into the Spear of Destiny, forming tendrils of red light over its surface. The Spear began to glow brighter, and the red tendrils turned to faint cracks in the wood. The cracks began to grow wider, and I heard the wood screaming. I stared in horror, ready to banish the Spear in seconds if those cracks grew any deeper.

NOW! Envy screamed, and I felt my arm point the Spear of Destiny at the doors to the chapel. A beam of purple light blasted out from the Holy Relic, slamming into the door like a speeding train even though it was barely as wide as my arm.

The massive burning doors rattled and groaned like a beast was on the other side trying to break through. The unnatural fire screamed and hissed, crackling and popping as it retracted from the door. Then the wood simply shattered, like ice on a frozen pond, and exploded outward.

Run! Envy screamed.

The floor behind me dropped and I felt myself almost fall backwards before I lunged forward and glanced over my shoulder. The floor was collapsing like one of those action movies where everyone has to sprint for their lives as the world crumbles in on itself behind them.

Good thing I'd watched those movies but, more importantly, good thing Envy's armor made me ridiculously fast. I raced forward as fast as possible, not even caring about the wall of flames engulfing the frame of the door I had just destroyed. Vines of blue and green fire lashed out at me, trying to grab me, but Envy's wings rose up from my back, shielding us, even as I heard Envy grunting and gasping in pain.

Claire was coughing in her delirium as I sprinted as fast as I'd ever run before. The halls were also on fire and portions of the exterior wall had collapsed already, letting in fresh wind and rain, which only served to make the fires flare hotter and fill the air with clouds of steam and smoke. The green and blue flames formed a net over the destroyed sections of the wall, preventing me from leaping or flying through them, but the front doors were currently free of the holy and unholy fire. Just a fuckload of regular fire.

I saw tendrils of blue and green fire snaking down from the ceiling and across the walls, struggling to cover said doors like they had read my mind.

I didn't dare risk letting Envy use the Spear for another blast that might permanently damage or destroy it. I let the Spear wink out and return to my soul.

The floor continued to collapse behind me, so I shielded Claire's face with my gauntlet and then used Envy's overcompensating shoulder armor to charge through the inferno that was now the entrance to this once holy place. The door exploded from the force of my blow, spraying burning timbers and planks and steaming stone out from Abundant Angel, and birthed from that madness was the same baby who'd once been abandoned on these very steps.

Except now she wore armor from Hell.

We hit the ground amidst an explosion of yet more embers and coals and rolled, Envy's wings protecting us as we tumbled down the steps and through puddles of chilly water.

We came to a halt and I just laid there on my back, staring up at the black clouds as heavy rain pounded at my cheeks and lightning crackled across the sky. I was exhausted but alive. Claire murmured fitfully against my chest and I squeezed her shoulders, letting out a loud laugh of joy. "We made it!" I wheezed.

I pursed my lips uneasily, spotting Greed's Halo clutched in Uriel's gauntlet. I frowned at it, realizing I should have sent it into the Seal of Solomon the moment I grabbed it. I felt like I wasn't firing on all cylinders since my thorough ass whooping at the Coliseum, but now that I'd bested Greed, I felt my confidence slowly returning.

"New guest, Obie," I chuckled. I carefully touched it to the Seal of Solomon, and it made a popping sound as it disappeared. Claire immediately whimpered and I grimaced, taking the soft sound as confirmation of my newest nightmare.

Had I just saved her only to bond her to an even worse fate? She'd been trapped in Greed's prison, and I'd just forced her into a symbiotic relationship with the jailor I'd saved her from. I hugged her close, simply relieved to hear her breathing.

Let me know if anyone looks like they want to kill me, Envy. I'm just going to lay here for a second and experience this moment.

I turned my head to look up the steps towards the church that had saved my life as a baby.

It was burning like the entrance to Hell, and I watched as the rest of the structure crumbled in on itself, sending geysers of embers and sparks up into the pouring rain. Smoke billowed like a living thing, fighting against the thunderstorm as Abundant Angel Catholic Church died a horrible, torturous death.

But I only noticed all of that in my peripheral vision because my eyes were firmly latched onto the top steps that had once touched the doors to my salvation.

The step where my mother and father had abandoned me to save me from angels and demons.

To save me from the Masters by setting me up to one day become a Master.

To continue their plan with Calvin and Makayla Temple to give their kids a future shot at winning the upcoming Omega War.

I sighed tiredly, turning away from the past.

I carefully sat up. Claire hugged me like a sleepy child, seeming to weigh a fraction of what she should. But she was alive. I was alive. Greed was trapped. Mammon was dead—

Callie? Envy asked me in a troubled tone.

We'll figure it out, Envy. Claire is strong and—

No, Envy argued. *We are not alone.*

I stiffened and lifted my head, searching for Uriel and whoever else had helped him set this fire up. I blinked to see a mass of very angry wizards glaring at me. Some of them were old and powerful and had milky white eyes.

"Motherfuckingmilkeyedshitweasels," I snarled, scrambling to my feet. I didn't call my claws, but I went into a defensive stance, ready to fight them all if need be.

41

The Conclave and the Shepherds had decided to leave Rome and go on vacation together. Destination number one? Abundant Angel Catholic Church in Kansas City. They would need to find new lodging.

They simply stared at me with a look of horror, disappointment, fear, anger, and sorrow. But none of them looked violent. I relaxed slightly, narrowing my eyes suspiciously. I glanced back at the smoldering ruins and winced. "That," I said, pointing at the missing church, "was like that when I got here."

One of the old men stepped forward and blindly pointed a thumb over his shoulder. "And that?" he asked in a soft, hurt tone. I followed his gesture to see a dozen massive fires in the distance and clouds of smoke billowing up into the sky. The sound of sirens filled the air, seeming to come from every distant direction. The thunderstorm was doing nothing to dampen the fires.

Kansas City was burning.

War had come to the City of Fountains, and we were woefully unprepared.

"I saved her life," I said, staring down at Claire, hearing how hollow it sounded in the face of the city burning and angels and demons running amok.

"That is good," the man said in a soft, empathetic voice.

Another old man piped up in a furious, judgmental snarl. "I hope her life is worth more than all of theirs."

I looked over at him with a dangerous glare. "What was your name again? I couldn't hear it through all your bravery and assistance."

He slipped back into the line of Conclave members and glared at me like a cowardly thug. The kinder man who had remained apart from his fellow wizards did not react to my comment with any emotion or anger. "I am Father Ignatius Rayebolera." He eyed my black armor with a strange look, and I cringed inwardly. Too late to hide it now. Thankfully, he didn't comment. Maybe he didn't know what it was.

This was the man Fabrizio had been bitching about? Maybe he was one of those passive aggressive, annoyingly cryptic old men like Mr. Miyagi.

"The perimeter is secure," a new voice said from my left and behind me. I snarled defensively as I twisted my neck to gauge the danger. A pair of nephilim stood ten paces away, and beyond them stood two more, and beyond them...

A quick glance in the other direction showed me the same thing. Dozens of nephilim, working in pairs, had formed a ring around the remains of the church, and all were heavily armed with swords and guns. The missing Kansas City nephilim, along with others who looked to be from all over the world.

They were all working for the Conclave now. Motherfucker. Did they know about the cuffs the Nephilim wore?

Abandon the armor, I told Envy as I scooped Claire up in my arms and rose to my feet. I felt the armor fade away like black smoke and hoped it blended in with the smoke from the church behind me or maybe came across as my clothes being damaged in the fire. Father Ignatius had looked at it strangely, but he was old, it was dark, my real clothes were dark, and the fire behind me helped distort and shade my appearance.

"As many disagreements as we have," I said calmly, "we face enemies who are far, far worse and who would stop at nothing to pit us against each other." Father Ignatius studied me calmly, nodding his agreement. "We should put a pin in this and stand against the forces of evil threatening to tear this city—and the world—apart at the seams."

Father Ignatius clasped his hands together in front of him and stared down at the ground for a few moments. He was a gaunt, frail old man with wispy white hair, and the pouring rain only served to make his shoulders look more like a coat hanger. His robes draped over him, plastered to his bony body, but I knew he would be a very fucking powerful wizard. Finally, he lifted his white eyes to mine, and I saw genuine compassion and tightly controlled fear. "You speak of Hell."

I nodded. "Yes." He could wait to hear about the whole shifty Archangels section of the story. I didn't want to blow up his pacemaker with a spoilery plot twist from his favorite book.

"I agree with you," he finally said in a resigned tone, making my flame of hope grow steadier in my chest. "But I am not a monarch, Callie Penrose," he said, glancing over his shoulder at the other members of the Conclave. Many I recognized but several I did not. "I am merely a humble servant chosen to represent the Conclave during these dark days." I kept my face calm, hating and appreciating him just a little bit more. He glanced back at his fellows and asked, "All those in agreement to bury the hatchet and unite together?"

There were a surprising number of votes agreeing to team up with me—I memorized their faces—but there were obviously more who shook their heads no. I sighed inwardly, accepting the fact that this next part wasn't going to make anyone any happier. I would have to flee. I couldn't fight this many wizards and nephilim while keeping Claire safe or revealing Envy's Hellpowered armor.

Father Ignatius turned back to me with an expression of sorrow, preferring not to drive the spike home.

I thought about Shadow Walking up to one of the nephilim and snapping away the familiar cuff on his wrist that would break his subservience and awaken him to his latent vampiric abilities, but I knew it would immediately be taken as an attack and said nephilim might very well go berserk, attacking his old allies on the spot as the bloodlust and rage at his captivity hit him.

"There has already been enough bloodshed this night," Father Ignatius said with a sad sigh, "and a House of God has fallen to Hell." Had his eyes briefly shifted to me, blaming me, or was it my imagination? The milky color made it almost impossible to tell.

"What about her?" a gruff voice asked from behind the members of the Conclave. "I don't trust her."

Father Ignatius pursed his lips, showing the first hint of anger as he glanced back over his shoulder, seeking out the strange voice. The members of the Vatican all huddled together, arguing amongst each other, but my eyes caught something in my peripheral vision from across the street.

My breath caught as I saw a man standing in the rain on the opposite sidewalk. Despite being alone, he looked to have four menacing shadows. His long hair was soaked but he paid the rain no mind as he watched us all with cold, merciless eyes. No one else had noticed him.

The Anghellian.

Envy whimpered nervously, not helping my own rising sense of fear. Whether Lucky was here to kill me or the Conclave, I didn't know, but both were equally as terrible. Thankfully, no one else seemed to have noticed him. He met my eyes and gave me the faintest of nods. I sucked in a nervous breath. I was about to Shadow Walk away when the Conclave parted enough for me to see they had the Easter Bunny in shackles. My panic slowly devolved to protective rage and I narrowed my eyes at them as they paraded Grace ahead of a man in a big dark hood. I narrowed my eyes, wondering how quickly I could neutralize him and grab her before Shadow Walking away, even though it would be taken as an act of aggression.

They'd already declined my peace offering, so why not poke the bear right now?

Grace met my eyes with a look of relief at my survival and regret at her current predicament. They must have caught her unconscious after Greed threw her through the window of the chapel. She wiggled her paws in what I took as an explanation for how she'd gotten caught. I translated it. *Shit happened.* The man behind her held her weapons on his belt, looking like a grim porcupine.

"She will be taken back to Rome to pay for her theft," Father Ignatius said. The hooded man stared at Father Ignatius, silently disagreeing with him. It looked like he wanted to handle the rabbit problem right here and now by adding her corpse to the bonfire behind me. "That will be all, Templar Killian."

My breath caught and my eyes widened. "Templar," I breathed, taking a step forward to try and stare into the dark hood of Grace's captor. A nephilim shouted out an alarm at my movement and then others seemed to notice Lucky for the first time. Blades and rifles were drawn as everyone spun to face whichever threat they feared most. The majority rounded on me, calling up magic or drawing down with their guns, but I heard many shouting at Lucky to announce himself and his business here.

Neither of us budged or cowed down. Lions don't listen to the bleating of sheep.

42

I split my attention between the hooded man and Lucky, reading the situation.

Lucky stared at them and then glanced at me with an amused smirk like Doc Holiday confronting Johnny Ringo in Tombstone.

What do ya' think, Darlin? Should I hate him?

I turned back to the Templar and Grace, deciding that Lucky could clean up his own mess. Nephilim peeled off from around the church, looking like they intended to arrest or kill him just to be safe. Idiots.

I stared down the Templar and I knew he was staring me down right back. I felt my lip curling in a furious snarl as he slowly pulled back his hood with one hand and met my eyes clearly. He did not look remorseful, but he did not look proud either. He dipped his chin in an *it is what it is* gesture.

"Beckett. Killian," I confirmed. My voice was as cold as ice even though my blood was boiling. Nephilim shouted at me and I saw a few Shepherds surround the Conclave in a defensive ring—to protect them from me.

I ignored the yapping dogs.

Beckett had been a detective here in Kansas City when I'd introduced him to the darker aspects of crime right beneath his nose. He had teamed up with the Templars after they promised to help him avenge his wife's murder, but they had neglected to inform him they were secretly werewolves. Claire had turned him into a shifter bear—a cute little sunbear, to be precise—to save him from the Templars forcing the werewolf lifestyle on him, and I hadn't heard much else from him since. I knew he had gone to Alaska with Claire's cave of shifter bears, but he'd also spent time hunting down the old commander of the Templars, Olin Fuentes. He must have formally taken control of the Templars and teamed up with the Vatican along the way.

"I wonder what a sunbear tastes like," I mused. I lifted my hand in a claw, pretending to wrap them around Beckett's throat for everyone to see. Then I squeezed and grinned at him.

His face contorted in confused rage as Grace's shackles fell to the ground and the Easter Bunny disappeared like smoke. The weapons adorning Killian's belt were suddenly gone and I watched as his pants fell to the ground because Grace had sliced the seams and button. He stood there with his dangly bits out and I momentarily considered hitting his lightning rod with a blast of electricity. Grace appeared beside me and I immediately snatched her paw and Shadow Walked us to Castle Dracula just as the gunfire started.

From the parting explosion, I wasn't entirely sure whether I had thrown the imagined bolt of lightning at Beckett or whether divine intervention had sent a bolt of lightning down to the ground in his general vicinity.

We hit the ramparts of Castle Dracula and Grace let out a triumphant laugh, clutching her leg with her free hand. "How's that for a lucky rabbit's foot," she hooted at the bullet hole in her thigh. But she was laughing deliriously, obviously not too hurt. I watched as it slowly started to heal before my eyes. "Just need some carrots and chocolate," she said with a bucktoothed grin.

Roland was standing in the archway with a startled look on his face, but he recovered swiftly, darting forward to take Claire from my arms. I let him, but I leaned in close to whisper in his ears. "She might have a similar parasite to the one I recently caught, but she's also in bad shape. Maybe you can have Aala look at her and then put her in a cell. A very comfortable not-prison-cell cell. Post a lot of guards but keep them out of her sight. Tell Kenai about the situation or send him to me before he visits her."

He pursed his lips and nodded. Grace gawked at her new surroundings and hopped over to the balustrade to stare out at Castle Dracula in stunned silence.

A man was waiting for me and it wasn't Ryuu.

Careful... Envy warned me. *Be very, very careful.*

I approached the Anghellian, not even bothering to ask how he'd escaped or why he had been there or returned here. His distraction had bought me enough time for Grace to pick the locks on her cuffs and for me to escape the Conclave and its overwhelming forces.

Lucky leaned his back against the balustrade, watching me approach with calm, eternally wise eyes. He looked like a saint. A madman. A sinner. A hero.

And...what Archangels were supposed to be.

But that could be a fallen Archangel or a Heavenly Archangel.

I studied his face as I approached. "Thought you were going for a long walk," I said carefully. "Seemed a little paranoid and cynical the last time we spoke."

He nodded faintly. "Justifiably."

I leaned my elbows over the railing with a tired breath. Honesty. "I think I've got it all under control, Lucky, but I can't be certain." He turned to duplicate my posture, leaning over the railing. "I de-winged Uriel," I admitted, "but I also killed Greed. They were working together."

Lucky grew still for a moment and then let out a soft breath. "That explains the fire at the church. I felt it from...very far away. Knew I'd find you at the center of it." He paused, studying me silently. "You also saved your friend at great risk to your life. You could have fled." He glanced over at Grace—who was pretending not to be spying on us—and he smiled wryly. "Two friends," he amended.

"Yeah. I don't have very many of them," I admitted, "and the new ones always get judgy and temperamental in the beginning," I said, aiming an accusatory look at him. He smirked, and I felt my chest relax to see a glimpse of the old Lucky.

"I...know what you mean. I get those looks as well. From absolutely *everyone*."

I winced, not having truly thought about it that way. I knew becoming an Anghellian had been a form of extreme mental and physical torture for him, forcing him to relive the traumatic events of three entirely different lives as Michael, Pride, and their shared Grace's experience in Purgatory were slammed together in a Big Bang. Talk about an identity crisis.

"So, are we cool now?" I asked.

He did not immediately answer. "That is to be determined. There are things you need to see. Qinglong is waiting for you," he said in a cryptic tone.

I frowned. I almost asked where when the look in his eyes said it all. "My mother's laboratory."

Lucky nodded. "You'd best hurry. We don't have much time before it all starts to fall down." He stared out at where the wedding arrangements were being finalized for the ceremony...tomorrow? Today? What time was it? "They really should reschedule," Lucky said, sounding sad.

"Do you know something?" I asked nervously.

"I know too many things, Callie," Lucky said tiredly. "But this is merely an obvious fact. The wedding will end in bloodshed one way or another. As to who spills the first drop?" he asked absently. "Pick a card, any card." I could tell he was referring to the numerous enemies in every direction. How the Sins and Archangels could even be here right now, disguised as allies.

"Is the Toymaker here?" I asked, wondering if Grace's claim was true, testing her word against Lucky's.

He nodded. "Not soon enough to stop the chaos, but she's already made some creations that will save lives tomorrow," he said, pointing down at the scurrying activity around the location for the wedding ceremony. "Like the ones at the Vaults, apparently. They can break through all illusions." I saw Carla walking around the perimeter, setting down vases in very specific areas as if she'd measured them out. She would glance left and right and then adjust the vase's position before leaving to collect another one.

"Go, Callie. There is nothing for you to do here and everything for you to face there," Lucky said, gesturing vaguely towards Solomon's Temple. "Grace may join you if you wish. It's always wise to keep grace close at hand. Your choice." He glanced at the rabbit. "And her burden to bear."

I grimaced uneasily, picking up on the double connotation. Grace was a virtue, and Grace the person was a remarkable warrior to have at my back, but it would mean revealing secrets and putting her in danger.

I wondered what the hell Qinglong had in store for me. I had intended to study my mother's Mem or E's, so this would let me kill two birds with one stone. "Is Ryuu okay?"

Lucky grunted. "Ryuu is working, and he truly enjoys his craft," he said with a wicked grin. "The city is in chaos, but he's holding his own. Your brothers are a big help," he said, obviously referring to Alucard and Gunnar.

I turned away to leave when another thought hit me. "I know about Claire's...situation already," I said cryptically. "Let me handle it."

Lucky glanced back at me pensively. He gave me a slow nod. "Okay, Solomon." Then he turned back to look out at Castle Dracula.

I walked up to Grace and grabbed her paw. Then I Shadow Walked us to the long hall leading to my mother's laboratory in Solomon's Temple. "Okay," I told her in a whisper, "I've got some stuff to tell you and it's probably going to make you shit an egg but you need to hear it if you're going to stick around."

Grace nodded firmly. "Ryuu told me enough to make my ears curl but I've already kind of taken a wild guess that I've only scratched the surface."

I caught her up to speed as I led her towards my mother's lab, sweeping my eyes from left to right to make sure we weren't being observed or followed.

Grace's ears did actually curl at a few points, believe it or not.

But she didn't run away screaming because the Easter Bunny ain't no li'l bitch.

43

I walked into my mother's laboratory after giving Grace permission to enter so she didn't suffer the same affliction as Solomon when he'd tried entering without permission—my mother's curse to keep this place restricted was hardcore. Having thorns grow out of your own body was a great way to discourage snooping.

The Azure Dragon was curled up on the floor resting his head on his lower back because his body was long and serpentine, more similar to the Asian dragon variety. He had long fleshy whiskers drooping from his cheeks, making him resemble a catfish. His eyes tracked me and Grace as we approached from across the room. Grace sat in one of the armchairs without a word, knowing she was here to observe and not interfere. I heard her draw a knife and start cleaning her nails in an absent manner. Qinglong snorted in amusement, his flesh whiskers swaying at the movement. His skin was a rich bluish green and seemed to change shades depending on how the light hit his scales. He was one of the Four Divines.

Why was everyone so concerned about them? Was it like Lucky had implied back in the library? That they were the key to breaking into the Garden of Eden? Anything was possible but it didn't make very much sense to me. They were not from the Christian pantheon. Not even remotely. The bulk of information I'd found on them had tied to Chinese and Japanese origins.

Lucky had said Azazel and Samzaya were similarly locked away, so what was all of this really about? How were the two related and why? He'd asked me if I knew where Sanguina was, but I still had no idea where she'd gone or how to find her.

I let out a frustrated breath, shaking my head.

Kansas City was burning as angels and demons fought for territory, the Conclave and its allies had returned with an army of nephilim and shifters, and Uriel was still out there somewhere fantasizing about my head on a spike. I'd expected him to be waiting for me outside the church after the fire, but he'd fled like a coward. Or maybe he'd sent the Conclave there to frame me for burning the place down. How many times had he secretly tried to kill me without me realizing it? He'd been working with Greed, so had he been behind the Coliseum attack as well as the trap at Abundant Angel?

And where did Raphael fit into all of this?

Regardless, Team Callie was not going to hold up well against an army of nephilim—not without an unacceptable amount of collateral damage. I needed to get the nephilim back under my control, but how?

"What is this all about, Qinglong?"

He pointed a claw behind me. "A satchel of Richard's."

Grace burst out laughing. "A bag of dicks!"

I blushed, biting back a smile of my own as I followed his claw to see the satchel Last Breath had given me before he'd died. How had it gotten here? Had I left it in the library after banging my head and accidentally entering Solomon's Prison?

I approached it warily. I finally flipped back the leather and reached inside, holding my breath. My hands came up empty and I frowned, glaring back at Qinglong. "What gives, Yoda?"

He did not smile. "Think of answers and you may find them." Then he rose up from his coiled position and silently left the room.

Grace frowned after him and then turned to me. "Are your mysterious meetings always so mysterious?"

I grunted, turning back to the satchel. My head felt heavy and so did my eyes. After the evening's fights, I felt exhausted. I heard Grace yawn behind me and mumble something about taking a nap. I nodded absently, focusing on the bag as I blinked tiredly. I almost convinced myself to wait until tomorrow so I could get some rest as well. My mind would be sharper...

My hand reached into the bag. *Answers*, I thought to myself.

Answers, Envy agreed. *Focus, Callie...*

My fingers touched something round and smooth. A marble. I pulled it out, blinking tiredly at the silver ball in my palm. It was heavy like metal. Like my eyelids. I sat down on the couch with a weary sigh. Was the room foggy or was it just my thoughts? Grace was sleeping peacefully on a wooden table, her leg hanging off the side and kicking occasionally as she dreamed.

I felt something pulling me under and the last thing I saw was the silver marble. Or mist.

I was King Solomon, staring up at a furious Uriel. I was in a closet and he was cutting me, torturing me, carving into my body. It hurt. It hurt so badly.

But not enough to betray my only family.

Callie was such a curious young woman. Always watching people with her scheming, calculating eyes.

I was proud of her. And Constance, of course. Such a devoted, determined woman. I wished she hadn't left us, but she'd given us a beautiful white rose to remember her by. Where had I put it?

Oh. Callie was the White Rose. So confusing. Where was Richard? He always helped me when I got confused. I hoped he hadn't told anyone about my dwindling mind. That would be embarrassing.

"You cannot have the Seal of Solomon. My demons will never serve you," I heard myself say as I coughed up blood. I wished I could see Obie again. I think I might have actually fallen in love with her. Had I told her that? I hoped I had, but everything was so confusing these days.

What would I have done without my dear friend Richard to keep reminding me of what I had forgotten? He would be good for Callie. Keep her safe after I was gone.

"She wears your armor, you know. Her parents stole it from you," I told Uriel. "No fiery sword for you. No chance to control or kill Azazel and Samzaya. You lied to everyone about...something." I coughed up more blood. "You no longer watch over Thunder and Terror." My tooth felt loose, but that was better than the ones that had already been ripped out. "Constance has them."

That armor comment made him angriest of all, but the others worked pretty well too. The angel of repentance was very focused. Pitiless as any demon. Not Obie. She was a treasured gem. All of my children were. I'd changed them...somehow.

A paradise or a prison? Both.

Uriel started poking and tearing me. I wished he had chosen a more dignified place to talk to me. A closet? There were much better places for torture here at my Temple.

Then my eyes stopped working and all I felt was burning where they had once been. The world was fire, darkness, and Uriel's snarling voice. I'd faced demons. So many demons. Uriel was worse.

"She has already taken the nephilim, Uriel. All will know of your cover-up soon enough," I heard myself murmur to the screaming Uriel. He screamed louder at that, but I was so tired and I couldn't be bothered to reply any longer.

"Why is the book empty?" Uriel roared, speckling my face with saliva. "Where is the original copy of the *Sev'n Most Sinist'r*? How do I get inside?"

I didn't answer him. I knew I had done something incredibly clever, but I couldn't remember what it was. Had I given my journals to Constance? Had she ever come back home? I missed her dearly. Probably a boy. I hoped he was a good one. Constance deserved a good man.

When I didn't reply, Uriel snarled, ripping the hard parts off of my fingers. That would make reading painful tomorrow.

Tomorrow wouldn't come, though.

I tried to smile. I should have taken a picture with Callie. That would have been nice. She could hang it up and smile at it after I was gone. Laugh about me tanning in my skins. I didn't care that they teased me about it. I loved Obie and she loved me. We liked to be naked by the pool. Nothing else mattered without her starry-eyed smile.

Maybe we had taken a picture. I couldn't remember.

Envy would help Callie. The White Rose and the Black Rose. A bouquet of beautiful death. Sanguina knew her job. She would find Azazel and Samzaya. I hoped they didn't kill her.

But Callie had so many friends to help her. She didn't need me any longer. I'd done a few good things, I thought. I could finally let go. Finally stop forgetting. Finally stop being a burden to my friend Richard. Maybe dream about Obie. Sitting at the pool and reading that silly vampire story she liked so much. That would be a nice dream. Naked, of course.

The shouting Archangel closed the door on me and I heard a strange hissing sound. I didn't like it.

I thought of Obie and smiled as a ray of sunlight hit my cheeks like a gentle kiss.

"Oh, gosh," I wheezed, wishing I could kiss her back. "I love you, Obie."

"My name is not Obie, King Solomon," a new voice murmured. It was gentle and compassionate and dangerous. But not to me. "Let me take your pain. You've been fighting long enough, Old One."

Sunlight hit my body and I gasped at the sudden absence of pain. A damp cloth gently dabbed at my forehead and I felt a loving hand cup my cheek, wiping away my joyful tears. He was crying too. For me. Holding my face like a wounded bird found in the garden. The Garden...

I needed to tell him about the Garden. He had a cruel and kind voice. Cruel to the unkind.

"Who would do such a thing to you?" he whispered, and there was an ocean of fury in his voice. A reaper of death had come to avenge me. I told him. I felt the tremor of rage in his fingers, but he was still gentle in cleaning my wounds.

"Who...are you?" I breathed, unable to see. "Why do you help me?"

"It is what Anghellians do. Hush. I will stay with you until the end. My name is Lucky."

He comforted me and I felt lucky to have Lucky watching over me. I talked to him as he kept his affectionate hand on me, filling me with warmth and stealing my pains. I felt hot tears hit my skin as the Anghellian wept to hear my tale.

"She...is good, Lucky. I know it in my bones," I assured him. "She has the Spear of Destiny. A key."

"I believe she is too," he rasped. "But she must be tested. For everyone's sake. They must see what we see. I will make sure they see her for what she is."

I cried quietly, wishing I could witness that moment. Where the world saw my Callie. Long lost but found again. Daughter of Constance. Friend to the Anghellian. I hoped Leviathan didn't give her too much pain, but it was necessary to give her Envy's Halo.

I was scared for her but Lucky helped me feel brave. "I will watch her."

"Watcher," I agreed. "Must save them from Uriel," I reminded Lucky. "Divines can break the Garden again, but one is missing this time. The

Spear and the Fifth Divine. *Sev'n Most Sinist'r*. It's a joke!" I coughed wetly and Lucky dabbed at my chin. "They've been hiding so long, waiting to save their brothers, Azazel...Samzaya..."

"I understand," he said kindly. I hoped he did. I'd forgotten who else I'd warned. "Don't be afraid. I am here," he said, and I felt safe.

"Not afraid. It's...Beautiful...Death...is only the beginning. There's truth in blood."

I knew the moment I died. In darkness, not the sunlight. Obie wasn't there.

But Lucky was.

I was not afraid. He walked me to Obie and handed me off to the love of my life. I stared into her starry eyes and felt like the luckiest man in the world. It was a beautiful death, thanks to Lucky. Who needed wisdom when you had love?

We laughed and stepped into the sunlight together.

Into a new beginning.

44

I woke up with a grunt to see a huge white bunny staring down at me, shaking me by the shoulder. "Get up! There's an angry old man in the hallway, and the snake drugged us."

"I am *not* an old man!" Roland roared from a short distance away, but I couldn't see him because a couch was blocking my view. I was sleeping on a fur rug near the fireplace, and I couldn't remember falling asleep.

"We're apparently late for a wedding," Grace said with a baffled expression on her face, shaking me again. "Drugs. Snake. Wedding. Get *up*."

Envy groaned, seeming just as groggy as I felt. She had no recollection of Grace's wild comments.

"Callie!" Roland barked. I sat up quickly, blinking rapidly to get my bearings. I was in my mother's laboratory still. Why was my memory so fuzzy? I felt anxious but I couldn't remember dreaming. I saw a pile of silver dust on the ground beside me and I frowned. "If you're late for the vows, the bride will personally kill everyone you love. She's in a tizzy," Roland shouted.

"I'm up," I mumbled, climbing to my feet so he could see me. "I'm up." I turned to look at him and smirked. He wore a tailored suit with a crisp white dress shirt that was unbuttoned enough to attract naughty librarians. I yawned dazedly and shook my head. Then my eyes bulged. "Wait. The *vows*?" I demanded, only just now processing his outfit and his words. "Right *now*?"

Roland nodded anxiously, pointing towards an open Gateway behind him in the hallway. Through it, I could see rows of white folding chairs facing Samael at the altar they had erected on the lower ramparts of Castle Dracula in a cute little pavilion with braziers and flowing red silks hanging from the columns and balcony railings. As I stared, I heard violins start playing the opening strings of *Here Comes the Bride*.

Godmotherfucker!

I muttered a curse and grabbed Grace's paw, tugging her after me as I sprinted for the Gateway, straightening my hair of tangles and curls along the way. Grace started helping, licking her paws and swiping at my hair in a blur as we passed the threshold of my mother's lab. Roland rolled his eyes at my clothes and let out a resigned sigh. Then he extended his elbow for me.

"Hey, d-hole," Grace growled, standing on his other side and glaring daggers at him. "*Two* ladies present."

He narrowed his eyes at her and I found myself smirking. "I didn't properly introduce you last night. This charming vixen is my new friend, Grace. She has killed over one-thousand people and she does charity work once a year." Grace beamed at my introduction and then glared at his arm pointedly.

He let out a resigned sigh and offered her his elbow. Then he ushered us through the Gateway at the speed of a spry old man power-walking to attract the blue-hairs gossiping at the mall's coffee shop.

"Too slow," Grace growled. "Let me handle this, Gramps."

The world blurred and I sucked in a breath as Grace Easter Bunny'd our asses to the front row in a blink.

My ass hit the chair hard enough to make me immediately flinch and almost fall out of my seat before Roland and Grace caught me on either side. I stared at the altar five feet away with very wide eyes.

I heard a familiar chuckle from behind me. "Are you *drunk?*" Quentin teased before letting out a surprised grunt, likely from Adrian's elbow. I heard Eae murmur a threat that shut them both up.

I ignored them so as not to draw attention to myself for being late and underdressed. I did casually crane my neck to glance at the aisle where Lilith was starting to make her special debut. She saw me and the smile of relief that split her cheeks was so heartwarming that my stomach fluttered. The tension left her shoulders and she shot me a loving wink.

Less than two minutes ago, I'd been unconscious—apparently drugged, although I didn't remember anything after seeing Qinglong curled up on the floor—and here I was sitting in the front row at my godparents' wedding. What the hell had happened last night in my mother's lab? Why would Qinglong drug us, and what did Lucky have to do with it? I didn't see either of them in the audience.

Lilith took her time walking down the aisle, staring at the overjoyed and overanxious Samael waiting for her at the altar. Slowly, facts started to trickle in as I assessed our surroundings. Lucky had warned me that the wedding was a terrible idea and that it would go horribly wrong.

And I didn't disagree at all. Within seconds, I was scanning the crowd for dangers, threats, unknown persons or weak defensible positions.

Ryuu should have been sitting next to me right now, but he was apparently still fighting in Kansas City with Gunnar and Alucard and a large portion of my shifters and vampires. That was why everything seemed quieter here than I had anticipated. Our forces had been split in half—at least. If I hadn't slept in, I could have made the rounds to check on Xylo and his men to make sure everything was in order.

Some monarch I was. Hopefully Cain and Xylo had seen to everything. Then again, Lilith had probably seen to all the security herself to make sure nothing would interrupt her moment. That actually reassured my anxiety— Bridezilla was not to be trifled with.

I felt like I was in *The Hangover*, unable to piece together anything since last night. Nothing at all. So, I made a list of all the things to freak the fuck out about. It was therapeutic to me.

I gritted my teeth, fighting back my frustrations and guilt. I would sit through the wedding, congratulate Samael and Lilith, make sure no one died, interrogate Lucky and Qinglong, and then go check in with Ryuu and see if I could hunt down Uriel, because that son of a bitch was still out there somewhere. It was way too naïve to think he'd died in the fires. Claire was now safe, but what had happened to the real Greta and Father David? Did Roland know I had destroyed Abundant Angel? I saw Fabrizio at the altar and my eyes widened in surprise to realize he was officiating the wedding. Had that changed? I could have sworn Roland had agreed to do that after I excused myself from consideration. I wanted to watch, not officiate, and since I was a target these days, it had seemed too risky for me to do it anyway. But...Fabrizio?

I felt my foot tapping anxiously as I became consciously aware of exactly how underdressed I was. Lilith had made me a special blood-red evening gown that fit me like a glove. I had really wanted Ryuu to see me wearing it today so I could suffer the consequences of his affections later tonight. Except Ryuu wasn't here and I wasn't wearing the special dress.

I wore my mother's black monster slaying clothes—slightly burned and bloody, but remarkably well-preserved, now that I thought about it. Next to Roland, me and the Easter Bunny looked like we'd just stumbled home without our heels after an all-nighter. I discreetly brushed my fingers through my hair, remembering that Grace had licked her paws before straightening it. I had a visual of looking like Mary in the infamous scene from *Something about Mary* and I felt my ears burn.

Grace set a paw on my thigh and glanced down at my tapping foot with an amused smile. I nodded and stopped the tapping as I swept my gaze over the gathered guests. There were surprisingly few chairs laid out for those attending the wedding. Maybe fifty or so. Eae, Quentin, and Adrian sat behind me and I felt one of them occasionally tugging at my hood or hair until Grace hissed at them with her murder-chompers on full display.

I saw Aala sitting all by herself, smiling coyly at Fabrizio at the altar. His bandages had been replaced with white silk sleeves under his suit jacket, and he actually looked pretty suave, even with his eyebrows missing. He merely looked extremely interested in absolutely everything he looked at. Unfortunately, Roland's librarian with benefits was absent. I didn't see any of the Divines, which made me feel suddenly guilty. They had all been as close as literally possible to Samael and Lilith at one point in their lives. Xuanwu and Qinglong had formed a Trinity with Samael, and Zoe and Bai had formed a Trinity with Lilith.

Yet...they had chosen not to attend. Had Qinglong really drugged us or had we simply passed out from exhaustion after a harrowing evening of war, crumbling buildings, and roaring fires?

I felt a general hum of power in the air and it took me a moment to realize it actually encompassed all of Castle Dracula. I cocked my head warily, recalling Pandora telling me that Solomon's Temple was the only thing keeping this place from flickering in and out of existence without Sanguina here.

In fact...the power I sensed kind of *felt* like Sanguina...

Was she back?

I tried reaching out to her through our recently muted bond and I frowned to learn that nothing had changed. I still couldn't sense her either. Lucky had asked me if I knew where she was, and it had seemed especially important to him to ask me that. Not necessarily because he wanted the answer, but almost as if he thought it vital that I needed to discover the answer and that he already knew it. I didn't see Starlight in attendance, which meant he hadn't found her on the Astral Plains yet either.

So...where was the sensation coming from if not Sanguina?

Perhaps the Castle was trying to warn me about the dangers of the Wedding. We had defenses in place, though, and there was nothing more left to do. My people had been promised a celebration and Lilith and Samael would not disappoint them. If I tried to shut it down now, they would disobey me and move their wedding down to the village where all the taverns and...entertainment houses were.

And they would hate me for ruining their moment. *Speak now or forever hold your peace.*

Most of the other faces in attendance were members of the Sanguine Council, Paradise and Lost were in the row behind us with Eae and my nephilim to keep an eye on Roland, and I saw Cain and Xylo glaring at everyone and no one in particular from their positions at the foot of the two sweeping staircases leading up to the pavilion, as far back from the altar as possible. Without climbing the walls, it was the only way to get to the pavilion. Was anyone watching the walls? Grace squeezed my thigh again with a shake of her head. I took a calming breath, wondering if I needed a Xanax or just coffee. I did a double-take to see my dad and Raidia seated across the aisle. My dad was decked out in a bespoke suit and his witch wore a very beautiful gown that looked to be designed a century ago. I smiled at the pair of them, feeling my pulse steady.

Terry Penrose glared at me and made a discreet *turn around* gesture with his finger. Then he smirked and winked at me. I grinned at him and nodded before turning back around.

"Let's just get this over with," I muttered impatiently.

Grace laughed at me. "Real romantic streak you got in that frigid diamond heart of yours," she whispered. "Who are these people again?"

I gave her a weak smile, realizing no one had told her. "My godparents."

She glanced at them and then me with a frown. "They're really good looking...and on the young side," she murmured, because they were currently in their human forms—a smoking hot, curvy redhead and a handsome, imposing man with silver streaks across his temples who looked like an oil tycoon in the prime of his life.

"They're Greater Demons," I whispered. "Samael and Lilith." I didn't even wait for her sharp intake of breath. "Yep, *that* Lilith."

As I watched my godmother, I frowned at a sudden thought. Lilith had been to the Garden of Eden because she had been Adam's first wife before Eve—wife numero uno hadn't been obedient enough for him, as she told it. Why hadn't I thought to ask her about the Garden of Eden sooner? I'd have to remedy that before they got to the consummation portion of tonight's festivities. Knowing them, that could be about ten seconds after the *I do's.*

Hell, *during* the vows wouldn't have shocked me.

"Be ready," I murmured to Roland and Grace. My old mentor set his jaw and gave a faint nod. He'd already been scanning the same security measures I had.

"For what?" Grace asked, reflexively checking her daggers.

I thought about it, eyeing the sky. Gargoyles swept through the air, patrolling every inch of Castle Dracula in anticipation of the chance of attack during the wedding. "The worst thing you can imagine," I said anxiously. "Whatever that is, in your opinion."

"Kids," she said without hesitation, shuddering. "Definitely kids. If I slip up once, I'll have fucking *octuplets.* If I'm *lucky!*"

I bit back a laugh until I saw the smirk on her face. It faded to a grim, professional scan of our surroundings, and I saw her checking for exits, examining security, and identifying potential pinch points if a battle erupted.

Lilith was finally passing the front row and I smiled sadly, only just now realizing that no one had walked her down the aisle. Had she wanted it that way or was it because everyone had left to go defend Kansas City?

She didn't look the least bit concerned about it so I dismissed it. She smiled up at Samael as she climbed the three steps leading to the altar. Then they were holding hands and staring into each other's eyes, lost in their own world. Fabrizio had to repeat himself a few times before they snapped out of their daze. Everyone in attendance chuckled and *awww'd.*

My foot started tapping again and my eyes darted about the area like I was an addict searching for a fix. I spotted the vases the Toymaker had set up but I didn't see her seated in the audience. I hoped they were as reliable as the illusion breaking guardians I had seen with Nate Temple at the Vaults in St. Louis. They looked like nothing more than rough stone and they weren't even engraved or anything. They did glow with red light from the inside, looking like more of an aesthetic decision than anything, as if someone had placed lanterns inside for ambiance.

The night sky was dark and breezy and calm, maybe seventy degrees. All told, everything seemed perfect.

My foot kept right on tap-tap-tapping, and I completely missed the vows.

Fabrizio's voice rang out loud enough to snap me from my thoughts. "I now pronounce you husband and wife. Samael, you may now kiss the unholy enchantress."

He did that with gusto and she melted into his embrace.

"Give it to her!" Quentin hooted, kicking off a round of cheers and applause from everyone in attendance.

And then a ball of crimson fire as big as a car slammed into the altar, burning all three of them to ash.

❦ 45 ❧

I flung up a shield at the same time Roland did, forming a conjoined ten-foot-tall wall of air to protect us from the blast of unholy magic. Because the air suddenly reeked of sulfur, I didn't need a signature on the fireball to know the Sins had arrived. Lilith's blackened hand hit the base of my shield and I caught a glimpse of her beautiful wedding ring before the secondary splash of fire incinerated it too.

I felt numb, staring at the ashes for an eternal second. And then my fight or flight mechanism kicked in.

Grace held a pair of daggers in her paws, spinning in a swift circle to keep any and all threats from reaching me. But...where the fuck were the threats? I didn't see our attackers anywhere, even though I heard screams in almost every direction, especially the castle proper, and out on the grounds below and beyond.

I almost summoned Envy's armor but then I hesitated. I didn't want that information too widely known yet. Instead, I called up Uriel's gauntlets and boots, and I saw a strange silhouette of full armor momentarily flicker into view before disappearing to just the gauntlets and boots again. I frowned. What the hell?

I didn't have Uriel's full set of armor...

I dismissed the thought as a wave of demons climbed over the railings lining our little pavilion. They'd fucking climbed it! I *knew* I should have been on security oversight! I started hurling blades of air at them as I turned to Grace. "Get my dad and his girl out of here!" I shouted, pointing at them through the chaos. He held his pistol in one hand and stood back-to-back with Raidia, but it was obvious he didn't know who to shoot. So, like all wise men, he followed his girlfriend's footsteps and only turned to pick off demons who got past her exploding vials of multi-colored fire.

If I had said any word but *Dad*, Grace probably would have completely ignored me. "And take them where?" she hissed as she threw a dagger at someone behind me.

Good question. Somewhere safe. "The Coliseum—"

A spear flew out from the chaos and stabbed my father straight through the heart hard enough for the tip to also stab Raidia on the other side. Both went limp, joined together by the spear, and toppled over. The vial in Raidia's hand shattered and lit their dead bodies on fire in a *whoosh* that made me jump.

My skin turned even colder than it had at Samael, Lilith, and Fabrizio's deaths.

I screamed.

A shockwave of power blasted out from me, bowling everyone within thirty feet back onto their asses, including Grace and Roland—friend, foe, inanimate objects.

I started hurling blasts of fire at any weak point in our defensive lines, but it was obvious that we were severely outnumbered. Everywhere I looked, enemies appeared as if by magic, running through Gateways or simply winking into existence.

I heard screaming, explosions, and blasts of power coming from within the castle. Gargoyles warred in the skies against angels, even though I hadn't noticed their arrival. Eae took one look at me, gritted his teeth in righteous vengeance, and took off for the skies to help the gargoyles.

Gateways continued flaring into existence, dumping wizards and Shepherds and Templar werewolves into the fight, attacking my allies from behind while they fended off demons from the front. My fireballs grew more erratic and wilder; I no longer cared what type of enemy I killed.

Terry Penrose was dead. The newlyweds were dead. Meatball was dead.

This pavilion would become their funeral pyre.

Xylo and hundreds of his skeletons held back what had to be three times their number in demons on one staircase leading up to the pavilion, and

Cain had another contingent of skeletons to defend the opposite staircase from a dozen bloodthirsty nephilim and a hundred werewolves. Those nephilim were each worth ten werewolves as I watched them slice through the skeletons.

Cain went down and I screamed again; my voice hoarse. I summoned up a wall of thorns and took down over one hundred wolves and most of the nephilim before they could trample Cain's corpse.

I tried turning off my emotions but they kept pummeling me, refusing to be ignored.

My. People. Were. Dying.

Demons, angels, and the Conclave had united to assault Castle Dracula.

My vampires tore through demons like schools of piranhas, but many of them were falling due to the sheer numbers side of the equation.

Because most of our forces were out in Kansas City, keeping everyone there safe.

I started targeting wizards, but they had formed a defensive line and thrown up shields. I screamed, drawing my claws as I sprinted for them. I was going to personally execute everyone from the Conclave this night.

Samael and Lilith dead seconds after marriage. My father and his girlfriend dead. Cain dead. Ryuu gone. My eyes locked onto Beckett Killian guarding Father Ignatius and I lost my freaking mind. The sunbear would die. I threw up a wall of thorns beneath them and killed half of the wizards in a horrifying bramble of screaming, dying, holy men.

I felt nothing but disappointment that I hadn't killed more.

I missed Beckett and Ignatius. Their eyes bulged at the brutality I had delivered, but they also looked horrified at the carnage they had started. They knew now that they had crossed a line. There were more dead bodies on the ground than living, and the tiles were slick with blood. I squared my shoulders and stormed towards them, extending my fangs.

I wasn't going to kill them.

I was going to *feast*!

I lunged forward with my claws outstretched, ready to drink every drop of blood in their bodies. Someone grabbed me from behind and heaved back, slamming me down to the ground. I rolled away and came face-to-face with Roland's lifeless eyes staring at me from the ground. His throat was slashed, forming a pool of blood between us. Not Roland too! I hissed, jumping to my feet so as not to touch his precious blood. "Get up,"

I whispered, nudging him with my practically humming demon-sensing boots.

He did not move.

I panted wildly, blinking rapidly, wanting to flee—

But I couldn't flee. This was my *home*. Whoever survived this—if anyone —would never again follow the White Rose if I abandoned them. The captain went down with the ship.

I turned to stare at whomever had been strong enough to physically manhandle me.

I snarled to see Uriel grinning at me. "This is what happens when you challenge—"

I retracted my claws and punched him in the throat with his own gauntlet, feeling his teeth shatter on contact as I screamed like a wild animal. Then I hit him again, screaming Roland's name. And again, screaming my father's name. And again, as I screamed the names of other fallen allies, enjoying the lovely way his head rocked back and forth like a speed bag as he coughed and choked on his own blood and bits of teeth. I grabbed him by the throat and lunged forward, my fangs starving and ready to drink him dry—

A fully armored Raphael swooped down from the sky and kicked me in the chest, sending me flying back on my ass. I hit the ground and rolled, bumping into a pile of bodies. I looked over to see Grace completely drenched in blood with a kukri in each paw, screaming as she faced two Archdemons who were perched on the ledge. They grinned in amusement, easily swatting her attacks aside without fighting back, only serving to infuriate the hostile, homicidal hare.

I jumped to my feet and grabbed her by the shoulder, pulling her back. She lashed out on instinct and I caught her wrist, jostling her. "It's me, Callie!" I shouted over her screaming.

She was panting and her eyes danced wildly. "I have to get you out of here," she abruptly said, wiping at her brow with the inside of her elbow. "I swore an oath to Ryuu!"

I shook her again and then lifted my gauntlet to indicate our surroundings. It had grown eerily quiet; although a few hundred people surrounded us, none of them were friendly. "Everyone is dead," I said in a cold, detached voice, feeling as if it wasn't really me saying it. Xylo and the skeletons continued fighting near the stairs because they couldn't be killed, but they were completely surrounded now and their enemies were simply keeping them occupied, seemingly toying with them.

There were supposed to be thousands and thousands of skeletons, not hundreds and hundreds. Had they gone to Kansas City to help, or...

I saw fires burning throughout Castle Dracula, not just here. The taverns and pleasure-houses were smoking, screams carrying on the wind, and I saw masses of bodies slamming into each other almost everywhere I looked. My mind raced, wondering if it was time for me to flee like Grace said.

But quitting was never an option, right? My dad had taught me that.

Stand up straight with your shoulders back and face the world as it is, not as you wish it to be.

Except...it looked like we had absolutely no opportunity whatsoever, because all of my enemies had rallied together. Heaven, Hell, the Templars, the nephilim, and the Conclave. Ryuu might have won the city with all of them here, but we'd merely traded places.

I saw Quentin and Adrian staring up at me with unblinking, lifeless eyes. A dozen demons surrounded them, but it had been enough to take down my only nephilim vampires. My only evidence against Uriel's crimes. Their claws weren't out either, so even dead they couldn't help me.

The few hundred surviving demons and werewolves had broken off into their respective groups rather than staying mingled together, and they had lined up on either side of us, leaving a wide clear path back to the castle proper, as if taunting me to try escaping. The nephilim had made their way past me to Father Ignatius, but not until Raphael gave them a brief nod of permission. So...that's who had brought the Vatican here. Raphael had given the nephilim to the Conclave—probably after I'd bumped into the Archangels outside the Garden of Eden. I put a cool mask over my features as I turned back to where the altar had stood. It was now a windswept smear of ashes that had once been my godparents.

No gargoyles flew in the skies overhead, and however many angels had been fighting up there were now all dead or fighting elsewhere. Since Raphael had dropped out of the sky to kick me across the pavilion, I was assuming the angels had been following his orders as well. I spotted a few of my gargoyles in the distance trying to help the rural areas, but it was apparent to everyone what had happened on this day of celebration.

Castle Dracula had fallen and would not rise again.

46

I grimaced as my eyes drifted over the Toymaker's vases. They had done absolutely nothing to help because no one had been hiding their identity like I had expected them to do. No one in attendance had actually been an enemy mingling in the crowd. They'd just made Gateways here in an all-out assault. Because with Sanguina gone, I had not been able to lock Castle Dracula down. The wards must have failed at some point in her absence.

Yet I could still feel that strange buzzing. It wasn't coming from the Toymaker's vases, so what was it?

Raphael had been kneeling over Uriel but I watched as he pulled the broken-faced murderer to his feet. Uriel's face was completely soaked in blood, but Raphael must have healed him. Or he'd healed himself.

I felt a cloak of cynicism settle over my shoulders. The only thing I had left in my heart was raw bitchiness. Unfiltered and on tap.

I met Raphael's cool gaze and lifted my bloody gauntlets, inspecting them. "I was trying to give them back but it wasn't working," I said apologetically. "So, I just kept trying. If at first you don't succeed..."

Raphael pursed his lips and shook his head, looking disappointed in my sense of comedic timing.

Uriel's face, on the other hand, really improved my mood. His eyes danced wildly with both panic and fury to have his ass so severely kicked in front of all of his pals. The wounds had been healed but his face was entirely covered in blood like someone had dumped red paint over his head. His nostrils flared and his chest heaved in and out like a winded horse. Something I hadn't noticed before was the pair of wings sticking out of his back.

I burst out laughing, unable to help myself as I pointed at the tiny baby bird wings just barely peeking over his shoulders. They were each the size of one hand with splayed fingers. "Ohmygod," I wheezed, feeling my eyes tear up. They looked absolutely ridiculous. He clenched his fists furiously and Raphael slammed a palm against his chest as he tried to take a step forward.

Uriel sneered at me. "My wings will grow back. Your leather workers will *not*. They died confused, thinking it was a game," he said, staring directly into my eyes as if to consume the pain his words would inflict. He...had gone looking for the wings I had stolen and had instead found Darling and Dear.

He'd killed them for knowing his humiliation. Two more casualties to my heart.

I lifted my hands in a unit of measurement as wide as my shoulders. "Your wings must be this long to get on this ride, Uriel. Sit down, stick a thumb in your mouth, and let the adults handle this, you petulant coward. Or I'll rip those jazz hands off your back like I did your other wings."

His itty-bitty wings flared reflexively. Their size and positioning made it look like he'd stuck his thumbs in his ears and waggled his fingers at me.

Grace roared with laughter and mimicked that exact gesture back at him. "I think you hurt his feelings, Callie," she said with mock sadness.

"I drink coffee stronger than his feelings," I muttered dismissively. "To see how far he's fallen is its own reward. From guardian of the Garden to..." I gestured disgustedly, "petty tyrant with feathered jazz hands on his shoulders."

Raphael slammed his sword into the ground between us, sinking it a few feet with a deep, chiming sound. "Enough! Lose with *dignity*, Callie Penrose!"

"I decided long ago that when I faced death, I would look him in the eye and laugh," I said, staring into his bright white eyes. I felt insanely serene— keyword *insane*. My heart body and soul were in too much shock from the abrupt catastrophe of defeat and cavalcade of murdered loved ones to do anything other than feel numb and detached. I was in denial, compartmentalizing my despair.

I wanted to hurt *everyone*. And if my only remaining weapon was my tongue, I would flay them alive.

Raphael let out a breath and actually dipped his chin respectfully at my comment. Bastard better stop doing things to make me almost like him or I'd have to do something drastic. I reminded myself that he knew all about Uriel trying to hide the nephilim secret and any momentarily redeeming qualities he might have had went up in flames.

I kept Grace close so that I could Shadow Walk to a safer area of Castle Dracula—like the Coliseum—if anyone other than Uriel looked ready to murder me. Because...everyone was just standing around watching me. Almost like they needed me alive for something. I put my haggling face on and read the faces of the power players before me.

Uriel's face was pinched and angry like an irritated asshole—not the adjective but the actual hole of an anus. Archangel Winky Browneye was on the case, and I realized that he was livid that the chaos had *ended*. He'd wanted to get something from me while everyone was distracted with the battle, but now that it was over, he could no longer risk exposing that desire in front of others. Was it about his armor or something more? He could call me out on that right now since I'd just pummeled him with it for everyone to see.

That cat was out of the bag, so what else did he want from me that he didn't want anyone knowing about?

Raphael was grim, resigned, judgmental—and possibly regretful? Whatever was going on in his Archangel brain was committed but willing to hear arguments. Whether he would accept said rebuttals was not clear.

Father Ignatius looked sad and disgusted at the horror show of bodies surrounding us. The white chairs were all shattered and destroyed, the altar was ashes, and the pavilion floor was literally one giant pond of blood, reminding me of my dream with Pandora—like I stood in the center of a crimson pool.

Blood is truth, I thought to myself, pensively. I felt a momentary flash of pain in my temples at the thought, sharp enough to make me suck in a breath. What the hell was that about? I maintained my composure and no one seemed to have noticed as they all checked on their own allies or tallied up death counts.

Beckett Killian looked just as grim as Raphael and just as committed, but there was no curiosity in those eyes. Just repressed guilt whenever they settled upon me. Not enough for him to do anything noble, though. Beckett was the kind of man who always talked about being noble and doing good, yet he always managed to cave in and give up when things grew difficult.

I slowly turned to the two Archdemons who were sitting on the ledge of the balcony, kicking their feet and chatting softly under their breath like this was a day at the park. I hadn't seen them participate in the battle, but someone had to have brought them to the party. "Hey!" I snapped. "Be careful up there. You might fall."

They wore black armor that looked better designed for light fighting rather than epic warfare. More like assassin armor than battlefield armor. Other than that, they basically looked like a human couple. Oh, and the red lesser demons bunched up in a row beside them.

Their faces were now uncovered, and I was surprised to see a very pretty blonde girl with smoky eyes and pouting lips. The other was a moderately handsome but easily forgettable man with mousy, tussled brown hair. The boy next door type. Both were thin and lithe, reaffirming my assassin assumption.

They stopped kicking their feet and chuckled at my joke. "Fallin' ain't so bad," the man on the right said in a deep voice. "Right Uriel?"

Archangel Winky's face puckered tighter and he was suddenly holding a sword, but Raphael restrained him again. Even as the austere Archangel held his corrupt brother back, I could see the nervous look in Raphael's eyes—that maybe the Archdemon had been right about his brother Uriel falling.

I'd heard it differently. The Archdemon hadn't emphasized the *ing* at the end of the word, so it sounded like a double entendre. *Fallen ain't so bad...* He must have known about Uriel working with Greed. Perhaps both translations were right. "Who are you?" I asked him. "You two forgot to wear your name tags."

"Gluttony," the clever man replied, shrugging. "This is a shit wedding. No bride for the dollar dance, and I don't see a scrap of food anywhere." He glanced at the bodies on the ground. "Oh. There it is."

"Take a step and you die," I growled, "even if I die in the process. Ask Pride what happens when an Archdemon calls my bluff. Or Envy. Or Wrath." I grinned, baring my fangs. "Oh, wait. You can't."

Gluttony folded his arms and sighed, looking bored rather than particularly concerned by my threat.

I turned to the other Sin, noted that she had armored but perfectly perky boobs, and then I gave her the gesture to proceed with her introduction. She laughed delightedly, and the sound sent chills down my spine at how malicious and sadistic it was. "Lust. I'm just here to watch you, Callie."

I knew how badly Lust wanted me dead—I had no idea why, exactly—yet she was wise enough to know she had no chance to take me with Raphael and Uriel here. This alliance was very fragile.

Could I shatter it? I thought to myself.

Watch those two, Callie, Envy warned. *And tell me when you are ready to flee or I will choose for the both of us.*

Okay, I told her, knowing she wasn't bluffing. Because it would technically be fulfilling her oath: to always serve my best interests, no matter what. Damn it.

I turned back to Raphael and then pointed over my shoulders at Lust and Gluttony. "I just detected the location of two Sins. Do your job and smite them, Archangel." He clenched his jaw unhappily, revealing that he was not pleased about the situation but not remotely surprised at their presence. And...that he wasn't going to do a thing about it. "I guess the band really is getting back together, eh? Did you guys carpool here?" He lowered his eyes reflexively and took a deep breath. I turned to Uriel and smiled. "How well did reuniting with Greed work out for you, Uri? Heard from her lately?"

His face went blank so fast that no one saw the change. Father Ignatius and his wizards frowned thoughtfully at this information.

Raphael furrowed his eyebrows and looked over at his brother with a dark look. "What is she talking about?" Lust and Gluttony leaned forward excitedly, grinning like mad.

Uriel pursed his lips. "It's called projecting, Brother. She spins lies as easily as one of the Sins. It is quite literally the only weapon she has left."

I lifted my gauntlets and grinned as I wiggled out a tooth from one of the joints. "Not my *only* weapon, buddy." I lobbed it to him and he swatted it away with a hiss, glaring greedily at my—his—gauntlets. "Memento from our first kiss. I've got a few more here," I reassured him, plucking out another tooth and pocketing it.

Grace shuddered. "Funny, but...ew."

I smiled at her. "Hey, do you know the Tooth Fairy, by any chance?"

She grinned, catching on. "I'll send you her deets."

I smiled at Uriel. "Dracula's making bank tonight, Uri. Thanks."

47

I still felt the vague hum of power blanketing Castle Dracula. It hadn't grown stronger or weaker throughout the ordeal and I felt myself growing twitchy. *If you're here, Sanguina, I could really use an assist.*

No response and no indication that she was anywhere close. Just my echoing request.

I did another quick sweep of the gathered crowd and shrugged. "Okay. I give up. What are we doing?"

"I'll take a wild guess and say we're waiting," Grace said, tapping her kukri together in a frustrated chime. I knew she was fast and could run around killing a few more people, but that would leave me open to attack. Also, Raphael would probably shut her down quickly, and she would only kill a few minions.

I smiled at Uriel. "Well, I've got plenty of stories to tell while we bide our time. How about we discuss White Rose Lane? What's left of it anyway. Remember our magical moment on the rooftop when I formally welcomed you to my city?"

Uriel might have looked panicked but I knew he was a clever bastard. He'd already manipulated me into taking the bait twice and I couldn't be certain this wasn't some other trap.

Raphael took a defensive step between us. "Why do you think I *brought* the nephilim and Conclave here?" he growled angrily. "You sliced off his wings and yet you stand here in a house of sin trying to claim the moral high ground! Even they might be better than you," he barked, pointing at Gluttony and Lust.

"Hey," Gluttony said with a frown. "That wasn't very nice. We *helped* you, Raphael. Don't think I won't let everyone know about you asking for our help."

"How desperate you must have been, afraid of this slip of a girl," Lust added, eyeing my ass and licking her lips. I frowned at her and made sure my hooded cloak was concealing my assets. I felt like I'd walked by a construction site after a once-over from her. "Delicious," she purred, amused.

I turned away. Raphael looked livid and rosy cheeked from Gluttony outing his request. But he wasn't very quick on his feet because he just chewed rocks and glared at the two Sins.

I jutted my jaw out at the holier than thou Archangel. "Yes, Raphael. I did rip his wings off. Maybe you should ask him *why*. Or we can talk about the nephilim and our private conversation outside the Garden. Another of your dirty little secrets. Why are your ears so red?" I asked, smiling. "We're just *talking*."

He gripped his massive sword in his knuckles and squeezed until they were white. I saw the nephilim stir uneasily at my words, frowning at the Archangels and Father Ignatius—who looked just as confused as them. "What is she talking about, Lord Raphael?" Father Ignatius asked, licking his lips nervously as he realized he had just demanded answers from an Archangel of the Lord.

"Enough!" Raphael shouted, leveling his sword at me with one hand, even though it looked like a two or three-handed weapon. I didn't care. The bastard was in on it. He *knew* about Quentin and Adrian and was in on the cover-up of the enslaved nephilim. I had caught them discussing it outside Eden. But he hadn't known about Uriel working with Greed. What the hell was going on here and how could I capitalize on their secrets? Everyone in this horrid family had secrets from each other. It wasn't as simple as Heaven and Hell. Envy had lied to the other Sins, Greed had likely been trying to take power for herself in Wrath's absence, and Uriel and Raphael were just as bad. "Your Castle has fallen and you have lost," he repeated.

I clenched my jaw at the reminder, seeing the dead faces of my friends flash across my mind's eye. "You'll never kill the skeletons. Literally." I blindly pointed back at them. The sounds of their battle continued. "They just keep going."

Raphael nodded, calming slightly. "Then we will bury them alive for a few hundred years when we turn this place into a wasteland. That will be the end of your curse, *Master Dracula*."

Uriel curled his lip disgustedly. "This place is a stain on the world of men. Salt the earth."

Gluttony cleared his throat pointedly. "I mean, if no one else wants it, we could take it as payment for our part in this," he said. "You see pillars of salt, I see potential. Might help still my wagging tongue."

Instead of replying, Raphael was staring over my shoulder with a baffled look on his face and I heard a general murmur of unease and confusion behind me.

Grace squeezed my wrist silently, telling me to take the opportune distraction as a chance to flee. I shook my head and turned to see Lucky calmly striding our way. He wore Timberlands and black jeans with a long white t-shirt that said *Fucked by Kindness* in cursive script. He held no weapons as he serenely approached, stepping between the rows of were-wolves and demons as if he didn't even notice them. He stopped about ten paces away from me, right before the imaginary line that would have put him in front of the Toymaker's vases.

"Nice shirt. Who the hell are you?" Lust asked, cocking her head curiously as she flashed her claws at him.

He glanced over at her and I sensed no power radiating off of him. "Just a man."

She scoffed, eyeing his hands dubiously. "How did you survive?"

He smirked faintly. "I'm just Lucky, I guess."

Father Ignatius stepped forward, frowning suspiciously. "We saw you outside the church last night."

Lucky nodded. "I was there for the end. It's kind of my modus operandi."

I felt a mild flash of pain in my temples, but nothing like before. On that cryptically chilling comment, I glanced back at Raphael. Whatever he'd been waiting on, this had definitely not been it. He returned my gaze before glancing back at Lucky. "Are you here to plead for your Master's salvation?"

Lucky turned to me and gave me a warm smile. "I do not make a habit of pleading for anything, Lord Raphael. I merely ask that people do the right thing and then I watch their responses."

Raphael furrowed his brow thoughtfully, looking intrigued. "And what is the right thing here?"

Lucky swept his gaze across the bloody floor with a sad look. "You've won the battle. Call off your men," he finally said in a calm, confident tone. "And women," he added, dipping his chin at Lust.

Uriel grunted. "Why would we do something so foolish? Why are we even *listening* to this human?"

I held my breath, wondering why they couldn't sense anything from him. Envy had, but she'd been bonded with me when she first saw Lucky, so maybe that had helped her see the truth. Greed had not noticed either, now that I thought about it. Not until he showed her his powers. But this was a huge gamble. As far as I knew, Lucky's body was most definitely mortal— weak, frail, and totally defenseless against these monsters. He was like a supernova within an egg shell.

Lucky cocked his head at Uriel. "Because you are Archangels and it is the right thing to do." He pointed at me. "Master Dracula is captured. Let her few surviving followers go. There are innocents here. Families. Children, even."

"They are all monsters!" Uriel snapped. "Let them all die!" he shouted at Raphael.

"It is better that ten guilty persons escape than that one innocent suffer," I heard myself say.

Raphael turned to me, cocking his head in surprise. Uriel shouted and argued but Raphael paid him no mind as he nodded thoughtfully, considering my words. "You refer to the destruction of Sodom in the Book of Genesis. The Lord told Abraham *I will not destroy it for the ten's sake.*" The Archangel studied me curiously.

I shot him a guilty smile and shook my head. "I was actually referring to Blackstone's Ratio, but I will admit that Sodom *is* one of the oldest examples of the concept. The theory didn't really gain traction during the Salem Witch Trials, though. Exodus 22:18, I think. *Thou shalt not suffer a witch to live.* Contradictions are a bitch, eh?"

Lucky coughed, biting back an amused grin. "She is correct, although sharp tongued."

"That doesn't make any sense," Gluttony murmured to Lust. She shrugged. "How am I supposed to buy this dump if they're already making caveats about saving freeloaders?" he grumbled. I glared at him and he winked back playfully. Then he pulled out a box of Girl Scout Cookies and started eating them with a satisfied hum.

Nate had been right. Girl Scouts really were the minions of Hell!

Father Ignatius was watching me curiously, seemingly surprised by my concern for my followers. Or maybe I'd had impressed him with my limited quoting of scripture. I only had a handful memorized. How evil did he think I truly was? I'd worked for the Shepherds, kind of, for quite a while, so he had to have heard the good things in my file—even if he chose to dismiss them overall.

A bolt of lightning struck the pavilion and everyone shouted, jumping back in alarm as four cloaked and masked figures stepped out of the blast. I groaned, suddenly realizing what Raphael had been waiting on, because he was the only one who did not look surprised to see the Four Horsemen of the Apocalypse.

I wasn't sure if it was better or worse that they were not mounted.

Death wore a skeletal mask that looked ancient and chipped and ominous. I saw what looked like an impact crater in the forehead, much like a metal target at a shooting range. He wore a wispy death shroud that whipped and cracked from an unseen wind. His skeletal claw wielded a scythe over one shoulder that looked big enough to kill six people in one swing. He was the only one armed, and I took that as foreshadowing. They weren't here to sell Girl Scout Cookies.

War glared at me from behind a red and white samurai mask which looked to be formed from flowing, molten lava that constantly shifted and drooped. His robes were charred and smoldering as if he'd just escaped a burning building. His overly large claws were red-hot steel and they dripped liquid metal.

Famine studied the gathered faces from behind a scarecrow mask that looked like a filthy, blood-stained burlap sack, and his robes were woven from dead and dried cornhusks. Claws that looked like thorned branches hung at his sides.

Pestilence, or Conquest, as he often went by, wore a plague doctor mask with a long, wickedly pointed beak. His robes were rotten and stained with green smears, but his bladed hands looked like scalpels.

Father Ignatius had practically soiled himself upon their arrival, falling back at the proximity of the lightning strike and then to abruptly see the four nightmares standing in its wake. Beckett Killian helped him to his feet and the nephilim formed a protective wall in front of him and the other surviving Shepherds and members of the Conclave. Their faces were nervous but defiant.

I turned to Raphael and suddenly started laughing. "You called the cops on me? For defending my home?"

Raphael pursed his lips and didn't answer me.

"We're here for Callie Penrose. And it is no longer a request," Death said, pointing a skeletal claw at me.

"Why?" I demanded. "You guys are worse than credit collectors. Did I forget to pay my membership dues or something?"

Famine grinned and War hit him hard with the flat of his fiery blade. "Oh, right. Serious faces."

Conquest was too busy ogling Lust to notice. She waggled her fingers at him like she wanted to play *Doctor*, and he stiffened—his spine, at least. Maybe his thermometer, too, but I couldn't verify that without a physical exam.

Death actually face-palmed.

War stepped forward, glaring at me. "You used the Mask of Despair against the wrong pantheon. The Dread Four have claimed jurisdiction over every other pantheon. This one is *ours*."

I blinked.

Envy, I growled, drawing out the length of the word in my best Ricky Ricardo impersonation. *You told me that you broke my Horseman's Mask at the Coliseum fight!*

She let out a huffy breath. *Well...I wasn't technically lying*, she whined. *I did feed off it, but only so I could help you punch Greed in the forehead. And using it against a Sin would have likely broken it anyway, just like he said—*

I burst out laughing at the voice in my head. The Four Horsemen did not find my manic break the least bit humorous. Grace eyed me nervously, as if to remind me her cottontail was on the line too.

"Fine, War. Let's walk through it together. After I was attacked and defended myself in single combat," I wheezed, "you came to arrest me for... jurisdictional disagreements?" I hooted. "This is just so fucking ridiculous I don't even know what to say right now. We're standing here with Sins and Archangels after mass slaughter, and *I'm* the bad guy." I glanced back at Gluttony and Lust to make sure they were still here. "Seriously. Is no one going to arrest them? He's eating cookies and she's flirting with anything with a pulse. And they started this whole shit-show the moment they came to town."

No one seemed very concerned about that key detail. Raphael pretended I hadn't said anything of note.

"And you brought a Sin to the Vatican for everyone to see," Father Ignatius said in a cool tone. "Without warning us."

Lust and Gluttony looked decidedly uneasy rather than smug like they had earlier. In fact, they looked ready to bolt after I'd repeatedly called them out and they glared at Raphael as if they suspected a trap—for them. Judging by the look on the Archangel's face, there was no alliance between them, just equal hatred and disgust. A necessary evil to take me down. A literal deal with the devil.

"Stand down, Horsemen," Lucky said in a dismissive tone, smiling at me. "I called first dibs and she was just about to tell an interesting story about Uriel and the nephilim before you interrupted."

The Four Horsemen bristled with menace, drawing blades as they shot the unarmed human very confused looks. *Who the hell is this idiot? Is he trying to get himself killed?*

I jerked my chin at the nephilim behind Beckett. "Slice off his bracelet and the truth will speak for itself. Uriel can answer any questions anyone may have—"

Uriel snarled and lunged forward in a blur. The only thing I saw were his jazzy wings fluttering towards me, and then Grace was yanked from my grip. He reappeared between me and Lucky, yanking the Easter Bunny's head back by the base of her ears and pressing a glowing dagger to her throat. He spun in a slow circle for everyone to see. "One more word from Master Dracula and the bunny gets it."

The crazed look in his eyes let me know he wasn't kidding.

Lucky burst out laughing. "The bunny...*gets it?*" he roared, laughing even harder. "That's the bold threat from the wingless Archangel? That you will kill a helpless hare?"

Uriel snarled. "Can someone kill this idiot and save us all from his preaching? Why are we even listening to him? He obviously has no common sense, meddling in our affairs."

He glared pointedly at Lust and Gluttony, but the two Archdemons shrugged. "It *is* kind of ridiculous to threaten a rabbit," Gluttony said.

"And the suicidal human says funny things," Lust added, pointing at

Lucky. She licked her lips with a long, forked tongue as she smokily eyed his junk. "I'll interrogate him later," she said in a husky purr.

"Dial it back, Skankalot," I muttered. "We all know you're easy."

She winked at me playfully. I stared at Grace and pursed my lips, ready to lunge for her and Shadow Walk the moment I saw an opening. She stared back at me with anxious, terrified eyes, and I could see that Uriel's glowing dagger was actually burning her fur.

Lucky stepped forward and my eyes widened as I realized he was stepping directly into the proximity of Carla's vases. His specter guardians instantly bloomed to life over his shoulders, looking like red and blue armored giants. Everyone gasped and drew weapons or called up balls of magic, taking steps back and murmuring warily. Even the Four Horsemen let out stunned grunts. Lust and Gluttony almost fell over the railing in their haste to sit up straight.

"I am an Anghellian," Lucky said in a voice that rang like a struck bell, "and the Four Divines are *mine*. Your petty squabbles are all about to end right here and now unless I take custody of Master Dracula and Grace."

Uriel sputtered incredulously and Raphael lifted his sword with a horrified look on his usually stoic face.

Lust and Gluttony looked like they'd finally decided to pack up and leave after shitting their armor and ruining their big night out.

❧ 48 ❧

Uriel looked panicked and confused as he clutched Grace tighter to his chest, his knife hand shaking nervously. "That's...*impossible!*" I could tell that he had heard an Anghellian walked the world again— Greed had most definitely told him—but that he hadn't *truly* believed it until this very moment, and he definitely hadn't realized Lucky was anything more than an annoying human he'd just been casually asking Lust and Gluttony to execute. Even now he eyed Lucky up and down with dumb confusion. And fear.

But I'd seen the flash of desperation when Lucky mentioned the Divines. He wanted them. Badly.

"You will come with us, Anghellian," Death said in a grim tone, taking charge of everyone's panic. "This battle is over and we must discuss this discrepancy in the covenants." He glanced at Father Ignatius and Beckett and the nephilim with a frown. "Privately. Strictly for...family."

I bit back my grin. Technically, that might include me since I was bonded to Envy.

Lucky nodded cooperatively. "I will remand myself to Uriel's custody as soon as he agrees to give me Callie Penrose and releases Grace. After all, he hasn't shown any grace thus far so it's a little late to try and hold it hostage."

Famine snickered at Lucky's barbed words and no one stopped him this time.

Uriel blinked incredulously at Lucky's offer, seeing a glimmer of opportunity. After all, he wanted the Divines more than anything. "Why would you trade yourself for her?" he demanded, searching for the fine print in the obvious trap.

Lucky glanced over at me and dipped his chin. "She was kind to me when no one else was. Now, we meet back in the middle after coming full circle," he said meaningfully, referencing his earlier cruelty to me in Solomon's library when he'd basically called me his enemy. But...what did he mean? Was he asking me to kill him, because he'd also said we would be on opposite sides of a thin line?

Or...was I missing something obvious? Because he'd made a one-eighty last night after seeing me save Grace and Claire at Abundant Angel, as if I'd regained his trust. What was I missing?

Qinglong. He'd sent us to my mother's lab where my night had abruptly gone fuzzy after encountering the Azure Dragon. I felt that flash of pain in my temples again and winced.

Lucky walked up to Uriel in slow, steady steps, holding his hands at his sides. His armored specters followed him like bouncers, crackling with raw, alien energy. "Do we have a deal, Uriel?" he asked calmly. It seemed as if everyone was holding their breath.

Uriel shoved Grace away and she fell down on her ass. She wasn't a threat because she was pretty much the only one left on my side who was still willing to fight. Lucky continued advancing on Uriel even though the Archangel held his dagger out in front of him, wary of a trick, as his eyes darted to the wicked specters hovering over Lucky's shoulders. The Anghellian continued advancing without slowing or speeding up.

Even as Uriel's glowing dagger touched his chest. Lucky took another step and the blade crackled as it slowly sunk to the hilt, spilling blood down the Anghellian's chest. Lucky stared down at Uriel, not registering even a flicker of his eyes or a wince of pain on his serene face, as if a glowing dagger wasn't stabbed into his chest at all. "You never should have lied to me, Brother."

Uriel's hand shook and his jazzy wings fluttered frantically as he stared at the Anghellian with wide, terrified eyes, not sure if he had won a prize or lost everything. His eyes darted down to the dagger as if to verify he had actually pierced the Anghellian's chest. Blood dripped freely and there was no hiding it. The dagger should have killed Lucky, but he seemed completely fine.

"W-we've never even *met!*" Uriel finally hissed, and then he tried to take a step back.

Lucky grabbed him by the shoulders, keeping him in place with what looked like absolutely no effort. Uriel fought and whimpered, trying to shake himself free but Lucky's grip was too strong. The Anghellian turned to Grace with a reassuring smile. "Do as your mistress commanded."

Grace frowned, momentarily confused. Then her eyes widened ever so slightly and she slowly turned to look at the nephilim in front of Father Ignatius. Her cute little whiskers wiggled as her face split into a predatory grin. And then she promptly disappeared.

Everyone shouted out in alarm, but then Grace reappeared at my side, hefting a sliced golden cuff in her paw like a baseball. She sheathed a dagger and held it up for everyone to see. I smiled. Finally.

Come to me, I thought to the freed nephilim.

Everyone spun towards Father Ignatius and his nephilim. One of them began to scream and then fell to the ground. My expectant smile slipped as the nephilim turned to ash and collapsed in on itself. Father Ignatius let out a shout of rage and horror.

Grace looked up at me with a stunned look. "You said to slice off his cuff! Did I do it wrong?"

I shook my head numbly, feeling my heart thundering in my chest. Grace had just unintentionally executed a nephilim in front of absolutely everyone. Uriel smirked discreetly—vindicated of my accusations—but his cheer immediately evaporated as he realized the development did nothing to help him escape Lucky's grip.

Raphael slowly turned his fiery glare upon Grace and raised his sword. "You just murdered a nephilim in cold blood," he accused in a hoarse tone. All Grace had done was remove his cuff, but she had moved too fast for anyone to visually corroborate that. They had only seen her move and then the nephilim had died. Did it only work if I did it? Or did I need to feed them angel blood after I did it? Or possibly bite them?

My mind was too fuzzy to recall what I had done with Quentin and Adrian. Turning them had been a happy accident involving Eae.

But Raphael knew the truth! Enough of it, at any rate. Why was he so protective of the nephilim when he knew they were brainwashed slaves? He glared at Grace with murderous fury in his white eyes and took a step towards her.

"You're *lying*, Raphael!" I snarled defensively, pulling Grace behind me. "You *know* what they truly are!"

"Take one more step, Lord Raphael, and your brother dies," Lucky said calmly. "Your choice, not mine."

Raphael hesitated, eyeing the specters over Lucky's shoulders. "You saw what she just did."

Lucky jerked his chin at one of the other nephilim. "Lift up your arms, nephilim."

Father Ignatius frowned, looking shaken, but he nodded for the nephilim to obey. The nephilim lifted his hands and I saw a second cuff on his other wrist. This one was identical to the first but it was black. A suicide collar. I saw Raphael's hesitation, frowning at the alien cuff. He hadn't known about it either. I slowly shifted my glare to Uriel, feeling my fangs slowly extending from my gums.

Lucky was staring at Uriel with a disappointed frown. "Insurance? Very clever."

"I don't know what you are talking about. Unhand me!" he snapped, even though he still had his dagger buried in Lucky's chest. His wings fluttered frantically as he tried, and failed, to break free. Lucky didn't even look like he was aware of Uriel's struggles.

"I am Michael and I am Lucifer," Lucky told him. Everyone gasped in surprise. Raphael's legs actually buckled before he propped himself up with his sword like it was a cane.

Uriel's face paled as he realized what that meant. His gig was up. Either Michael or Pride knew things that Uriel thought had been safely buried.

"You no longer deserve these," Lucky said in a calm tone. And then the hulking gauntlets of his specters each reached over Lucky's back and grabbed Uriel's baby wings. They squeezed, crushing them, and then they tore them out like weeds in a garden. Uriel screamed as the wings and the holes now in his back both erupted with green flames.

Having his wings ripped off twice was not enough repentance for my current tastes.

I was relieved that Uriel was finally paying for his crimes, but all I could think about was my utterly destroyed army. Why had I thought I could lead them against powers like this? Sure, I was strong, but my people were not on their level. My pride had led to my downfall. Lucky should have just let me die.

He'd shown up at the end, but too late to save my friends—

"Hey! Asshole!" a voice shouted from behind us in the direction of the castle. We all spun to see Darling striding towards us, and he looked furious as his eyes locked onto Uriel. "I specifically heard my wife say the safe word."

Uriel stared incredulously back at him. "That…is not possible," he stammered. "I killed you."

"And my *wife*, you satchel of Richards!" Darling roared, still storming towards him as if he intended to physically throttle him despite how outnumbered he was.

"Bag of dicks!" Grace snorted, and then she abruptly froze with a very confused look on her face.

I felt a mental bolt of lightning zap down from my skull to my tailbone and I groaned. It was gone a moment later and I saw stars in my peripheral vision. I frowned, blinking rapidly at a sudden sense of deja vu. Grace laughing at the term *satchel of Richards* and blurting *bag of dicks!* I shared a meaningful look with Grace and our eyes shot wide open, suddenly recalling the events from last night. They hit me in a staccato of memories and I felt my heart start to race as I panted desperately.

No one seemed to notice my conniption because they were too busy gawking at Darling's miracle revival.

Qinglong had given me one of the satchels and told me to look for answers while reaching inside. The room had been slowly filling with a fog, putting us to sleep as he left. Solomon. I'd touched a marble with Solomon's memories. Within heartbeats, I relived his fractured, confused, determined mind. His love for Obie. His fatherly love for me and my mother. His internal war. And then the horrible, brutal memories of Uriel torturing him for information on the demons within the Seal of Solomon, controlling the nephilim, the Watchers, the Garden.

Uriel had been after power by any means necessary. Lucky had been in the memory, helping ease Solomon's pain during his last moments and staying with him until the end.

I was there for the end, Lucky had told Father Ignatius earlier. *It's kind of my modus operandi…*

Ohmygod. Lucky had been *there*. He knew *everything*. He'd mentioned testing me. Was that why he was here right now? Why he wanted me for himself? Had Lucky somehow brought Darling back from the dead? My thoughts ran wild, but I put them on the back burner as I stared at Darling, feeling just as confused at the current situation as my mind was about last night.

"But she used the safe word," Darling continued, "so you should have left her alone."

"Safe word?" Raphael asked in a baffled tone. "What is the safe word?"

Darling grinned wickedly as he lifted his arms high. "Bridezilla!"

Uriel stared at him, still gripped in Lucky's embrace.

Lucky was grinning at me. He winked, but everyone was too busy staring at Uriel and Darling.

"She did not say...that," Uriel said warily. As if it would have made any difference to him even if she had. He was grasping at straws and still trying to fathom how Darling was still breathing.

Darling glanced over his shoulder with an annoyed scowl. "BRIDEZIL-LA!" he shouted louder.

And the air behind him abruptly rippled, revealing thousands upon thousands of—

"What. The. *Fuck?*" Grace wheezed, latching onto me.

49

Two Greater Demons stood behind Darling, towering over him in their armored, monstrous forms. My godparents, Samael and Lilith. But behind them were so many more allies.

I stared at a horde of faces I had thought never to see again. All the men and women I had watched die right here in front of me, and many, *many* more. What had to be five times the number of warriors had returned to avenge...*themselves*.

The shifters, the vampires, Roland standing with his werewolves, Paradise and Lost, on either side of him, Quentin and Adrian glaring at Raphael and Uriel with their silver claws out and looking hungry for blood, Eae, Fabrizio and Aala, and faces I only knew in passing. Terry and Raidia grinned savagely, and my father winked at me before pointedly straightening his spine and stretching his shoulders back in a silent reminder to me. My eyes grew blurry with tears and I felt a wolfish smile split my cheeks as I nodded back.

Samael was a titan of scales that looked to be made of charred black coins with huge horns sprouting from his head. His eyes blazed with red fire and his huge black wings flared out from his back, rattling like a diamond-back rattlesnake. He was shorter but stockier than his brand-new wife, reminding me of a warrior dwarf.

Lilith was a ten-foot-tall, mutant crocodile with rough gray scales that looked more like armor. She was buff with more pectoral muscle than breast, and she wore a fur skirt that stopped at about midthigh. Her beady black eyes contained the righteous wrath of a bride who'd received bad news from the caterer.

And now everyone had to die.

Everyone who had been here when the attack started. It...was impossible. It hadn't been an illusion because I still stood in their blood. I could still see their dead bodies surrounding me, for crying out loud. What the actual fuck had the Toymaker's vases done?

The invaders of Castle Dracula seemed rooted in place, struck speechless as they looked from the dead bodies littering the ground to the same exact faces now lining up to charge them.

Lust and Gluttony abruptly winked out of existence with a muttered, "Fuck this!" abandoning their small army of demons without a second thought.

Dear sauntered up to her husband and rested her cheek on his shoulder with a weary sigh. "Shall we dance in their skins, my love?" she asked in an eerily calm but surprisingly loud and hopeful voice.

"We shall, Dear. You will laugh this day," Darling vowed in a lifeless, merciless rasp.

Their eyes burned with black fire and I saw a strange distortion around them as if they were about to finally reveal who the fuck the infamously scandalous and scary leather workers really were.

Lilith and Samael stepped in front of Darling and Dear and lifted their claws to point at various targets. I saw a blast of black smoke where the two leather workers had been standing, but my bulky godparents' forms had concealed Darling and Dear's apparent transformation. Damn it!

The author of my story was a sadistic sociopath!

"When you fuck with Castle Dracula," Samael snarled, "Castle Dracula fucks back!"

"KILL. THEM. ALL!" Lilith roared, and a platoon of gargoyles erupted out of the depths of Castle Dracula, screaming as they filled the night sky and then dove down to exact their revenge on the invaders. The wedding attendees charged, shrieking like lunatics in their posh formalwear.

Lucky glanced over at me and shrugged with a shit-eating grin and a wink.

I found myself grinning from ear-to-ear as I heard shouting and death screams from behind me. Grace was laughing and hurling daggers at the now distracted demons and werewolves, because thousands of skeletons had crawled up the walls of the ramparts to sneak up behind everyone while they'd been distracted by the newlyweds' army. I saw Xylo shove his hand through the back of Father Ignatius' neck and out the front of his throat, his crimson cowl whipping in an unseen wind—like he shared an alternate plane with Death—and his eye sockets billowing black smoke.

Cain buried daggers in the foreheads of two nephilim and then it was madness as an ocean of living, cackling bones wielding silver blades swamped over everyone from the Vatican, turning them to fountains of blood and horrified screams.

Roland roared like an animal as he sank his fangs into the neck of one demon and incinerated three more with his free hand as he drank his fill. The fire grew larger and hotter with each drop of demon blood to hit his tongue, as if it was powering him up.

Everywhere I looked, my previously victorious foes were surrounded by the hordes of Dracula on all sides, fighting for their lives, and unable to even take the time to escape. I did see the Four Horsemen staring at their would-be prisoner—me—with stunned and furious looks on their faces.

I grinned and blew a kiss at Death before he disappeared.

Lucky was staring out at the Coliseum with a smug smile on his face, and I sucked in a breath of surprise as I realized how similar this was to the effects of the Dueling Grounds. I blinked and licked my lips nervously as it hit me. He had...somehow turned all of Castle Dracula into the Dueling Grounds! That was why they had all returned after waking up back in their beds! Holy shit. Was that the source of the strange power I'd felt swamping Castle Dracula? Or maybe it had something to do with the Toymaker's vases.

Either way, I didn't really care. Lucky had done something and everyone who had died seemed to have been in on the con rather than confused about being alive again.

This had been planned. Orchestrated. Was this why Qinglong had drugged us? To keep it a secret?

Uriel managed to break free of Lucky's grip while he was distracted. The wingless Archangel lunged at me with a furious snarl. Lucky noticed at the last second and lunged after his escaping quarry. Uriel dodged a slash of my claws and latched onto my forearm just as Lucky latched onto Uriel's shoulder, connecting the three of us at the exact same instant.

We were torn from Castle Dracula as either the Anghellian or the Archangel chose a place for us to grab a night cap rather than hang back for the necromantic battle at Castle Dracula.

The sounds of murder and mayhem abruptly ended, replaced by a harsh, whistling wind.

I looked up to see the three of us standing before the gates to the Garden of Eden. The massive and worn-down rock wall surrounded a wild, untamed forest—the only hope for sustained life in this realm. The massive golden gate was pitted and bent as if large armies had laid siege to it but had ultimately failed to overcome it, dying of starvation within full view of the luscious paradise beyond. The only testament to their efforts was that some of the letters had fallen free of the arch over the gate, renaming *The Garden of Eden* to *The den of Ed*. A few missing letters was the sum total of the combined victories in attempting to defeat the gate.

Thousands of years of acid rain had ensued, pitting away at the gate and devouring the bones of all those who had died trying to get inside. Behind us was a windswept wasteland that resembled a desert, but I knew the sand was actually bone dust. Angel and demon bone dust. Large trees peppered the dunes, but they were hollow, calcified shells, looking more like the masts of ships that had sunk beneath the depths of the ever-shifting ocean of ash.

Mounds and pillars of salt also rose up from the ashy hills, looking like giant abandoned, half-melted candles, and weapons and angelic armor sprouted up here and there like persistent weeds. Some of those weapons stood upright with flags and banners somehow enduring the passage of time. I read a few of them in my quick glance and they sent a chill down my spine even though I had already seen them once before.

Non Serviam.

Defiance.

Arete.

The same words on Nate Temple's family Crest. Maybe his ancestors had vacationed here once, thought the slogans were catchy, and then plastered them on their own crest to one-up a neighbor.

The sky was burnt orange despite there being no sun in sight, casting a rusty stain over the barren wasteland. Even though this wasn't my first time seeing the setting of the Angel War, it was just as haunting and chilling as the first time Michael had shown it to me. And here I was again with Michael...kind of.

Uriel looked just as surprised to be here as I was, letting me know that Lucky had been the one driving the bus. "Now," Lucky said in a strangely energetic hum as he stared at the bewildered Uriel, "I think it's time the seven of us go treasure hunting like that old children's story, *Sev'n Most Sinist'r.*"

And then he drop-kicked Uriel in the chest so hard that the Archangel flew the fifty yards to the gate, slamming his wing sockets into the metal bars and screaming in both confusion and agony at the reminder of his wounds.

I recalled Solomon's memory and how Uriel had been furious that the book Lucky had just mentioned had been blank or some kind of fraud, and then him telling Lucky that the book was a joke. Half of Solomon's cryptic thoughts and comments were bizarre and amorphous, but I understood the important bits.

Uriel had intended to kidnap me from Castle Dracula to steal anything and everything from me in order to get his hands on any kind of power that would keep his head above water, whether that was the nephilim, my demon prison, or his armor, he didn't really care. The answer was simply, he wanted it all.

And he'd missed his moment to do it quietly when Raphael arrived, kicking me away. Granted, I might have actually killed Uriel if Raphael hadn't intervened, but it still resulted in Uriel missing his chance to nab me. Had he hoped to become the new boss in Gabriel's absence, or had he merely wanted to cover up the past crimes with the Watchers and nephilim that Envy had told me about? I decided I didn't care.

I turned to Lucky with a sad smile. "You stayed with him," I whispered.

He glanced over at me and dipped his chin slightly. Then he lifted his arm, inviting me in for a brief hug. "Solomon believed in you, Callie. Even though his mind was torn to pieces, he was certain of that and a few other things."

"And you had Qinglong drug me," I said in a low growl.

Lucky winced guiltily. "Yes. You needed sleep and I needed to be certain you didn't go haring off with the hare on some misguided adventure and get yourself caught by Uriel. Like checking on Ryuu or hunting the Archangel down," he said meaningfully, knowing that was exactly what I had intended to do. "You didn't need me to *tell* you what I'd seen with Solomon, you needed to *live* it. To see what he endured to keep you safe from Uriel. And you were the bait for the wedding trap. Can't catch an Archangel without some cheese." He let out a light laugh. "I still can't believe the Divines were able to amplify the Dueling Grounds effects. It's why I came out. To stall everyone while Xylo and his men gathered your people who had woken up from their beds, armed them, and then sent them to their positions. It was Ryuu's idea, to be fair. We hashed out the details with the Divines—and here we are."

I detached myself from Lucky and shot him a wide-eyed stare at a sudden thought. "Is Ryuu the fifth Divine?" I whispered, thinking of the mysteriously absent golden dragon I had once seen carved on Xuanwu's front door.

Lucky considered it for a few silent moments. "I have no idea. Maybe. They are very secretive about it."

I nodded numbly, processing the rest of his claims. "They were all in on it?" I asked, thinking of my allies willingly going to the wedding, knowing they would die terrible deaths and that the Dueling Grounds spell might not actually work.

He nodded solemnly. "They wanted payback for the Coliseum. They love their Master Dracula. They believe in you, Callie, just like Solomon did. Like I do."

I smiled, nodding. Then I saw the dagger wound in Lucky's chest and I winced. "Lucky!"

He saw and waved off my concern. "It doesn't matter. We have more important things to worry about," he said, jerking his chin at the Garden. "Watch. This will be beautiful and terrible, Callie," the Anghellian said, his eyes glittering with excitement.

He grabbed my hand and we turned towards the Garden. Uriel was on all fours, moaning deliriously and I felt myself snarl. It was time to deal with this motherfucker, and I was going to make it memorable. For Solomon and Obie. And myself.

I gasped as four towers of light at equidistant points around the Garden abruptly shot up into the sky, piercing the rusty clouds above, and filling the air with a steady hum like I was too close to an electrical power plant. It was kind of the opposite of what I had felt at Castle Dracula with the expansion of the Dueling Grounds.

"The Divines?" I whispered, staring in awe.

Lucky nodded.

The beams of light bent down from the clouds and met in the middle over the Garden of Eden, connecting to form a Cross Pattée shape and making the Garden look like a giftbox with a ribbon of light. The combined energy blasted down from the cross and slammed into the center of the Garden, but not before a crackling dome of blue light screamed into existence to protect the Garden. The golden light struck the dome with the sound of a struck bell and the ground shook in every direction like an earthquake, almost knocking me back on my ass.

I stared in stunned disbelief at the Garden of Eden, which now looked like a snowless snow globe.

With a severely cracked dome.

Because all the snowflakes were out here—the bone dust from the angels and demons.

The end had begun.

50

U riel was slowly rising to his feet, looking dazed.

"He'll fly away," I urged.

Lucky chuckled. "Not with the green fire I burned into his roots. It will take days for him to get that power back. Days he doesn't have. He's trapped. Still strong but he can't run. Everyone knows he's been playing all sides now. He has no credibility. The rest of his armor and the sword of fire are his only hope at reasserting his power. With the sword, he can execute or control Azazel and Samzaya—which means he will control the nephilim completely, with or without the cuffs."

I shuddered at the thought. I'd heard only vague stories about the sword of fire that protected the Garden of Eden, and I'd also seen vague references to Uriel wielding a fiery sword. This was so far out of my wheelhouse of Biblical lore that I just had to trust Lucky—Michael and Pride. But I could tell that Lucky had a personal stake in this. To him, this wasn't necessarily about stopping Uriel. It was righting a wrong of some kind. What had Uriel done to Michael and Pride?

Regardless, if Uriel gained absolute control over the nephilim, we were fucked.

"Solomon said my parents stole his armor," I said, staring at the shambling Uriel, "so how the hell did they get inside to put the rest of it in the locked Garden?" I asked.

Lucky pointed at the Divines and smirked. "The same way we're about to."

I decided to just roll with it. All would become clear soon. I wasn't here for Bible studies. I was here for blood and vengeance against a monster. To stop him before he grew even more monstrous. Uriel would die.

I watched as said monster tried to force his wings to grow by hunching over and straining like he was dropping a deuce before the holy gate, but it only resulted in green flames shooting out from his open wing sockets and him crashing to the ground in squealing agony. I grinned. Maybe this wouldn't be so hard—

Raphael slammed down to the ground between us and Uriel. His armor crackled ominously. His gleaming sword hung at his side rather than pointing at our faces, so I smiled politely. "I thought you would return to the scene of the crime. I cannot let you enter the Garden."

My smile evaporated.

Lucky narrowed his eyes. "You are not the guardian. *He* is," he growled, pointing at Uriel, who was now seated on the ground with his eyes closed and a look of intense focus on his face. I felt a twinge of unease. What was he doing? Healing himself? "You've seen what he's become. Imagine an Archangel with that hunger for power getting it all back."

Raphael studied Lucky curiously, as if still struggling to accept the claim that this man was truly Michael and Lucifer. "Perhaps having his armor stolen is what turned him into this. He is desperate and afraid."

Lucky considered that and finally shook his head. "He became corrupted the moment he lied to everyone about the nephilim. When he told Michael he would do as commanded and kill them all."

"Uriel followed Gabriel's orders, not yours—Michael's," he corrected himself.

Lucky stepped forward and Raphael tensed, gripping the hilt of his sword. "Perhaps Gabriel is the one who *told* him to enslave the nephilim. You have not seen Gabriel lately, Raphael. He is working hand-in-hand with Wrath. They both tried to kill me." He pointed a thumb at me and I flinched, so engrossed in the conversation between Archangels that I had momentarily forgotten I was the most easily squishable person here. "She worked with the Divines to reunite Michael and Lucifer with their Grace in purgatory. That is what was done to us, Raphael. We were ripped into thirds and then pitted against each other, told to fight an endless war when our Father left to start new projects."

Raphael glanced at me sharply and I took a step back, realizing I wasn't supposed to have heard that last bit about their pops. I mimed zipping my lips closed and tossing away a key. His eyes narrowed suspiciously but he turned back to Lucky. "Father is the Creator, we are the managers. If He does not continue creating, He dies."

Lucky nodded knowingly. "That doesn't mean He's to be congratulated for His failures."

Raphael sighed. "I hear Lucifer speaking through you yet also remnants of Michael," he admitted with a tired smirk. He didn't look completely sold on Lucky's claims, but he did look open-minded to it. "These are old, endless arguments." He glanced up at the beams of light attacking the Garden's protective ward and clenched his jaw. "I know what they can do, but what *are* they?" he asked, obviously referring to the Divines.

Lucky was silent for a few moments. "Watchers, brother." Raphael froze, his eyes widening in shock. I might have gasped as well. The Divines were Watchers? Holy shit. Lucky nodded. "Azazel and Samzaya caught wind of what Uriel and Gabriel were planning for them, so they secretly sent four Watchers out into the world as insurance."

I didn't say anything, but my mind instantly perked up at that. Four secret Watchers...or *five*? Raphael licked his lips and glanced at his meditating brother with an uneasy, thoughtful frown. "Uriel...would have known. He would have hunted them down."

Lucky smiled sadly. "They lived like nomads, wandering the world as lonely, beneficent travelers, splitting up to hide their identities and their abilities as best they could. They helped strangers and then kept walking. For centuries. Homeless and kind, living off the gifts from the people they helped. Enough time went by that they evolved into something different. Something...better, perhaps. They healed my mind after my ordeal," he whispered. He glanced up at the beams of light. "They are totally selfless, Brother. They are what we *should* have been."

Raphael stared up at the beams in silence, shaking his head. "So, they became symbols," he mused. "The Four Divines. Our Father must have known the truth or we would have never heard of them. Yet their stories were shrouded in mystery and fear."

Lucky nodded but then shrugged. "What better way to hide their true nature than to create monstrous legends? Perhaps they are the ones who spread their own myths to keep Uriel and Gabriel far, far away from them." He shot me a smirk. "Until a Solomon found them, of course."

He studied Lucky and a hint of a familiar smile crossed his face. "I cannot believe it is truly you, Michael."

Lucky snorted. "I'm just as much Lucifer as I am Michael. You are only seeing one-third of the picture, Brother. That is why you fail. Your perspective isn't broad enough." He pointed at Uriel. "He tortured Solomon to try and get access to the demon prison. When he realized Callie was the new warden, he grew furious, demanding to know how she awoke the nephilim from their enslavement."

Raphael's face grew pale and he glanced over at his brother, who was still peacefully meditating, breathing deeply. "Do you have proof of this?" he asked softly. They both turned to look at me.

"I...have been looking, but every time I get close, he tries to kill me and paint me as the fall guy," I admitted, even though I felt like throttling Lucky for not bringing me in on his grand scheme. I would have trusted Envy a whole lot sooner if Lucky had corroborated her claims. Then again...maybe that had been Lucky's concern. He had doubted my ability to withstand her influence until he saw me save Claire and Grace at risk of my own life.

I knew Envy hadn't known about Lucky's involvement or awareness of Solomon's ploy, because she had been terrified to discover the Anghellian's existence. So, I had two independent sources verifying the same story. Before I could feel too righteous for Lucky's lack of trust in me, I mentally reminded myself that trust was in short supply these days. I had not trusted many of my allies in recent days because the events at the Coliseum had truly shaken me. My confidence had been broken, and it had taken me time to pick the pieces back up and glue them together. Humility was a bittersweet fruit.

"What I don't understand is why does everyone seem so surprised about the nephilim secret?" I asked both of them. "They've been around forever, so it's blatantly obvious that Uriel lied about killing them all. This is not a newsflash. How he might have accomplished it could have been a mystery, but each of you had to know that the nephillim weren't wiped out by the Great Flood like the Good Book says. Why have none of you questioned this before?" I understood why Lucky was hazy on the details because it had taken him some time to reconnect the pieces of himself after becoming an

Anghellian. Another question on my mind, although I didn't ask, was why the Divines had agreed to heal him. Had *they* told him their true origins as Watchers?

"Uriel lied," Lucky said, but only after it became apparent that Raphael was not going to answer. "He claimed that he missed some of them, and Gabriel covered for him. They concocted a way to make more nephilim without the thirst for angel blood, or so we were told. We did not know the extent of how many nephilim he had truly missed or how he had actually enslaved them to the will of the Archangels—namely, Gabriel. As we are now aware, he crafted the cuffs to restrain the nephilim and use them for good. Little did we know how tentative that leash was and that whoever controlled the last two Watchers—Azazel and Samzaya—could control the nephilim. In the book of Revelations, Uriel is the one prophesied to execute Azazel and Samzaya with the fiery sword."

Raphael shook his head, looking frustrated and overwhelmed. "This can't be so simple and complex at the same time. You have given me explanations but no *facts*," he growled.

Lucky smiled sadly. "Sometimes, you just have to have faith."

"Don't you dare," Raphael snarled, clenching his blade tightly.

Lucky arched a cool eyebrow. "Both Michael and Lucifer could best you at the sword, Brother. Do not make a decision you and I will both regret..." And there was absolutely no confusion on what Lucky meant.

He would regret killing Raphael, because that was the only possible outcome.

I held my breath.

Do you feel lucky? Well? Do ya, punk?

R aphael hesitated.

Lucky pointed at Uriel. "He is the one who has been manipu-lating everyone, and at the behest of Gabriel...and likely Wrath. I wish only to take that danger from his hands and give it to another."

Both of them glanced at me. Lucky smiled encouragingly but Raphael narrowed his eyes. "She is not worthy of such terrible responsibility. She is human and tainted by sin."

I arched a cool eyebrow. "Remind me...who hired Lust and Gluttony to slaughter my people?"

He clenched his jaw so hard that I could practically hear his teeth grinding together.

"If we can't trust the blood of Solomon, who can we trust?" Lucky asked. "She has the Spear of Destiny within her. She healed it, as a matter of fact," Lucky added in a hopeful tone. I managed not to wince as I recalled Envy helping me weaken it yesterday. "If that's not a testament to her worthiness, I don't know what kind of proof you would accept." He let that sink in and I held my breath, watching Raphael closely. "Gabriel and Uriel have betrayed us. Perhaps this power was never intended for Archangels. Nephilim are half human, after all, and the Garden was given to man. Not angels. Perhaps Father was wiser than I gave him credit for."

Raphael turned his back on the two of us and Lucky shot me a patient look, imploring me to remain silent and look like a good little church girl. I had never been good at that, but I tried. Raphael paced back and forth, muttering under his breath.

Sharp cracks could now be heard, sounding like lightning, as the dome of power protecting the Garden of Eden grew weaker under the onslaught of the Four Divines. Each sharp retort made Raphael flinch in anger and I realized it was only serving to push him further from Lucky's persuasion.

Solomon had mentioned us needing a fifth Divine to break it—or had it been my Spear that was the key?

Raphael finally turned to face us. "Who stole Uriel's armor and locked it in the Garden of Eden? If he had his armor, none of this would be happening because that is the original key to Eden—given to him by our Father."

Lucky sighed and hung his head. "Constance Solomon. Daughter of King Solomon and mother of Callie."

"But I didn't know any of this until recently," I argued defensively.

Raphael set his jaw. "So, I am to believe that the thief who made all of this possible had altruistic intentions, giving those stolen goods to her daughter, and this makes her more trustworthy to guard Eden than my own Brother, who was given the responsibility to protect this place...directly from our Father."

Lucky nodded. "When you say it like that, it doesn't sound very good. My way was better. Want me to repeat it for you?"

Raphael shook his head. "I agree Uriel has many questions to answer. While we await his trial, I will take this responsibility of protecting Eden for myself." He gave me a sympathetic look. "You can either give me the pieces of his armor that you do have or I will take them from you. Choose wisely."

Lucky held up his hands to diffuse the tension and took a step forward. "Let's take a deep breath and reconsider—"

Then he punched Raphael in the throat hard enough to send the Archangel flying off into the distance at what looked like the speed of light. He struck one of the hollow trees and obliterated it, sending the hulking shell crashing to the ground in a cloud of bone dust. I gasped in horror. "What the *fuck*, Lucky?" I demanded, scanning the ground for any serviceable weapons. Dozens were within reach, all divine weapons abandoned during the Angel Wars. A black sword caught my eye, looking long, thin, and graceful, stabbed down point-first into a mound of bone dust. It looked only mildly damaged by the passage of time.

"Ye old sucker punch. Works every time." Uriel was sprinting for us, sensing an opportunity to defend Raphael and hopefully gain an ally. Unfortunately, his meditation seemed to have healed him to some extent, because he looked much more confident and determined than before, no longer fearing the Anghellian.

"Which one do you want?" Lucky asked, grinning.

"You said you were better than Raphael, right?" He nodded. I took a calming breath and walked over to the black sword I had seen. Before I could even touch it, the hilt flew to my hand and throbbed warmly in greeting. The rust fell away like dust, revealing an elegant black katana that gleamed silver on the polished edge. Hadn't it been a two-handed sword moments ago?

Lucky stared down at it warily. "That...was Envy's sword, Callie," he said, studying the black blade. He pointed at a rose engraved into the hilt. "One of her symbols was the black rose."

I felt Envy purring longingly within my chest, finally joining the conversation.

I trust you, Envy, I thought to her. *Let's get changed into something more appropriate.*

I felt a loving warmth rush through me. Uriel's gauntlets and boots winked out and Envy's black armor rolled over my body, replacing the warmth with cold mountain air. I saw Raphael racing back towards us and I turned to Lucky with a calm expression.

"I would rather convince him than kill him, Lucky. I will show him how adept I am at managing the darkness. I am the darkness, yet I still walk in the light. You take Uriel. Michael has unfinished business with him for lying all those years ago."

Lucky studied me curiously and then nodded. "Okay, Callie. White Rose. Black Rose. Whatever you are."

I smirked, eyeing him up and down. "Two sides of the same coin, just like you. Go."

His specters suddenly shimmered into view over his shoulders as he spun and tackled Uriel to the ground, cracking the earth where they struck.

Raphael hovered over me, looking surprised that Lucky had turned to fight Uriel and left me for him. He slowly drifted to the ground in front of me with great sweeps of his wings. He eyed my armor and narrowed his eyes suspiciously. I repeated what I had told Lucky—with a few tweaks.

"I am the Horseman of Despair, and yet I am still optimistic. I was born an orphan yet I have made several families. I was given great powers in the Doors and I abandoned them to protect Solomon's Temple. I healed the Spear of Destiny. I wear the armor of Envy, yet I still don't desire to kill you. I was born and raised by treachery and darkness, yet I still reach for the light at the end of the day."

"What do you desire, Callie Penrose?" Raphael asked me, his eyes flicking to the Garden as another sharp crack announced further weakening of the dome.

"To learn from my mistakes and those of others."

Raphael slowly drew his sword. "You desire wisdom. For power?"

I laughed and almost said no. Then I hesitated. "Only if I can use that power to help those less fortunate." I eyed him thoughtfully. "I do desire two other things," I admitted.

"Oh? Pray tell."

"Your trust, for one."

His bright white eyes locked onto my katana, recognizing it. "My trust is earned, not given, Black Rose."

I nodded, not bothering to hide my smile. "That's where the second desire comes in." He waited curiously. "I desire to beat you bloody and then lift you back to your feet and shake your hand. I call it woman-splaining."

He stared at me as if I'd just announced the sun rose in the west. "What makes you think you can best an Archangel at the sword?"

"Because I'm no longer hiding what I am," I said, holding out my hands to show off Envy's armor.

"A Sin," he said flatly, staring at Envy's sword.

"A sin-*ner*," I corrected as Lucky and Uriel went tumbling by between us, cracking the earth and grunting as they pounded on each other, neither wearing armor but both taking the punches like they were. The ground shifted between me and Raphael. Neither of us lost our balance or broke eye contact with the other.

He arched an eyebrow as if wondering whether I might be deranged.

I lifted my long, curved katana—which was longer than I was used to but easier to wield than any blade I had ever touched. I lifted it to my forehead and dipped my chin at Archangel Raphael.

He did the same, shifting his huge sword into something more like mine, except his was white.

"Oh," I added, "And I was trained by Ryuu, the Halo Breaker."

Raphael's features instantly grew wary and he gave me a slow nod, the words stabbing deep into his confidence. "You are becoming very, very interesting, Callie Penrose. But I *will* kill you. This is not training with wooden swords. We are not friends."

I drew a line in the sand between us. "They always say that at first."

"Who?" he asked in a low growl.

"The foes who I let survive," I said calmly, sinking deeper into the flow state I'd learned from Ryuu. To become one with my surroundings, a part of it rather than a foreign force reacting *to* it.

Raphael rushed at me, sword held high. He did not look calm.

❧ 5 2 ❧

I fought for respect. I demanded it.

Raphael's emotions and piety made him easy to predict. He genuinely believed me to be an upstart human. A person to respect, but only insomuch as I was the more fascinating of the other bugs he'd observed in life. I stood motionless as he lunged for me with the tip of his white blade, my face as calm as a winter pond.

Then I pivoted, turning my body an inch to the right so his blade whispered past me, almost grazing my armored belly, as I lifted my elbow and hammered him in the nose, using his own momentum against him. He took it like a champ, snarling as he stumbled past me, but I wasn't finished. I kneed him in the lower back and then slammed the hilt of my katana into his abdomen when he recoiled from the knee strike.

I leapt back with a great sweep of Envy's wings and held my sword vertically between us as he rounded on me, his chest heaving with outrage. "Dance with the devil, Archangel," I purred.

He closed the distance between us impossibly fast, swinging his sword down at my neck. I was forced to slide back on my heels as I blocked, blocked, blocked, gritting my teeth at his power.

I Shadow Walked behind him and stabbed him in the thigh, my blade slicing through his armor with surprising ease. He stumbled and cursed, swinging his sword to swat me away and gain some distance.

Uriel and Lucky were beating the living fuck out of each other at the gate, slamming each other into the stone wall with concussive cracks that echoed the thunderous booms now threatening the Garden's dome.

I turned back to Raphael to find him missing. I felt him shimmer into existence behind me and I heard the whistle of his sword in the air as it raced to sever my wings like I had done to his brother, Uriel.

I let Envy's wings vanish and felt the rush of air as his sword slammed into the dust. He might have shaved off a bit of my ass if he'd been any closer. I froze time and summoned my wings, launching myself up into the air behind him. Then I lashed out with one of Envy's Hellchains and let time resume right before contact.

He growled to see me suddenly missing, but the sound turned into a spasming choke as my chain wrapped around one of his wings, hitting him with a full blast of Sulfuricity. He dropped his sword as his body stiffened. I wasted no time in yanking him up into the air towards me. Then I dove to intercept him, doubling the impact of my fist aimed at his face. I released Envy's chain and punched him in the jaw hard enough to shatter his perfect mask and whip his head to the side as his body rocketed down to the ground.

He hit and cracked the earth, leaving a substantial crater and ring of dust.

I floated back down to the ground and calmly walked over to the sword he had dropped. I scooped it up in my free hand and compared the two blades thoughtfully. This felt right. Two blades felt right.

I dismissed the thought and walked up to him as he climbed back to his feet. He glared at me; his face was bleeding, and his nose was smashed. He had one massive scar from temple to opposite jaw, and part of the skin was burned as if from acid, pocked and cratered and pink.

I smiled compassionately. "You are still beautiful, Raphael. Scars build character." Then I tossed him his sword. He caught it with a bewildered frown, and I could tell he wasn't quite sure what to be more startled by—my compliment or that I'd shown mercy.

Except it hadn't been mercy, because I settled myself back into fighting stance, letting him know we were not finished. He narrowed his eyes at me, showing a much healthier respect now.

He would no longer hold himself back.

The trick to my confidence was that I had already weighed my healthy fear for Sins and Archangels. Everyone claimed they were the most powerful beings around, and that was arguably true. But this was a sword fight and I wore the same weapons and armor as him, putting us on relatively equal footing.

For him to be such a great swordsman, he would have had to fight count-less duels against stronger and more talented opponents. Yet...those opponents didn't exist. He had spent his formative years already knowing he was one of the biggest honchos in Heaven, and his only source for improving his bladework was sparring against his fellow Archangels in a controlled environment.

True mastery was learned in war. Fights for your life.

I'd been in countless life or death situations. I'd lost quite a few fights as well. Learned a fair bit. Like the Coliseum, for instance. That had really messed with my subconscious, and I hadn't shrugged it off until my fight at A2C2 with Greed.

But the Archangels had only been in one war. Here. And they hated themselves for it. So, he probably hadn't touched his sword in quite some time, merely carried it around as a symbol of his might. He hated the thing. All Archangels probably did. It was a trophy of his glory days, and he'd grown a beer gut and a bitter attitude while staring at it hanging over the mantel.

The Sins, however, worshipped their blades after suffering a humiliating defeat here.

They had been cast down into a pit where it was kill or be killed. Outma-neuver your foes or suffer the consequences of being outmaneuvered your-self. The Sins had sharpened their blades whereas the Archangels had sheathed them.

I would have been more scared of fighting Uriel because he had a clear goal in mind and a dedication to achieve it by any means necessary.

Raphael dipped his chin and approached in slow, shuffling steps, closing the distance without losing his center of gravity. I lunged, testing him on basic skills. He blocked, if inelegantly, and I began to realize that meeting your idols, or confronting a legend, was all about your own confi-dence and attitude. Your perception of them was always larger than the truth.

Our swords flashed, sending up sparks as they clanged together. We spun, danced, dodged, and parried. My face was calm and amused. His was strained and annoyed. Doubt was creeping into his thoughts like vines slowly creeping up a wall and crushing the structural integrity over time.

I did not need the Horseman's Mask to give him despair. I was Despair.

I glanced down to see a few slashes in my armor, showing thin lines of my blood where he'd scored a strike, but his armor was practically shattered. Some of it had fallen off or was hanging by threads of...whatever held it to his body. Some of the pieces smoked, leaking tendrils of vapor like my wings did when I went into the air.

He lunged for me and I cracked him across the head with the pommel again, then I swatted his ass with the flat of my blade as I pirouetted past him. He snarled and tried to grab at my wings. I let them wink out and he stumbled off balance, having put too much momentum into the grab. He was like a great lumbering bear, furious at the nimble wolf.

I knew a bear could still destroy a wolf if he got the right opportunity, so I didn't let arrogance cloud my mind. My thoughts were blank and I was one with the scene. He swung for my head and I ducked, slicing the upper thigh of his other leg.

I rolled clear as he tried to rip me in half with a backhanded swing, but I wasn't quite fast enough because his sword raked across my lower back hard enough to make me grunt and stumble. I glanced down to see blood dripping at my feet and then I gave him a congratulatory nod.

That pissed him off even more—to accept a compliment from a human.

Envy was working double-time to heal me but I could tell she was exhausted. Raphael flapped his massive wings at me, sending a cloud of bone dust my way and making me cough. I squinted, holding my sword up, but I couldn't see him. He tackled me out of the cloud, and I only barely missed the edge of his blade as I struck the ground on my back with him on top of me, bleeding all over my face. Some of his blood hit my tongue and I gasped as a rush of power hit me like a blast of adrenaline.

My fangs ripped out and I was halfway to chomping for his throat when I remembered my goal here—to earn his trust. I kicked him off me and up into the air. Then I Shadow Walked into the sky above him and punched him in the throat as his wings were unfurling to steady himself in the air.

I Shadow Walked again, appearing below him and grabbing his boot. I swung him down to the ground hard, slamming his shoulder into the center of a ring of swords that were stabbed into the sand. I landed atop him with my knees on his chest and I bared my fangs at him as I pressed the katana against his throat.

He stared up at me with wide eyes, realizing he could actually die right now.

I consumed that fear—the moment an immortal realizes they aren't quite so invulnerable.

"I killed Ares," I snarled. "I killed Leviathan and Mammon. I defeated Michael in single combat. I'm friends with the Easter Bunny, and I've about had it with trying to prove myself to you assholes!" I shouted.

His eyes bulged, processing my words.

"All I have to do is press down and your life is ended, Raphael. I am the Halo Breaker, but I do not want your crown on my conscience."

I pulled back my katana and slammed it down into the earth by his ear, slicing through part of the thin cartilage to let him know how easily I could have ended it.

"Do. You. Understand?" I demanded.

He nodded faintly. "Yes."

"Good." I rose to my feet and yanked my katana from the ground. I slipped it onto my hip out of habit, only realizing too late that I had no sheath. Yet the blade whispered against velvet and let out a faint click. I glanced down to see a glossy black sheath engraved with rose vines and I smiled to myself.

Part of the armor, Envy cooed. *You whooped the piss out of the poor boy,* she said smugly.

I chose not to feed her comment as I glanced down at Raphael. Then I held out my gauntlet to help him up. He stared at it for a few moments before clasping my hand in his. I pulled a very confused and quiet Raphael to his feet and steadied him with my other hand on his shoulder. His armor was still battered and broken but he didn't seem concerned. He held his sword at his side, the point resting in the dirt as he silently suffered an identity crisis.

I let him.

I stepped out of the ring of swords and glanced up at the sky above Eden. The dome of blue light let out a series of thunderous cracks and I glanced up to see that the spiderweb of fractures had almost reached the stone wall. The Divines' beams of light boiled the air, warping it whenever I tried to look directly at it.

Raphael gasped in terror.

I heard a sharp laugh and looked down to see that Uriel was holding a very limp and bloody Anghellian by his throat in front of the gate. Both men were battered and bloody, but Uriel's drive for power had exceeded Lucky's vengeance. The Anghellian's eyes were closed.

53

U riel glanced over his shoulder at me, met my eyes, and then slammed the back of Lucky's head into the gate with a resounding clang. "Foolish child," he muttered. "Keep the armor. I have the Anghellian."

"No," Lucky croaked in a soft, maddeningly calm voice, his eyes weakly fluttering open. "The Anghellian has *you*." I didn't have time to chastise him for stealing my lines before Lucky sliced through the arm holding him by the throat with a rusted, jagged dagger he must have scooped up off the ground during their brawl. Uriel screamed in outrage and agony as his stump spurted blood all over Lucky's face.

Then he snatched up a huge sword from the dust behind him and stabbed Lucky in the gut, ramming the blade to the hilt. Lucky grunted and his eyes bulged as his apparitions crackled to life over his shoulders and started flickering in and out like dying light bulbs.

"NO!" I screamed, throwing my arm forward without consciously choosing to do so. The Spear of Destiny flew from my hand and screamed through the air towards Uriel's back just as a sword sliced into my thigh from behind. I grunted and fell to one knee as my peripheral vision caught Raphael's katana hitting the ground in front of me and him falling to his knees from shame. I blindly struck him with a blast of power that sent him flipping across the wasteland as I stared at my Spear in the air, wanting to see the moment it—

Uriel spun at the last second, somehow sensing it, and my Spear slammed into Lucky's heart.

My own heart stopped as the apparitions above Lucky's shoulders winked out entirely. The Spear of Destiny glowed brightly as if drinking in his power.

The spear tip had struck the gate behind Lucky with a thunderous chiming sound that threatened to make my ears explode, and I watched as the dome of power protecting Eden finally shattered with the sound of calving glaciers, raining down shards of blue glass-like pieces over the Garden.

The Divines' pillars of light did not wink out, though. Instead, they lashed out like tentacles, meeting down in the center of the Garden of Eden and flared even brighter.

Uriel looked stunned as he stared at the Anghellian—his lost prize—in disbelief. He reached for the Spear of Destiny and it zapped the shit out of him, making him jump back with a shout. He gripped his bleeding stump and I saw that he had somehow staunched the blood with his healing abilities.

I rose to my feet, my wounded leg almost giving out on me, and unfurled my wings. *Those healing abilities would be a great idea right about now*, I muttered to Envy.

Do you have any idea how much faster I just made you? She snapped in a sleepy tone. *Look at your armor.* I glanced down to see it smoking and steaming, just like Raphael's armor but not quite as badly damaged.

Oh, I admitted guiltily. *Well, do what you can, because I think we're just getting started*, I said, launching up into the air and racing for the gate.

I saw the moment Uriel recognized his opportunity because he glanced up at me with a slow, wolfish smile. Then he reached for the gate and pulled it open, swinging Lucky's pinned body to the side. He took off in a blur, sprinting for the Garden's center.

I pursued him from the air, summoning the Spear of Destiny back to my hand. The spear hit my palm and I winced at the blood covering the blade and much of the haft. Lucky's blood. *Are you in there, Lucky?* I asked hopefully, recalling how the Spear had blazed brighter.

No response.

I gritted my teeth and pressed on. Lucky had wanted this more than anything. I would mourn Lucky from a position of victory as I stared down at Uriel's cold, dead corpse.

I winced uneasily as I reached the threshold of where the dome had been, fearing I was about to resemble a bug splat on a windshield, but I sailed through without even a flicker of power touching me.

I poured on the speed, racing for the beams of light as I flew above an overgrown forest of prehistoric flowers the size of cars, ponds rippling with crystal blue and green water, and craggy mountains hiding stunning waterfalls and hot springs. Two colossal trees flickered in and out of existence in the distance, never seeming to grow closer no matter how much ground I was covering. They looked as big as mountains and touched the orange clouds high overhead.

The Tree of Life. Adam and Eve had lived beneath it.

The Tree of the Knowledge of Good and Evil. This was the dreaded apple tree. Even as I looked, I spotted millions of flecks of red blanketing its limbs. Enough to feed the whole world. Ironic that man was never supposed to touch it when it seemed to be the answer to all the problems ever.

My parents had sent Uriel's armor here. One of these trails might have been walked by them. It gave me a sudden sense of peace, even as my thigh throbbed, dripping blood in my wake. As beautiful as the Garden was, I kept my eyes low for Uriel.

This was a hunt, not a sightseeing trip.

I had no idea what I was looking for, exactly. My only leads were the convergence of the Divines' light and trying to locate Uriel through the thick foliage below. Since I could no longer see him, I decided on the light, finding it oddly ironic after my talk with Raphael.

I always seek light at the end.

He's after the flaming sword, Envy whispered. *The weapon that can kill Azazel and Samzaya. You promised to save them for me*, she sobbed.

"I haven't quit yet, Envy," I growled as I finally came upon the center of the Garden. "Trust me. And I can't believe it's called the flaming sword. That is the lamest name for an all-powerful weapon that I've ever heard."

I squinted at the miniature sun in the center of the Divines' light as I spun in a slow circle, scanning the area for Uriel. It was a wide, grassy clearing in the middle of an exotic jungle. Glossy shrubs with leaves big enough for me to use as a hammock lined the edge of the forest of black and white trees. I saw birds flitting through the air, startled by my presence.

I saw a black pond surrounded by a ring of trees near the center of the Divines' light, but it wasn't anything remarkable. I couldn't see anything more than that because the light was simply too bright for me.

I came down to the ground faster than I wanted to, but I didn't want to waste a single moment in case Uriel zipped across and stole...well, whatever the hell he wanted, first.

As my feet touched the ground, the beams of light from the Divines winked out and the Garden grew utterly silent. I spun in a slow circle, wary of unintended consequences, like the dome of protection suddenly slamming back into place and locking me here forever.

I gripped the Spear, comforted by its steady hum of power.

I froze as my eyes latched onto the spot where the light had conjoined. Now that it was gone, I saw a large, metal cube sitting in the center of the grass. Moss had been growing up its sides, but the cube was glowing red from the apparent heat of the Divines' light.

Resting peacefully atop the cube was a long, elegant sword. The gleaming blade flickered with fire in a gentle, crackling tone like a fireplace on a cold winter night.

I sprinted for it.

A green bird swooped down from the sky and clawed at my face with a furious squawk and I cursed, stabbing up at it with the spear. "Goddamned Holy pigeons!" I hissed, feeling blood dripping down my forehead where it had gotten me.

I looked up in time to see the green bird falter in midair as if I'd managed to damage one of its wings in my wild stabbing. Then I let out a shout as it materialized into a one-armed Uriel. He slammed into the metal cube with a grunt and all the grace of a bag of frozen sliced potatoes dumped onto a hot skillet.

But his good hand landed on the hilt of the sword, even as the metal cube hissed and crackled, sizzling his flesh. He screamed and flopped off the cube, panting wildly as his good arm lifted the fiery sword before him.

He met my eyes and let out a shout of joy, lifting the holy sword high. "The nephilim are mine—"

The fire winked out of the blade and he froze, staring up at it with a perplexed frown.

I blinked, cocking my head in confusion.

"What did you do to it?" he snarled, pointing it at me with a trembling hand. "You were here first!"

I lifted my Spear defensively. "Maybe it needs gas," I said, just as confused as him. But my eyes darted to our surroundings, wondering where my mother might have put the rest of his armor—the second treasure he wanted from the Garden.

I froze as two glowing figures calmly walked out of the woods behind Uriel. I sucked in a breath, feeling like I'd been punched as I slammed the butt of the Spear down into the grass and held onto it like a lifeline. My eyes filled with tears. The sky darkened and I heard thunder rumbling in the skies above as the clouds grew dark and foreboding. I stared, shaking my head back and forth, terrified.

"No-no-no-no-no," I whispered. Envy's armor evaporated. A gentle breeze picked up, billowing my cloak and hood in the wind, but I couldn't look away.

Upon seeing my reaction, Uriel spun around and abruptly gasped at the two figures.

"Mom...and...Dad..." I rasped, feeling my lip trembling in disbelief. It had to be a trick. The Garden's serpent fucking with me, because what I saw was horrifying.

Constance and Titus were in the Garden of Eden.

They smiled at me proudly and dipped their chins, looking emotional but wracked by guilt. They were each fidgeting, dry washing their hands nervously.

And they were on fire.

54

U riel pointed the holy sword at them. "Get back!" He roared like
he was a lion tamer and the beasts were licking their chops
at him.

My parents were fiery silhouettes of themselves. Specters or ghosts, I
wasn't sure. Upon Uriel's threat, their faces had morphed into feral snarls
and then they started to advance, fire blooming to life in their wake. Uriel
shrieked and ran back to the block of glowing metal, touching the sword
against it. The sword flared back to life and he hooted triumphantly, spinning back around to face them.

The sword winked out again and he started to panic.

My parents relentlessly strode closer at a steady, foreboding pace like a
spreading wildfire. The grass smoldered behind them, leaving blackened
footprints.

I stared, transfixed, knowing Uriel stood no chance. And that felt right
to me.

He swung the flameless sword at them when they came within striking
distance and the blade crumbled to ashes. "Who are you?" He squealed frantically.

"Thunder," my mother said in a strange tone that seemed to resonate on
multiple planes of existence. The dark clouds above rumbled louder,
growling their agreement.

"Terror," my father said, in a frigid, inhuman growl. Fat droplets of rain started to fall, hissing as it struck their shoulders, but their fire did not go out.

Uriel looked terrified and utterly bewildered, as if he had no idea what that meant. Or maybe as if he thought those terms had meant something else entirely and he didn't know what to make of their claims.

He tried to run.

My parents grabbed him. The Archangel erupted into green flames, screaming as his skin and hair smoldered and crackled like frying bacon. I licked my lips nervously and took a step back, wondering if these were just lookalikes of my parents.

Thunder and Terror, they had said. I remembered Solomon mentioning those words in his last moments. They were something he was supposed to watch over within the Garden. Did that mean they needed to be protected, or did it mean that the world needed to be protected from *them*.

Unfortunately, I had no idea what the answer was. Lucky might have known, but he was dead. I felt a throb of pain in my chest at that, and my eyes darted to his blood coating my Spear, but I squashed it down, staring at the screaming Archangel. What would Raphael do when he found out? I had no witnesses to defend me, and he seemed to unconditionally love his brother, despite Uriel's flaws.

Thunder and Terror—my parents—hadn't said a word to me and they had seemed savage and primal rather than human. Like two wild predators disturbed in their natural habitat by unwelcome intruders.

Uriel's blackened, smoldering corpse crashed to the ground, crumbling to embers and sparks. His Halo winked into existence, and then bounced and rolled across the grass, coming to a rest at my feet.

I stepped back, grimacing at it.

My parents looked up at me and their primitive features slowly softened, returning to a semblance of humanity. I held my breath, not knowing whether to trust my lying eyes and walk into the fire or to make a run for it.

"Oh, Callie," my mother said, lifting a trembling hand to her mouth. My father wrapped an arm around her shoulders to support her and I saw molten lava dripping from their eyes. Tears.

"Mom? Dad?" I rasped, taking a step closer.

"In the barest sense," my father, the mighty Titus, replied in a hoarse voice. "We are so goddamned proud of you."

My mother swatted his chest, eliciting a dash of sparks into the air. "Language," she scolded.

"How?" I whispered, panting heavily. This couldn't be real. "What happened to you?"

They shared miserable looks and sighed. "When we brought the rest of Uriel's armor here, we destroyed the fiery sword so he could never use it to kill Azazel and Samzaya," my father said.

"But it didn't work out as we planned," my mother whispered. "We had hoped to return to you when the work was finished, but the sword was not so easily vanquished."

"The moment we destroyed it, the flames split in two and consumed us, locking the Garden back down on us even stronger than before. Too strong for the Divines to break back in and free us," my father said.

I stood as stiff as a board, trying to keep my face blank as I listened, but I felt hollow and fragile.

"We *became* the new flaming swords, splitting the original in half. Thunder and Terror," my mother said, holding out her hand. A fiery sword flickered into view, narrower and lighter than the larger sword I had seen Uriel claim from the metal block. My father did the same, summoning up his own blade.

Noting my silence, they hung their heads and the flames winked out.

I closed my eyes and took a calming breath, forcing my pulse to steady. "Prove who you are."

They smiled sadly and nodded. "We left you with Father David at Abundant Angel Catholic Church," my mother whispered, hanging her head in shame. "I abandoned my baby and left her outside in the rain, wanting to kill myself even though I knew it was the only way to keep you safe from them," she sobbed angrily, glaring down at Uriel's corpse.

My father squeezed her shoulder reassuringly. "You held a piece of Excalibur," he whispered, unable to meet my eyes.

I nodded, steeling my heart for disappointment. Being locked up in the Garden, they would have had no way of knowing those things. Before I could open my mouth to interrogate them further, my mother spoke.

"Even though we couldn't be together, your father and I always wanted to be touching you. When we stole Uriel's armor, we each chose pieces to give you," my mother whispered, smiling sadly. She pointed at my hands and my gauntlets flickered to life with a warm throb, tightening around my ring finger. "You always used to clutch at my fingers as a baby, so I wanted to always clutch yours after...after we, l-left you." She burst into tears and almost fell to her knees if not for Titus catching her.

He was silently weeping as he held her up, twin streaks of lava flowing down his cheeks. "And I," he rasped in a voice like gravel, "always used to pinch your toes because it would make you giggle. You had such a beautiful laugh, daughter. I would walk through Hell to hear that sound again." He lifted a trembling hand and pointed at my feet.

My boots flickered into being with a ticklish pinch on my toes. I dropped my spear, unable to see them clearly through my tears.

"Can...I have a hug?" I whispered.

My mother let out a sob and rushed towards me in a spray of sparks and molten tears. She hit me hard and wrapped her arms around me tightly, but the only warmth I felt was from the overwhelming flood of love that hit me on contact, like I had caught a hold of her heart and read it like a book. She whispered into my ears like a broken record, "I'm so sorry, so sorry, so sorry, so sorry..."

I squeezed her back and felt myself bawling like a baby. I couldn't form a response, and she didn't expect one. She sniffed at my hair and clutched me like the world was ending. Or...like she'd been waiting to do this for over twenty years. She finally pulled away and squeezed me by the shoulders, eyeing me up and down. "You wear it so much better, my love," she laughed.

"Step aside, woman!" Titus snapped with faux anger. But he didn't hug me. He just stood there, staring at me as more tears leaked down his cheeks and his lips trembled uncontrollably. Then he fell to his knees and bowed at my feet, resting his forehead on my angelic boots. His back shook as he wept, clutching at my ankles. "I missed you so goddamned much," he whispered, shaking violently.

I knelt down and wrapped him up in a tight hug as he sobbed into my shoulder. Then his arms wrapped around me and he squeezed, mumbling incoherently. I blinked rapidly, unable to even see him through my tears. "I did it, Dad," I whispered. "I didn't break. It's okay."

He cried harder, and then my mom joined us on the ground and we held each other, grieving and loving.

"How much time do we have?" I whispered miserably.

They slowly pulled away but kept their hands on me as they averted their eyes, both glancing at the Spear of Destiny in the grass. "As long as we want, but the only way you can claim the flaming swords is to give up the Spear." He took a deep sad breath. "And the moment you claim the swords, our battle will finally end," my father said.

"But then you will always hold the fire of our love in your hands," my mother whispered. "A symbol of us anyway."

I felt the Spear of Destiny grow warmer even though it was not in my hands. It felt...right. Like this was my destiny. To hold Thunder and Terror in my hands and give up the Spear.

They are right, Callie, Lucky said in my mind, feeling like a soft breeze through my soul. *The Spear was merely the key to unlocking the Garden. The key to creating the Fifth Divine...*

I looked up sharply and my eyes widened to see the Four Divines seated before the metal cube. They smiled sadly, shedding tears of their own as they watched me. But atop the cube was a sinuous golden dragon with a mane of dandelion-light fur that seemed to float of its own volition. It looked like Qinglong's bigger cousin.

"It was a beautiful death, White Rose," Lucky, the golden dragon said. "The Spear and my blood were the transformational power surge needed to unlock the garden and to bring me properly into my new family," he said, trotting in a circle across the top of the cube to show off his wings and long, golden body. He was much like Qinglong in style, the serpentine dragon look —except for his wings. "I knew what my destiny was long before I came here. We all did," he said, smiling.

I met the faces of the other Divines and found them all nodding reassuringly and their eyes drinking in a portion of my sorrow at the news of my parents' limited reunion. They felt guilt for not being able to save my parents from their fate long ago, but my parents merely smiled at them.

Xuanwu the black tortoise gripped his frosty sword in a trembling claw, blinking dejectedly at my mother.

Qinglong smiled apologetically for drugging me earlier, his long blue body curled up in a serpentine ball.

Zoe was tucked up close to the metal cube, feeding off its heat, her red feathers burning warmly.

Bai had her head on her white paws, tears streaking down her cheeks as she stared at me and my parents.

Then they slowly rose and turned their backs on us, giving us privacy.

My throat ached, realizing what my parents hadn't said out loud about me abandoning the Spear for the fiery swords, Thunder and Terror. "But...*you* will be gone."

They nodded sadly. "But we have this moment," my dad whispered, smiling crookedly as he held my mother's hand.

I clasped each of their hands and nodded, forming a circle with our knees touching. "That's more than I'd ever hoped for," I whispered.

We didn't speak for some time. It could have been days. It could have been moments.

But in a way, it lasted over twenty years, making up for every second of their absence.

I looked up to see the Five Divines peeking at us from behind the metal cube. The moment I saw them, they ducked out of view. Well, Xuanwu ducked his head inside his shell, but he was too large to hide. I laughed. "Get over here."

With shouts and sounds of glee, the Four Divines bounded up to my parents, hugging on them and curling up next to them with purrs, chirps, and growls. My parents laughed delightedly, and I watched them catch up with each other and start sobbing all over again.

Lucky curled up beside me and rested his head in my lap. His scales were very warm and I felt tension easing from my shoulders. "Family," I said, smiling as I set my palm on his neck, stroking lovingly.

We talked back and forth for a long time, and I realized that I had barely scratched the surface on their secrets. I listened in stunned disbelief, asking questions when necessary, but committing most of it to memory for later thought.

The things they had gone through for me...

Love didn't even start to describe the sacrifices they had made for me.

55

After some time, my father rose to his feet and cast me a sad smile. "It is time, daughter."

My mother scowled at him but I knew he was right.

I climbed to my feet and picked up the Spear of Destiny. It grew warm in my hand, and I saw that the cracks from using it with Envy were no longer as wide.

"Okay," I said, gathering my courage.

"Stab it into the cube," Lucky said.

I pointed the Spear at the cube and felt it grow warmer in my hand. The cube grew warmer as well, resonating with the Spear. I held my breath and took a step closer, staring down at the weapon. Miraculously, the cracks slowly closed and I felt a slightly magnetic pull in the direction of the cube. The weapon practically sang in my palm, begging to go home.

I walked up to the cube with my parents on either side. The Divines stayed back, watching us with somber faces, knowing what price I was paying.

I touched the blade to the block and gasped as the Spear seemed to let out a sigh of relief.

"I love you, Mom," I said.

She wrapped me in a hug and kissed me on the forehead. "I couldn't be more proud of you, daughter. Oh, and you look splendid in the full set," she added, eyeing me up and down.

I blinked, glancing down at my body to see I wore a full set of Archangel armor. "How long have I been wearing this?" I whispered.

"Since I just gave it to you, daughter. We wanted to hide it in case Uriel managed to come back before you found us."

"Your mother loves her little tricks," my father said with a smirk as he stepped up and kissed me on the forehead. "Whenever you're feeling sad, just think of me pinching your toes," he said with a loving grin.

I nodded. "Okay. I love you, Dad."

They set their hands on my shoulders and squeezed encouragingly. I pushed the Spear and it slid into the stone like it was made of garden soil. With hardly any effort, the Spear slipped fully into the cube with a pleasant chime.

Then a blast of power shot up from the cube and I stared in awe as the blue protective dome reformed over the Garden of Eden, the Spear of Destiny rebuilding it.

"The Garden is now yours to guard, Callie Penrose," Lucky said in a formal tone.

I nodded and turned around to embrace my parents one last time—

But only their smiling faces remained as sparks swirled away from their bodies to rematerialize in my hands.

"We love you," they said before fading away entirely. I looked down to see two fiery swords in my hands.

Thunder and Terror.

Constance and Titus.

I turned to Lucky with a smile. "If the Garden is now locked up," I said, looking up at the fully-formed dome overhead, "then let's go home."

Lucky grinned. "You can come here the short way whenever you want, but everyone else has to use the front gate—which is always locked."

I smiled and then noticed Uriel's Halo in the grass. I grimaced, briefly considering leaving it here, but I had no idea who else lived in my new property. I called up Envy's Gauntlet—the counter to an Archangel was a Sin—and picked up the Halo. Then I touched it to the Seal of Solomon with a wicked smirk. Uriel was going to be so pissed.

He had wanted the demons in Solomon's Prison. He'd gotten what he wished for.

The Halo winked out of existence and I felt Solomon's ring grow warm for a heartbeat. Then I ripped open a Gateway to Castle Dracula.

The Five Divines followed me as we stepped onto the ramparts. I'd prepared myself for chaos, almost having entirely forgotten about the battle I'd been pulled away from. But...everything was peaceful. Well, there were a lot of people cleaning up blood with mops on the pavilion below, but there was no fighting anywhere, and the fires throughout Castle Dracula had been put out.

I cocked my head at a new thought. "If you turned this place into the Dueling Grounds—a"

"Temporarily," Lucky corrected. "Now it's back to normal."

I nodded. "Then all the people we killed. The Conclave, the nephilim, the demons...they are still alive too."

Lucky nodded. "The war has only just begun, White Rose. And we must soon leave to save Azazel and Samzaya before the nephilim lay waste to your city."

"Let's go right now," I said, rolling my shoulders and eyeing my new fiery swords.

Lucky shook his head, glancing back at his four brothers and sisters meaningfully. They had passed out right on the ramparts, snoring away like a pile of puppies. Lucky shrugged. "They need to recover from all the work they did tonight."

I sighed. "Then I need to check with my general—"

"Got him!" a bubbly, familiar voice cheered from behind me, and then I felt something slam into my back. It was big and strong but I didn't budge. My armor kept me grounded. I recognized his scent and spun around to grab Ryuu. He was glaring at Grace a few paces away, and his hair was tussled, so she must have rabbited him here at supersonic speed.

Her shit-eating grin confirmed it.

Ryuu smiled and pulled me close, letting out a breath of relief. "It worked," he said, kissing my hair.

I nodded and hugged him back, feeling my stress level relax significantly. "No more secrets," I told him.

He laughed. "We're both guilty of that, but Lucky wouldn't let me—"

"Blame it on the dragon, *sure*," Lucky said in an annoyed tone. Ryuu's eyes widened as he saw the golden maned dragon standing by my side.

Ryuu grinned broadly. "It *all* worked?"

"Like a charm," Lucky said haughtily. "Ye of little faith. By the way, Callie beat Raphael in a duel."

Ryuu's eyes widened incredulously. "Congratulations, White Rose," he said in an official tone, bowing. I swatted him and he grinned. "Looks like I owe you some daggers, after all. An Archangel is worth three."

Grace cleared her throat off to the side and I saw her cleaning her claws with one of said daggers.

"Make it four. You gave her three," I said. Ryuu chuckled and nodded. I noticed Ryuu's clothes were torn and speckled with blood. "Are you okay? What happened?"

"War," he said. "We'll need to move on Kansas City as soon as possible. It's madness out there."

I felt a shudder of fear ripple through me. "Show me."

He told me where to open my Gateway—and he was very specific about where to do so without being noticed and murdered on the spot. I ripped open a Gateway to Xuanwu's estate, on the front lawn, per Ryuu's request.

I stared up at the sky and my eyes widened. "What are those?" I asked, counting hundreds of falling, burning comets tumbling from the sky.

"I think they are falling angels," Ryuu said in a solemn tone.

I lifted my swords and stared up at them. "No. They are reinforcements. All heaven is about to break loose. I think Gabriel and Wrath have finally made their play. We're going to need to save the Watchers a lot sooner than we'd hoped, Lucky," I said, glancing down at the golden dragon. "We will need every single nephilim to stand a chance against that. Get someone to help you bring the Divines to Aala's Healing Pond." He nodded and ducked back through the Gateway.

Azazel, Envy sobbed.

There were still so many questions left unanswered. Where was Sanguina? Were Father David and Greta dead? Was Claire okay? How was Greed enjoying her vacation? How was I going to tell Obie about Solomon's last memory? Where was Raphael? What were the Four Horsemen going to do? I was certain they would have something to say about angels falling from the sky. There would be no more concealing magic from the world after one camera caught wind of the sky over the City of Fountains.

I sighed and turned to Ryuu, my lover, wanting to run away and hide with him in bed.

But neither of us could or would do that. He was my general.

My swords throbbed warmly in my palms. Thunder and Terror. I was going to need them. I left the Gateway open for Lucky to start bringing the Divines across with the help of some of my vampires he had corralled into the effort. They looked very confused and startled by the golden dragon barking orders at them, but they saw me through the Gateway and their faces paled upon seeing my Archangel armor and the fiery swords in my hands.

There were no more questions or hesitations after that.

I pulled Ryuu down to the grass and we watched the falling angels as I caught him up to speed. I listened to everything he had been through, but most of it was battle related rather than answers to the questions plaguing my thoughts. Grace was perched in the grass a few paces away, listening intently as she rolled her daggers over the backs of her knuckles and studied me with her bright blue eyes. I saw the reflections of burning angels in them and my resolve hardened.

I met both of their eyes. "No more hiding what we are," I told them. "Here is what we're going to do..."

Callie Penrose will return in ANGEL DUST in June 2021...or sooner.

*Turn the page to read a sample of **OBSIDIAN SON** - The Nate Temple Series Book 1 - or **BUY ONLINE**. Nate Temple is a billionaire wizard from St. Louis. He rides a bloodthirsty unicorn and drinks with the Four Horsemen. He even cow-tipped the Minotaur. Once...*

(Note: Nate's books 1-6 happen prior to UNCHAINED, but they crossover from then on, the two series taking place in the same universe but also able to standalone if you prefer)

Full chronology of all books in the TempleVerse shown on the 'BOOKS BY SHAYNE SILVERS' page.

TRY: OBSIDIAN SON (NATE TEMPLE #1)

There was no room for emotion in a hate crime. I had to be cold. Heartless. This was just another victim. Nothing more. No face, no name.

Frosted blades of grass crunched under my feet, sounding to my ears like the symbolic glass that one would shatter under a napkin at a Jewish wedding. The noise would have threatened to give away my stealthy advance as I stalked through the moonlit field, but I was no novice and had planned accordingly. Being a wizard, I was able to muffle all sensory evidence with a fine cloud of magic—no sounds, and no smells. Nifty. But if I made the spell much stronger, the anomaly would be too obvious to my prey.

I knew the consequences for my dark deed tonight. If caught, jail time or possibly even a gruesome, painful death. But if I succeeded, the look of fear and surprise in my victim's eyes before his world collapsed around him, it was well worth the risk. I simply couldn't help myself; I had to take him down.

I knew the cops had been keeping tabs on my car, but I was confident that they hadn't followed me. I hadn't seen a tail on my way here but seeing as how they frowned on this kind of thing, I had taken a circuitous route just in case. I was safe. I hoped.

Then my phone chirped at me as I received a text.

I practically jumped out of my skin, hissing instinctively. "Motherf—" I cut off abruptly, remembering the whole stealth aspect of my mission. I was off to a stellar start. I had forgotten to silence the damned phone. *Stupid, stupid, stupid!*

My heart felt like it was on the verge of exploding inside my chest with such thunderous violence that I briefly envisioned a mystifying Rorschach blood-blot that would have made coroners and psychologists drool.

My body remained tense as I swept my gaze over the field, fearing that I had been made. Precious seconds ticked by without any change in my surroundings, and my breathing finally began to slow as my pulse returned to normal. Hopefully, my magic had muted the phone and my resulting outburst. I glanced down at the phone to scan the text and then typed back a quick and angry response before I switched the cursed device to vibrate.

Now, where were we?

I continued on, the lining of my coat constricting my breathing. Or maybe it was because I was leaning forward in anticipation. *Breathe*, I chided myself. *He doesn't know you're here.* All this risk for a book. It had better be worth it.

I'm taller than most, and not abnormally handsome, but I knew how to play the genetic cards I had been dealt. I had shaggy, dirty blonde hair—leaning more towards brown with each passing year—and my frame was thick with well-earned muscle, yet I was still lean. I had once been told that my eyes were like twin emeralds pitted against the golden-brown tufts of my hair—a face like a jewelry box. Of course, that was two bottles of wine into a date, so I could have been a little foggy on her quote. Still, I liked to imagine that was how everyone saw me.

But tonight, all that was masked by magic.

I grinned broadly as the outline of the hairy hulk finally came into view. He was blessedly alone—no nearby sentries to give me away. That was always a risk when performing this ancient rite-of-passage. I tried to keep the grin on my face from dissolving into a maniacal cackle.

My skin danced with energy, both natural and unnatural, as I manipulated the threads of magic floating all around me. My victim stood just ahead, oblivious to the world of hurt that I was about to unleash. Even with his millennia of experience, he didn't stand a chance. I had done this so many times that the routine of it was my only enemy. I lost count of how many times I had been told not to do it again; those who knew declared it *cruel, evil, and sadistic*. But what fun wasn't? Regardless, that wasn't enough to stop me from doing it again. And again. And again.

It was an addiction.

The pungent smell of manure filled the air, latching onto my nostril hairs. I took another step, trying to calm my racing pulse. A glint of gold reflected in the silver moonlight, but my victim remained motionless, hopefully unaware or all was lost. I wouldn't make it out alive if he knew I was here. Timing was everything.

I carefully took the last two steps, a lifetime between each, watching the legendary monster's ears, anxious and terrified that I would catch even so much as a twitch in my direction. Seeing nothing, a fierce grin split my unshaven cheeks. My spell had worked! I raised my palms an inch away from their target, firmly planted my feet, and squared my shoulders. I took one silent, calming breath, and then heaved forward with every ounce of physical strength I could muster. As well as a teensy-weensy boost of magic. Enough to goose him good.

"*MOOO!!!*" The sound tore through the cool October night like an unstoppable freight train. *Thud-splat!* The beast collapsed sideways onto the frosted grass; straight into a steaming patty of cow shit, cow dung, or, if you really wanted to church it up, a Meadow Muffin. But to me, shit is, and always will be, shit.

Cow tipping. It doesn't get any better than that in Missouri.

Especially when you're tipping the *Minotaur*. Capital M. I'd tipped plenty of ordinary cows before, but never the legendary variety.

Razor-blade hooves tore at the frozen earth as the beast struggled to stand, his grunts of rage vibrating the air. I raised my arms triumphantly. "Boo-yah! Temple 1, Minotaur 0!" I crowed. Then I very bravely prepared to protect myself. Some people just couldn't take a joke. *Cruel, evil,* and *sadistic* cow tipping may be, but by hell, it was a *rush.* The legendary beast turned his gaze on me after gaining his feet, eyes ablaze as his body...*shifted* from his bull disguise into his notorious, well-known bipedal form. He unfolded to his full height on two tree trunk-thick legs, his hooves having magically transformed into heavily booted feet. The thick, gold ring dangling from his snotty snout quivered as the Minotaur panted, and his dense, corded muscles contracted over his now human-like chest. As I stared up into those brown eyes, I actually felt sorry...for, well, myself.

"I have killed greater men than you for lesser offense," he growled.

His voice sounded like an angry James Earl Jones—like Mufasa talking to Scar.

"You have shit on your shoulder, Asterion." I ignited a roiling ball of fire in my palm in order to see his eyes more clearly. By no means was it a defensive gesture on my part. It was just dark. Under the weight of his glare, I somehow managed to keep my face composed, even though my fraudulent, self-denial had curled up into the fetal position and started whimpering. I hoped using a form of his ancient name would give me brownie points. Or maybe just not-worthy-of-killing points.

The beast grunted, eyes tightening, and I sensed the barest hesitation. "Nate Temple...your name would look splendid on my already long list of slain idiots." Asterion took a threatening step forward, and I thrust out my palm in warning, my roiling flame blue now.

"You lost fair and square, Asterion. Yield or perish." The beast's shoulders sagged slightly. Then he finally nodded to himself in resignation, appraising me with the scrutiny of a worthy adversary. "Your time comes, Temple, but I will grant you this. You've got a pair of stones on you to rival Hercules."

I reflexively glanced in the direction of the myth's own crown jewels before jerking my gaze away. Some things you simply couldn't un-see. "Well, I won't be needing a wheelbarrow any time soon, but overcompensating today keeps future lower-back pain away."

The Minotaur blinked once, and then he bellowed out a deep, contagious, snorting laughter. Realizing I wasn't about to become a murder statistic, I couldn't help but join in. It felt good. It had been a while since I had allowed myself to experience genuine laughter.

In the harsh moonlight, his bulk was even more intimidating as he towered head and shoulders above me. This was the beast that had fed upon human sacrifices for countless years while imprisoned in Daedalus' Labyrinth in Greece. And all that protein had not gone to waste, forming a heavily woven musculature over the beast's body that made even Mr. Olympia look puny.

From the neck up, he was now entirely bull, but the rest of his body more closely resembled a thickly furred man. But, as shown moments ago, he could adapt his form to his environment, never appearing fully human, but able to make his entire form appear as a bull when necessary. For instance, how he had looked just before I tipped him. Maybe he had been scouting the field for heifers before I had so efficiently killed the mood.

His bull face was also covered in thick, coarse hair—he even sported a long, wavy beard of sorts, and his eyes were the deepest brown I had ever seen. Cow-shit brown. His snout jutted out, emphasizing the golden ring dangling from his glistening nostrils, and both glinted in the luminous glow of the moon. The metal was at least an inch thick and etched with runes of a language long forgotten. Wide, aged ivory horns sprouted from each temple, long enough to skewer a wizard with little effort. He was nude except for a massive beaded necklace and a pair of worn leather boots that were big enough to stomp a size twenty-five imprint in my face if he felt so inclined.

I hoped our blossoming friendship wouldn't end that way. I really did.

Because friends didn't let friends wear boots naked...

Get your copy of OBSIDIAN SON online today!
http://www.shaynesilvers.com/l/38474

Turn the page to read a sample of **WHISKEY GINGER** *- Phantom Queen Diaries Book 1, or* **BUY ONLINE***. Quinn MacKenna is a black magic arms dealer in Boston. She likes to fight monsters almost as much as she likes to drink.*

TRY: WHISKEY GINGER (PHANTOM QUEEN DIARIES BOOK 1)

The pasty guitarist hunched forward, thrust a rolled-up wad of paper deep into one nostril, and snorted a line of blood crystals—frozen hemoglobin that I'd smuggled over in a refrigerated canister—with the uncanny grace of a drug addict. He sat back, fangs gleaming, and pawed at his nose. "That's some bodacious shit. Hey, bros," he said, glancing at his fellow band members, "come hit this shit before it melts."

He fetched one of the backstage passes hanging nearby, pried the plastic badge from its lanyard, and used it to split up the crystals, murmuring something in an accent that reminded me of California. Not *the* California, but you know, Cali-foh-nia—the land of beaches, babes, and bros. I retrieved a toothpick from my pocket and punched it through its thin wrapper. "So," I asked no one in particular, "now that ye have the product, who's payin'?"

Another band member stepped out of the shadows to my left, and I don't mean that figuratively, either—the fucker literally stepped out of the shadows. I scowled at him, but hid my surprise, nonchalantly rolling the toothpick from one side of my mouth to the other.

The rest of the band gathered around the dressing room table, following the guitarist's lead by preparing their own snorting utensils—tattered magazine covers, mostly. Typically, you'd do this sort of thing with a dollar-bill, maybe even a Benjamin if you were flush. But fangers like this lot couldn't touch cash directly—in God We Trust and all that. Of course, I didn't really understand why sucking blood the old-fashioned way had suddenly gone out of style. More of a rush, maybe?

"It lasts longer," the vampire next to me explained, catching my mildly curious expression. "It's especially good for shows and stuff. Makes us look, like, less—"

"Creepy?" I offered, my Irish brogue lilting just enough to make it a question.

"Pale," he finished, frowning.

I shrugged. "Listen, I've got places to be," I said, holding out my hand.

"I'm sure you do," he replied, smiling. "Tell you what, why don't you, like, hang around for a bit? Once that wears off," he dipped his head toward the bloody powder smeared across the table's surface, "we may need a pick-me-up." He rested his hand on my arm and our gazes locked.

I blinked, realized what he was trying to pull, and rolled my eyes. His widened in surprise, then shock as I yanked out my toothpick and shoved it through his hand.

"Motherfuck—"

"I want what we agreed on," I declared. "Now. No tricks."

The rest of the band saw what happened and rose faster than I could blink. They circled me, their grins feral...they might have even seemed intimidating if it weren't for the fact that they each had a case of the sniffles —I had to work extra hard not to think about what it felt like to have someone else's blood dripping down my nasal cavity.

I held up a hand.

"Can I ask ye gentlemen a question before we get started?" I asked. "Do ye even *have* what I asked for?"

Two of the band members exchanged looks and shrugged. The guitarist, however, glanced back towards the dressing room, where a brown paper bag sat next to a case full of makeup. He caught me looking and bared his teeth, his fangs stretching until it looked like it would be uncomfortable for him to close his mouth without piercing his own lip.

"Follow-up question," I said, eyeing the vampire I'd stabbed as he gingerly withdrew the toothpick from his hand and flung it across the room with a snarl. "Do ye do each other's make-up? Since, ye know, ye can't use mirrors?"

I was genuinely curious.

The guitarist grunted. "Mike, we have to go on soon."

"Wait a minute. Mike?" I turned to the snarling vampire with a frown. "What happened to *The Vampire Prospero?*" I glanced at the numerous fliers in the dressing room, most of which depicted the band members wading through blood, with Mike in the lead, each one titled *The Vampire Prospero* in *Rocky Horror Picture Show* font. Come to think of it...Mike did look a little like Tim Curry in all that leather and lace.

I was about to comment on the resemblance when Mike spoke up, "Alright, change of plans, bros. We're gonna drain this bitch before the show. We'll look totally—"

"Creepy?" I offered, again.

"Kill her."

Get the full book ONLINE! http://www.shaynesilvers.com/l/206897

MAKE A DIFFERENCE

Reviews are the most powerful tools in my arsenal when it comes to getting attention for my books. Much as I'd like to, I don't have the financial muscle of a New York publisher.

But I do have something much more powerful and effective than that, and it's something that those publishers would kill to get their hands on.

A committed and loyal bunch of readers.

Honest reviews of my books help bring them to the attention of other readers.

If you've enjoyed this book, I would be very grateful if you could spend just five minutes leaving a review on my book's Amazon page.

Thank you very much in advance.

ACKNOWLEDGMENTS

Team Temple and the Den of Freaks on Facebook have become family to me. I couldn't do it without die-hard readers like them.

I would also like to thank you, the reader. I hope you enjoyed reading *HALO BREAKER* as much as I enjoyed writing it. Be sure to check out the two crossover series in the Temple Verse: The **Nate Temple Series** and the **Phantom Queen Diaries**.

And last, but definitely not least, I thank my wife, Lexy. Without your support, none of this would have been possible.

ABOUT SHAYNE SILVERS

Shayne is a man of mystery and power, whose power is exceeded only by his mystery...

He currently writes the Amazon Bestselling **Nate Temple** Series, which features a foul-mouthed wizard from St. Louis. He rides a bloodthirsty unicorn, drinks with Achilles, and is pals with the Four Horsemen.

He also writes the Amazon Bestselling **Feathers and Fire** Series—a second series in the TempleVerse. The story follows a rookie spell-slinger named Callie Penrose who works for the Vatican in Kansas City. Her problem? Hell seems to know more about her past than she does.

He coauthors **The Phantom Queen Diaries**—a third series set in The TempleVerse—with Cameron O'Connell. The story follows Quinn MacKenna, a mouthy black magic arms dealer in Boston. All she wants? A round-trip ticket to the Fae realm...and maybe a drink on the house.

He also writes the **Shade of Devil Series**, which tells the story of Sorin Ambrogio—the world's FIRST vampire. He was put into a magical slumber by a Native American Medicine Man when the Americas were first discovered by Europeans. Sorin wakes up after five-hundred years to learn that his protégé, Dracula, stole his reputation and that no one has ever even heard of Sorin Ambrogio. The streets of New York City will run with blood as Sorin reclaims his legend.

Shayne holds two high-ranking black belts, and can be found writing in a coffee shop, cackling madly into his computer screen while pounding shots of espresso. He's hard at work on the newest books in the TempleVerse—You can find updates on new releases or chronological reading order on the next page, his website, or any of his social media accounts. **Follow him online for all sorts of groovy goodies, giveaways, and new release updates:**

Get Down with Shayne Online
www.shaynesilvers.com
info@shaynesilvers.com

facebook.com/shaynesilversfanpage
amazon.com/author/shaynesilvers
bookbub.com/profile/shayne-silvers
instagram.com/shaynesilversofficial
twitter.com/shaynesilvers
goodreads.com/ShayneSilvers

BOOKS BY SHAYNE SILVERS

CHRONOLOGY: *All stories in the TempleVerse are shown in chronological order on the following page*

FEATHERS AND FIRE SERIES
(*Also set in the TempleVerse*)
by Shayne Silvers

UNCHAINED

RAGE

WHISPERS

ANGEL'S ROAR

MOTHERLUCKER (Novella #4.5 in the 'LAST CALL' anthology)

SINNER

BLACK SHEEP

GODLESS

ANGHELLIC

TRINITY

HALO BREAKER

NATE TEMPLE SERIES
(*Main series in the TempleVerse*)
by Shayne Silvers

FAIRY TALE - FREE prequel novella #0 for my subscribers

OBSIDIAN SON

BLOOD DEBTS

GRIMM

SILVER TONGUE

BEAST MASTER

BEERLYMPIAN (Novella #5.5 in the 'LAST CALL' anthology)

TINY GODS

DADDY DUTY (Novella #6.5)

WILD SIDE

WAR HAMMER

NINE SOULS

HORSEMAN

LEGEND

KNIGHTMARE

ASCENSION

CARNAGE

SAVAGE

PHANTOM QUEEN DIARIES

(Also set in the TempleVerse)

by Cameron O'Connell & Shayne Silvers

COLLINS (Prequel novella #0 in the 'LAST CALL' anthology)

WHISKEY GINGER

COSMOPOLITAN

MOTHERLUCKER (Novella #2.5 in the 'LAST CALL' anthology)

OLD FASHIONED

DARK AND STORMY

MOSCOW MULE

WITCHES BREW

SALTY DOG

SEA BREEZE

HURRICANE

BRIMSTONE KISS

MOONSHINE

CHRONOLOGICAL ORDER: TEMPLE VERSE

FAIRY TALE (TEMPLE PREQUEL)

OBSIDIAN SON (TEMPLE 1)

BLOOD DEBTS (TEMPLE 2)

GRIMM (TEMPLE 3)

SILVER TONGUE (TEMPLE 4)

BEAST MASTER (TEMPLE 5)

BEERLYMPIAN (TEMPLE 5.5)

TINY GODS (TEMPLE 6)

DADDY DUTY (TEMPLE NOVELLA 6.5)

UNCHAINED (FEATHERS...1)

RAGE (FEATHERS...2)

WILD SIDE (TEMPLE 7)

WAR HAMMER (TEMPLE 8)

WHISPERS (FEATHERS...3)

COLLINS (PHANTOM 0)

WHISKEY GINGER (PHANTOM...1)

NINE SOULS (TEMPLE 9)

COSMOPOLITAN (PHANTOM...2)

ANGEL'S ROAR (FEATHERS...4)

MOTHERLUCKER (FEATHERS 4.5, PHANTOM 2.5)

OLD FASHIONED (PHANTOM...3)

HORSEMAN (TEMPLE 10)

DARK AND STORMY (PHANTOM...4)

MOSCOW MULE (PHANTOM...5)

SINNER (FEATHERS...5)

WITCHES BREW (PHANTOM...6)

LEGEND (TEMPLE...11)

SALTY DOG (PHANTOM...7)

BLACK SHEEP (FEATHERS...6)

GODLESS (FEATHERS...7)

KNIGHTMARE (TEMPLE 12)

ASCENSION (TEMPLE 13)

SEA BREEZE (PHANTOM...8)

HURRICANE (PHANTOM...9)

BRIMSTONE KISS (PHANTOM...10)

ANGHELLIC (FEATHERS...8)

CARNAGE (TEMPLE 14)

MOONSHINE (PHANTOM...11)

TRINITY (FEATHERS...9)

SAVAGE (TEMPLE...15)

HALO BREAKER (FEATHERS...10)

SHADE OF DEVIL SERIES

(Not part of the Temple Verse)

by Shayne Silvers

DEVIL'S DREAM

DEVIL'S CRY

DEVIL'S BLOOD

DEVIL'S DUE *(coming 2021...)*

NOTHING TO SEE HERE.

Thanks for reaching the last page of the book, you over-achiever. Sniff the spine. You've earned it. Or sniff your Kindle.

Now this has gotten weird.

Alright. I'm leaving.

Made in the USA
Middletown, DE
16 May 2021